The Seventh Blessing

R.L.Baxter

Table of Contents

Prologue

How long has it been? How long have I been wandering through this cold and frightening place, alone? Ten billion years perhaps? No... Much more than that. I am so cold and tired. I just want to rest, in a place that I can call home.

Chapter 1: Unholy swordsman

Under a dark and windy night, within a large field, I stand opposite a magnificent being. Its body is brighter than the sun, and its attire consists of long silk and a golden gown that sparkles as though it were filled with endless stars. A large swirling halo hangs just above its head, as the being glares nervously at me. It is nervous, not because of my physical appearance. After all, I am just a young man. What it fears, is my capability.

Sporting a white robe, I hold a feisty grin - crossing my arms. Dancing around me, a mysterious thin black sword levitates by my side. Breaking the silence between the glowing being and me, I address the foe.

"What's the matter? You don't look so confident... For a god. Are you not embarrassed?" I ask, tauntingly.

"How dare you insult me? I will not stand for such talk!"

Upon a small chuckle, I slowly blink and respond, "Sigh... Please remind me of your name again? Oh, that's right, it was Gaudium, correct? Listen – we both know how this is going to end. Tell me everything I need to know if you want to keep your immortality."

The godly being shivers before shouting "You... You do not scare me. On the contrary, it is you who should be scared... By the likes of I: Gaudium!" Arms stretched forward, the god releases a blinding beam of light from its hands.

Standing firm, I bat not a single eyelid, as the large surge of light races directly towards me. Speaking in a monotone fashion, I whisper to the dancing sword, "Adamas."

On cue, the sword zips protectively in front, as the projectile arrives only inches apart from me. Astonishingly, the sword cuts into the light – causing the beam to ricochet into the distance before colliding and exploding against a distant mountain. The explosion sweeps outward and rises to the heavens, as I keep a focused stare – watched by the now speechless deity.

"That… That's not possible!" Gaudium shouts – leaping towards me. Fists clenched, the god swings its arms to crush me – however, I dodge the attack with lightning evasion. Instead, the fool strikes the ground – causing the entire field to split in two. The earth screams as smoke and debris shower the area. "Where are you… Where did you go?" Shouts the hysterical being, unable to catch sight of me. Such pitiful antics from a being, claiming to be a god. If my opponent was less hysterical, he would have already noticed that I am in fact behind him.

"Sigh… - Adamas, finish him."

Obeying my command once more, the sword spins through the air – like a deadly boomerang before homing in on the opponent. With ease, the sword cuts through Gaudium's body – amputating its limbs continuously. "Stop, stop it!" He screams - begging me to have mercy. The being is terrified beyond words, terrified at the prospect of no longer living. I can somewhat empathise with its fear. Imagine possessing an immortal life, with no concept of death – only to have such a luxury, abruptly taken away from you? It must be a truly horrific pill to swallow.

With his arms and legs completely severed, the god falls flat to the ground – looking up at me as I step onto its chest. "I warned you, this was how it was going to end. How does it feel, to be under the heel of a human? O how I love the face of despair and shame your kind display when humbled by me. I could spare you, if you talk that is?"

To my surprise, a smile opens on the god's face before it replies, "Hehe… You really want me to tell you, how to get to The Land of The Gods? Do you realise how foolish such an attempt is? Do you realise how stupid you sound?" He gloats – causing me to flinch. Gaudium laughs manically, before speaking forth once again. "The other gods warned me about you. You are Luna the evil messiah, the one with a most laughable scheme. Are you truly doing all of this, in the hope that you'll find your sibling? The Seventh Blessing already claimed her, and there's nothing you can do about it! Your sister no longer exists... Hahaha!"

At that moment, I lose control. In fact, losing control would be an understatement. I am pissed off, and the being's annoying laugh is only making it worse. Yanking the hilt of my companion sword, I viciously stab the god's face and body - screaming to the top of my lungs.

"Curse the Seventh Blessing! If it wasn't for such an awful thing, my sister would still be alive. Why... Why did your kind create such a horrid thing?"

The being disappears into traces of light – leaving me as the victor. However, I feel far from accomplished. Standing under the dark sky, I slowly compose myself and breathe deeply. I remain still, soaking in the silent sounds of grass beneath me before whispering to myself, "Dammit... I was unsuccessful in getting any information out of him."

"Yeah, you can say that again" responds my sword. Yes, not only can the weapon move on its own, but it can also talk – much to my annoyance at times. "You really need to control yourself, sometimes."

"Shut up, Adamas."

"Sigh - you are so mean... Luna."

Chapter 2: World of Popla

We return to our temporary abode. For the past month, this sword and I have been staying in a small town called: Belgrave. To be blunt, the place is an absolute shithole, filled with the worst characters I've ever met. Residing in the south-east of this land, Belgrave is a place where wanted criminals go to hide, men who have lost their way go to rot and underground deals are made. Swordsmen, mages and many more, live together in this notorious den, making end's meat, through bounty rewards, mostly.

In the central area, lies the town's main place of social gathering: The Provider – a multipurpose bar for eating, gambling, drinking and beating the shit of each other, from time to time. As a final selling point, the bar advertises a range of jobs, which we are free to take up. Of course, these are not your average nine to fives but instead, missions that involve killing, capturing or stealing someone or something. So far, the reward money has usually been enough to keep us earning our keep. More importantly, they offer an opportunity to hunt my prey... The gods.

"Uh... I am so exhausted!" Adamas moans as we enter the doors of the Provider.

"Exhausted? You're a sword, moron."

"So what? I can at least pretend that I am tired" The floating sword replies, as I shift my eyes to the multitude of punters within the bar. It's noisy and overcrowded with overly excited brutes – drinking, arm wrestling and laughing together. Honestly, you'd think they'd do something more constructive. Such a waste of time. I'd be lying if the thought of killing them all didn't cross my mind.

Squeezing our way to the bar at the far side, I sit upon a stool and wait to be served, as my sword companion rambles on.

"Luna - if you're gonna keep losing your temper, then we'll never get where we need to go!"

"Ok, jeez! I heard you the first time!"

"That's what you always say but, time and time again, you end up killing gods before getting the information we need from them. You and I are in this together, remember? A little consideration goes a long way, ya know?"

Nodding my head before turning away, I produce a small chuckle – finding my companion's statement amusing. My name is Luna Ray and I am on a mission, to find a place that no man has ever set foot in: The Land of The Gods. This world is ruled by an untold number of deities. The gods control everything in this world and at times reveal their presence to us. Most of us are expected to worship and submit to them – however for some, we have refused. I fall into that small category, for a simple reason. My sister... she was taken from me by the gods, which is why I am searching for their land, to bring her back. Simple.

As for the badgering sword here – well I found it, some time after losing my sister. It too is looking for the Land of the Gods but doesn't quite know why. It has no knowledge of how it came into existence or even its purpose, other than the fact that it desires to reach their abode. A living, talking sword, which just so happens to have amnesia. Unfortunately, we have been unsuccessful in finding the Land of The Gods. Nobody knows a thing, which is why we have taken up certain missions, to hunt the gods down, in hopes to force the whereabouts of their land to us. Unfortunately, as we witnessed earlier, this is easier said than done.

"Hey there, my gruesome twosome! I see you were successful in killing the god Gaudium" comes a familiar voice from my left side. Turning my gaze, I see a woman sitting next to me – sporting a long red cloak and a large pointy hat. Displaying a great smile, she goes by the name of Trista. She is the agent whom we go to, for our mercenary work. She's also a witch – although the only fancy thing I've seen from her is her ability to appear when we least expect it.

"Nice to see you again. Yes, we were successful in killing the god. Do you have our reward money?" I ask unwaveringly - extending my open palm to her.

"Oh, looks like you're not in a very talkative mood. What's wrong? You didn't fail the mission – so why the long face?"

Before I have the chance to reply, the badgering sword interrupts and says, "Luna lost his cool once again, failing to obtain any information about finding the Land of the Gods..."

"Enough Adamas! Nobody asked you anyway!" I utter - rolling my eyes in annoyance. Upon a brief pause, the witch looks upward in thought before speaking in a bright and cheerful manner.

"Ah, don't beat yourself up over it... Shit happens. You should know by now, the type of beings the gods are. They rule our world of Popla and expect us, mortals, to forever stay beneath them. As such, it would be very unlikely for one to do as you say, even on the verge of death. Furthermore, what makes you think that such a place exists in the first place, Luna?"

"It exists. It must do. The gods must come from somewhere, right?"

Sighing to herself, as though having had this conversation with me on many occasions, Trista scratches her forehead and replies "Yes, that may be true. However, even if there were such a place, the next task would be getting there." Taking off her large hat, the witch reveals her long brown hair.

Twirling her hat between her fingers, she continues, "To make matters worse, there is still the issue of the Seventh Blessing to worry about. If you're not careful, even you may wind up..."

"That's enough, Trista. If you don't have anything else to offer, please hand me my reward money and let's call it a night."

"Very well" she responds - clicking her fingers to summon a medium sized bag from out of thin air. Upon the bag magically appearing, it lands gently into my hand. The sound of many coins can be heard from inside it, from which I produce a relieved nod. "There... That should be sixty-one thousand biscoins."

"Nice doing business with you," I say before leaving the counter and walking towards the exit of the bar. "Adamas, you coming or not?" I call to my sword companion, at which point he follows behind me.

After squeezing through the rowdy customers, before finally approaching the exit – the red-dressed witch shouts to me, from the far end of the bar.

"Hey, wait a second..." she calls, clicking her fingers once more. By her command, a small envelope appears in my hand. "You asked me to do a little favour for you, the other day, remember? Well, within that envelope is good news. I hope it helps you."

We leave the Provider and emerge out onto a dark and quiet street, save for a single dim lamppost. Bearing right, we stroll under the night sky – glancing up at a sea of stars, kept company by two moons: one red and one blue. As I look up at the cosmos, I am reminded of fond memories, not too long ago. However, now's not the time for sentiments. Casting the memory aside, I look away from the sky and focus on the street in front – spotting our hotel up ahead.

"Jeez, my feet are killing me. I can't wait to finally get some sleep!" Adamas expresses – to which I roll my eyes and laugh.

"Ahaha... How many times do I have to remind you? You're a sword. What do you know about pain or sleeping?"

The blade pauses, giving off a surprising aura. It was just for a minor second, but I could have sworn the sword had just felt sadness... Or something along the lines of longing. Glancing to Adamas, I await his reply.

"Well, nothing I guess. However, it's nice to imagine what it would feel like. I am especially fascinated with the concept of dreaming. Tell me, what happens within a dream?"

"Huh? Are you serious?"

"Yeah. Dreams sound so fascinating! I was told that all kinds of people within our life can appear, all at once. I was even told that it's possible for those who are no longer alive, to exist again."

Stopping my stroll, I tilt my head with curiosity and ask "Adamas, who have you been talking to?"

"Trista told me."

Rolling my eyes, I continue walking onwards before expressing "I should have known that nosey witch had something to do with this. Ignore her, Adamas."

"Ah come on Luna! You don't have to be like that. She only wanted to tell me what dreams felt like."

"There is nothing special about dreams. Dreams are lies, made to give us a temporary retreat... From this harsh reality. However, once we open our eyes, they abandon us and we are left to fend for ourselves. Consider yourself lucky."

Finally arriving at our hotel, we enter its doors. Once inside, we slowly ascend towards the seventh floor, where our room resides. Climbing these stairs always feels like forever – especially after such a long night like this one.

"Where do you think you're going, wise guy!" A voice calls to me from behind, as we pass the sixth floor. Startled, I jump before turning around. To our surprise, we see the landlord, Lloyd – looking to us with his hands beside his hips.

"Christ almighty, Lloyd. Did you really have to spook me like that? I almost tripped and fell down the stairs!"

"Hahaha, sorry but I couldn't help myself" The man responds. The landlord is quite a nice guy if I must say so. He's one of the few that I take to. Not sure why though – however, he possesses a character that is warm and pleasant. He reminds me of a dopey father: the kind that can easily disregard their child's mood swings. "So, do you have the cash to cover your room for the night?"

"Huh? Oh yeah... Right. The cover is thirty thousand biscoins for one night, correct?" I reply, reaching into my inside pocket to search for our rent money. For some reason, however, I can't seem to find it. "Hey, Adamas – what happened to our reserve money I always keep in my inside pocket? Do you have it?"

"Haha, and where would I keep it? I am a sword, remember!

Perhaps you dropped it when we left the Provider? Oh, come to think of it, I noticed something falling out from your clothes - however, I forgot to tell you."

"You forgot to tell me? Why would you not say anything? Do you realise, if we can't pay our god damn rent, we'll be homeless, numbskull!"

"Oh... Sorry Luna. I'll go out and find it, right away!"

"Forget it, it's probably already taken now."

Laughing at the pair of us, the landlord smiles and says "You two are hilarious! Relax - you don't need to worry about the rent, today. After all, you never cause me trouble, unlike some of the other tenants here. Go get some rest."

"Many thanks, Lloyd" I respond, before stomping up the stairs. Finally entering our room, the first thing I do is leap onto my single bed, as the living sword floats and lands upon a nearby desk – its favourite spot.

Together in the small room, we lay in silence, reflecting on the night. Laying to my side, I look through the window at the twin moons above - appreciating the silence of the night. Of course, quietness never stays for long, as Adamas just loves to keep talking, like a pesky child.

"Hey, Luna – you're not sleeping, are you?"

"Sigh... Would it be a problem if I was?"

"Wait... Before you go to sleep, we need to figure out what our next move is. How are we gonna find the Land of the Gods?"

"I don't know. The gods we encounter never want to spill any info, even with the prospect of death. Someone has to know something, in this land."

Hopping onto my chest, the sleepless blade utters "Luna – we both came to Biscus about a month ago, right? So far, we haven't made any progress. Was there a reason that we came to this land in particular?"

Staring into space, I ask myself the same question. Why did we come to this specific land in the first place? Oh... Now I remember. Someone from long ago recommended Biscus because apparently, something special is sealed away here... - Something that could help us. However, I haven't had any luck finding it either.

Like a light bulb flicking on, I remember the envelope given to me by Trista the witch. I remember that I asked her to look for the sealed thing for me. Reaching into my pocket, I pull out the envelope and waste no time opening it. I gasp with surprise by what I see - mouth wide open. Eventually catching my breath, I produce a small chuckle and whisper to myself.

"Hehe... Well, I'll be damned. The witch really outdid herself this time."

Chapter 3: God of Giving

The next morning, under a bright blue sky, Adamas and I sit in the back of a wooden carriage – escorted by a horse and its rider in front. We have been travelling for just over an hour – feeling the warm rays of the sun and observing the peaceful landscapes that pass us by. As I sit, arms folded, eyes closed – I can't help but keep a wide grin on my face.

"Hey, Luna – what's with the face? You've been smiling, ever since we woke up today. Furthermore, do you mind telling me where we're going?"

"Hmm? Oh… I guess I can't hide my excitement. If you must know, I am happy because of the info found in Trista's envelope. Apparently, there's an old legend about a monster, said to have been sealed away, some five thousand years ago. We're going to meet it."

"Huh? What does that have to do with finding The Land of the gods?"

Opening my eyes, I glare to the sword, confidently. "It could be our ticket. I can imagine a being as old as five thousand years would possess some knowledge about our ultimate destination. Good idea, right?"

"Oh wow! That's awesome, Luna! I hope the monster is friendly?"

"Hahaha" I giggle – closing my eyes once again and slumping into my seat. As usual, my overly attached sword can't help leaving me in peace and right on cue, it clobbers my head before asking me a question.

"Luna - did you dream last night?"

"Ouch! Yeah, I did. Although, I can't quite remember what it was about."

"Oh come on! You're lying again. Just tell me. I wanna know!"

"Sigh… It's the truth. Ah, wait… I remember now. Haha, it was quite a funny dream. I was a bird, flying across the world – eavesdropping on everybody's conversation. Then, I stopped by an old hut and found you there. However, you didn't look as you are now. You were a grumpy old man, who complained about almost everything!"

Dancing through the carriage, my sword laughs hysterically – clearly amused by my dream. "Aahahaha, I was an old man? That's incredible! How did I look, how did I look!"

"Hmph, you had barely any hair and no teeth. You looked vile, to say the least."

Falling flat onto my knees, as though overwhelmed with my telling, the sword breathes a cheerful sigh and utters, "I so wish I could dream as you do. It sounds all so beautiful."

"Adamas, are you serious? Of all the things you could wish for, you'd wish to dream? Honestly, you say the most absurd things."

Suddenly, our escort stops abruptly and addresses us. "Here we are. Welcome to: Brightin."

"We're here… already?" I ask, slowly poking my head out the carriage to take a clear look at our destination. It's a port town, situated by a clear and wide sea. Breathing in the ocean air settles me, as though I were on vacation, on a trip to the beach. "Thank you, for the free ride. It is much appreciated" I say to the escort while climbing out the carriage along with my sword.

"No problem at all. I was already heading in this direction anyway. Have a good day" He responds pleasantly, before riding off into the distance.

Entering the port town of Brightin - Adamas and I stroll through the many streets, searching for the monster that is said to dwell somewhere here. Hiding the sword within my robe, not to attract attention to ourselves, it's clear to see the locals are your average townspeople. Unlike the rebellious and dangerous people of Belgrave, these people seem normal enough. However, at the same time, something seems quite troubling about this place – yet I can't quite put my finger on it.

"So, Luna, any idea how we're to find the monster you're looking for?"

"Hmm, well I thought the best thing we could do is ask around? I figured that would be the most direct approach."

"Agreed. Let's ask some store clerks or something."

Nodding my head, I look around and spot a flower shop – opposite the street from where we are. Strolling along the cobbled ground, I notice the door is shut. "Hmph – must be closed today" I whisper, before casting my eyes to a nearby cafe. To my surprise, it too is closed, for reasons beyond me.

"Hey Luna, why is a café and flower shop closed, on a bright morning?"

"Beats me. Clearly, they must not care about making a profit. Imagine the amount of money to be made off visiting tourists."

Laughing aloud, the sword flails under my robe and responds "Well, they're not losing out with us being here. We don't have a penny to our name! Hahaha!"

"Shut up, will you? And stop prancing about under my clothes. Your constant poking is annoying me. Come on, let's find a place that is open."

Carrying on, we search for an open establishment – however, not one place seems to be open. We continue, for many hours, only to come across the same outcome. What first began as a vague suspicion of the town, grows into a cause for concern. Everything from: Cafes, stores, markets and pubs are closed. I would simply ask a passer-by, but it would seem they are not very approachable. Not in a threatening or hostile way, but in a nervous way. A heavy air of fear and suppression fills this town – I can feel it. Something is wrong.

Having explored close to every nook and cranny of Brightin, Adamas and I rest by the seafront area – at the end of a long pier, looking out at the ocean.

"So, are all seaside towns as boring as this one?"

"No, like hell they are. This place might as well be a ghost town. Nobody looks our way or even speaks. Everything they have here is kept behind closed doors."

"Do you think it has anything to do with the monster we're trying to find?"

Scratching my forehead with distress, I reply, "Maybe... or maybe not. I just wish somebody would fill us in. Uh... where's that bothersome witch when we need her!"

"Hey, are you all right, kiddo?" Comes an unfamiliar voice. Looking to my right, I see an elderly man, approaching me with a walking stick. Not being able to see my companion sword under my robe, the man must be thinking that I am talking to myself, like some suicidal nutcase.

"Huh? Oh... I am fine, thank you. I am just thinking out loud, that's all. You're the first person to speak in this whole town."

Standing next to me, the man looks outward to the sea – holding his silence for many moments. Keeping a pleasant smile, he takes a small breath and addresses me, once more.

"We don't get many visitors here. I can hardly remember the last outsider that stumbled here."

"Is that so?" I ask – using this one in a million chance to pry further. "May I ask why that is? After all, this is a very beautiful town."

"Oh... Tradition. Please forgive us. You must have been shocked to find nothing open. Although it is troublesome and hard for us living here, it's the only way... to remain under the protection of the god: Praecipio."

Slapping my forehead, I forgive myself for not realising sooner. Of course, the cause of such ridiculous actions would be because of a god. I imagine that the being has hidden the monster I am looking for, somewhere troublesome.

"Is that so?" I reply to the man – with a curious and innocent tone. "What exactly would this town need protecting from?"

"Hmm... The calamity. Legend has it, at some point in history, it almost destroyed the world and attempted to usurp the greatest of gods. It was defeated however and imprisoned ever since. For its crime, it was sealed away – where it will remain for the rest of eternity."

"That's quite a story. However, I am not sure I believe it. The world is overrun with false tales" I say – subtly taunting the man. Like a fish being caught, he falls for the bait. Pointing outward to the sea, he rants on.

"Are you calling me a liar? It's the truth! Over there, by a nearby island is the home of Praecipio who keeps watch over the calamity!"

Indeed, looking outward to the sea I spot a small island – roughly a mile away. Bingo – so that must be where the monster is being kept. Now all I must do is find a way to cross the sea. Peering to the elderly man with a cold gaze – I drop my polite façade and ask sternly "Old man, I need to get to that island. Tell me where I can find a boat to get there."

The man flinches with fright – caught off guard by my direct and surprising question. Hesitating for a few seconds, he takes a step back and responds "No… we don't have any boats here. Besides, even if we did, you wouldn't be allowed on that sacred island. No human can set foot there. It is forbidden!"

Ignoring the old man's words, I lean over the very tip of the pier and moan "Sigh… is there anything this pitiful excuse for a port town has? Looks like I'll have to take matters into my own hands." Throwing caution to the wind, I jump off the pier and plummet towards the sea below. As I fall, the black sword panics and rants.

"Huh? Have you lost your mind, Luna? Why have you just leapt off the pier like that? Do you hope to swim all the way to that island!"

"No, of course not" I reply, as we continue to fall: wind rushing upward from beneath me.

"Well then, if you can't swim, what the hell are you doing?"

"Sigh, just shut up and watch, will you?"

Eyes closed, I clap my hands as I hit the surface of the sea. However, I do not sink but instead land gently upon it, as though my body were like a leaf.

"How the hell did you do that? You never told me that you could use magic!" Adamas screams – amazed and shocked by the little trick I just pulled.

Hands held in prayer position like a holy monk, I begin strolling towards the distant island – walking on the sea. "This isn't magic, Adamas."

"Huh? Well, if it's not magic, then what is it?"

"It is called a miracle art. I already told you this... a thousand times before! Do you ever listen to anything I say?"

The sword frustrates me to no end. It is constantly surprised at everything I do, no matter how many times it sees me do it... especially miracles. I possess a benevolent power, to cast living miracles. I aquired such power, sometime ago, shortly before encountering the blade. Adamas and these miracles of mine are what have made me one of the most feared individuals, in this land.

Before we know it, we reach the shore of what is supposed to be the home of a god and the prison of the one we're looking for. Observing our surroundings, we see a multitude of trees and a deep forest. By the entrance of the forest, a large golden statue can be seen. Walking to it, we inspect the monument, which looks to be of a heavily armoured knight, bearing six arms – each holding a rapier sword.

"So, I am guessing this must be the statue of the god who dwells here. He looks very proud."

"Aren't they all? That's just the kind of self-centred beings they are. Come on – let's get moving."

Suddenly, as I take a single step forward – the ground shakes violently, as though a thousand giants were stampeding towards us. "What in the world..." I whisper – sensing several powerful presences which seem to be mowing down the many trees from within the forest. As the sounds grow nearer, I begin to sweat. "Adamas, can you feel that?"

"Yeah... looks like we have company."

At that moment, a dozen four-legged beings emerge into the open. Bearing the faces of bearded men, equipped with large wings upon bodies resembling gryphons, the creatures charge towards us - emanating a radiant light that sends shivers down my spine. Thinking fast, I call my sword to action.

"Adamas – go!"

"I am on it!"

Shooting forth at the speed of sound, the black sword flies before stabbing the first beast with a clean and fatal strike. Screaming in agony, the first of the twelve falls to the ground, as the others gallop around – watching with caution. As they circle around me, my dancing sword companion speaks.

"Luna, do you know what those weird creatures are? Oh, let me guess... you plan to tell me another time, right?"

"Wrong. What you see are the steads of the gods, known as Cherubim. I've only read about them in rare texts, so it's shocking to actually see them in person."

"Is that so?" Adamas asks, taking the offensive - piercing through six of the riding Cherubim. As they scream on their way to death, I cover my ears from the sheer volume of their cries, while the magnificent sword zips to my side once again. "The gods seem to have everything: Gifts, love, faith, loyalty and even their own steads. I wish I had a stead."

"Sigh, must I keep reminding you? You're a sword... act like it."

Spinning to the five remaining Cherubim, Adamas finishes off the last of the beasts – severing their bodies in half.

Upon their the defeat, they each burst into a trail of light that rises into the clouds. Seeing no more enemies, we breathe a sigh a relief – soaking in the sound of the peaceful waves.

"Hmm, it seems that was the last of them. I sure hope so anyway. Their screaming was enough to shatter my eardrums. Regardless, thanks for getting rid of them, Adamas."

"Hey? Are my hilts deceiving me? Are you actually paying me a compliment?"

"Yes... don't get used to it. Come on... we have work to do."

As we prepare to resume our journey, another earth-shaking sound of a stampede is heard, this time greater than the last. "Sigh... what now?" I mumble, hearing countless trees being trampled on.

"Be careful Luna. I sense something powerful... more than I've ever felt before!" Adamas warns, levitating in front of me, protectively.

Bursting into the open, we marvel at a gigantic Cherubim, bearing three heads and eight large wings. Upon its back, a deity can be seen, covered in golden armour, bearing six arms that each wields a shining rapier sword and a glowing halo above its head.

"Shit, it's the god. Adamas go!" I order – commanding my sword to launch directly to the rider and its stead. To my disbelief, the heads of the large Cherubim open their mouths and catch the blade in their jaws. "What in the..."

"Uh... let go of me!" Screams Adamas – trapped within their locked jaws. Laughing aloud, the six-armed god summersaults off its stead and commands the Cherubim to plummet into the sea, along with my companion sword.

Landing elegantly, minor meters apart - the multi-sword wielding god faces me, as I stand defenceless. "Shit!" I whisper to myself – keeping my eyes glued to the opponent who stands with a piercing stare and a bold grin. He assumes a strange fighting stance - standing on one leg and rotating his arms hypnotically. This god is not like the others. Unlike the rest I've encountered, he actually bothered to anticipate my actions – using his Cherubim to keep my sword at bay.

"Mortal, give me your name?" He asks softly yet clearly – exuding an impatient aura, like an unwavering king. Reluctant to Comply, I answer him.

"Its... Luna."

"Luna? Tell me... what are you doing here, especially with the god-slayer weapon: Adamas?"

I flinch, surprised at his knowledge of my companion sword that can slay the gods. I do not answer him – knowing that he most likely will answer his own question anyway.

"That cursed sword you possessed, is supposed to have been kept in the holy land of Lelail. How did you manage to get a hold of it, especially when such a weapon is supposed to be so heavily guarded?"

"I dunno… You tell me?" I ask brazenly. It probably wasn't a good idea to respond so carelessly – however, it's the best thing I could think of, to buy time. Damnit, what's taking that blasted sword so long to return!

Taken back by my boldness, the being pauses for many seconds before laughing. "Hahaha, what do I care anyway. It's none of my concern. My purpose is to stay on this island… forever. Such a boring fate, don't you think?"

To my curiosity, I notice a slight look of sadness upon the opponent's face. I am not exactly sure why and neither do I care. However, his brief break of focus is all I need, to take the initiative.

Clapping my hands into prayer position, I take a deep breath and exhale. As I do so, the whole world stops. Everything from the water, wind, clouds, to the trees and flowers. Everything in the world has frozen in time, except for me of course. I must hand it to this particular god, for trying to catch me off guard – however, I am always one step ahead; I have to be. Only an idiot relies on just his weapon to fight – which is why at times like these, I utilize my trump card: miracle arts.

Wasting no more time, I dart past Praecipio and sprint into the vast and dense forest. The ability that I used to stop time, only lasts for a short period. During such a crucial time, my plan is to find a hiding spot within the forest, long enough for Adamas to eventually return… if he does ever return that is. Spotting a pack of bushes, beside a large tree, I take my chances and hide within them – just as time begins to resume again.

"What in the…" I hear the baffled god gasp – most likely speechless at my disappearance. Peering through a tiny gap from within the bush, I see the confused deity by the shore. He turns to face the direction of the forest and with frustration he shouts, "I know you're in there, somewhere!"

All I have to do is stay still and be quiet. Finding me right now would be the same as trying to find a needle in a haystack.

To my disbelief, however, I watch as Praecipio extends all six arms outward before unleashing a great light that fills the entire area. "What in the…" I close my eyes as the light comes my way – blowing me off my feet. I fall and tumble – keeping my eyes closed as the sounds of trees being destroyed can be heard, all around me.

Slowly opening my eyes, I gasp with shock at the aftermath of the light. The large and dense forest that once was, is no longer. Now, it is nothing more than a desolate wasteland. Such power.

At that second, the sound of a blade can be heard from behind, followed by a stern threat.

"Move an inch and I'll kill you… mortal."

Peering slowly from the corner of my eye I see the six-armed god, pointing one of his swords, inches from my neck. With no further tricks up my sleeve, I do as he says and remain still. A somewhat tense moment of silence fills the desolate grounds between us. Although I cannot see his face expression fully – I feel his piercing gaze, as though he were looking into my soul.

"Mortal, the way you evaded my sight earlier, should not be possible – even by magic standards. You used a miracle, didn't you!"

My silence is all he needs to confirm his guess was correct. With his sword still aimed at me, he slowly treads to my front – holding a cautious glare.

"I've experienced such a miracle once before. You used: Time Stop. However, an art such as that one is not widely shared. In fact, it is only revealed to the elite disciples of the grand order of Lelail. Wait… are you a disciple? Answer me now!"

Damn, he's good. For a god that has been left here for thousands of years, he seems clued up. Even so, I really don't want to have to tell him any more about myself. Shit, what do I do?

"Lunaaaaaa, hang in there!" shouts the familiar voice of my companion sword, soaring to my aid from the distance. Hearing him tearing through the wind, I let out a relieved sigh.

"Took you long enough, Adamas!"

Within seconds the black sword descends in between my foe and I. Flinching with caution, the god shuffles backwards a few paces and curses, "Damnit. So, you broke free from the jaws of my loyal stead."

"I did more than break free from that filthy pet of yours. I made sure to cut out all its teeth before slaying the vulgar thing. It dragged me miles under the sea. I could barely hold my breath!"

Rolling my eyes, I stand to my feet and take hold of the blade with both hands. "What are you babbling on about? You don't need to worry about breathing. You don't have a mouth!"

"Oh yeah? Well if I don't have a mouth, then how am I speaking?"

"Beats me. I didn't create you. More importantly, we have bigger issues right now. We need to kill that god!" I state – entering a strong fighting stance and glaring to Praecipio. Not to be intimidated, the deity glares back at us – wielding its six blades.

"Hmph, don't get cocky, just because you have a sword by your side. The odds are still weighed against you. For not only do I have six blades, but I am also one of the best swordsmen among all the other gods."

"Is that supposed to scare me? Well, it doesn't!" I shout – pouncing forward to duel against the six-armed being. Our blades strike continuously; my one sword against his six. His movement is fast, inhumanly fast – stabbing at the speed of sound. However, despite his lightning-fast thrusts, I manage to dodge each attack – like a fly evading a storm of raindrops.

"What in the..." The god stutters – unable to believe his eyes at my swordsmanship. Upon each successful dodge, I counter with a quick swipe, which although doesn't quite make contact against his body, still manages to surprise and impress him. "... How are you able to fight so well?"

"Save the compliments" I state, as we run side by side through the island – continuing our showdown. Not only do I hold my own against the multi-sword wielding god, but my attacks also begin to slowly become more precise. The reason for this is simple. Everything in this world has a pattern. The sun rises every morning, only to be surpassed by the moons at night. The flowers bloom by certain seasons, only to wither when their time is up. Everything has a pattern and the gods are no exception.

Praecipio's fighting style is terrifying, for if I were to slip for even for a second, I'd lose my life. However, it only took me a few seconds to figure out his fighting style. The first two arms come against my right side, while the next two come to my left. The fifth arm attacks from the centre, while the sixth defends. Rinse, repeat, rinse repeat.

"No, you are not just an opponent" the deity utters – showing a great smile upon his face. "You are a blessing!"

"A blessing?" I respond, dumbfounded by his remark. In fact, I am so dumbfounded that I let my guard down for but a second. However, that one second is all my opponent needs during such a heated battle. Wide open, all it takes is for one of his blades to finish me. Astonishingly though, he chooses not to attack with his blades but instead with a kick. I am sent flying before tumbling across the ground. Hitting against a large stone slab I drop my companion sword.

"Shit!" I whisper, before reaching to pick it up. However, before I have the chance, the deity steps onto my blade and addresses me.

"Luna, was it? I think this is where I say: checkmate?"

"Fuck!"

"Haha, Relax. Although you lost this round, I'll offer you an opportunity for a second bout. Come to the centre of the island, by the great stage and I'll be waiting. Don't disappoint me!"

At that moment, the god disappears into a burst of light – causing me to cover my eyes. As the light disappears, I open my eyes and scan the empty surroundings. Exhausted from the intense dual, I sit in silence – breathing deeply to catch my breath.

"That was a close one, right Luna?" Adamas says – standing upright before leaping onto my chest. "I wonder why he chose to not kill you? We must have given him a good impression, don't you think?"

"Huh? Yeah… I guess…" I reply, becoming concerningly more exhausted. In addition, I begin to lose my breath and sweat immensely. Shit… I don't feel so good.

"Hey... you don't look well, Luna. What's wrong?"

"I am... fine... I... am... fine..."

Without warning, I close my eyes and hit the floor – hearing the screams of my hysterical companion sword as I lose consciousness.

Chapter 4: Blessed Battle

Sitting upon a rooftop, I am looking up at the majestic stars above – gazing at the twin moons. The light from the celestial wonders illuminates all that is beneath them, and I am captivated… Lost in their grace.

"I think I know how they got there; the moons I mean" a voice comes to my right side. Turning my head, I see a girl, also looking up at the sky – eyes filled with wonder. Biting her lips, I can see she is trying to piece an explanation together, as to why such beauty exists.

"Hmm, well go ahead, sister" I utter with curiosity – eager to listen. Already, I can assume that whatever she is about to say, will be something enlightening. That's just the kind of person she is.

"Well, what if the moons are places where people live, much like how we live on Popla? What if they're also looking at us, wondering about our world? What do you think, brother?"

Holding my silence, I ponder her theory. She has a point – however, I am not sure I entirely agree. Staring up at the stars once again, I reply "I dunno… who can say? Perhaps there's no reason for why they exist at all? I mean, what if they're just there to be admired? Why must they have a reason?"

She smiles and shrugs her shoulders – impressed by my response. With a grin, I sit back… and close my eyes.

"Hey, Luna! Wake up will you!" Comes a hysterical voice into my ears.

"Huh? Sister, are you ok!" I panic – opening my eyes and sitting upward. However, I am no longer on the roof of the dark night, but under the bright blue sky of the small island.

"It was a dream…" I whisper to myself – realising where I am.

That's right, I came to this island, in the hope of finding some-thing that would help me locate the Land of The Gods. However, I was stopped by a god called Praecipio. He spared me, and I don't remember anything else, after that. I must have dozed off.

"Oh Luna, don't scare me like that. You had me so worried!" Rants Adamas – bouncing into my line of sight like an annoying puppy.

"Huh? Oh, don't worry about me. I'll be fine..." I say dismis-sively – slowly pulling myself up. As I stand to my feet – I take a deep breath and stretch my arms wide. Suddenly without warn-ing, I cough forth blood, before tumbling to the ground. "Shit!"

"Luna, are you ok? What's going with you!"

"I am fine... It's just a reaction. It will pass."

"A reaction, from what?"

Upon a brief pause, I get back to my feet and reply "A reaction from using a miracle, moron. Come on, I'll explain along the way", I state – walking onwards, further into the island, where the god awaits.

Floating by my side, Adamas asks "So, are you gonna tell me what exactly a miracle is and why you're acting so weird?"

"Very well, Adamas. So – are you aware of the type of arts in this world? I am not referring to the typical kind, such as music, painting or science. I am referring to the art of a supernatural kind. There are two main types. The first type is magic. Using spells, one can manipulate the natural energies within this world. However, the second type is miracles. Only a certain few can use miracles and I just so happen to be one of them. Such arts allow me to create or negate the principles of this reality. Sim-ply put, anything I imagine can be realised. Earlier I used a mir-acle called time stop, to buy me enough time while facing off against Praecipio. Almost anything is possible, with a miracle."

"Wow! That sounds amazing Luna! Wait... So how come you can use it?"

Being careful to answer, I pause for a few seconds and reply "It... it's a long story. The downside is: using it saps my lifeforce. Which is why I often use it, sparingly. Overuse of such an art is too much for the human soul to bear – hence the reason for my sudden lack of energy earlier. For me, my daily limit is only three uses. Any more than that and I risk losing my life."

"Really? Wait... so seeing as you used it twice already today, does that mean you only have one more left?"

"Precisely. The final catch is: I can't use the same miracle twice in one day either. It has to be a different miracle." At that moment, we see a large coliseum up ahead. It is gigantic – fit together with numerous stone pillars that look as though they have lasted since the dawn of time.

"So – it looks like we found our impressed opponent. I am willing to bet that the monster we're looking for, is somewhere there also" I say – strolling onwards, arms crossed.

"Yeah, you're right. I can sense Praecipio, along with another aura. It feels strange. I've never felt anything like it before. By the way, do you have a plan for how to beat Praecipio? He's quite strong, don't you think?"

"Hmm, unfortunately, we're dealing with a tough deity. Beating around the bush, especially on his turf won't work. My idea is to simply defeat him with sheer skill alone. If I find myself in a pinch, I'll just use my last remaining miracle. All you need to do is be a good little sword for once and stay within my hands."

Blocking my path once more, the sword cries, "No way, Luna! I hate being wielded. Besides – I can handle him by myself and..."

"Ha! Have you forgotten the last time you whizzed around? You got caught in the jaws of his stead and dragged to the bottom of the ocean. No, for this fight, you're staying in my hands, whether you like it or not." Taking hold of the hilt of the black blade, I grip it tightly and approach the entrance of the Coliseum. We stop at the entrance – consisting of a large golden door, with ancient symbols inscribed upon it. An eerie silence fills the air, as we prepare for our second encounter with the fearsome adversary.

"Hey, Luna."

"What is it now Adamas?"

"One last thing troubles me. So, today, you used miracles to walk on water and stop time, right?"

"Right."

"If that is so, how do you explain your swordsmanship? I find it hard to believe that a human could fight on par with a god, with just skill alone – especially a god that has six arms."

"I... I had a good teacher... That's all."

Taking a step forward I place my hands against the large golden doors and shout aloud, "Hey Praecipio – I've come, as requested! Are you gonna open these doors or shall I barge my way through?"

My voice echoes and reverberates against the golden doors, amidst the faint howling of the wind. Upon a short moment of silence, the doors slowly open wide. Holding the sword tightly, I take a deep breath and carefully stroll inside.

As we enter, I glance around and notice an abundance of material possessions, placed on the surrounding spectator seats. Everything from: flowers, dolls, clothes, food, drinks and many more. I am aware that certain gods require material offerings, but this is a little overboard. There are literally thousands of items.

At the centre of the Coliseum, we see our opponent – sitting calmly on the dusty ground. Upon drawing near we stop, roughly ten meters apart from the six-armed god. Disturbingly, he looks pleased to see me. From the outside looking in, Praecipio and I probably look like old friends, instead of enemies.

"Welcome, Luna. You are the first mortal to have pricked my interest. You are a blessing to me", he says – along with a respectful head nod. I am not impressed. In fact, his praises are creeping me out.

"Are we going to start or are you going to keep kissing my ass? I don't have all day" I say bluntly – pointing my sword in front. Annoyingly, the god isn't phased by my words and instead glances around at the various items on the surrounding seats.

"Look around you, Luna. Do you see all these offerings and gifts? They came from the people of that port town: Brightin. For thousands of years, the tradition was to offer their best gifts, to please me – in the hopes that I kept the great calamity sealed. Although I admire their efforts, not a single gift has ever made me happy. What I long for and desire is something that no material possession could ever replace. I long for... the thrill of a battle!"

Taking a step backwards, I flinch at the sight of his excited facial expression. Like a child opening a long-awaited gift, he glares at me as though I were the sun. "Hmph – so the one thing you've always wanted in this world, was a mere fight?" I ask curiously, surprised by the god's honest desire.

"No! I don't crave a mere fight. What I want... Is a battle of dreams!" He shouts forth – emanating a radiant aura from his body and halo. "For millennia, I have experienced the same reoccurring dream. Within it, I am fighting the most amazing battle I've ever witnessed. My opponent is someone that could kill me, with a single strike. Then, my dream always ends, with myself as the loser - however at peace and fulfilled that my longed-for wish was granted. Unfortunately, not a single foe in the real world has ever matched my skill... until now."

Standing to his feet – wielding his six blades, Praecipio enters a fighting stance and says, "Although you probably won't last long against me, please do your best to keep this joy upon my face – even if it's for but a fleeting moment!"

Launching forth, my opponent pounces towards us. Holding my companion blade within both hands, I ready for our second bout. "Here he comes!" Adamas warns – stating the obvious.

We do battle – clashing blades continuously, under a now looming sunset. Each swipe from my foe is countered by my blade and each attack I perform is blocked by one of his six swords. The sound of steel reverberates rapidly through the coliseum – testament to our skills and swordsmanship. Looking into his eyes, the same smug smile remains on my opponent, as though this dangerous duel were but a thrilling sport.

"Beautiful... Beautiful... Beautiful!" He says repeatedly, upon each strike. Like masterful performers, we dance around the stage of gifts – attempting to take the life from the other.

"Block... Evade... Attack... Block..." I whisper to myself – memorising Praecipio's battle style further and further. With each second, I become more familiar with his techniques. With each second, he becomes predictable. Hmph... Godly swordsman my ass.

"Mortal - when I fight you, I feel like I am within my dream!"

"Well then, allow me to put you to sleep, permanently!" I threaten – slipping past his blades before performing a mighty forward stab. As my blade gets closer to him, a smile opens on my face. It is a smile of accomplishment, upon having figured out his fighting style. Do you know that feeling of putting together a jigsaw puzzle or puzzle cube? That's the sensation I am having now.

Suddenly, inches before my blade makes contact, Praecipio evades my strike and summersaults backwards to safety. Shit. Serves me right for speaking too soon. I was so close!

"Whoa, Luna! You almost had him!" My sword companion says excitingly.

"Be quiet, will you? I am trying to concentrate!"

Such a missed opportunity will cost me - for although it looks like I have the upper hand, if I continue fighting like this, I'll lose. Even the best fighter in the world is bound by his bodily limitations. Such is the annoying hindrance of being a human. On the surface, I am portraying a calm and collected pose. However, in reality, my body is screaming with exhaustion. Each quick movement I used to attack, evade and defend against this god greatly drained my energy. It won't be long before my speed and strength begin to wane. I must think of a way to end this, quickly. Perhaps I should use my final miracle?

To my surprise, the opponent emits a blinding flash of light. As the light fades, I gaze with shock at what I see. The once six-armed god now possesses over one thousand arms – each wielding a shining blade. "Holy shit!" I gasp – overcome with nerves, while my opponent smiles to me.

"Young mortal. Although our duel was fun, I am afraid this is where it all ends. I told you that I am one of the best swordsmen among the other gods, didn't I? Well, now you know why."

"Hmph... With so many hands, something tells me that playing card games against you would be a pain in the ass" I respond sarcastically. I really should be more tactile with my choice of words, especially at a time like this. However, it can't be helped. I am nervous and my soul won't stop shaking. Sigh, to hell with it... It looks like I have no choice but to use my final miracle. Here goes nothing!

Clapping my hands together, I cast my third and final miracle for the day. Within seconds, a great light exudes from my body.

"Hey, Luna – what kind of miracle did you use just now?" Asks my companion sword. Holding him elegantly in my left hand, keeping my right hand in a prayer stance, I produce a sinister smile and reply to him.

"Watch and see. Let's go!"

Shom – at that second, I blast forth like a torpedo. I am fast, faster than I ever was before – closing the distance between my foe who blinks with surprise.

"What in the..." my opponent gasps – unleashing the entire might of his one thousand blades. As his numerous arms extend and launch towards me, I dance past his attacks with ease – moving at the speed of sound. "... So fast!"

"Whoa, Luna! You're like a human thunderbolt!" Adamas adds – as I continue to dodge each strike from Praecipio. Not only has my movement increased but so has my cognitive ability. His thousand arms that relentlessly come at me, seem as though they are moving at slow motion. I can see them, I can see them all!

"Mortal – I couldn't tell you how long it has been since I felt such exhilaration. Although you clearly are but a man, you fight like one of us, the gods!"

"Hmph, such an insult to assume that great skill equates to godliness. I am sorry to break it to you, but my potential as a human being cannot be compared to anything!"

Taking the offensive, I sprint past his swords and cut off one of his many arms.

"Ughh, you bastard!" Praecipio shouts as I keep a focused glare – watching as his severed arm falls to the ground. One arm down. Nine hundred and ninety-nine remaining!

Pushing forward – I zip around my foe, cutting off dozens of his arms as I dart from left to right. "Twelve… Fifteen… Ten… Eleven…" I whisper - counting the number of limbs I manage to cut down by each second.

"Slow down Luna. You're moving me too fast, I am getting dizzy!" The badgering companion moans, due to my flurry of strikes. Rolling my eyes, I ignore him and continue cutting through my foe.

"Nine hundred and ninety-eight, down!" I cheer – having cut off all but one of his arms. Standing shocked and helpless, Praecipio looks along the ground at his severed limbs.

"You… You managed to…" He stutters, trying to catch a clear sight of me as I continue to run rings around him. "This… This is just like my dreams. You… you were the adversary of my dreams all along!"

Darting past him once more, I chop off both legs, causing him to fall to the ground.

"Ahhhh!" He screams as I stand a meter apart from his torn body. Remaining still, I watch my defeated foe – who simply looks up at the orange sky.

After many seconds of silence – hearing nothing but the howling of the wind, I finally let go of my sword. Crossing my arms, I slowly approach the god that I bested in combat. Showing no mercy, I step onto his chest and look into his eyes.

"Praecipio: god of giving – I Luna have defeated you."

"Indeed… You have. Hmph… All this time, what I thought was a mere dream was, in fact, a prophecy… Of my own demise. However, I am far from sad. On the contrary, I am relieved. Thank you human… For giving me the best feeling I've ever had. If I ever have the chance to fight you again, I would like to do so… As a mortal."

There he goes again, with the compliments and random spiel. It almost makes me feel a little sorry for him. This is the first time that I've met a god that desired to be like one of us: mortal. Not to be distracted by such ponderings, I gently increase the pressure of my foot on his chest, before addressing him.

"I have two questions for you, although I am quite convinced you'll refuse the second one. First: where have you kept the so-called great calamity?"

"The great calamity? Hehe... We're standing on it. The great calamity is sealed under this very coliseum."

"Is that so? How do I unseal it?"

"Worry not, for my body itself was the seal. Once I perish, the great calamity will be free."

With an understandable nod, I utter "Very good. Now for my second question. Where can I find the Land of the Gods?"

The deity pauses – looking up at me as though attempting to understand my motives. Upon a short moment, he smiles and asks "The Land of the Gods? What business do you have with such a realm?"

"That's none of your business."

"Wrong... It's everybody's business. Whatever your reason, you would be foolish to go there."

"Hey, I didn't ask for your opinion. I asked you where I could find it!"

"Mortal – even if I wanted to, I wouldn't be able to tell you. You see... the Land of the Gods is a place so sacred that its where-abouts can not physically be uttered. It can only be shown, not said. However, the calamity you wish to awaken should know... How to get there."

Taking a step back, I gasp mildly and absorb his revelation. So, the location cannot be uttered, even though he has the know-ledge of its whereabouts. Fascinating and yet frightening at the same time. Peering to the floating sword by my side, I nod and command "Adamas... Finish him off, will you?"

With a straight stab into his chest, Praecipio lets out a short and quick squeal before slowly disintegrating into traces of light. Once he disappears, I stand silently – looking up at the sky.

"Hang on, sister. I am slowly getting closer..." I whisper to myself. Breaking my daydream, I fall to my knees with exhaustion – coughing relentlessly in the process. "Shit… as usual, the adverse effects of using three miracles have taken their toll."

"Luna, you ok?"

"I am fine Adamas. I just need to catch my breath. Besides, the worst is over now."

Suddenly, an unfamiliar voice responds to me from underneath the ground. Surprisingly, the voice sounds cheerful and menacing at the same time.

"The worst is over? Bwahahahaha… oh, how wrong you are. The worst has yet to come, for all of you!"

At that moment, the earth shakes violently, so much so that various pieces of the coliseum begin to crumble. Additionally, the sky turns pitch black as a great and thick cloud of darkness blots out the sun. "Luna… I am scared. Maybe it was a bad idea for us to come here?" Adamas whimpers – staying close to my side.

"Shut up, will you?" I order, also nervous at the frightening scene before us. Although I won't say it, I too am regretting coming here. A dark and malevolent force can be sensed, slowly coming towards us. What on earth was I thinking, awakening such a thing?

Suddenly, a great pillar of fire erupts from the spectator's seat to our left, which rises to the heavens. The sheer force and intensity of the fire is so strong that the entire collection of gifts are burnt to ashes. Traces of my robes are also singed, due to the great flame before us.

To my relief the pillar of flame ends – however in its place, we see a single female. Looking more like a teenager, she bears a single red horn on the left side of her head while sporting a dark cloak that covers her entire body from the neck down. Looking to Adamas and me with bold and wide eyes, she holds a playful grin before addressing us.

"My name is Ten: supreme overlord of the underworld! I don't know why you freed me from my prison, but you have my thanks. As a reward, I'll make sure to devour you… Painlessly!"

Biting my lips, I hold a firm stare – kicking myself for coming to this island in the first place. I am all out of energy and I have no miracles left to use.

"Shit... I fucked up!"

Chapter 5: Old Pain and New Wounds

As the dark cloud disappears, the waning sunset shows itself once more – allowing for us to take a clear look at the dark and mysterious girl. Her hair is long and black, and upon her forehead, a third closed eye can be seen. Behind her, a long scaly tail shows itself, extending down to her feet. On close inspection of her so-called cloak, they look to be wings, folded to resemble that of a cloak. More importantly, what should I do right now? If she comes at me, I won't have the energy to fend her off. My only choice is to perhaps persuade her not to fight me.

Slowly standing to my feet, I hide my nerves and state "My name is Luna and I have come here, requesting your help. I seek the Land of the Gods and I believe you know where it is."

Eyes perked with interest, she responds "The Land of the Gods? Hmph, if you knew anything about that land, you'd know that its whereabouts cannot be spoken" confirming the words of the defeated god moments earlier. Shifting her gaze to Adamas, her smile drops and she utters "Furthermore – what are you doing with Adamas? It doesn't belong to you!"

"Huh? How does she know my name?" Asks the surprised sword – looking to me for answers.

"How the hell should I know?" I reply to it – equally surprised by her knowledge of my companion sword. None of this makes sense. If she knows of Adamas, then does that mean it too was alive over five thousand years ago and played a part in the so-called calamity? If that's true, why doesn't it know of her?

Suddenly, the demon girl unfolds her dark wings – revealing a tight vest and short skirt. Shouting forth she says "I asked you a question, worm! What are you doing with Adamas? Everybody knows that it belongs to only one other person!"

Within the palm of her hand, a great ball of fire appears and grows larger by the second. "Shit... Could this day get any worse?" I whisper, watching as the fireball grows to be the size of a house. Holding it above her head, she screams to me.

"You're dead meat, mister!"

With no hesitation, she tosses the flaming projectile towards my position. It's coming so fast, there's no way I can escape it. "Adamas, protect me!" I command – causing the sword to react and dart straight ahead to the gigantic ball of fire. As they collide into each other, a great explosion ensues – blowing me off my very feet as my sword spirals into the distance.

"Uhhhhh!" I shout, blown backwards by the force of the explosion that is so great, the entire coliseum obliterates into pieces. Upon crashing to the floor, I lay still as a great shroud of smoke and debris covers the area. "Such power. Shit... Where the hell is Adamas?"

At that moment, I feel a single footstep on my chest as I lay helpless. It's the she-demon. Looking up at her grumpy face, she glares down and says "I see you've managed to brainwash Adamas into fighting for you. What have you done with the original wielder?"

I can't answer her. Not because I don't want to, but because I have no idea what she's talking about. However, something tells me that no matter what I say, she will kill me anyway. I close my eyes and prepare for a swift death. I am sorry, sister.

Suddenly, at that second, I hear a familiar voice addressing the demon girl.

"There's no use killing him. The original wielder of Adamas is no longer of the living. After all, it has been quite a while."

Opening my eyes, I am stunned and relieved by the sight of Trista the witch, who has miraculously appeared inches next to the she-demon. Caught off guard and equally surprised, the demon shrieks before leaping backwards with fright. "Eeeek! Who in blazes are you?"

Laughing hysterically, clapping her hands with amusement, the witch replies "Haha... Sorry, I couldn't help myself. My name is Trista and I am a witch. If I am not mistaken, you are Ten, the demon overlord that has been sealed away... For five thousand years."

Flinching abruptly before pausing like a statue, the girl stares blankly at Trista, shocked by her words. Nothing but the gentle whistling of the wind can be heard, for many moments, before the girl takes a single step forward.

"Five... thousand years? You're not messing with me, are you?"

Twirling around on the spot, Trista smiles and replies "No, I am not. Just look around you. Have you noticed any differences?"

Glancing up at the now early evening sky, along with the twin moons and numerous stars, the she-demon responds, "Come to think it, everything does look rather displaced. I didn't realise that I was sealed away for so long. Does that mean all of my friends have... died?"

Vanishing into thin air before reappearing next to the demon, Trista casually places her arm onto Ten's shoulder and utters, "Yes... including your most famous friend. You still remember him, don't you?"

The demon displays an almost terrified face, as the witch holds an amused grin, displaying a mysterious side that I've never seen before. It's clear that Trista seems to know more than she's letting on. Jeez, this day has been full of surprises.

Facing my direction, the witch says to Ten "That boy wishes to go to the Land of the Gods. Of course, his reasons are none of your concern, but he is the current wielder of Adamas: The immortal slayer. You'll need his assistance, where you're headed. After all, you want revenge, right?"

Looking at me as though pondering my worth, the she-devil slowly approaches me. As she gets closer, I sit upward and brace myself for anything. Stopping inches apart, she extends her right arm to me. "Very well. Let's be on our way."

Sheesh, finally she doesn't want to kill me... thanks to Trista I might add. I guess I could put our little altercation aside and proceed with using her help, to find the Land of The Gods. However, I am not a fucking idiot.

"Go fuck yourself" I respond, before standing to my feet and turning my back to them both. "Do you honestly think I would team up with a she-devil who almost killed me? You've got to be out of your godforsaken mind. Thanks, but no thanks. I'll find another way, thank you very much."

Lost for words, the demon girl and witch gasp at my refusal. Taking a step forward, Trista says "Hey, are you serious? But Ten can help you find the Land of the Gods. She knows the way!"

"Oh yeah? Then you go with that crazed demon. It's obvious that you have motives of your own also, Trista. Anyway, please make sure to magic up a boat for me to get off this island, will you?"

I begin to stroll away from the Coliseum of rubble, leaving the pair baffled.

"Adamas, where the hell did you go?" I shout to my companion sword, remembering that it was lost while trying to defend me, moments earlier.

"I am over here Luna. Could you give me a hand?" He responds, nearby. Looking to a pile of bricks, I see its hilt, sticking halfway out from a small piece of rubble. Crouching down, I pick it up.

"Moron, you could have easily lifted yourself out. It's not as though you can get tired."

"Sorry Luna, but this time it's the truth. That girl's fire... it's really strong, so strong that since getting hit by her flames, I've been unable to move."

"Oh really?" Interesting, for her to immobilise even Adamas here, which so far has proven himself invincible. Oh well... more reason to avoid such a troublesome person. What a waste of time this day has been.

With sword in hand, we carry on and head to the outskirts of the island, to the same spot we first arrived. Under the night sky, the moons and stars shine brightly – reflected upon the sea. By the shore, I see a small canoe, fitted with two oars. "Thanks, Trista" I whisper – strolling to the boat. Pushing it into the water before climbing aboard, I begin rowing, as my companion sword remains quiet.

As we slowly sail, on our way to the port town of Brightin, I converse with Adamas – slightly concerned.

"You're awfully quiet, for once. What's the matter?"

"Huh, oh me? Nothing special. Well… I was just thinking about what that demon lady was saying earlier. She seemed to know a lot… about me."

Looking up in thought, I recollect our interaction with the girl known as Ten, before agreeing "You're right, she did seem to know much about you. Adamas, tell me something: What is your earliest memory?

"My earliest memory? Well, my earliest memory was when you found me. I know nothing of before that, especially ever being wielded by someone else."

"Hmph, according to that she-demon, you were around, four thousand years ago. It seems like you have a bad case of amnesia. Haha, you are the most human sword I've ever met."

"Oh really? Do I really behave like a human being? By the way… what's amnesia? Is it a sickness of some kind?"

"I'll tell you another time."

Being quiet once again, we continue sailing under the peaceful sky and calm sea. After a short moment, the sword asks "Say, Luna – why are you so hell-bent on reaching the Land of the Gods? Nobody else seems to desire such a thing."

"Huh? Did I not already tell you this before?"

"No… at not in depth anyway."

Ah shit… I guess this is one of those heart-to-heart moments, right? Now, all we need are a few violins. Putting down the oars before folding my arms, I think back to when I first met the strange weapon.

"Ok – I guess it's only right that I tell you everything about me, seeing as we'll be stuck together until we reach our goal. I am from the famed country of Lelail, the richest, powerful and feared nation in the whole world. Within Lelail, my sister and I lived in poverty, within a shoddy town. Our parents were killed by some bandits when we were young, so we had to rely on each other. Many years later, my sister caught a vile sickness. This sickness was so nasty that not even magic could stop it. It had no cure, and still doesn't, to this day."

Moving its hilt with surprise, the black sword responds "A sickness that has no cure? Where would such a thing come from?"

"I personally believe it may have something to do with the gods. All I know for certain is that once you catch it, you're as good as dead... usually within seven days. Once the blessing comes upon you, it brands your right hand or palm with bizarre markings. Mankind has come to name this sickness: The Seventh Blessing. To my knowledge, such a thing has always existed with us humans, snatching our lives with no remorse. For some reason though, the gods seem drawn to those who have passed away by the vile sickness, and often times they hover around the grave of the claimed victim."

I pause and look out over the sea, taking a deep breath to compose myself, as my mind recalls my many griefs. Hanging onto my every word, Adamas asks, "So – what exactly are you looking for, within the Land of the Gods?"

"...The origin... of everything. It is common knowledge that above all the other gods resides one supreme god: The Great Observer. This supreme god apparently thought up all that we see into existence. My idea was to ask of its whereabouts, to find it and request that it save my sister. Seeing as it thought everything into being, it could just as easily think into existence a cure or something. I went to Lelail's capital city: Babylon city, to seek an audience with the Messiah. The Messiah is a human whom all the gods fear and respect as an extension of the Great Observer. However, he refused to help me and as such, my sister died."

"I... I am sorry to hear that Luna. Wait, so if your sister has already passed away, then why are you still looking for the Great Observer?"

Blinking quickly, as if its question were almost an insult, I reply "...To bring her back, to life."

The sword goes abruptly quiet, as though trying to understand the logic behind my intentions. I don't expect it to understand. I don't expect anybody to understand, for that matter. Regardless, I won't be deterred from my goals.

Picking up the two oars, I begin sailing once more while conversing further. "So, seeing as I had nothing left to lose, I decided to sneak into the church of Babylon and initiate a ritual that would allow me to also become a messiah and use miracle arts. I found you by mere chance, in one of the church's sealed rooms. You probably remember the rest from then, for when I pulled you out, you spoke to me and we left the land of Lelail."

"Yeah, that's right. So, by becoming a messiah, you hoped to force the other gods to tell you the whereabouts of the Great Observer."

"Bingo... - although as you have witnessed so far, this has proved very difficult indeed. If Praecipio's words are to be believed, asking for directions will be meaningless. Nevermind – we'll have to find another way. Perhaps we could capture the next god we come across and force it to physically guide us? Hmmm..."

"Luna, why don't we just use that demon girl's help? After all, she does know the way."

Rolling my eyes, I shake my head and respond "Yeah and attract a whole bunch of attention to ourselves while we're at it, right? I am not interested in partnering up with explosive demons. Before I know it, she'll stab me in the back and feast on my carcass. Let's think of a plan tomorrow."

Arriving at Brightin, we stroll through the empty streets and exit the sorry excuse for a seaside. With no escort to ride us back to Belgrave, we have no choice but to walk. Correction – I have no choice but to walk that is, through the cold of the night. Jeez, I can't wait to climb into my warm bed and put this whole farce of a day behind me.

Two hours pass and we finally reach the old shithole. As much as I love to hate this place, I feel a warm relief, coming back here. In a strange way, it kinda feels like home. Oh god, am I going crazy? I can't believe I just said that. Clearly, I am tired and need to get to bed.

We make our way to the hotel. Strength rejuvenated, Adamas resumes floating by my side, as we enter. Stepping into the reception, we traverse up the stairs – passing the many floors as we make our way to the seventh. As we prepare to ascend from the sixth floor, I can already foretell what will happen. The landlord Lloyd will jump out from nowhere and request his money. Shit, we don't have any Biscoins to give him!

"Boo!" Right on cue, Lloyd leaps out from behind to surprise me. I turn around and pretend to be shocked – holding my chest dramatically. "Haha... gotcha!"

"Christ Lloyd. Must you always frighten me like that? You're gonna give me a heart attack!"

"Well, serves you right for not being more aware, haha. I am surprised you've been able to survive for so long in these lands. How was your day?"

"Meh, disappointing. Anyway – please accept my apologies, for I don't have the cash for yesterday and today. I promise that I'll get something for you tomorrow."

With a puzzled stare, the man tilts his head and responds, "Huh? But your wife already paid it off."

"My what?"

Lost for words, I stare at the landlord as though he were crazy. A 'wife'? I don't have a wife. He must be pulling my leg.

"Yeah, your wife" He reiterates with a simple head nod. "She arrived about an hour ago actually. You should have told me that you have a woman."

Whispering to me, the black sword utters "Luna – what's he on about?"

"I don't know but there's only one way to find out" I reply, before darting up the stairs to my hotel room. As we enter, Adamas and I gasp with shock at the sight of our once moderately kept room. Now, for some reason, the place is an absolute mess. Everything from half-eaten pizzas, sandwiches and burgers can be found on the floor, alongside empty beer cans. "Who the fuck did this?"

"Whoa, it looks like a storm hit it."

Looking at the bathroom nearby, we hear running water and a person singing. "Someone's in our friggin bathroom" I mumble – slowly walking towards it. "Get ready for anything Adamas" I prep my sword companion, while reaching to the door handle. To my surprise however, the bathroom door swings open from the inside, revealing the she-demon, Ten from earlier this evening. Body wrapped in a white towel, holding a toothbrush in her mouth, she looks to us with mild surprise. "What the hell…!"

"Oh, hey boys. Glad to see you made it back. Took you long enough" She says casually, before stepping past us to sit on my bed. Adamas and I simply stare, lost for words at the audacity and sight of her. Upon pinching myself – wishing it was but a dream, I address her.

"What the hell are you doing here, demon!"

"Bwahaha, isn't it obvious? I am here to find the Land of the Gods with you."

"Like hell you are. I already told you that I am not using your help! Furthermore, how did you know where I lived?"

Taking no notice of me, she spits out the toothbrush, my toothbrush in fact before reaching to the messy floor to pick up a pizza slice… like an animal. Clearly, without simple manners, she answers while eating, "Trista told me where you lived. Relax… I'll promise not to get in your way."

"Is that supposed to be a joke? Look at the mess you made of my room! Furthermore, you're using my towel and toothbrush. Get out now!"

"Uh, is that the thanks I get for paying the charge of your hotel room for you? God, it's no wonder why you're having trouble finding help, with an attitude like yours."

"With an attitude like mine? Are you forgetting that it was you who tried to kill me earlier after I freed you from your prison? Also, why did you tell our landlord that you were my wife?"

"Sigh... yes, I tried to kill you earlier, but that's all in the past now. Furthermore, I had no choice but to tell him that we are married. How else was he going to give me a second key to your room? It's not my fault that I arrived here before you. Besides, you should consider it an honour to be within the same sentence as the great demon overlord."

To my surprise, Adamas bursts into laughter by the she-demon and my argument. Glaring to my so-called companion sword, I grit my teeth and shout "Adamas, why are you laughing?"

"Hehe, I am sorry Luna – Ten sounds really funny, especially when she's talking to you."

"Moron... you're supposed to be on my side!"

Throwing the towel to my face, Ten says, "I told you before: Adamas does not belong to you!" Looking to the black sword, she smiles and then asks it "So, what do you think, Dimmy? You're happy with me joining you, right?"

"Dimmy? My name is called Adamas."

Rolling her eyes before slapping her forehead, the demon rants "Oh jeez... are you honestly telling me that you've forgotten your nickname also? What happened to your memory? Well, I guess it has been five thousand years since I last saw you. Come on – let's drink and reminisce together!" She says cheerfully while picking up a fresh can of beer from the floor.

"Are you blind? How can Adamas drink with you? He doesn't have a mouth. He's a sword!" I say to the girl, shaking my head – still in disbelief at the whole situation.

Shrugging off my point, Ten replies "Don't be such a party pooper. Dimmy can simply pretend to drink. "Now, let's all relax and be merry!" She shouts, before tossing a can of beer to me.

Catching it within my right hand, I casually throw it back to her and respond "I don't drink. I am going to bed... downstairs!"

Turning around I exit the hotel room – leaving Adamas with

the annoying girl. With a deep sigh, I storm down the stairs, back to the ground floor reception area and crash to sleep, on the cold sofa. Fuck my life.

Chapter 6: The Dark Trio

Sitting upon a rooftop, I am looking up at the majestic stars above – gazing at the twin moons, once again. The light from the celestial wonders illuminates all that is beneath them, and I am captivated... lost in their grace.

"Ok, this time I think I know for sure, how the moons got there" comes the familiar voice from my sister.

"Hehe, very well Lucia. Let's hear it" I utter with curiosity – eager to listen to her.

"Well, what if each moon is, in fact, the home of a god? That would kinda make sense, right?

"I guess it's possible, I suppose. However, without us physically going there, we'll never know."

Upon staring in silence for many moments, she stands up, stretches her arms to the night sky above and proclaims "Someday... I'll find a way to the moons and see for myself, who lives there."

Rolling my eyes with amusement, I close my eyes and respond "Hmph, suit yourself, sister. Just don't come crying to me, if you discover that there's nothing there, at all. You would have wasted all that time and effort, for nothing."

"Dear brother, if that were the case, what would make you think that I'd feel disappointed? In fact, even if I were to never reach the moons and stars, it still wouldn't be pointless. After all, having a goal or purpose is better than having nothing at all."

"As ambitious as ever. Are you done? It's getting late and we need to get some sleep. Hey Lucia, are you listening? Lucia..." Opening my eyes I expect to see my sister, under the night sky –

however as I do, I find I am no longer upon the rooftop.

"Shit, it was another dream... Another recurring dream" I mumble to myself, recognising the hotel and cold sofa that I fell asleep in. It is now morning and the numerous windows by the four walls welcome the bright sun rays. With a deep breath, I close my eyes and sigh – taking in the slightly unsettling yet peaceful start to the day. "Morning already? I wonder what kind of day I'll have this time?" I ask myself – briefly casting my mind back to the events of yesterday. To my shock and surprise, the familiar voice of a certain witch addresses me.

"Are you gonna lay there all day? You don't have the luxury of time, Luna."

Upon a great sigh, I stay put – not reacting to her. By now, I am getting used to her predictable appearances. As such, I take my time, slowly opening my eyes as I sit upright on the sofa. Opposite from my position, I see Trista, sitting on a wooden stool - arms and legs crossed, looking to me with a shamelessly proud grin. Displaying an unfriendly gaze, I utter "What do you want, troublesome witch?"

"Oh my... You don't seem very happy, even after everything I've done to help you so far."

"Help me? Do you think that telling some she-demon where I lived was helping me? I already made it clear to you both yesterday. I don't want her anywhere near me. All I wanted, was information on finding the Land of the Gods. Nothing about her tagging along."

"Haha, but you know now that speaking the whereabouts of the Land of the Gods is impossible. Besides, what's so wrong about her accompanying you?"

"I'll tell you what's wrong: Everything about her! In case you've forgotten, I escaped my homeland of Lelail after stealing Adamas from the country's most powerful church. Essentially, I am a wanted man. With her around, it won't be long until the Messiah of Lelail comes after me."

Squinting her eyes for some time, as though unable to understand my reasoning, the witch bursts into laughter and responds "Aaahahaha... Is that your reason? Oh, honey, you don't have a clue, do you? Your actions alone this past month, have already spread far and wide. People have coined you the title: Luna the dark messiah."

"Bullshit. I don't believe you. Why has nobody said that to my face then?"

"They don't say it to your face because they're all afraid of you. After all, you're one of the only warriors here that can take on my toughest missions. It's not every day that we meet someone who can kill immortal beings. Curse all you want, but it's the truth. Your name is currently being spread far and wide and will eventually reach Lelail. So, if anything, having Ten with you will ensure your safety."

I hate to admit it, but she has a point. If what she's saying is true, then it's only a matter of time before the Messiah of Lelail finds out where I am. If he finds me, then it's game over.

Leaning forward, the smiling woman asks "So, have you made up your mind, misery guts?"

"Yeah, I'll allow her to escort us to the sacred land. However, I'd like to know something."

"Go on."

"Why are you doing this, Trista? This kind of assistance is well beyond your job description, as a mediator between clients. It's clear that you have some agenda of your own. Out with it."

Staring into space while caressing her chin, the witch stands to her feet and responds, "Well, I'd be lying if I said that I wasn't curious by The Land of The Gods - home and origin of all that is - brought into existence by a mere thought, supposedly."

"I see. So, your idea is to get me to do the hard work, while you watch from the sidelines. You're really a piece of work, you know that? But I guess it's to be expected, in this dog eat dog world. Anyway, I had better fetch the other two. I guess seeing as the she-demon knows the way, I have no further reason to stay in this shoddy town. So long, insufferable witch."

Standing up before turning my back to her, I begin strolling towards the staircase. However, as I take the first step up, the witch calls to me.

"Uh, you might as well save yourself the trip upstairs. Ten and Adamas had already woke up, hours ago and left."

"Left? To go where?"

"Haha, they went to the Provider. You can find them there."

Upon a pleasant chuckle, she exits the hotel – singing to herself joyfully. While standing alone in the hotel reception area, I am troubled. The stupid sword is supposed to be my companion, and yet as soon as some she-beast comes along, he forgets who I am. Well, I guess moaning to myself won't help. I had better meet up with them.

After a short while, I leave the hotel – waltzing through the town of Belgrave. It is an exceptionally busy day today, most likely thanks to the good weather. Market stalls of all kinds populate each turn – drawing in hundreds of locals. Not sure why people are so quick to buy anything from here though. Most of it is stolen and will only be sold to another person. The only thing worth buying here is the food, which in all honesty is pretty good. Speaking of food, I am starved. I sure hope Adamas and the she-demon have made themselves useful and grabbed some food, at least.

Before long, I reach the Provider – standing outside its doors. As I prepare to enter, I hear the sounds of cheering and clapping. Although I may be mistaken, it sounds much louder today. Is there something special going on inside? Gosh, the atmosphere feels so positive today. I guess it should be a good thing.

Opening the doors, I step inside and to my amazement, the bar is completely jam-packed, crowded than ever before. "What the hell…" I whisper to myself, trying to figure out the reason for such a huge clientele this morning. The punters all seem to be huddling around something in the centre of the bar. I would call out to Adamas and the devil girl, wherever they are, but the noise is so great, it would be pointless. Squeezing through countless sweaty and excited brutes, I attempt to find the two. As I struggle further into the centre of the bar, I begin to hear the voices of Adamas and Ten, laughing and shouting. Something tells me that those two are the reason for all the commotion.

Finally pushing to an opening, I am stunned at the sight of the she-demon, sitting at the centre of a small table. Kept company by the floating sword next to her, I catch Ten in the middle of an arm wrestling match, against a large man.

"For crying out loud..." I mumble, as the crowd scream and cheer with excitement - watching as the grinning she-demon's grip overpowers her nervous opponent. By the edge of the table, I spot a large open bag, filled with hundreds of Biscoins. So, it looks like they're competing over money. Such a barbaric concept.

At that moment, Ten completely overpowers the man and slams his arm onto the table, so hard it breaks in half. Money flies everywhere, while the crowd cheer louder, as the man lay on the ground, possibly with a broken arm. Paying no mind to his cries of agony, the girl laughs victoriously.

"Bwahaha... You lose, sucker! Taste defeat at my incredible strength. I am Ten, supreme overlord of the underworld. Now, pay up!"

"That's right, you heard her. Pay up, otherwise, we'll smash your face in!" Adds Adamas – sounding like he has been influenced by the demon's distasteful nature.

"Adamas, Ten... What the fuck are you doing!" I shout – stepping into the centre. As he instantly hears my voice, the sword freezes with surprise, as the whole crowd also pause with silence – petrified by my sight. Ten, however, simply rolls her eyes and yawns – like a teen whose fun has been spoiled.

"Oh, look who it is. It's the party pooper. Nice to see you're awake, finally."

"Quiet, she-devil," I say - casting my eyes to the black sword. "Adamas - in case you've forgotten, you're my weapon, remember? You can't just go running off whenever you want, especially with that monster."

"I am sorry Luna, but..."

"No buts! And I don't approve of you entertaining such petty sports and using vile language."

"But, you use vile language all the time!"

"I am different, moron. And for the last time: You are a sword, act like it!"

Interrupting me with an angry grunt, Ten steps forth and says "Hey, leave little Dimmy alone, asshole. He was merely supporting me, while you were lazing around. We managed to make over five hundred thousand Biscoins. A little appreciation wouldn't go unnoticed, jerk!"

Five hundred thousand Biscions? Come to think of it, that's a lot of money to be made in one morning. I guess I can't argue with that.

"Ha, I know what your thinking. You're most likely regretting your little outburst. Now that you've seen how much money I can make us, you've changed your tune, right?" She says with a smug grin. I gotta hand it to her. She's right, I suppose. Of course, I am not about to admit it to her. Her ego is already big enough, it seems.

"Sigh... Very well. Just grab the money and let's get out of this town, but not before getting something to eat first. I am starved."

As Ten begins to collect the coins scattered on the ground, I cross my arms and glance at the crowd of punters. With mouths open wide, they continue to stare at us – whispering to one another. I can already tell where this is going to go. Those blockheads are most likely thinking up rumours that will soon spread.

"Don't even think about spreading any falsities about me and the she-demon here. If I hear anything about us, I am coming to claim all your heads!"

Shaking with fear, they bow continuously and apologise profusely. Having crammed the earned Biscoins into a large pouch, Ten slings it over her shoulder and says "All done. Shall we get going, Lulu?"

"Lulu? The name's Luna."

"I know, but Lulu's easier to remember. Never mind, you'll get used to it."

"Sigh... Whatever."

Suddenly, the doors of the bar burst open and a single man storms in – erratic and terrified. "Guys, we got trouble. Hundreds of gods have appeared, asking for the calamity and the dark messiah!"

"What?" I gasp – knowing full well that the calamity would be Ten, and the dark messiah would be me. "You had better not be messing around with us. I am not in the mood for jokes today."

"I promise you, I am telling the truth. They said that if you don't come out, they'll destroy this whole town!"

The scared look in the man's eyes and trembling tone are enough to convince me. Shit – I really wished he was lying. I am not in the mood for fighting right now, especially on an empty stomach.

The crowd of brutes are equally shaken – wondering what I'll decide to do. If I stay hidden inside the bar, the gods won't be able to spot me – however, the town will more than likely suffer the consequences. The most efficient thing to do would be to run away and allow this town of degenerates to perish. However, as much as I'd love to do it, there are some people here worth saving. Lloyd the landlord of our hotel and Trista would be the main two, and I guess the loud brutes here have put a warm smile to my face, in times of boredom.

Putting the frightened sissies out of their misery, I turn to the exit door and casually stroll towards it, arms crossed – causing the men to whisper at my seemingly bold action.

"Well, are you two coming or not, or do I have to sort this out by myself?" I address Adamas and Ten – who upon a brief pause, follow behind me.

"This will be fun" Chuckles the she-demon, walking while holding the bag of money over her left shoulder.

"I sense so many strong presences, all around us", adds my companion sword – zipping to my side.

Upon leaving the bar and stepping outside, we marvel at the sight before our eyes. Vast in number, an army of gods, each bearing a large halo fills the sky. Exuding a bright and majestic light, their collected presence makes the heavens look almost golden. Hanging in the air, holding dazzlingly bright weapons, they look down at our position and stare at us, like judges within a courtroom. Hmph, the fucking liar said there were hundreds of gods, when in fact there are around one thousand in number.

"Mortal – are you the one known as the dark messiah?" One of them asks me – in a voice so great, the ground rumbles. "The one who stole the cursed sword Adamas? The one that killed our brethren and awakened the great calamity?"

"Yes... I am" I reply coldly – tapping my feet impatiently. I hate it when people ask questions they already know the answer to. If it's supposed to be a scare tactic, then it failed miserably. "Let's cut to the chase, shall we? You want me to surrender to you, correct? Well, clearly I am not planning on doing so, anytime soon. So, let's screw the words and let our blades do the talking!"

Together, they react with a slight flinch – taken back by my fearless reply. As they stay speechless, I glance to the demon next to me. She grins with amusement, as though impressed by my bold talk. Shifting my eyes quickly to the bar behind, I see the pack of brutes, huddled by the window – staring at us in suspense.

"Mortal – do you truly fail to grasp the magnitude of your actions? You are becoming an enemy to your overseers. Doing so is an act, punishable by death."

Bursting into laughter, Ten drops the bag of money and holds her stomach; hysterical by the god's words.

"Bwahahaha! That's the funniest thing I've heard in ages. A measly group of gods, asks my husband whether he truly understands the magnitude of his actions? No, it is you who do not understand the magnitude of your actions. Clearly, the past five thousand years of my imprisonment have made you forget the despair I brought to this world. Allow me to remind you, why I am the great calamity!"

Stretching her wings apart – Ten unleashes a fiery and dreadful aura. With fists clenched, she crouches briefly and shouts forth "I am the one and only: Overlord of the underworld. You are all my prey!" Soaring into the sky, she does battle with the multitude of gods. Instantly, the sky erupts into a series of fiery explosions – followed by bodies of deities that fall from the sky, crashing to the ground and houses.

With a watchful gaze, I notice that she uses no weapon to fight. Only her bare fists, which upon connecting with the gods, results in a gigantic explosion.

"I was the one who once brought the world to its knees!" She states – easily evading the attacks from her foes before countering: severing their bodies in half. "I am the one who once made it: To the Land of the Gods and will go there once again!"

She continues – soaring through the army, leaving a trailblazing fire in her wake. The opponents do not back down however and unleash a collective beam of light from their halos. However, she summons a great ball of fire within the palm of her hands and tosses it to them. The result is a great explosion, which completely obliterates hundreds of gods, in one go.

"Impressive..." I whisper to myself – watching the spectacle with Adamas by my side. So, she has the power to destroy immortal beings too". Is she using magic arts or something else entirely?

To our surprise, the entire townspeople can be heard cheering from within their homes, bars and stores – as Ten lays waste to the uninvited guests above.

"Whoa, she's so cool Luna!" Says Adamas – dancing with excitement, while I stand calmly – arms remaining folded. "Shall we help her?"

"No, let's allow her to enjoy herself. She has been locked away for some time, after all. Besides, we should be worried about ourselves right now." Right on cue, we see a further army of gods, running towards us from the far end of the main street we're on. Like a stampede, they charge towards Adamas and I – glowing brightly with swords held in front.

"Let's get to work!" I state - taking hold of my companion

sword before running fearlessly towards the horde before us. Wasting no time, I take on the numerous deities – cutting swiftly yet aggressively through their ranks. With each step, evasion and counter I make, a limb is lost from the foes – a testament to my unrivalled swordsmanship.

At this point, the townspeople are ecstatic – blown away as Adamas and I take on the celestial beings below, while Ten battles them in the skies. The town becomes a bed of chaos, as buildings, towers and homes crumble. Despite the carnage, however, the people of Belgrave continue to chant our names: "Horray dark messiah" and "Horray the calamity".

Almost two hours pass and the godly intruders are finally no more. Against the strength of Adamas, Ten and myself, the deities were no match. Standing in the middle of a large street, I sit on the ground – heavily exhausted from it all.

"That was amazing Luna! We were so cool!" says Adamas – clearly overjoyed by our battle against seemingly uneven odds.

"Hmph... That's easy for you to say. You're not the one who must deal with getting fatigued. On top of that, I am starving!"

"Bwahaha, the cup of victory should be more than enough to quench your hunger. After all, you've earned it" comes the voice of the she-devil: Ten. Looking up at the sky, I see her – bat-like wings outstretched, looking down at me with arms crossed. Slowly descending to my position, she holds a genuinely pleased and intrigued smile. Landing to the ground, she stares at me, as though evaluating my character.

"What? Why are you looking at me like that!" I ask her – bothered by her peculiar gaze. Upon a jolly head nod, she crouches down and extends her arm to me.

"You're not so bad after all, Lulu. The way you fought all those numbskulls was incredible. Your fighting style reminds me, of an old friend of mine."

Keeping her arm stretched forth, I look to her in silence – hesitant to reciprocate her gesture. I admit I wasn't too pleased with the way she tried to kill me yesterday, and the way she trashed my hotel room. However, she does make a good companion, as well as a hopeful tour guide to our destination.

"You fought well also" I respond to her – taking hold of her hand before standing up. Glancing around, we see the aftermath the battle had on the town of Belgrave. Almost everything is demolished. Some buildings are partly destroyed, while others are completed gone.

"What shall we do, guys? Our fighting has made quite a mess here. It will take weeks or months to fix everything" utters Adamas – displaying a tone of concern.

Turning her back to us, the she-demon rolls her eyes and replies "Pffftt... It's not my problem. The mortals here should be thankful we kept them all safe". Such an irresponsible response, befitting a person like her.

Rolling my eyes also, I utter "It's not my problem also. But even so..."

Clapping my hands together, I cast a miracle art – summoning a great sphere of golden light to envelop the entire town. Before our very eyes, the broken houses, buildings, stores and streets of Belgrave, astonishingly repair all by themselves. As though having a life of their own – each brick and stone begin to levitate and drift through the air, forming multiple large ques, throughout the entire town. Watching as the city slowly reconstructs itself, Ten and Adamas freeze in shock.

"What... What is this?" She asks – mouth opened wide.

Hands pressed together – surrounded by the light, I reply to her "It's called a miracle. What? You've never seen anything like this before?"

Looking to me with a baffled gaze, she pauses briefly and says "Yes I have, but not used like this. When did humans acquire the power of the gods?"

Judging by her concern, I'd hazard a guess that miracles weren't used by humans, in her time.

Breaking our conversation – the residents of Belgrave step into the open, from around a nearby corner. Upon staring quietly at the three of us, they begin clapping their hands – cheering and whistling our victory. As we stand speechless – more residents can be seen, surrounding us from all sides. I must admit, I am quite overwhelmed by their gratefulness. Looking to the ground, I hide my blushing cheeks, while Adamas hangs by my side.

Unequipped with the same modesty – Ten beats her chest and shouts battle cries of victory, like a gorilla.

"That's right worms... I, the great Ten saved your sorry souls! With the aid of my husband and his deadly blade, we obliterated the weak gods!"

Yanking her by the horn, I whisper to the loudmouth demon "Hey, why the fuck are you telling them lies? I am not your husband!"

"Ah relax, Lulu! Rumours like this help to spread our name, far and wide. You want to be feared, don't you?"

"No, I don't... Silly she-demon. I just want to get to the land of the gods, with as little trouble as possible. Come on – we've wasted enough time as it is. Let's grab something to eat on our way to leaving this dump!"

Together - Adamas, Ten and I make our way towards the exit of Belgrave, watched by the entire townspeople who follow behind us, clapping and cheering continuously. It almost seems like we've acquired our very own followers, with the intention of remembering us for years to come. Briefly stopping by a bakery, we stock up on food supplies, using the money earned within the Provider, before departing the town.

Upon leaving, being roughly a dozen meters outside of Belgrave, I stop and take a deep breath – turning to take one last look at the old shithole that accommodated Adamas and me for the past month. Miraculously repaired, the town looks good as new, which brings a smile to my face, as the people can be heard singing and laughing. Upon a small nod, I turn around and resume my journey – along with Ten and Adamas.

A further two hours have passed since departing, and the three of us have been walking along a single road, surrounded by nothing but expansive fields. Biting through a steamed bun, I follow behind Ten, who continues to glance about her surroundings – mumbling to herself. Drifting between us, the floating sword observes the land before us also.

"So, you've been a little quiet, ever since we left. Are we going in the right direction, she-demon?"

"Huh? Oh... To tell you the truth, I am not sure."

"You're not sure? What is that supposed to mean? I thought you knew the way?"

Stopping in her tracks, Ten turns around and replies "Well, it's not so easy, seeing as much has changed since my imprisonment. Everything is so darn different in this world."

"Oh yeah? Like what?"

Pointing upward, the girl responds "Well for starters, the sky is all messed up. Last night, I noticed two moons. However, in my day, there were four."

Pausing with shock, I remain silent – taken back by her revelation. Four moons, once existed? I admit I find that quite hard to believe. If there were two additional moons at some point, what caused their disappearance?

Slapping her forehead with distress, the she-demon turns her back to me and continues leading the way, as Adamas and I trail behind. "Worry not, Lulu and Dimmy. Once I get my bearings straight, we'll be at the Land of the Gods, in no time!"

"Hmph, I won't hold my breath. On a similar point, you mentioned earlier that the Land of the Gods cannot be uttered. Does that also apply to clues? nearby locations? Anything?"

"Forget it, Lulu. I can't even mention whether its north or south. If I try, the words do not leave my lips. It's annoying and troublesome. The Great Observer most likely put it in place, to ensure its safety from man and us demons alike."

Grinning with a slight surprise, I perk up at her mention of the Great Observer: The originator of everything – residing in the Land of The Gods. "I am happy to know that you too are aware of the Observer. Nowadays, most people talk of it and its sacred land as though it were a fairy-tale"

"Pffft... I assure you, it's no fairy-tail, Lulu. In my time, everybody knew it as fact, Which was why so many attempted to find it. Men, women and beasts of all kinds, risked their lives trying to find the Great Observer and the Land of The Gods, to have their wishes granted. Of course, everybody failed... including me."

Holding her head low, I sense a feeling of sadness coming from Ten. Knowing myself all too well, I stay quiet and not ask any further. However, that doesn't stop my pesky companion sword from chiming in.

"Ten – how did you fail? I thought you said you once found the Land of The Gods?"

Stopping once again, she turns to Adamas and says "Yes, I made it. A lot of my friends made it. However, many of us suffered grave consequences. My price was imprisonment and..." Pointing to her forehead, she gestures to us the single red horn on the left side of her head and the absence of what is supposed a second horn, on the other side. By the look of things, I assume that she was met with some strong opposition. Perhaps even going up against the Great Observer herself.

"The Land of The Gods is not a place to be taken lightly" She utters - resuming her stroll. "Many comrades have become bitter foes because of it. Even your best friend may become your greatest enemy. Hell, even I could become your foe."

"Well, we'll just have to cross that bridge when we get there, won't we?" I ask – finishing the last of my steamed bun. As we continue, I ponder her last words. It's clear that she has some good yet unsettling knowledge about our destination. It kinda makes sense, for people to fight over the prospect of a wish. After all, mankind has fought for less. Regardless, even if it means killing a friend, I wouldn't think twice – if it meant seeing my sister alive once again. I'll happily be the bad guy, for all of eternity.

"Hey guys, I have an idea!" Shouts Adamas cheerfully. "Why don't we simply purchase a map? That way, Ten could simply point to the destination, without having to say it, right? It would surely make our journey that much easier, right?"

Looking to one another, as though not having thought of it

earlier, Ten and I gasp with surprise.

"Aha! That's a great idea, Dimmy! You're a genius!" She says – yanking him by the hilt before waving him around frantically. "How could I have forgotten such a convenient thing? Although I am no pro, I know enough about the world to spot where the Land of the Gods should be located, on a map, at least!"

"I must admit, that's a pretty neat idea Adamas. If the sacred land can't be uttered, we'll just have Ten show us on a map. Excellent work!" I compliment the black sword – watching as he is flailed around by the ecstatic demon girl.

"Luna, make her stop, will you! She's holding me so tight, I might lose my breath. Either that or I may puke from being so dizzy!"

"Sigh... You're a sword, Adamas. So, it's settled then. The next place we stop at, we'll buy a map and head for the Land of the Gods!"

Chapter 7: Who we are... Who we were

Sitting upon a roof with my sister Lucia, we look up at the majestic stars above – gazing at the twin moons, just like every other night.

Sensing a slight worry from my sister, I turn to her and ask "What's the matter? You seem sad or concerned about something."

"Huh? Oh... No, I am fine."

"Like hell you are. I can read you like a book. Come on... Out with it."

"Ok. Well... I was just wondering where mother and father might be."

Holding my silence, I look down with a frown – reminded of our tragedy. Because of a bunch of criminals, our parents were taken from us. I always knew the world was a dangerous place, but I never imagined anything would happen to my family. Now, it's just me and my sister.

"Sister... Wherever mother and father are, I am sure they're happy."

"Yeah, you're right..."

Suddenly - someone calls out to us from below.

"Excuse me, would you like to play with me?"

Surprised, we blink in every direction before looking down at the main street. To our surprise, we see a single boy, roughly the same age as us. Dressed in white and gold robes, too large for his small and slim frame, he looks up at us eagerly. Straight away, I can tell that he's not from here. Not just by his clothes, which look to be made of the finest quality, compared to me and my sister's ragged attires, but rather... something about his presence. Putting it simply... he seems special.

"What are you doing in the middle of the night, all by your-self? This town isn't safe, especially for outsiders."

"Huh? What's an outsider?" He asks with a naïve and curious look.

"An outsider is someone who isn't a local" replies my sister – amused by the interesting boy.

Upon scratching his head, displaying a thinking stare, he responds "Oh... Well I guess I am, haha! So... will you play with me?"

"No! Just go home, before something bad happens to you."

Swaying his head with refusal, the boy turns his back to us and says "Nah, I am not ready to go home yet. Don't worry about me, I'll just find someone else to play with. Have a good night!"

Astonished, we watch as he slips into the night – long and baggy robes shuffling along the soiled ground. Is he insane? Running around in this poverty-stricken village is not a good idea at this time of night, especially by himself. If he's not careful, he'll run into trouble.

"Brother, we gotta go after him!" Advises my sister – concerned just as I am. Wasting no time, we climb down the roof, onto the ground before chasing after him.

"Hey, come back will you!" We shout, just as he readies to divert past a corner into an alleyway. Being roughly twelve meters from us, he pauses before looking at us with surprise.

A spontaneous smile appears on his face. "You'll have to catch me first!" He laughs, before sprinting into the alleyway, to our dismay.

"Hey, stop!" I shout – chasing after him, along with my sister close behind. He leads us into the alleyway, then a back garden and then the main street. Before we know it, my sister and I are sent on a wild goose chase – pursuing the mysterious boy past endless twists and turns. He seems to be enjoying this unintentional game of cat and mouse, laughing hysterically, while my sister and I grow more frustrated. Bothered by the rants, laughs and constant running – villagers can be seen peering out from their homes, telling us to clear off and get lost.

The pursuit goes on for many hours into the night, before we finally track him down in a small field, by the outskirts of our village. Tripping over his long robe, he falls flat to the ground, much to our relief.

"Quickly, don't let him get up!" Shouts my sister, as I pounce on top of him – pinning him to the ground.

"Gotcha!"

Looking up at me with cheerful eyes, he simply chuckles as I display a tired, exhausted and extremely angry glare. Strangely enough, another feeling is stirred from within me – a feeling of familiarity. As bizarre at it seems, I feel as though this isn't our first-time meeting.

"Haha... that was fun!" He states – like a clueless and irritating child. "You win!"

Slowly releasing him, I roll my eyes and say "Ok, you've had your fun. Now, you really should be going home. Where are you from, anyway?"

Standing to his feet, brushing the dust away from his robes, the boy turns around and points to the far distance. Between a trio of mountains, a tall tower can be seen. "My house is over there," He says simply – causing my sister and I to flinch.

"Do you mean: Babylon City?" My sister asks – aware that the tower resides in perhaps the most powerful and envied city in the whole world. Babylon City is the home of our land's richest and most blessed people. It is also the home of a messiah, who leads an army of powerful gods that maintain order within our world.

"Yes, Babylon City is my home," He says nonchalantly – along with a proud nod of his head. I guess now that explains the attire. However, why come all the way here just to play? Before I even attempt to piece a question together – the sun can be seen, from behind the clouds.

"Ah! It's sun-rise already? Oh shoot, I need to get back!" Says the mysterious boy, full of panic. Turning his back, he prepares to depart. However, he pauses for a moment and says "Oh, please excuse my manners. I didn't even introduce myself. I go by the name of Orion. What are your names?"

With a small step forward, my sister replies "My name is Lucia. Nice to meet you, Orion."

Stepping forward also, I place my hands on my waist and say sternly "My name is Cassius. Now hurry home, before you get us all in trouble!"

"Haha, it was nice to meet you... Lucia and Cassius. I had a great time. See you again tomorrow!" Waving his hands, he races off into the sunset – back to his home city, as my sister I remain baffled. Did he truly say that he'll return tomorrow? Sigh... The last thing we need is another night like the one we just had. However, despite all the trouble that he put us through, there is a part of me that wishes to see him again. Orion.

"Luna - get up, will you?" comes the voice of a certain blade. Immediately I open my eyes – looking directly up at the sky, which has now become a glistening orange colour. Sitting upward, I glance about my surroundings – finding myself in a large field, kept company by Adamas.

"Hey, what are we doing here? Last I remember, we had already left Belgrave and were looking for a place that sold a map."

"You don't remember? You were complaining about wanting to rest, so you decided to take a short nap."

Upon a wide yawn and stretch, I respond "Oh that's right. How long have I been asleep for anyway? Also, where is Ten?"

Whizzing around me, the sword replies "You were asleep for about three hours. Ten couldn't wait any longer, so she decided to go on ahead."

Springing to my feet by my sword's information, I shout "What did you say? So, she just up and ditched us? Why didn't you wake me up sooner, idiot?"

"Well, I was afraid you'd get angry and shout at me like you always do."

"Sigh... if you're gonna keep acting stupid, then, of course, you'll be shouted at!" I rant, turning my back to the incompetent blade - strolling through the quiet field. "Did she even mention the direction she was headed?"

"Yeah. She said that she will continue northward. She should be at the next town we find… I guess."

"You guess, huh? Well, I guess there's only one way to find out."

Together we walk northward, along a small path. In no mood to communicate, I display a vexed stare, as the black blade follows behind. The sheer audacity of that she-demon. She could at least have had the decency to wait until I woke. Now, I must find her and pray that she hasn't made a mess of things and purchase a world map while I am at it. Jeez – can I at least have a day that goes as planned?

To my surprise, I hear crying, coming from behind. From the corner of my eye, I glance back and see my companion sword, moaning and trembling.

"Adamas… are you actually crying?"

"Sniff… no… I am ok. I am just a little tired… that's all" He replies, which of course is a complete lie. Adamas is never tired and is unable to sleep. He must indeed be crying, which is beyond me, seeing as he is nothing more but an object. Regardless, I attempt to find out what is wrong.

"Why are you crying?"

"Sniff… well… sometimes… when you call me names… it hurts my feelings."

"Feelings? Are you serious?" I ask – shocked to the point that it's almost laughable. I can't believe that I am about to have an emotional talk with perhaps the world's most powerful sword. Sigh… why me?

Stopping to face the blade, I cross my arms, lean into it with a stern gaze and say "Adamas – you really shouldn't worry about what I say. For the most part, I am merely cursing my situation. Not you in particular. Imagine that one day, you are walking through a field, before hitting a large rock. You swear at the rock, but it's not the rock you're truly angry at. After all, all the rock did was be a rock. The truth is, you're angry at your own misjudgement. It's the same principle with how I sometimes communicate with you. For me, you are that rock. Understand?"

Instantly, the blade bursts into further crying – screaming to the hilltops. "Lunaaaaa – that's a horrible thing to say. Not only am I a stupid sword, but I am also as useless as a rock!"

"No, no... that's not what I meant. Ok, look... I am sorry. From now on, there'll be no more name calling from me. Happy now?"

"Do you really mean it?"

"Yes, I do."

Oh god, what am I thinking? I know myself better then to make promises I most certainly cannot keep. Having this sword feels more like having a child. If I knew that Adamas was, in fact, a talking sword, with the mind of an unbearable child, I probably wouldn't have taken it in the first place. I wonder how the previous wielder coped with Adamas? If I remember correctly, the she-demon mentioned that there was an original owner.

With a curious tone, I ask the blade "Tell me something – did Ten talk to you about your past, after I left you both in the hotel room, last night?"

"Huh? Oh... well, she intended to tell me everything about who I was and of the person who used to wield me. Unfortunately, she got drunk and passed out before saying anything."

"Haha, go figures" I laugh – strolling onwards under the looming sunset as my blade skips around me. "Still, it is strange that you don't remember anything from the past. Perhaps if you did, you might have been useful in helping us locate the Land of the Gods."

"Yeah... sorry, Luna. I wish I knew why. I also wish there was a reason why I can talk and think for myself. All the other blades I've seen so far can't speak or move by themselves."

"True. Maybe you used to be a human? But because of a cruel spell, you became a terrifying immortal slayer! Haha!"

Spinning through the air with excitement, my companion blade shouts "Wow, what if it's true, Luna? What if I really was, in fact, a human being? The thought of it alone makes me so happy. Oh, I do hope it's true. If so, all we need to do is find the evil witch or wizard who cursed me and..."

"Whoa, don't get ahead of yourself. It was just a hypothetical example, which probably is far from the truth... whatever the truth is, mind you. Listen, why don't we ask the devil girl, once we regroup with her? Perhaps she could shed some light on your past?"

"Bwahaha – it really is a funny sight, listening to you both" Comes a familiar voice, from above us. Looking upward, I see the she-demon, swimming through the air with her usual bold grin.

"Ten, how long have you been up there, eavesdropping on us? Furthermore, are you not supposed to be acquiring a world map, seeing as you decided to rush ahead without us?"

"Uh, you're quite bossy... for a mere mortal. What did your last slave die of? For your information, I have been eavesdropping on you, ever since you woke up from your little nap. I already made it to a nearby town and purchased a world map, long before you woke" She says with a relaxed tone – pulling out a rolled-up map before tossing it down to me. As I catch it, Adamas praises her quick handy work.

"Wow, you're so fast, Ten! With a map of the world, we'll be able to..."

"Don't speak too soon, Dimmy. Unfortunately, the map is useless."

"What makes you say that?" I ask her, as I unfold the map and glance over it. It looks fine by me. The same as it has always looked.

Closing her eyes, she sighs and replies in a bothered manner. "Sigh... trust me, I know what the map of Popla is supposed to look like, and that one is not it. The world map you see today portrays a world of only a slew of countries. In my time, the real-world map reflected a world of almost a hundred lands."

"So, what you're indeed telling me is that most of our world has been intentionally blotted out? Mind if I ask how much of the world has been left out, according to you?"

"Hmmm... I'd say about seventy per cent."

"Bullshit! That can't be possible."

Laughing at my outburst, Ten responds "Bwaha – you'd better believe it, Lulu. It's as I told you before: everything in this world today is all messed up. It's clear that someone has systematically tried to make sure that nobody ever finds the truth. Firstly: The stars, which once consisted of four moons, have been reduced to just two. Secondly: The original and true world map, which at a point in time revealed everything discovered in this world, including the Land of the Gods, has been dumbed down. Lastly: Adamas, who once knew the way to the sacred land, now seems to have lost his memory, along with all knowledge of the way."

Gasping with shock by her last sentence, Adamas and I look to one another.

"I... I once knew the way?" The blade says.

"Yeah, you once did. However, don't let it bother you too much, Dimmy. There are many ways to skin a cat."

Tucking the map into my sleeve, I call out to the she-demon and request "We need to talk."

Short moments later, the three of us find a creek to rest near. Sitting by the bank, I take in the slow and serene sounds of the stream, as the night sky begins to appear. Laying on the ground beside me, sipping a can of beer, the demon holds a relaxed demeanour, as the curious sword hovers between us.

"All right Lulu, fire away. I'll give you ten minutes to ask all you want. After that, I'll probably be too drunk to respond, so make it snappy!"

"Sigh... typical. Tell me – has Adamas always been a living sword? How was he created and what was the reason for his creation?"

"Yeah, little Dimmy has always been a blade with identity issues. However, even I, with all my superior knowledge can't understand why. Everything from his creation and purpose is a mystery. Next!"

"Sigh... fine. Earlier, you mentioned that someone else originally wielded him. Did the original bearer of Adamas, know anything at least?"

Sitting upward, as though impressed by my question, Ten replies "Ah, finally – a good question! You must be referring to Septimus. Not only was he the original swordsman of Adamas, but he was also one of my best friends too. He was a mortal like you, with a similar fighting style – however, he was a lot nicer."

Rolling my eyes, I glance to the black sword and ask "Well, does the name Septimus ring any bells?"

"Hmmm... sorry, Luna, it doesn't."

Shrugging her shoulders, Ten continues, "Well, as I was saying: Septimus was the one who first possessed the blade. Come to think of it, he did know quite a lot about the nature of Dimmy. However, I wasn't very interested at the time... hence why I am unable to tell you anything about Dimmy here.

"Hmph - so you had the opportunity to know about Adamas, but you chose to ignore it out of ignorance. How stupid."

Yanking the sword before sitting it flat on my lap, I begin to stretch and rub my fingers together.

"Hey, Luna! What's the big idea?" It moans as I prepare to cast a miracle art.

"Quiet you. Can't you see, I am trying to make you remember" I reply – clapping my hands together before uttering the phrase "Remember"!

By my command, a sphere of light surrounds the blade, which also lights up the dark creek. A strong force expands outward, like a strong wind, which sways the grass and river nearby.

Shom – suddenly, before my miracle begins to take effect, a barrier appears around Adamas – cancelling out my miracle. Like a battery that short-circuits, my light disappears.

"Shit, what the hell happened?" I shout, surprised and baffled by the mysterious force field that blocked my powers. "Why didn't it work?"

"Well don't ask me, Lulu. However – if I had to guess, it would seem that miracles do not work on little Dimmy."

Swatting the blade away from my lap, I produce a deep sigh before laying back to the ground. "Damnit, this is all so annoying."

Finishing her can of beer, the she-demon tosses it into the river and says "Relax, Lulu. There is always a way to success. Even if all the doors are closed, we'll simply smash open a new path. Say... where did you find Dimmy, anyway?"

"I stole Adamas from a place called Babylon City, the most powerful city in the world. It lies in my home country of Lelail – many days from here by ship."

"Is that so? Tell me... in that place called Babylon City, was Dimmy found with anything else?" She says with a strangely uncomfortable gaze – looking at me with a side glance.

"What do you mean by that?" I ask suspiciously – looking to her with the side of my eye also.

"Hehe, what do you think I mean, Lulu? Did you see any other weapon when you found Dimmy? Perhaps... another talking sword?"

Flinching – eyes perked, I reply "No, I didn't. What... is Adamas supposed to come as a set?"

Upon a slight pause, she stands to her feet and stretches her arms before replying "Never mind Lulu. Forget I said anything." Walking over to the stream, she kneels by it and washes her face.

"So... That witch friend of yours told me that the Seventh Blessing still exists. Such a troublesome thing. Even in my time, it was a sickness that became an automatic death sentence when caught. She also told me that it was what claimed your sister?"

"Trista talks too much. Regardless - she is correct, and I blame the gods for it. I am certain that the Seventh Blessing has something to do with them."

"Aha... so that explains your reasons for finding the Land of the Gods. You want to wish your sister back to life. Mind if I ask why?"

Slightly offended by her direct and amateurish question, I reply "Was that supposed to be a trick question? I want to wish her back to life because she's dead."

"Bwehe... you don't say. However, seeing as she's already dead, why not just let her remain dead?"

"Because she didn't deserve to die... bitch!"

There I go again, losing control of myself when the topic refers to my sister. Looking to the she-demon, I watch as she stares at me, with an unphased grin. Taking a short breath, I utter "Sorry for my outburst."

"Ah, don't apologise, Lulu. I kinda like it when you mortals give into your emotions. Your desire is so laughable, and yet you are deadly serious about it."

"Well, maybe if you had a sister, you'd understand?"

"Bwahaha... as a matter of fact, I do" She responds – looking up at the starry sky, with eyes of sentiment. "However, unlike you, I am not going to the Land of the Gods for her sake. My sister is the complete opposite of me. She's sensitive, naive and inno-cent. My reasons for entering the sacred land again is to avenge someone I cared deeply for. I'll never forgive the great Observer for what it did." A vengeful look appears upon her face, as a cold aura fills the area, sending a chill down my spine.

"Ten - we should get some sleep for a few hours. Let's carry on by sunrise."

"Fine by me. Have a good night, Lulu and Dimmy!" She says with a wide yawn – taking flight into the night sky. As she disap-pears beyond the clouds, Adamas slowly hops to my side.

"Ten said some interesting things, right Luna?"

"Well, I guess. I just wish there weren't so many obstacles. Any-way, we'll resume by tomorrow morning. Get some sleep."

"Ok... um..." A sad tone can be felt from Adamas. Oh shit, I should have remembered. The blade is unable to sleep. Sigh... now, what do I do? When we were at the hotel, he would stay in the drawer, at night. Seeing as we're outside, with no form of shelter, I kinda feel bad and awkward, for sleeping in front of him.

At that moment, an idea comes to mind. Undressing the top half of my body, I throw my robe over the blade, like a blanket.

"Here... now you can pretend you're one of us mortals and at least act like you're sleeping."

"Oh... really? Thank you, thank you! I'll pretend to sleep, right away!" It says cheerfully – tucking under my robe. Watching as the sword behaves like a child, I let out a small chuckle.

"Hehe, you are really bizarre. You know that, right? Oh... guess what? I had the most amazing dream while I was napping."

"Huh? Did you? Was it about me, Luna!

"Yeah. You were a builder that made gigantic houses. In my dream you built a tower that was so tall, it reached the heavens."

"Oh wow! A tower that went up into the clouds? Oh jeez! I wish I was there. You always dream the most amazing dreams, Luna; especially about me!"

With my back turned, I stand to my feet and respond "Yeah... well, we're comrades, right? I am going to find a place to rest nearby. See you in the morning". Strolling into a nearby small forest, I leave the sword by the peaceful stream.

Hearing nothing but the sound of a distant owl, I waltz through the forest for roughly ten minutes before finding a suitable spot to rest. Sitting upward, against a large tree – I prepare to fall asleep. However, as soon as I close my eyes, I begin to cough manically – producing blood that shoots from my mouth. Doing my best to stop it, I cover my mouth with my hands. "Shit... this is what I get for using two miracles in one day" I whisper – as my coughing fit slowly subsides.

"Awww, you are so sweet... giving up your clothes so that the sword wouldn't feel left out" Comes a familiar voice of a certain witch. Glancing from left to right, I attempt to spot her, but to no avail. "Up here..." She says.

Looking upward at a tree branch opposite, I see the one and only: Trista the witch, sitting gleefully on a single branch.

"Sigh... what do you want? I thought I saw the last of you?" I ask the insufferable woman. She laughs of course, before replying to me.

"Haha... It's nice to see you too, Luna. I thought I'd say hi, seeing as it's been so long since I saw you last."

"It's only been a day since we left Belgrave."

"Yeah, I know, but you're one of my best clients. Not to mention, you've become quite the talk of Belgrave. It's great to see you, Adamas and Ten bonding. I almost shed a tear, when you told Adamas of the dream you had about it."

"You saw that? Hmph - I wish people would stop spying on me, every ten seconds. Besides, the dream wasn't that special anyway."

"Well, of course, the dream you had of Adamas wasn't special. After all, it wasn't even real. You made it up, just to make the blade feel better, didn't you? Even a fool could see through that."

Once again, the witch proves how annoyingly perceptive and wise she can be. Around her, I always seem to get the feeling that she knows a hell of a lot more than what she's letting on. Now, I can't even tell a simple white lie, in peace. Yes, I have been lying to the sword about my dreams. The truth is, I have never once dreamt about it. The only dreams I have, are of the past where my sister is still alive.

With a smirk, the witch takes off her hat and spins it around her index finger, playfully. Displaying a taunting gaze, she continues, "I must say, you do have a particularly bad habit of lying. I mean, I understand your reason for doing so, but being untruthful to your comrades may not be the wisest decision."

"Nobody asked you. Besides, it's not like the sword and anybody else are important to me. Whether I tell a lie or not, makes no difference in the end."

"Haha... there you go again, with the lies. You can fool everybody else that you're without compassion and loyalty, but you can't-fool me. Underneath that cold and heartless exterior, you are and will always be... Cassius."

Blinking with shock at her last word, I stare at the taunting woman with an angry glare. The reason for this is because she addressed me with a name that I have long since buried. Furthermore, I don't ever remember disclosing it to her, which makes her audacity even more blatant. With no hesitation, I clap my hands together - ready to perform another miracle, to banish her from my presence.

"Not so fast, Mr dark messiah. Have you forgotten that you've already used up two miracles for the day? You wouldn't waste your third one on little old me, would you?" She says tauntingly.

"Begone!" I shout, ignoring her - going ahead with the casting of my third miracle, causing a prism of light to surround the witch. Within seconds the prism disappears, along with the troublesome woman – banished from my sight. Left alone in the quiet forest, I breathe a sigh of relief – whispering to myself.

"Hmph… I guess she wasn't as perceptive as I thought. I never gave her permission to use my original name. Cassius no longer exists."

Chapter 8: Dragoon

The following morning, Adamas Ten and I resume our journey. After roughly three hours of strenuous walking, we arrive at the gates of a city which goes by the name of Wellington. The city is large – consisting of moderately tall buildings and structures. Strolling inside, under a sunny day, we see many city folks, going about their daily activities.

"At last, we've finally reached the next city. Remind me to purchase a horse next time. My feet are killing me."

"Bwahaha… Are you always this cranky, Lulu?"

"Quiet, she-devil. It's easy for you and Adamas to say. After all, both of you can fly."

Dancing around, the sword laughs "Haha, flying isn't that convenient. As a matter of fact, I'd prefer legs, like you!"

"Why doesn't that surprise me. What is it with you and your fascination with being human? If you're not careful, I'll use a miracle to temporarily turn you into a human!"

"Ah, would you really do it? That would be amazing Luna! Do it, do it now!"

"It was a joke, sheesh!"

Watching our banter, the she-demon bursts into laughter. "Bwahaha… I could literally listen to you two squabble, all day. What's so amazing about being human?"

"Well… Humans can fall asleep and dream."

"So what? I can do that too, Dimmy. And I am not as weak as those pitiful mortals!"

Zipping to her side, the black sword asks "Oh really? What do you dream about?"

"Nothing much… Other than the destruction of the world or

something of that nature."

Strolling through the city, we browse the busy streets. As Ten and Adamas continue conversing, I glance about my surroundings – looking for any clues. By clues, I mean any sign of gods or god worship. You never know when we'll encounter a deity. Our names have started to spread, after all.

"Hey, Adamas – do you sense any gods within this city?"

"Huh? Um… No, I don't think so. Everything seems pretty normal to me."

"That's good to hear. If you sense anything out of the ordinary, just let me know."

"Roger!"

At that moment, the demon takes my arm – forcing me to walk hand in hand, like a pair of lovers. With a sarcastic expression, she says "Aww, relax honey Lulu. You're way too on edge for your own good. Let's enjoy the day and explore!"

"Explore? This isn't a vacation, silly fiend. We're supposed to find a way to reach the Land of the Gods. While we're on the subject, did you manage to think of any ideas since last night?"

"Nah – I was far too tired."

"Useless! Why the hell did I free you from your prison if you weren't gonna use your brain at least?"

Full of laughter and good cheer, she pulls on my cheeks while Adamas chuckles at my plight. "Awww, you're so cute when you're angry and frustrated. You look as though you have the weight of the world on your shoulders."

"The only weight I have on my shoulders is you" I respond sternly – pushing her arm off from me as we approach a street corner. Taking a deep breath – hands placed on my hips, I state "We need to be serious about this. We're not about to waste time fooling around – so I propose that we split up, for now."

"Huh? Split up?" Asks the black sword, finding difficulty in understanding my simple request.

"Yes, that's right. We're not gonna make any progress, huddled together like this. So, I need you to lay low and find anything this city may have that will help us. Ten – I need you to do the same. Anything relating to the sacred land, report straight to me, got it? Let's regroup at the end of the day."

"Roger, I won't let you down!"

"Whatever you say, Lulu... Bwehehe."

Rolling my eyes, I turn my back and hope for the best. With orders issued, the three of us split up. Adamas soars into the air, while Ten waltzes in the opposite direction from me. Taking a nearby turn I begin walking down a small street, keeping my wits about me. In all honesty, I am quite doubtful that we'll find anything pertaining to our goal in this city, let alone anywhere else. If all the maps available are a lie, combined with the fact that the sacred land cannot be uttered, reaching our destination will not be easy. However, there are some keys to a solution. Take Adamas' memory for example. If somehow, we were able to make it remember, then we'll be a big step closer. Another possibility is that of the world map. If by some slim chance there still exists an original version, then we'd be able to locate the Land of the Gods.

Moments later, catching my eye I notice a large library, across the street. Many statues of men, holding globes representing the world hang on the outside. I freeze, not by its impressive design, but because of the information libraries naturally contain. "Interesting..." I mutter – slowly approaching its doors. If there's anything more underrated and overlooked in this world, it's your local library. As a child, I rarely had the opportunity to visit such things – however, when I did, I always found something enlightening. Here's to hoping I find something useful.

Inside, I see a single library clerk by the counter to my right, in a heavy sleep. Haha – looks like this place doesn't get many visitors I suppose. It's a shame, for as I progress inside, I am met with rows of narrow shelves that contain an abundance of books. "Other than the sleeping library worker, it looks like I am the only one here" I whisper to myself – relieved. I prefer to explore in peace – without the presences of others.

Taking in the dusty and familiar smell of pages, I stroll through the aisles, gently brushing my fingers over the vast number of books. "No... no... no..." I confirm, upon each book that I find of no interest. Suddenly, my fingers and eyes stop by one book, titled: Modern Day Biscus. In all honesty, I am not sure why I find this so intriguing. It's not as though I am in any way interested in this land. However, I am reminded of just how little I know about this country.

Taking the book, I sit down upon a nearby bench to read. I skim read through most of it, before coming to a page concerning this country's current ruler. Apparently, a god governs this land and dwells in the country's capital, a place called: Gin. It says here that the god is called Gigas and apparently has stored the world's most prized possessions, from the beginning of time within its chambers. "Ah ha... this is what I'd like to hear" I mutter, imagining the kinds things the ruling god of Biscus holds.

At that moment, I hear the doors of the library open, along with sounds of heavy footsteps – treading slowly inside. Immediately I become suspicious. Something about the sound of their movement is not natural, as though they're after some-one. Sigh... please don't say it's me.

Placing the book inside my sleeve, I keep quiet – trying to figure out how many there are. Sounds like two... maybe three.

Stepping into my line of sight, by the far end of the aisle in front, I spot one individual. Dressed in full knight's attire, the person stands to the side – Looking to my direction, sporting a helmet fashioned like that of a dragon. By his waist, a large sword can be seen, sheathed in a metallic scabbard, and upon his back, I notice a pair of mechanical wings. Something tells me, he hasn't come for a pleasant read.

"May I help you?"

The person doesn't answer and remains focused on me – exuding a murderous aura. Guess it won't take many guesses to figure out what his intention is. However – why has he come for me?

Hearing footsteps from behind, I glance back and see two other mysterious knights, sporting the same armour as the first in front. Looks like they wish to make sure I don't make it out alive. Of all the times to be without Adamas – now would most certainly be a bad time. It's not the end of the world, however – for I do have the power of miracles at my disposal. This will be over in a flash.

"I don't know who sent you, but I am going to give you five seconds to turn back. You're in the midst of the dark messiah, in case you haven't heard?"

As expected, they ignore my warning and begin to unsheathe their blades. Very well, if they want to do this the hard way, then let's do it the hard way.

Clapping my hands together, I cast a miracle – releasing a blinding light that fills the whole library. Upon a sound of a great trumpet, the light disappears – revealing the leftovers of what once was the three intruders. I say leftovers, because now the only thing remaining of them, are pillars of salt.

"I warned you..." I say to the defeated fools that tried to come against me – casually standing up and waltzing to the window. Peering outside I call to my blade "Adamas – get back here, wherever you are!" Hoping it returns, sooner than later. God knows how many of those weird soldiers are after me.

Suddenly, without warning – the ceiling above is smashed open, as a fourth knight crashes into the library to face me. Shit, now I am slightly concerned.

Turning tail, I leap out the window of the library, onto the street of the city. To my annoyance, I find a dozen additional knights, coming at me from the front. "Shit – an ambush!" I shout – doing a sharp left, sprinting through a busy street. Gasping and screaming, the nearby onlookers scatter around with panic – watching as I am pursued by the mob of knights. I could finish my pursuers with another miracle, but I'd rather not waste another one. Furthermore, this street has way too many blind spots for me here. Damn, it would be a hell of a lot easier, if that blasted sword was around.

"Adamas! Get your butt here now. I need you!" I shout aggressively, as my attackers begin soaring through the air with their mechanical wings, akin to jetpacks. At the speed they're going, it won't be long before they catch up to me. Darting around a nearby corner, I find an open park square – surrounded by a slew of stores. "This open space should be good enough..." I say to myself – stopping in the centre before turning around to face the flying knights. "Give it your best shot, assholes!"

Charging at me, the first knight swings its weapon to strike – however, with a quick dodge I snatch the attacker's blade and stab him through the heart.

"Urrrghhhh!" He screams as blood stains the ground. The rest circle around me, as I begin juggling with the fallen foe's sword. Hmph, I don't need Adamas to take care of these numbskulls. Confident in my raw swordsmanship, I take on the mysterious attackers – parrying, dodging and defending their swords before countering with precision. All it takes is one single stab for me to kill each one, before moving on to the next. Although I am unable to see their faces, I sense an air of fear, which increases as I progressively take the lives of their comrades.

"Who's next?" I state coldly – spinning and darting through their ranks – leaving a bloody mess upon every successful kill.

"Arrrrggghhh!" Cries the final knight – falling onto my blade. However, unlike the rest, I intentionally miss his vital organs – leaving him alive, just long enough to explain himself. Yanking his helmet off his head, I look upon his bloodied face and address him.

"If you want me to save you, tell me why you and your comrades came after me. Hurry up. You don't have much time left!"

Slowly looking to my face, coughing forth blood, the knight replies "You... you and your cursed sword are wanted... by the King... of Gin."

"What? The King? Wait... isn't the King of Gin a dragon god? What does he want with me? Speak!"

Shakoom – at that moment, the ground beneath me explodes and I am sent spiralling backwards before hitting the ground hard. Smoke and debris shower the area, as I struggle with the disorientation. Shit, I also lost the weapon I had in the process.

"Whahahaha! Not bad, Mr dark messiah" Comes a deep and husky voice. Clearing my eyes, sitting upward I see a single knight – arms crossed. However, unlike the other knights, this one is much larger, with humongous golden gauntlets and grieves that look as though they could crush men with ease. Sporting a unique colour of black and red, the large and intimidating knight continues laughing at me, as I prepare to speak.

"So, you must be the leader of those flying fighters that tried to kill me?"

"Indeed I am. My name is Vast: commander of the dragoon soldiers. We have come all the way from the city of Gin to claim your head, as there have been reports of a mysterious troublemaker, killing the gods that protect our land and way of life. I expected someone a lot stronger and brighter though. However, what I find is a skinny wimp before my eyes, without his rumoured deadly sword. Such a disappointment."

Wow – he sure seems full of himself. If there's one thing I hate about people, it's their arrogance, and he smells of it, big time. It's only right that I put him in his place, via a miracle. I wonder what I should do? Turn him into a pillar of salt or turn him into a piece of excrement. Hmph… the latter seems far more appropriate.

Standing to my feet, I take a deep breath and clap my hands together to cast the miracle. However, as I do, nothing seems to happen. No lights, sounds or wonder. "Now what?" I whisper, trying to understand the reason my powers are not working.

"Whahaha! What's wrong… Your little fancy miracles aren't working? Aw, that's a shame!"

Wham – thrusting his fist forward, the huge knight performs a mighty clothesline tackle that hits me full on. Within seconds I am thrown backwards, out of the park before smashing through the window of a clothing store. Tumbling inside, along with shards of shattered glass, I lay on my back as clothing falls on top of me – hearing the terrified customers screaming. "Ouch. That hurt like a bitch" I mumble in agony - injured from head to toe.

"Bwehe… Looks like trouble seems to follow you everywhere, Lulu". Tossing the items off from my face, I see the she-demon

Ten, standing over me – sporting a pair of sunglasses while holding many bags of expensive looking clothes.

"Sigh... Where the hell have you been!" I ask sternly, to which the girl shows a confused stare.

"Huh? Well isn't it obvious? I've been doing a bit of retail therapy. Can't an overlord unwind from time to time?"

"Stupid demon. You were supposed to be looking for clues! Furthermore, could you not hear and see the commotion outside? I've been fighting for my life for the past twenty or so minutes!"

Lowering her sunglasses, she smiles and replies "Yeah, I was gonna help... After I stopped at one more store. After all, I've been unable to keep up with the latest trends for at least five thousand years."

"Materialistic wench... Just help me the hell out, will you? You can spend all you want after we kill that oaf!"

Dropping her bags, Ten looks outside – watching as the armoured knight charges towards us both. "Sigh... Very well, Lulu. As usual, it takes a woman to do a man's job!"

Pouncing forward – propelled by her wings, Ten races dead ahead to the humongous attacker – fists clenched. Upon a mighty jab, she hits him, square in the chest, with such force the entire ground shakes. To our surprise, however, her fists barely harm him – merely pushing him mere meters backwards.

"Hmph, is that all you got? You'll have to do much better than that, demon!" He taunts. Holding a firm fighting stance, she displays a slightly worried face – as though unable to understand how a mere human could withstand one of her blows.

"Oh wow – it seems you don't go down easy. I hope you can put up a good fight?" She responds – brushing off her mild concerns before leaping to him once more. Upon a rapid twirl, she hits him with a strong kick – however, he simply bats her attack aside. "What the hell is going on?" She lets out – becoming even more bothered by the futility of her strikes.

Upon a quick step forward, Vast performs a perfect thrust of his left gauntlet, which connects directly against her face. The force of the impact is so great, the surrounding houses crumble from the shock, and as Ten receives the brunt of the knight's fist, she is sent skyrocketing through rows of buildings.

"Fucking hell!" I gasp – gobsmacked at the power of this so-called leader of the Dragoon soldiers. Leaning against the side of the destroyed shop entrance, I shake my head in dismay – as buildings continue to crumble from the aftershock. "Come on..." I say to my hands – clapping them together, hoping that whatever prevented them from casting a miracle has worn off. However, as much as I try, nothing seems to work. "Why isn't it fucking working? And where the hell is Adamas!"

"Lunaaaaa... Hang in there!" Comes the voice of the familiar blade. Before I know it, my companion zips to my side from above – apologising profusely. "I am so sorry I couldn't help you earlier. I ran into some trouble along the way. I was ambushed by a bunch of flying swordsmen and..."

"Say no more, I can fill in the rest myself" I respond – snatching him by the hilt before pointing the sword to the direction of the gloating knight ahead. "We have bigger fish to fry. That gorilla over there is supremely strong. In fact, he managed to knock Ten off her feet. To make matters worse, my miracles don't seem to work. Any guesses why?"

"Oh... I can't explain it but, it feels as though someone is using some form of magic to suppress your miracles. I don't know where it's coming from, but I am sure of it!"

"Huh? So, there is another individual around here, somewhere. Shit, it looks we were set up to be ambushed from the beginning."

Shakoom – at that second, Ten can be seen smashing her way out from the rubble of collapsed houses before taking flight into the sky above. She looks angry while exuding a hot and dark aura.

"Whahaha! You've come back for another beatdown, have you? Well, give it your best shot!" Vast says – opening his arms wide, in an unthreatened fashion. This triggers her anger to heighten – sending her in a fit of rage.

"You won't be laughing after I've burnt you to a crisp," she says – producing a ball of fire within her hands. Holding the project- ile above her head, she shouts "Say goodnight, shithead!" Toss- ing the fireball, directly to Vast. As it descends to him, he stays put – showing not a hint of nerves. Suddenly, as it gets within inches of his body, he swats it away, as though it were a soccer ball. This wouldn't be a problem, had he not knocked it straight to my direction.

"Fuck!" I gasp – while the fireball is redirected towards my position. "Adamas, protect me!" I order – tossing the sword to the oncoming projectile. Shit, I just remembered... The last time Adamas got in the way of Ten's fireball attack. It paralysed him.

Shaboom – the fireball explodes against Adamas, causing an explosion that sends me tumbling across the ground. Smoke, debris and fire engulf the area, as I lay with more injuries. My body is in excruciating pain and I notice that I am bleeding from head to toe. To top it off, I think I've broken my right arm. Damn, I hate to say it, but it looks like we're not gonna get through this one.

Struggling to lift my head, I see Ten and the powerful knight, continuing their fight. Amongst the embers, I watch as she con- tinues to struggle against him – throwing mighty blows, only for him to defend and inflict twice as much against her. She doesn't seem to give up, and upon each knockback, she tries harder and harder. As for me, well, there isn't much I can do right now. Shit... even with everything I have... I am still not able to change anything.

"Lu...naaa... Are you ok?" Says the companion blade, which I spot laying by the ground nearby. "You're not dead, are you?"

"No, I am not dead. However, I might as well be. We don't stand a chance in hell against him. Your strength is most likely sapped from protecting me. Sorry about that."

"Huh... did you just apologise? Luna, you're really not sound- ing like yourself" replies the blade, as Ten and Vast can be heard continuously fighting in the background. "You're not ready to give up, are you?"

Closing my eyes, I stay silent – feeling sorry for myself. It really isn't easy, carrying on sometimes. For the most part, I try my best to not be a victim of circumstance... - however, when faced with times like these, I am forced to realise my powerlessness. I have always been powerless... unable to change anything. Right sister?

As I drown in my sorrows, I hear my companion blade, standing upright, attempting to hop towards the battle to support Ten.

"Hey... What are you doing? You don't have any strength left!" I say – wondering what is going on with the black sword. Stopping, it turns around and responds to me.

"Yeah... But we have to keep fighting, no?"

I gasp, taken back by Adama's short and clear words. He's right... my body is in so much pain and our chances of survival are slim. However, what does that have to do with giving up? All I've ever experienced was pain, in one way or another. So why should this be any different?

Struggling through the agony of my broken arm and injured body, I sit on my knees and take a deep breath. "It's only pain... it only hurts". Fighting through the pain of many glass shards, lodged in my knees I stand to my feet. "It's only pain... it only hurts". Scooping Adamas into my only working arm, I slowly sprint towards the armoured knight and scream with unwavering might. "It's only pain... it only hurts!"

Tearing into the fray with Adamas held tightly, I somersault forward and perform a vertical strike to Vast's front armour. As expected, my blade bounces off his tough suit, but not before leaving a noticeable tear. It is small, however, but a good indicator that victory is possible.

As I shift backwards, being only a few meters apart from the foe, Ten stands nearby – holding a fierce fighting stance. Displaying a frustrated face, she says to me "The son of a bitch is as tough as an ox."

"I know. His armour is insanely strong, and someone or something is using magic to suppress my miracles and your strength. However, don't give up" I respond – holding a defensive stance.

"Don't give up? Who said anything about giving up? As a matter of fact, I could have ended this easily, if it weren't for you and everybody else here!"

Blinking with surprise, I wonder what she means by her comment. In a curious manner, I ask "Wait, are you suggesting that we're somehow distracting you?"

"No, that's not what I meant!" She says harshly, as Vast charges to us with both fists clenched. "Now's not the time for discussions, Lulu. Just make sure you keep hitting him with Dimmy. I'll support you!"

Wham – swinging both gigantic gauntlets downward like a guillotine, Vast tries to crush us. However, Ten and I both leap out of harm's way – causing him to instead pound the ground, resulting in a great eruption of smoke and debris to sweep outward.

"Now's my chance!" I whisper to myself – somersaulting over his head, to his exposed back. With a mighty cut, I tear into his armour, leaving a deep graze to his protective suit.

"Quickly turning around, the large knight shouts "I don't know what you're trying to accomplish, but you should just give up!" He says before throwing a left punch directly towards me. However – just before I prepare to dodge, Ten leaps into harm's way and blocks his gauntlet fist.

"He's wide open. Lulu, go for it!"

Wasting no time, I continue with two quick slashes to his front amour before sliding through his legs – striking his grieves along the way. Engaging him from behind, I ready to attack further, while Ten holds him from the front. With all the strength left in me, I stab and swipe everything from back, waist, helmet and shoulders. As I thrash manically, I hear sounds of his amour, slowly giving way. It's working... it's working!

Breaking free from Ten's hold, he performs a lethal kick to her stomach – sending her tumbling backwards before hitting a nearby stone slab. As he turns around to face me, I pounce away, creating space between him and I.

Standing opposite one another, amidst the now burning city around us, I display an exhausted posture, while my opponent shows a frustrated stance. This would most likely be due to the state of his armour, which now looks ripped, battered and damaged, thanks to Adamas.

"Hmph... Don't get cocky, just because you managed to inflict some cheap shots. Your scratches still could never hope to penetrate my armour" He says, with a not so confident tone. Entering a humorous grin, I respond to him.

"You sure about that? I wouldn't downplay those so-called scratches if I were you."

Suddenly, right on cue, Vast's whole armour begins to shatter and crumble – save for his pair of golden gauntlets. His helmet is the last to fall to the ground, revealing an old bald male, with many scars on his face, like a seasoned war veteran.

"Uh... How..." He stutters, lost for words as I hold a relieved grin – feeling my companion sword shake excitingly within my hand.

"We did it, Luna!"

"Yeah... We did. However, let's not let our guard down yet. He still is equipped with those deadly gauntlets. All we need is one more opening, to land a killing strike."

From the corner of my eye, I spot Ten, picking herself up from the ground, ready to fight once again. I gotta hand it to her. She can take a ton of damage, that's for sure.

Looking at one another for a few seconds, we nod our heads – gesturing to do a collective attack against the defenceless knight. Standing in silence for a few tense moments, we keep our gaze against Vast, who now displays a worried expression.

"Now!" I shout to the she-demon, signalling for us to engage him together. Side by side we dart towards him, ready to finish him off. With my sword in hand, I muster every ounce of my strength, as Ten readies her fiery fists.

Suddenly, a mighty force blasts us backwards – preventing us from going any further. To our shock and surprise, we see a second knight, standing protectively in front of Vast. Although the newly appeared knight is not as large as Vast, an even greater aura can be felt from the sudden opponent. Catching my sight, I notice the new foe holds a sword hilt but with no apparent blade.

"Shit, just how many of these pesky men are there?" Moans the she-demon – echoing my thoughts exactly. It's clear this dragoon team consists of strong members. Not only that, they seem to possess weaponry that I can't seem to understand. Will we be able to stand against Vast and this new knight?

At that moment, the mysterious companion takes hold of Vast before soaring into the air and disappearing beyond the clouds.

I am not entirely sure why they retreated, but I am certainly not complaining. Ten and I take a relieved deep sigh, surrounded by the now scorching city.

Chapter 9: Wanted and Needed

Later that evening, after departing the doomed city of Wellington - Adamas, Ten and I stopped by a mild creek. The reason I refer to Wellington as doomed is that the last thing we saw as we left, was of the city burning to the ground. I could have saved the city if it weren't for my arm being broken. Thanks to a bunch of groupies and a giant oaf, I ended up breaking my right arm, which means that I am unable to use miracles. Oh well… Shit happens.

Sitting by a log, broken arm held together by a small plank of wood - I am kept company by my companion sword who sits on my lap. Opposite from me, the she-demon lays by the small river – lost in thought. We've been resting like this ever since – recuperating our strength after the eventful day we had. Upon a deep breath, I address the two.

"So – did any of you manage to at least find some clues pertaining to our journey, before we got ambushed?"

Turning around, Ten faces me - sporting a pair of flashy glasses. I don't even know why I bothered to ask the question. While I was out busting my ass, she was busy on a shopping spree, wasting our money. "I'll take that as a no, Ten."

"Sorry Lulu".

"Sigh… Don't worry about it."

Standing upright on its hilt, Adamas surprises me and says "I managed to find some info! Not about the Land of the Gods, but about those soldiers that attacked us. I overheard them talking about where they're from. I think they called it: Gin.

Eyes perked wide, I gasp – wondering why the name sounds so familiar. Oh, that's right… Gin is the name of this land's capital city. One of the men also mentioned hailing from that place. Reaching into my robe, I pull out the book I acquired from the library: Modern Day Biscus. As I flick through its pages, I converse with the pair.

"So, those pesky knights came from the capital city of Gin. What a coincidence that it is the same place that might contain what we're looking for."

"What do you mean by that, Lulu?" Ten says, while slowly cracking open a can of beer. With a hopeful smile, I reply while staring at the contents of the book.

"Well, it says here that an all-powerful god named Gigas dwells in the nation's capital. He is said to be the leader of all the gods here in this land, and he also has ancient treasures. My guess is, the original map you were referring to, could be locked away in his chambers somewhere."

Dropping her can of beer, frozen by my words – the she-demon shakes and responds "Gigas? Did you just say what I thought you said?"

"Yeah... Have you ever heard of him?"

Crawling to my side before snatching the book from my hand, she peers at the pages and answers. "Gigas... I can't believe he's still alive, after all these years. Gigas is an immensely powerful god. He's also a dragon, at that."

"Wow! So, he's a dragon god?" Asks the black sword – curiously excited about the so-called being that sent shivers down Ten's spine.

"Yes, he's a dragon god. Before my imprisonment, my comrades and I were constantly being pursued by him."

"Mind if I ask why he was after you?" I say with a wise gaze. Handing the book back to me, she stands up and yawns – looking up at the night sky above.

"He was after Dimmy. He's a massive hoarder, who seeks to claim every known treasure in the world. Hmph... now I get why those knights came after us. News must have gotten to Gigas that you are in possession of the blade."

Tucking the book back into my robe, I lean back and take a

deep breath – overcome with a burden. It seems like every day our situation gets worse. I might as well just assume that the whole country is aware of us.

"Is he someone that we can beat?" I ask Ten, hoping her reply will be something positive. Based on her non-immediate response, I can assume that my answer will be met with a no.

"Lulu... Perhaps we should avoid Gigas? Victory is out of the question" she says with a concerned and deep reply. It is the first time I've ever sensed weakness from her, which quite frankly surprises me. Between the three of us, we stay quiet – listening to the mild movements of the surrounding tree branches.

Breaking our silence, we hear a noticeable chuckle, nearby.

"Teehee... You three aren't ready to throw in the towel yet, are you? Stop thinking and go for broke!"

Following the direction of the voice, we spot Trista, standing on the opposite side of the small creek. In typical Trista fashion, it's almost as though she were there the whole time – dwelling in the background of our blind spots.

"Sigh... What do you want, wench!" I call to her – in no mood to entertain her taunts. However, this doesn't stop the witch, and upon vanishing into thin air, she appears in the middle of us three – causing Ten and Adamas to jump with fright.

"Jeez, Trista! Do you have to scare us like that?" Shrieks Ten – pouncing backwards before accidentally falling into the shallow river.

Frightened also, Adamas leaps out of my lap before unintentionally poking me in the eye with his hilt. "Fuck sake!" I shout as the witch claps her hands with amusement and laughter.

"Aahahaha... You three are priceless! I do a little teleportation, and you lose your minds. No wonder you were so unprepared against Vast and his dragoon comrades earlier."

"So, you were observing everything that happened today? Thanks for not helping us" I utter - rubbing my now sore eye. "Have you come to provide any useful advice, or have you just come to be a pain?"

"That all depends on if you can keep up with me. It's about

the big soldier you fought against earlier. I bet you're wondering why your miracles were not working, correct? I'll give you a clue. One of the opponents you confronted, used an art. However, it wasn't magic or miracles."

Failing to understand her words, I respond "Not magic or miracles? But, those are the only kinds of supernatural arts in this world."

"Wrong. In fact, there are many kinds in this world. You just are not knowledgeable enough. Take Ten's powers for example. They consist of old arts called: Demon arts."

Climbing out the river, Ten chimes in and says "So, what kind of art do you think was used to suppress our power today? The only guess I have is that it could be dragon arts. However, neither of the foes today were dragons."

"Are you sure about that? After all, the second knight who saved Vast was covered from head to toe in armour."

"Hmph, so you're saying that the smaller knight was most likely a dragon, underneath? No way. I've seen dragons before, and he looks nothing like one" Ten responds with frustration.

Meanwhile, I stay amazed by the revelation of the many arts that exist in this world. Such a fool I was, to think that there were only two types. As well as miracle, magical, demon and dragon arts... Just how many are there in total?

Strolling to my sword, the witch holds him gently and says "You were the star of the show today. If it wasn't for you Adamas – Ten and Luna would have been finished."

Tossing her glasses to the ground, the she-demon interjects with anger and says, "Hold your tongue, miss know-it-all. Lulu might have been in danger, but I wouldn't have kicked the bucket. I am an immortal being, in case you've forgotten? Furthermore, I could have crushed that bulk headed knight easily... If I wasn't holding back."

"Well then, why were you holding back?" asks the witch, with a sly and cunning tone, as though somehow knowing the answer to her own question. She does have a point. If what Ten is saying is true, then why didn't she go all out? It doesn't make sense at all.

Slowly strolling to the demon – Trista stares upon Ten's face and points to her third eye, which since meeting her has always remained closed. With a taunting grin, the witch utters "All you had to do was... Open... Your..."

"Back off!" Shouts Ten - raising her hand to strike Trista. However, at that second the witch disappears into thin air. Her voice, however, continues to fill our ears, like an ominous phantom.

"Teehee... Ok, I'll quit playing around and leave you three in peace. Just bear in mind, Vast and that other knight will never leave you alone... Not until they got what they wanted. Gigas has his eyes set on you three, so trying to avoid him is pointless – especially considering he most likely has what you need. As bleak as it sounds, you're better off heading straight to his abode."

"No... no, no Trista! Gigas is too powerful for us and you know it. Going straight to him will be more than dumb" shouts Ten – fists clenched with frustration at the advice of the witch.

"Teehee... Oh Ten, a little positive thinking wouldn't go amiss. The future is not set in stone, after all. Till we meet again, my loves!"

As her voice reverberates through the air, I ponder her words of advice – stroking my chin in thought. Turning to face me, the demon asks "So, what do you wanna do? It's your decision after all."

Holding my silence for a short while, I reply "let's head for the capital city of Gin and kill the dragon god: Gigas. Any other ideas will simply prolong our goal. I have no doubt that he's as strong as you say, but we have to at least give it a shot."

"Sigh... Very well, Lulu. Just don't blame me when you die" she responds while slowly strolling away into the distance.

"Hmph... you should take Trista's words into account. The future isn't set in stone" I state in a bold and confident tone. Stopping in her tracks, she turns around and leaves me with one final warning.

"You're right: The future isn't set in stone. However, it all means nothing... To a being who can see the future."

Before long I retire for the night and drift to sleep. Within my sleep, I dream of memories that are dear to me... memories that I never speak about, to anyone.

"Cassius, Lucia... I think I know where the moons came from" Suggests our new friend Orion, whom we met about a month ago. Ever since our first encounter, where he had us chasing him around all night, the mysterious boy has met us every night, without fail. We don't know much about him, other than his name and the fact that he hails from the most blessed city in the world.

"What if the blue moon is just a massive pile of blueberries? Also, what if the red moon is a humongous cluster of strawberries? That would explain why they look the way they do!"

Bursting into laughter, my sister and I clutch our stomachs – unable to control ourselves. "Hahaha... Blueberries and strawberries? That would have to be the most ridiculous assumption ever! Orion, you say the funniest things!"

"What's so funny? It could be true... You never know" responds our new friend.

"You have a good point, Orion. It could be true... - However, with no way to reach the moons, I guess we'll never find out" Utters my sister, with a pleasant tone. Sitting on our favourite roof, the three of us remain looking up at the stars. After many moments of quietness, the robed friend claps his hands and gasps for our attention.

"Aha! I just remembered something... Something that will allow us to know for sure, where the moons came from. Where I am from, many people speak about a place called: The Land of the Gods. They say the creator of everything resides there. What if we were to go and meet the god of everything? Then it would tell us why the moons got there!"

Scratching my head, I display a face of doubt, as my sister also seems unconvinced.

"The Land of the... What? Gods? I've never heard of that before."

"It's true, Cassius. As a matter of fact, where I am from, such a place is common knowledge."

"You're from Babylon city, right?" My sister asks, showing a look of curiosity. Leaning forward she continues "Is it also true that your city is protected by powerful gods?"

Chuckling innocently, the boy replies "Not just gods... but angels too. They look a little scary at first, but they are really nice, once you get to know them."

Lost for breath, my sister and I stay astonished. We have never seen a single god before but only heard about them. They are the champions of celestial justice – said to bring order to this world. Rumours have it that looking into just one of their eyes could vaporize your soul. They sound so strong and infinitely powerful. However, Orion seems to speak of them without any fear.

Reminded of another rumour, Lucia asks "Oh, I also heard another story too. Doesn't a messiah rule your city? I've heard stories about a person who can wield the power of the gods, even better than the gods themselves."

Wow, my sister really is privy to all the rumours and news of Babylon city. I can't blame her, to be honest. After all, it is supposed to be a place of wealth, beauty and wonder. Nothing like this crap head we live in here. Yet, even though Babylon city is envied by all the world, I am unable to find its allure. I guess it simply doesn't have anything I'd want. My sister is all I need… in this world.

Orion answers my sister in a reluctant manner, twiddling his fingers together. "Um… Well… The messiah of Babylon city isn't that special. For the most part, he leaves the ruling to his advisors and family."

"Oh really? He sounds lazy."

"Haha… He definitely likes to sleep, especially during the day-time" replies Orion, before shimming to the edge of the roof. "Well, I need to get going now. It will be sunrise soon and I need to make sure I am back before anybody notices."

"Ok, we'll walk you to the end of the village."

In the dark and quiet night, we climb off the roof and make our way to the ground. Remembering which direction needed to continue, I glance from left to right. Curiously, from the corner of my eye, I notice our friend becoming uneasy. Staring into space, the robed boy seems to shiver.

"Hey, Orion... Are you ok? You look worried or something."

Slowly turning his head to me, he replies with a worried tone. "Something... Something is coming!"

At that moment, two large beings pounce towards us from the shadows and before I know it, I am snatched up by one of them and taken through the village. Orion too is plucked up by the second one – leaving my sister to watch as we're stolen into the night.

"Brother!"

"Luciaaaaaa!" I scream to my sister, helpless to break free from whoever has captured Orion and me. To my shock, I notice that the speed we're going is fast... faster than any average human being. Feeling the tight grip of my kidnapper, its skin feels scaly and cold. Mustering the courage to look at the shadowy being, I am petrified by its sight. Its face is pale white, consisting of scales and a split tongue that constantly emerges and retracts. Eyes darker than the abyss, it's clear that this is a monster. However, why have they taken me and Orion?

Heart racing, I glance to Orion, who can be seen carried on the shoulder of the second reptilian being. However, to my surprise, he looks far from scared at all. In fact, he is smiling, as though it were just a game. "What in the..." I whisper – confused by the whole scenario. Regardless, I am relieved they didn't bother to get my sister. If they end up eating me, I wouldn't mind, for at least Lucia will be ok.

Leaping onto the houses – hopping from rooftop to rooftop, my kidnapper speaks in a chilling tone and asks "Boy... Which one of you is the Messiah? Reply with an untrue answer and I'll rip your fucking neck apart!"

"Huh? What are you talking about? Are you referring to the messiah of Babylon city? None of us is the Messiah. You've got the wrong people!" I plead to the creature. Why on earth would it think that Orion or myself is the messiah of Babylon City? Can it not tell that we're just kids?

At that moment, the creature stabs its claws into my stomach, filling me with the most excruciating pain that I've ever felt. I try to scream, but the beast covers my mouth and whispers a terrifying threat to my ear.

"That was only the beginning. If you don't want to feel any more pain, then you'd better tell us what we wanna hear, maggot!!

Taken to the outskirts of the village, by a thick forest, our two kidnappers toss us to the ground and stand over us. On my knees, I sit in pain – losing blood from the open wound the creature inflicted.

"Idiot! You weren't supposed to harm any of them! The plan was to hold the Messiah for ransom to issue our demands to the gods of Babylon city. We can't do that if he ends up dying because of us!" The second creature scolds the first.

"Hmph, don't blame me. He frustrated me by not revealing which one of them is the Messiah!"

"That's not the point..."

As the two reptilian creatures bicker and argue, Orion sits close and comforts me. With a concerned face, he sees the blood that runs from out from my wound. I am sweating and losing strength... Becoming increasingly dizzy by the second.

"Orion... I don't think I am gonna make it. Everything feels weird and I feel really tired."

He doesn't answer. Instead, he holds a stern gaze, troubled by the pain I am in. Placing his right hand onto my wound, he whispers into my ear and says "Everything will be ok. Trust me". Removing his hand from my injury, I gasp with disbelief, finding the wound to no longer be there at all. Furthermore, I am no longer weak, dizzy and in pain. I must be hallucinating. Either that or...

"Hey, which one of you is the messiah of Babylon city!" shouts the second kidnapper, with a tone as scary as the first. However,

Orion shows no fear and simply stands to his feet – back turned to the two. "Answer us! Otherwise, we'll torture you in ways your tiny little bodies would never imagine. Which one of you is the Messiah?"

Turning around to face the creatures, Orion replies "I am the Messiah... of Babylon city!"

I gasp by what I hear – as the two monsters smile with the excitement of having found what they're looking for. However, almost immediately, their joy falls as a great aura and wind exudes from my friend. With his long sleeves and attire flowing hypnotically, he slowly strolls towards the two, like they are nothing but mere insects. To my amazement, I notice that upon each footstep, he leaves behind a handful of multicoloured flowers that sprout within seconds – as though he were adored by nature itself. A feeling of overwhelming majesty exudes from Orion, or should I say the messiah?

Looking at him, I feel as though I am gazing into the mysteries of this world. No, on second thought... I feel like I am staring at the creator of it all. The two reptilian creatures sense it too, hence why they now look terrified, as though Orion could crush their very existence, without batting an eye-lid.

"Please... Forgive us..." They weep – falling to their knees and planting their heads to the ground, like peasants. The sight before me is so profound, I doubt anybody would believe me if I told them. Two fiendish beasts, with the strength to kill most men without much effort, are bowing at the feet of one small boy.

"Leave this place and never return," He says to the two, like a mighty god issuing a holy command. Wasting no time, the pair stand up and retreat into the distance, bowing continuously as they go. Once gone, Orion takes a deep breath and turns around to face me. As his mighty aura disappears, he strolls to me as I remain on the ground. "Well... I am glad that's all over, haha!"

"Please don't hurt me!" I shriek – still overcome with nerves. He steps backwards, pauses and laughs once more before reaching his hand out to me.

"Hahaha… Relax Cassius. I am not gonna hurt you. I'd never harm you. After all, you're my friend, remember? Sorry that I didn't tell you sooner, about me being the Messiah and all. Come on… take my hand. I'll help you up."

Reluctant to move, I look to the ground – slowly gaining the strength to shift my gaze upward before looking into his eyes. His eyes are like before: Innocent and familiar. I still can't believe that after all this time of knowing him, Orion is, in fact, the messiah of Babylon city. The Messiah of the world's most powerful city, filled with the world's most powerful gods, is my friend.

"Ok…" I respond humbly, extending my hand out to him. However, just before I can take his hand, the sky lights up. However, this isn't your average light. This light is golden and so bright, I feel as though my eyes could go blind. The sound of trumpets fills my ears as a feeling of benevolence surrounds me. Within seconds I marvel at the sight of twelve beings, as tall as a skyscraper, standing around Orion and me. Are these… gods?

"Oh dear… It looks like I am in trouble, haha!" chuckles my friend – looking up at the celestial figures pleasantly.

"Blessed one - please return home. This place is not deserving of your presence" One of the gods says.

Kicking the ground like a spoiled child, Orion sighs and responds by saying "Yeah I know… I was only gone for a little while, sheesh! Ok… let's go home then."

Kneeling low, one of the gigantic gods places its huge hands onto the ground, allowing for Orion to step onto it. As he does, Orion turns around and stares upon at me – not saying a word for many seconds. As the light continues to intensify, I can barely see Orion's silhouette. With a quick head nod, he leaves me with a fond farewell and says, "See you again, my friend…"

At that moment, the being cradles the Messiah into his hands, and upon a great burst of light, I am knocked off my feet – tumbling backwards.

To my astonishment, I find that Orion and the dozen gods have disappeared, along with the blinding light. Left alone within the dark and quiet forest, I simply lay... taking in everything that occurred. "Orion..."

Before long, I hear the voice of my sister – calling to me from nearby. "Brother... brother, are you ok?" Taking a deep sigh of relief, I call out to her.

"Sister, I am fine. I am over here!"

Emerging from behind a bush, I spot Lucia and she spots me also. With no hesitation, she runs straight to me and gives me a big hug... a tight hug at that.

"I am ok. I am not hurt". She doesn't reply but instead continues to hold me close. I hear her sniffing – which probably means that she's been crying. Damnit, now I feel bad, although it wasn't my fault. I realise how much I mean to my sister... I am all she has left, and she is all I have left. Had it been the other way around and she was taken, I don't know what I what have done. I don't know what I'd do, without my sister.

Chapter 10: Iron Angel

The next morning, Adamas, Ten and I resume our journey before taking a brief detour by a pond. To be honest, it wasn't my idea to stop here – however, the she-demon just had to take a dive into it. Full of intense steam and bubbling water, it's obvious that such a pond is not meant to be used... By normal people anyway. If myself or any other human were to jump in, we'd probably burn within seconds. However, Ten seems to have no trouble swimming within the dangerous water. As a result, we've been stalling for the past twenty minutes. Standing by the edge of the pond, looking up at a grey sky, I sigh impatiently.

"Ten – how long are you gonna fool around? We have a lot to do, in case you haven't noticed?"

"Ah relax Lulu!" She replies – splashing around like an immature adolescent. "It's not as though the world is going anywhere. You need to relax a little."

"That's not the point. Where is your sense of urgency? Do you not realise that we're probably enemy number one within the whole country?"

"Hmph, it wouldn't be the first time... For me anyway."

Slapping my forehead, I turn my back – already fed up of her antics. For a being who's lived for thousands of years, she clearly doesn't know how to act her age.

"Luna, how is your arm?" Adamas asks concerningly - choosing a time when I am least in the mood for small talk. What is it with these two? If they're not doing something pointless, such as swimming in a boiling pond, they're saying something utterly useless and unchangeable, such as the state of my broken arm. Nevertheless, I'll cut Adamas some slack. After all, he did pull through for us yesterday.

"My arm is better. The pain has mostly worn off. Now, all it needs is time to heal."

"Oh, I see. How long does it take for most humans to recover from an injury like yours?"

"Hmm... without any healing ointments, I'd say about a week."

Laughing at our conversation, the she-devil boasts, "Bwa-haha... You humans are so weak and fragile. It's a mystery as to why you were created at all. Yet, despite your feeble mortality, you still wish to go toe-to-toe with Gigas the dragon god."

"Yeah, well I am not exactly planning to fight alone. Hence the reason why you're here.

Laughing once more, she turns her back and glances from the corner of her eye. "Bah... don't get in over your head, Lulu. I am strong, but I am not Gigas strong. Therefore, if our backs are against the wall, don't expect me to stick around. Sorry, not sorry."

"Excuse me? You'd actually ditch us if the worst were to happen?"

"Why are you surprised, Lulu? I am a demon, after all. What did you expect... loyalty?"

"Sigh... I should have left you in your prison, to rot for all eternity."

Hovering over to the smiling girl, the black sword asks, "Ten, didn't you once say that you were immortal? If so, why are you so worried about the dragon god Gigas?"

"I'll tell you why. Like me, Gigas has the power to kill other immortal beings. If I slip up, then I am as good as gone."

A cold sweat comes over me, upon hearing the power of the dragon god who rules this land. Perhaps I am in over my head after all? However, if we turn back now, what do we do then? Where will we go?

Taunting me, as though reading my thoughts of concern, Ten advises, "Maybe we need more comrades? No, scratch that...

we'd need an army to go up against him."

"I've heard enough. We can figure out a plan of action, on the way. Hurry up and get out the pond."

Finally, we continue our journey to reach the city of Gin – home to the dragon god Gigas. Staying clear of open and main paths, we instead trek through woods, lakes and fields. God knows how many people are after us. Wouldn't wanna run into that overgrown knight again, that's for sure. Of course, the downside is that we may come across worse enemies.

By a large and rushing river, we approach a wooden bridge that stretches out for many meters. The bridge looks old and worn, as though it could break at any moment. "Hmm... I don't have a good feeling about this. Is there not another way to reach the other side?"

"Awww... What's wrong, honey Lulu? You afraid of falling and getting a little wet?"

"No. I am afraid of falling to my death. Hitting such an intense flow of water will most likely prove fatal."

Patting my shoulder, she grins and says "Well, if you'd like, I could always carry you across? After all, I do have wings."

Brushing her away, I roll my eyes and reply "Thanks but no thanks. I trust you, as far as I can throw you."

"Bwaha... Well, suit yourself, honeybee. We could try and find an easier route, but it will add a few extra days to our journey. The choice is yours."

With a grieved sigh, I push her aside and step onto the wooden bridge. "Fine, I'll walk along this shitty looking bridge. Just remember to catch me, if it falls apart."

"I'll do my best... Bwehehe"

By my side, Adamas speaks in a helpful manner. "It will be ok, Luna. I'll stay close to you and help you, every step of the way!"

"That's cute."

Walking onwards, I progress slowly along the bridge. As expected, it is far from stable. Each step causes it to sway slightly, as a plank or two falls to the river below. It also doesn't help that the she-devil has chosen to also traverse the bridge, following behind me.

"Ten, why in god's name are you on here as well? Clearly, you are able to fly."

"I know that, Lulu. I am merely trying to offer you some support and encouragement."

"The only thing you're offering me is dead weight. I swear, if I fall to my death because of you, I promise that my soul will torment you forever."

"Bwahahaha... Sounds like fun. Now I am kinda tempted to push you off myself."

"Don't even think about!"

Whizzing around me, the companion sword says "Ten's only playing around. Just focus on getting to the other side. Come on, just concentrate on the road ahead."

"Sigh... You're right, just concentrate on the road ahead. Easy does it..." I mutter – stepping ever so carefully. As I slowly but surely make progress, I am once again disturbed by the she-demon. To my annoyance, I hear her giggling hysterically to herself. "For crying out loud... What is so funny, Ten?"

"Bwehehe... You're walking so slow. I imagine it'd be almost night time when you finally reached the other side."

"Sigh... That's the last straw" I mumble – reaching my only working hand forth to take hold of Adamas. "I've had enough of you and your shit!"

"Awww, come on Lulu. Can't you take a little joke?"

"Not when I am trying to concentrate. I've made up my mind. I am cutting your tongue out so that I can at least think straight. I refuse to continue this journey with a bunch of motor mouths."

Wrestling within my hand, the companion sword begs "Calm down Luna. Let's not lose our heads. Besides... I don't want to hurt Ten."

"Quiet you! I am your wielder, so you'd better do as I say!"
"No!"

Resisting my hold, Adamas attempts to shake free from my grip, while I try to position it to the direction of the she-demon who simply cries with laughter. On the wobbly bridge, my sword and I struggle against one another. This day is already turning out to becoming another shit show.

"Stop resisting and do as I say!"

"No Luna, I won't let you hurt Ten. She's nice!"

"Nice? In what world? You two are really starting to piss me off. You're lucky I am unable to cast miracles right now. I'd surely turn you both into nothing but cockroaches!"

With all my strength, I force the blade downward to submission. However, being in such blind fury, I find that I have accidentally struck the old bridge with a clean swipe.

"Shit..." I shout – hearing the bridge giving way. Within seconds, the entire structure splits in half, with me in the middle. To no surprise, I fall and plummet towards the deadly river below, with Adamas held tightly. "This is all your fault!" I scream to Ten, as she watches from above. "Hurry up and save me!"

Wings widened, she responds, preparing to rescue me. "Hang in there, Lulu! I'll be there in a..."

"Don't worry, I'll save you!" comes an unfamiliar voice. Within seconds, I am caught in mid-air, by something from behind. Glancing back, I gasp at the sight of what can only be described as a mechanical, human-sized robot. Bizarrely enough, it resembles a young child – with eyes consisting of yellow bulbs and body made of seemingly old pieces of tin. Hovering in mid-air, by what looks to be feet that expel harsh steam, the metallic samaritan smiles at me. "You have nothing to fear... Malcos is here!"

"Malcos? Is that your name?"

With a chirpy nod, the robot whisks me upward, to the other side of the river before settling me and Adamas down. Feet happy to touch the ground, I breathe a sigh of relief, as the mysterious helper remains stationary, in flight.

"Well, seeing as you're no longer in danger, I had better get going. If you need any help within this region, come and find me. My house is just over there..." The robot says – pointing to a large manor that can be seen, not too far amidst a dense forest.

Taken back by the act of kindness, I remain silent before turning to the friendly robot.

"... Many thanks."

Standing at attention, like a soldier, the robot soars away into the distance – leaving its steam to trail behind. I stand mesmerized, as Adamas stays lost for words also.

"Woe... just who was that person, Luna?"

"How the hell should I know. Either way, he saved my life. His name was Malcos, right?"

"Yeah, Malcos. He seemed friendly."

Breaking our conversation, the she-demon swoops down to our side. "Wow, who the hell was that?"

"Someone helpful... not like you'd ever know about that. If it weren't for that robot, I'd most likely be finished."

"Aww, that's not true. I was gonna save you. Although... it would have been amusing to see you hit the river. You looked so terrified as you fell... Bwahaha!"

Rolling my eyes, I turn my back and face the path ahead. "Never mind. Let's get moving."

Obstructing my path, the companion sword rants "Hold on Luna. Let's go and meet that friendly person again! Didn't it say that it lived just over there, in that old house?"

"Huh? No... forget about it. Besides – I already thanked it" I reply, swatting Adamas from my sight before strolling onwards. As enduring as ever, the sword once again zips in front and babbles on.

"Oh come on, please? He looked so different from anything I've ever seen so far."

"That's because he's a robot, Dimmy" responds Ten.

"But what's a robot?" The blade rants on, like a baby who's entered its terrible twos. Yanking it to eye level, I proceed to speak in a slow yet firm manner.

"A robot is what you just saw, pipsqueak. Body made of metal held together by nuts and bolts. Unlike the rest of nature, robots are created by humans and usually given a basic set of orders to follow. Nothing special... now move it!" I state, tossing the sword to one side. As it spirals, Adamas gasps with excitement by my description.

"Wow! That thing was made by a human being? Now I am even more intrigued. Say, what if Malcos could help us on our journey?"

"Like how?"

"Well, for a start, he may have something that could fix your broken arm?"

I pause – biting my tongue for not thinking of such a possibility. That robot just may have something to heal me, along with any information on our destination. Reading my expression, as though already predicting my change of heart, the winged girl chuckles menacingly.

"Quiet, she-devil!" I let out, before turning to my companion sword. "Ok Adamas, you convinced me. Let's go to the home of that robot. However, don't get any ideas of overstaying our welcome. Once we've got everything we need from the robot, we will resume our journey."

"Yay!"

And so, as decided, we make our way towards the manor of Malcos the friendly, mysterious robot. I'd be lying if I said that I wasn't a little intrigued myself. Although I've never seen a living robot before, there have been many stories about them. They are typically seen as the result of hard work, by certain outcasts of society called scientists. As one can imagine in this god serving world, those who have abandoned faith in the gods, in favour of natural laws are either something to be feared, shunned or both.

After walking through a thick forest, we come to an opening where a large manor can be found. Catching our attention, we see a huge mansion – consisting of old mouldy brickwork that is covered partially by many leaves and vines. To the left of the mansion, a small chapel can be found, barely visible under a pile of brown leaves. By the entrance of the manor, a short and rusty gate surrounds it. An atmosphere of old memories can be sensed, just by observing the space that looks to have held many special moments.

As the three of us stand outside the gate, we hear the sky breaking – followed by the arrival rain.

"Hmph, looks like it was a wise decision to come here after all. We can also use this place for shelter until the rain subsides" Ten points out – using her wings to act as umbrellas against the rain.

Being the first to enter the gates of the manor, I respond "Yes, well at least we can agree on something. I'll go ahead in front. Ten – please stay close by and watch out for any signs of danger. For all we know, this could all be a trap."

"I wanna go first!" Shouts the living blade – zooming past us like a naïve child. With a deep sigh, shrugging my shoulders, I watch as the sword flies ahead to the front door. "Hello! Malcos... are you in there?" Adamas asks – tapping the door with its hilt.

As it waits, hopeful that the door will open, Ten and I stand back and brace ourselves. We hear running footsteps, coming from inside the house and the sound of the friendly robot calling out "Just a second... I'll be there in a flash!" The door swings open, revealing Malcos with a welcoming smile. "Never fear... Malcos is here! Oh, it's you..." says the robot.

"Yes, we're the people you helped a little while ago. My name is Adamas. The other two are Luna and Ten!"

"Oh wow, I have never met a talking sword before."

"And I've never met a robot before. Haha!"

As the two remain fascinated by each other, Ten and I join in and make our intentions known. "Hi again, Malcos. We have come seeking any help and advice you may have. Not to mention, our friend here is quite impressed by you. May we come inside?"

With a cheerful gasp, the robot shows a bright smile and replies, "You need my help? Of course, I'll be happy to help with anything you need. That's why I was created, after all. Please, come in."

Gesturing us to come inside, the three of us enter the mansion. Once inside, Adamas Ten and I marvel at our surroundings. Directly in front, we see a wide staircase that leads to numerous rooms from left to right. Many lamps, chandeliers, vases and furniture can be seen, sparklingly clean and polished.

"Wow, this sure is a swanky place to live. It must have cost a fortune to buy" Ten says with a smirk.

Standing opposite, the friendly robot replies, "Actually, it was built by my creator, long ago. It's beautiful, right? Although, it takes quite a while to clean every day."

"Oh, do you maintain this place all by yourself?" I ask – strolling to a nearby clock, finding not a speck of dust.

"Yes, I am the only one here," the robot says, in a simple and compliant manner. Its answer fills me with questions and mild assumptions. Who would create a robot, just to be friendly and helpful to strangers… living alone in one huge mansion?"

From the corner of my eye, I watch as the she-devil strolls to a vase before casually picking it up. Sticking her tongue out with disgust, she comments "Ugh, as much as I like the décor – you didn't have to clean it so much. After all, if you live alone here, what's the point? It's not like you have to answer to anybody."

Nodding politely, the robot responds "I can't help it. It's part of my programme to keep this place clean."

"Hmph, I guess it sucks to be you, Bwahaha," She says rudely – placing the vase back where she found it.

Circling around Maclos curiously, Adamas asks "What exactly is a programme?"

"A programme is a set of instructions that I follow. It's written into my system. My main three instructions are: Treat everything with respect, help everybody and never cause harm. Oh, and I also am bound to stay within two miles of my creator's home."

Interesting indeed. It's clear that whoever made this machine, had good intentions in mind. I guess there are nice people out there, in the world.

"Bah! That sounds like an awful set of instructions. What was your creator thinking?" Asks Ten, not impressed by the robot's purpose. "I am surprised you managed to survive this long, without getting yourself killed."

"Not everybody is as selfish as you, demon!" I shout to her, in defence of the robot. Truth be told, Ten does have a point and I do agree with her. As idealistic as those rules are, they are filled with a ton of errors. Nevertheless, it's thanks to Malcos' instructions, which saved me.

Facing the robot, I say "Please excuse my ill-behaved comrade. She hasn't had the best upbringing. Anyway, let's move onto more serious matters. Firstly – do you have anything that will help this arm of mine? It's broken."

Startled, the robot gasps and replies "Oh, it's broken? Please forgive me. I had no idea. To answer your question, yes, I can repair your arm, right away. Please, come with me!"

Pulling on my attire, the robot leads me through a set of corridors, as Ten and Adamas follow behind. Catching my attention, I spot a series of photographs, hanging on the walls. Each photograph consists of Malcos, alongside an old man who sports a long clinical styled jacket. Before long, we are taken into a large room, consisting of many desks that contain screwdrivers, needles and many more.

Led to the far side, I am seated down on a surgical chair, next to a large vertical window that reveals a wide garden outside. It's still raining – however, from inside, it's a pleasant sight. This type of mellow afternoon rain feels refreshing – the kind one would experience on a Sunday afternoon.

"Allow me to take a look," Malcos says before gently holding my broken arm. Paying no mind, I allow it to do so, as Ten and Adamas nose around. To my amusement, I notice the robot gently prodding my injured arm with its metallic hands.

"Hehe, that tickles... Are you sure you know what you're doing? What's the point feeling my arm? It's not like robots have the capacity to feel physical touch."

"I am afraid you're mistaken, Mr Luna. As part of my system, I was installed with nerves and pain receptors. My creator said it would better help me develop empathy. Although, I don't really know what empathy is."

Taken back by his words, I pause with surprise before asking "Wait, you don't know what empathy is?"

"Correct. My creator intentionally left it out of my internal library. He said that once I figured it out, it would have a stronger meaning. It's been fifty years though since he left and I still have no idea what it means."

"Fifty years? So, fifty years you've been living in this mansion… all alone." With a concerned gaze, I look at the robot with pity. It is quite unfortunate indeed, to live in such a secluded place such as this. Of course, what's even more tragic, is the fact that the machine probably has no idea how sad its life seems to others. Looking through the window, I spot three tombstones in the garden. I am guessing at least one of them belongs to his creator.

Glancing at the walls of the room, I see more pictures of Malcos, with the same older man. Curiosity getting the best of me, I go ahead and ask, "Those pictures… they are of you and your creator, right Malcos?"

"Oh… Yes they are. His name was Doctor Stone. When he was alive, we used to do so many nice things together: Picnics, hikes and games. We also used to help the local animals and feed them. He said that all life here on Popla, needs love. To him, there was no such thing as a bad person. Everybody just wants to be loved and if we could find a way, then everybody in the world would be able to get along.

A warm and fuzzy statement, I must say. Unfortunately, such a statement I find rather naïve. It's not the fault of Malcos of course, but of his creator whom it seems had lost touch with reality. Most people in this world, don't even know what they want, let alone to be loved. But of course, such a machine would never know that… being in this old place.

Catching my eye, I notice a photograph, unlike the rest, by a desk beside me. This picture looks much older than the others and doesn't include the robot. Within it, I see the Doctor, looking noticeably younger - standing next to a woman and a boy. Seeing the source of my gaze, the robot smiles and says "That is doctor Stone with his family. Unfortunately, I never had the chance to meet them. I was created after they died" The machine says bluntly. I wonder what caused the death of his wife and son? Whatever it was, it clearly led him to create this robot, with a set of idealistic instructions. At least I know the reason for the other two tombstones.

Crack – suddenly, a sharp pain is felt to my broken arm. "Fuck!" I shout – voice reverberating through the whole room. Looking to the robot, I ask "What the hell are you doing?"

"I fixed your arm for you. It wasn't exactly broken but merely dislodged. Worry not, for I snapped it into place for you" The machine says, performing a jolly salute. Hesitant to believe him, I slowly move my left arm, with ease. Other than mild pain, it seems to be working again.

"Amazing. You really fixed my arm. I owe you again. Thanks, Malcos."

"Oh, haha... Don't mention it, Mr Luna. It's what I was programmed for."

Covering her mouth, as though ready to burst into laughter, the she-devil approaches and says "So, all you needed was a little elbow grease, to fix your arm? I could have done that for you, Bwahaha!"

"Hmph... You probably would have torn my arm off."

Standing at attention. The robot asks "So, what can I do for you next?"

Remembering our destination, I prepare to ask the machine anything it knows about the land of the gods. However, before I do, my sword zips in front and babbles "I wanna see the rest of your home, Malcos!"

Bulblike eyes flashing rapidly, the robot says "Ok, it will be my pleasure. Come on, let's go!"

Rolling my eyes, I sigh and turn away, as the robot and blade hurry towards the exit door. Noticing the she-demon and I staying put, Malcos asks "Oh, are you two not going to join us?"

"No thanks. I'll wait till you and Adamas are done."

Sharing my same intentions, Ten responds to the robot "I am

not interested in this overly clean home of yours. I'll also sit tight here. Have fun, Tinny and Dimmy."

With a firm nod, Malcos exits the room with Adamas, leaving the she-demon and I alone in the quiet room – kept company by the gentle raindrops that hit the window.

The two of us remain quiet, for many moments – appreciating the calm atmosphere. Perhaps it has something to do with the house and the machine. An air of relaxation flows throughout this mansion.

"So, Lulu… What do you think of Tinny?"

"Tinny? Sigh, must you always think of ridiculous nicknames for others? To answer your question, I am quite fond of that machine. I am even contemplating, asking him to come with us."

"It's a pretty thought… However, you know that such an idea would be the worst decision for you, honeybee. Its master created it with the instructions to treat everything with respect, help everybody and never cause harm. However, the idiot didn't think to include things such as self-preservation and the ability to defend itself. Poor tinny would be a massive liability."

"Yes… Not to mention the fact that we're being hunted by that fat knight and his cronies."

Suddenly, the two of us hear a fierce roar – so loud the entire mansion shakes. Startled, we jump to our feet and gaze out the window. As the roar continues, we see an abundance of small animals, entering the garden as though fleeing from something dangerous.

"What the hell is going on?"

"Well, how the hell should I know, Lulu!"

The roar slowly subsides, and as it does, Malcos followed by Adamas comes bursting inside the room.

"Oh no… She's come back again!" Panics the robot, seemingly familiar with the dreaded sound.

"Malcos, what was the cause of that sound and where was it coming from?"

Eyes dim and low, as though expressing an ill feeling, the machine replies "It's the Starlight Queen!"

Chapter 11: Queen of the Stars

Slumping backwards against the window, I cross my arms and sigh with burden – already knowing whatever the machine is about to say, will be something bothersome. "Ok Malcos... just what on earth is this Starlight Queen?"

"The Starlight Queen is a creature that comes out on nights when the stars shine bright. She first appeared in these parts, about a month ago, preying on the local animals and travellers. Since then, she has continued to come here – sending a violent roar during the afternoon, as a warning of her appearance later."

"Hmph... so how have you managed to stay alive?" Ten asks with a curious smirk.

"Well, seeing as it isn't within my programme to fight or defend myself, I simply stay inside my home and hide. However – it's becoming increasingly difficult, as the local animals have started to hide here for shelter. With each appearance, she comes closer to this mansion. It's highly probable that this time, she will not only get all the animals but destroy this entire manor in the process."

The machine looks to the ground as though helpless. Naturally, this would be the part where one of us would step in to help. However, as cold as it may seem, I am not in the habit of risking my life for a bunch of animals and an old house. "Malcos, why don't you just leave this place and find a new home, somewhere else? Then, you won't have to worry about the beast."

Shaking its head, the robot replies "No, Mr Luna. I can't just leave the animals behind. It goes against everything I was programmed for. I was created to protect this area."

"Bwahaha... Well it's not like your presence here changes anything, Tinny" Says the she-demon – gently tapping his metallic head in a patronising fashion. "The most you can do is hide those animals in this home of yours. However, you said so yourself... the next time she appears, she'll probably destroy this entire manor."

"I know... I know..." The robot says repeatedly – reluctantly agreeing with Ten. "I've tried everything to reason with her, to show that all she needs is love. I've tried: talking, pleading, giving gifts and even offering food. However, nothing has worked so far."

Strolling past the machine with a taunting grin, Ten responds, "Well, no shit. Even an idiot would know that negotiating with a beast is pointless... especially one such as the Starlight Queen."

"Really? Why is it pointless? I don't understand. All I want for it and everything else is to feel love, not hate. So why is it terrorizing everything?"

"Sigh... Do you really need me to spell it out for you, Tinny? A monster such as the Starlight Queen has no issue with loving itself. On the contrary, it loves everything it does. It loves to install fear in the hearts of its prey, before gobbling them up. The fact that this means others must suffer for its joy, means nothing to it. Welcome to the real world."

Exiting the room, the she-demon leaves the robot to ponder her words, as Adamas and I stay quiet.

"So, if the Starlight Queen loves what she's doing, then how can I protect the animals here? I wasn't programmed to harm anything – only instructed to treat everything with respect and protect all life. How... how does that solve anything? Why wasn't I given other instructions for situations like this?"

Eyes pulsating, as though in the midst of a minor malfunction, the robot desperately tries to make sense of its helplessness. Although it's just a machine, I can sense its frustration. Malcos was made to be bound by a set of rules that it could never escape. For the first time in its life, it has come face to face with its limitations. Perhaps in the future, its objectives will be more appreciated. However... That time is not now."

Strolling to the machine, I place my hand on its shoulder and say "Don't worry about it. I'll think of something." Walking towards the exit door, I glance at Adamas and say, "Hey – keep your new friend company, while I get some fresh air for a while."

An hour or so passes, and it is now sunset. Finding our way onto the roof of the mansion, Ten and I sit together and discuss Malcos and the Starlight Queen.

"So Lulu... How do you wish to deal with the monster?"

"Deal? Slow down, Ten. I never mentioned anything about fighting the beast."

"Bah! Don't play dumb with me, honeybee. We're still here, after all. We could have left this place, ages ago. However, you have chosen to stay, knowing full well that the night is drawing near. Of course, it doesn't bother me. I'd love to flex my muscles against such a legendary monster."

"You seem to be quite familiar with the Starlight Queen. Is she a friend of yours?"

Quick to correct my assumptions, she displays a repulsed expression and replies "Not in a million years. The silly hag has been alive, longer than most beings in this world and yet she still is unable to say a single phrase that makes sense. Nevertheless, it still doesn't stop her from being one of the most terrifying demon beasts in the world. She is called the Starlight Queen, not only because she comes out on star filled nights, but because the stars literally give her power."

"Sounds troublesome. Any idea how we can kill her?"

Standing up, stretching her wings and arms wide – Ten yawns and replies "Unless you can figure out a way to extinguish all the stars, her source of power, your guess is as good as mine. Let's do our best!"

With a wink and a smile, she leaps off the rooftop – leaving me to ponder her words. Looking up at the orange sky, I mutter to myself.

"Extinguish... All the stars? Hmph, that would take a miracle."

A further few hours pass and with the sun gone, the twin

moons can be seen amidst a cold night. Covering the sky, a legion of stars hangs beyond the clouds. Outside the front gates of the manor – Ten, Adamas and I stand with our backs turned to the mansion. From the safety of his home, Malcos stays inside with the animals, watching us through the window. Facing an open and large space, we await the arrival of the Starlight Queen.

"What's taking her so long? We don't have all night!" Ten expresses with an annoyed face. As usual, she is far from intimidated.

"Ten, are you not the least bit nervous? If she is as strong as you say, then I wouldn't be looking forward to meeting her" I say worryingly. I'll admit, I am slightly spooked. The howling of the cold wind, combined with what the stars represent this night, is giving me the shivers. I used to admire and adore the stars. Tonight, however, they terrify me like a bad omen.

"Why should I be nervous, Lulu? After all, I am the demon lord of the underworld. Bwahaha... I can smell the fear on you though!"

"I am not afraid, silly demon!"

Hovering by my side, the companion blade says to me, "Don't worry, Luna. I am afraid too. We can be afraid together."

"Quiet, you. For the last time, I am not afraid!"

At that second, the terrifying roar from earlier can be heard. Its sound sends my body shaking with fright, along with Adamas who zips behind me. Laughing at us, the she-demon rolls her eyes.

"Bwaha... Pathetic, both of you. Anyway, it looks like our Queen from the Stars has arrived. A further screeching roar is heard, followed by heavy footsteps that are so loud, the ground trembles. Emerging into the opening, we see our target. Large and wide – twice the size of the mansion, the monster bears pale white skin. The lower half of her body is like that of a snake or slug – sliding along the ground, leaving a dark green liquid trailing behind. The top half is without arms – consisting of four moth-like wings. Her face is gigantic, with a tongue that looks like a large spear which protrudes out her mouth.

"Yuck... as hideous as I imagined" I mumble to myself – keeping a firm gaze to the beast. "Ten, Adamas... let's make this quick. Her sight is turning my stomach."

"Very well, Lulu. I'll go on the offensive while you cover me!" responds the she-demon – entering a battle stance. Fists clenched together, she generates a pair of fireballs within each palm. "Here we go!" She shouts – tossing the blazing projectile to the beast. The Starlight Queen is hit full force and upon a great explosion, she is obliterated. Smoke and debris shower the area from Ten's powerful attack. As the smoke subsides, the beast can be seen no more – save for a large crater from the devastating fire blast.

"Eh? Is that it?" I ask openly, expecting much more from such a creature. With a haughty laugh, the she-demon pats herself on the back.

"Bah, so much for being one of the strongest demon beasts. I wasn't even getting started."

With a sigh of relief, I close my eyes and cross my arms. Nudging my shoulder, however, the companion sword speaks with concern. "Luna – something doesn't feel right. I can still sense that monster, somewhere. She's still here."

"Are you sure about that? You saw how Ten destroyed her..."

Suddenly, bursting from underneath the ground, the Starlight Queen appears inches in front of Ten who remains unprepared. "Shit! Look out!" I call – however it is too late. With her piercing tongue, she stabs Ten through the chest – impaling her to the ground.

"Waaaaaaaaahhh!" My companion screams. How on earth did the beast appear? I saw her explode into flames!

Wielding my sword in front, I race to help Ten. Pouncing forth, I strike the creature's deadly tongue, shattering it to pieces – freeing my winged comrade. The beast screams in agony while I sprint around it – ready to initiate my next attack. Somersaulting to the hideous creature once more, I aim for its neck. With a strong and vertical swipe, I cut its head clean off from its shoulders. As its face hits the ground, I run to Ten's side.

"You ok?" I ask – kneeling while she sits upward with remarkably no heavy wounds.

"I'll be fine, Lulu. I was just caught off guard, that's all. Nice moves by the way."

"Yeah, well this time, I am certain we killed her," I say confidently – watching her lifeless and decapitated head and body. To our surprise, her body vanishes into thin air, like some sort of apparition. "What in the... where did she go? Adamas, help me out will you?"

"I can still sense her. She's near the mansion!"

"What? But didn't we just..."

Looking to the mansion, we gasp in shock at the sight of the Starlight Queen – alive once again. Hovering over the house, she readies to demolish it – large face already in motion to crush the building. Damn, we're too far away to stop her!

Thinking fast, I clap my hands together and cast a miracle – freezing time completely, save for only Adamas and I. "Go on!" I order the blade – commanding it to race towards the monster. Wasting no time, the blade cuts into the beast – slicing it into hundreds of pieces. With the monster finished off, the blade returns to my side, as time begins to resume. "Great work Adamas," I say – looking to the dead carcass of the Starlight Queen, with a far from pleased stare. The beast has been killed three times now.

Standing shoulder to shoulder, the demon looks on with a thinking stare. "So, the old hag truly does have the favour of the stars. No matter how many times we kill her, she constantly respawns. What a cheater!"

Once again, before our very eyes, the beast fades into thin air – causing us to stand on edge, wondering where she'll strike next. On full alert, the she-demon and I stand back to back – glancing continuously from left to right. The moment is eerily quiet, and as each second passes my heart grows with anxiety. It almost feels as though the monster is purposely trying to scare us. Even Ten, who at first showed a confident demeanour now displays a worried face.

"Lulu... maybe you should get out here? This is a battle of endurance. At this rate, she'll keep coming at us, until she gets what she wants."

"No. I still have one card up my sleeve. I just need to make sure it's worth it."

Suddenly, the Starlight Queen materialises in front of us – laughing in a fiendish cackle.

"Kakaka... Neither of you are going to survive this night. As long as the stars shine, I will never die!"

Her voice is dark and terrifying – causing me to sweat profusely. With a fretted look, Ten responds to the gigantic monster. "So, you can speak after all. You're just full of surprises... aren't you?"

With an unsettling grin, the creature peers only to Ten and converses with her. "Demon lord Ten, it truly is a shame to see you in such a state. Once again, you have allowed your love for humans to hinder you. Just like days of old, you always seem to rub shoulders with a mortal man. Remind me again... what was the mortal's name you used to trot around the world with? Ah, yes: Septimus. Kakaka... you, Septimus and his mighty pair of swords ventured around pathetically. Oh, I am forgetting someone else. What was the name of your sister?"

"Shut your hole!" Screams Ten – angered by the grinning beast. Whatever the creature is referring to, has clearly gotten under Ten's skin – as I notice an aura of flames that begin to surround her. The heat is so strong, I step away, feeling my skin growing hotter. Laughing even more, the Starlight Queen taunts my winged comrade further.

"Oh, are you going to open your third eye? I'd be careful if I were you. We've all heard about what used to happen when you opened that eye. Well, it doesn't bother me. For me, death is not a concept, thanks to the stars. However, I am not so sure your new friend there will survive? Mortals are such delicate creatures, wouldn't you agree?"

Gritting her teeth, full of frustration, she looks conflicted. By what the fiend is saying, Ten is able to access a hidden power, within her ever closed: third eye. However, whatever that power is, it's enough to harm all those around. I am intrigued, I must say but not intrigued enough to find out.

Stepping in between Ten and the monster, I interrupt in a nonchalant and brazen fashion, as Adamas hovers protectively around me.

"You really have quite the mouth. I preferred you when you were roaring like a mindless monster" I say – offending the Starlight Queen. Taken back by my cocky comment, the creature gazes with a threatening stare.

"You, how dare you speak to me like that? You are just a mortal. Know your place, Worm!"

"Ha, I am not just any mortal. My name is Luna the dark messiah. Starlight Queen, it is you who should know your place!" Clap – pressing my hands together, I look up at the twinkling sky and shout forth "Disappear!"

At that instant, the stars within the night sky vanish, all at once. Their sparkling light that shone down, are no more, thanks to my second miracle. Frozen in astonishment, Ten, Adamas and the foul monster stare in shock and awe.

"Lulu... how..." The she-demon says – amazed by my powers.

"Incredible..." Adamas says, with an equally gobsmacked tone.

Shaking and shivering with nervousness, the once grinning monster glares at me and says "How... How in the world did you do that?"

With a cold and strong gaze, I reply "I already told you. I am the dark messiah!" Taking hold of Adamas I run fearlessly towards the beast and shout "You should have kept your mouth shut, regarding the stars being your source of power. Now they're gone, I am almost certain you won't be able to respawn... Ever again!"

"Kaaaa... Get away from me!" The Starlight Queen screams, taking flight by using her large wings, in hopes of escaping.

"Go!" I shout – commanding my blade to soar towards the fiend. Like a deadly boomerang, Adamas lobs off each wing before returning to my side. The monster plummets and crashes to the ground – writhing on the floor hysterically.

"Curse you... Curse you!"

Arms crossed, I stand calmly, looking to the beast as Adamas dances around me – ready to obey my next order. To my surprise, however, Ten strolls past me from behind, with a firm and focused gaze to the Starlight Queen.

"Queen of the stars, you said something about me being hindered earlier, because of humans. Do you still believe that... Seeing as you've been bested by a mere mortal?"

The foul monster doesn't answer. Trembling continuously, the once confident monster that sought pleasure in terrorising others begins to weep.

"I... I don't want to die. Why... Lord Ten? Ever since you met that bastard Septimus, you changed. Can't you see? The mortals are a lost cause. Their fate is already sealed... By that wretched affliction known as the Seventh Blessing. Eventually, it will claim all of their lives!"

Holding a firm stare, Ten creates a single ball of fire within her right hand. As the flame grows, she responds to the wretched and pitiful beast.

"Save it." With the fireball enlarged to the size of a boulder, the she-demon tosses the projectile to the monster. She explodes – letting out a deafening scream.

As the blast disappears, not a trace can be seen, save for small embers that litter the sight of destruction.

As my miracle wears off, we notice the stars reappearing within the sky again – however, with no sign of the Starlight Queen. "Adamas, please tell me you no longer can sense her?"

"Yeah, I can't sense her at all."

"Thank the heavens for that" I state with relief – falling on my behind and letting out a deep breath. "That fight really took it out of me. I am glad that's over!"

At that moment, I hear a nearby door open. I turn to the mansion and see the friendly robot Malcos, slowly stepping outside. He approaches us – keeping his sights glued to me alone. Stopping roughly a meter apart, he bows his head with gratitude.

"Thank you... For protecting the animals here. I am forever in your debt."

Picking myself up off the ground, I fold my arms and reply within an unbothered manner, "Think nothing of it. I was merely returning the favour. I am sure you would have done the same, had it been the other way around."

Looking down to the floor, Malcos pauses briefly as though troubled. With a slight head nod, he says "Yes... I would have done the same. However, because of my objectives, I am not able to."

"Hey, are you ok?" Asks Adamas – sensing a certain sadness from the robot. Although I can't be too sure, I'd hazard a guess the machine is starting to resent its nature. The robot doesn't reply and simply remains silent with its dim bulblike eyes.

Stepping in between us, the demon yawns aloud and asks "What are you sobbing about, Tinny? You're supposed to be a helpful robot, so act like it. You can't continue to watch this place, feeling sorry for yourself."

"Yeah... You're right Mrs Ten..." he responds, before lifting his head to address the three of us. "So, now that the Starlight queen is no more, the animals can now live safely, once again. If there's anything I can do to repay you, please don't hesitate to ask. You're welcome to stay the night before resuming your journey?"

"Hmm, thanks for the invitation, but I am afraid we'll have to decline" I reply, to which at that point, Adamas and Ten rants with an objection to my decision.

"Hey, come on Luna! I wanna stay here for a little while longer!"

"Yeah, honey Lulu. Can't you see it's already late? Why are you in such a hurry to leave already?"

Rolling my eyes, I reply "Sigh... In case you have already forgotten, we are being hunted by Gigas' men. We need to keep moving – otherwise, we risk putting our new friend here in danger.

Eyes flashing brightly, Malcos steps forward and says "Gigas?

Are you referring to the dragon god of this country?"

"Yes. Long story short: We intend to reach his city, in the hopes of obtaining something that will help us find the Land of the Gods."

"The Land of the Gods? I've never heard of that before. However, I have heard of Gigas and his city of Gin. In fact, I think I know of a way that will help you reach there, in no time!"

Short moments later, we are led to the chapel of the manor, just next to the mansion. Brushing away the many leaves that cover the entrance, we are taken inside. The chapel is dim, cold and eerie – as though it hasn't been used for decades.

"Hmph, this is clearly a place of worship. Malcos, what does this have to do with our destination?" I ask curiously – watching as the friendly robot strolls further inside, towards the podium which can be seen at the far end of the chapel.

"Come on, we're almost there. It will all make sense, once I show you". Reluctantly we follow his lead.

"Ugh, such an unsightly place. I hate chapels!" Moans Ten – partially covering her eyes in a dramatic fashion."

"Oh come on Ten. What's to hate about this place? It looks so mysterious and peaceful" says my companion sword, to which I chuckle to myself. I find it astounding at the very fact that the three of us are together on this journey, despite how opinionated we are. We never seem to agree on anything and yet somehow, we consider ourselves comrades.

Stopping at the podium, the robot pauses for a moment before pointing around at what used to be a congregation.

"A long time ago, long before my master built his home on these grounds, this used to be a place of worship. Doctor Stone knew nothing of the people that once filled this congregation or of the deity they worshipped. Apparently, when he first explored this area, everybody was long gone. However – one day, he found something extraordinary here."

Walking to a nearby lever by the wall, Malcos pulls down on it - causing the podium to open forth like a trap door. Looking down to where the stage once was, we see the entrance to a tunnel, as the robot carries on his explanation.

"My master discovered a secret pathway that apparently led directly to the city of Gin: Gigas' home city. Doctor Stone didn't know why such a tunnel was built. However, he was convinced that it was used by many, at some point in the past."

"Unbelievable!" I gasp – pleased by the shortcut revealed to us. Peering into the dark tunnel, I ask Malcos "How long do you think it'd take for us to reach Gin?"

Shrugging his shoulders, he replies "I am afraid I do not know. Neither do I know what dangers await inside. I am sorry that I couldn't be of any more use."

Facing him with a strong and firm look of respect, I place my arm on his head and say "You have nothing to apologise for, my friend. You have done more than enough. Thank you."

The robot looks down, exuding a body language of sadness. I could ask him what the problem is, but I doubt it would help. Furthermore, I think it's already quite clear the reason for his sorrow. He wants to be free and live a life without being bound by rules.

"Sigh... Are we gonna stand here forever or are we gonna get moving? See you down there, chumps!" Moans Ten - casually strolling past us and leaping into the tunnel.

Hovering to the machine's front, Adamas bids a final farewell also. "Malcos, it was a pleasure to meet you. I hope we can meet again... someday."

"Me too..." responds the mechanical friend, with a reluctant tone. The black sword drifts into the tunnel also – leaving only Malcos and I in the dark chapel. He keeps his head held low, as though afraid to look into my eyes and say goodbye. With a heartfelt tone, he addresses me.

"Mr Luna... Have a safe journey. If you ever decide to visit, I'll be here... I'll always be here... Whether I like it or not."

Wow, I didn't think saying goodbye would be this hard, especially to a robot. If I left now, without doing something, I'd feel like a complete jerk. After all, he caught me from a falling bridge, healed my broken arm and revealed a way to the City of

Gin. Wait... How many miracles have I used today?

Like a light bulb shining in my mind, a bright idea comes to me – causing me to smile immensely. Why didn't I think of such a thing earlier? Well, here goes nothing.

Clapping my hands together, I cast my final miracle for the day and utter the word "Freedom". The robot lifts its head and stares at me – feeling something different about itself, although not quite sure why.

"Mr Luna, what did you just do to me?"

"I freed you. You are no longer bound by the rules of your creator. Now, you can do whatever you want with your life."

"Are you serious?" Malcos asks – eyes shining brightly.

Turning my back, I reply and say "Yes. Now there's nothing keeping you here. My friends and I probably won't be returning here ever again. However, if you ever wish to find us, we'll be at the Land of the Gods. Farewell... my friend."

The robot's eyes shine with wonder at my parting words, as I enter the tunnel. He pulls the lever – causing the podium to close behind me.

Now, all alone in the chapel, Malcos stands with a confident and hopeful gaze. "Am I truly... Free?" He asks himself, turning around before exiting the church. He strolls outside and looks up at the starry night, filled with a newfound perspective.

"The world... It's so big and full of amazing people, like Mr Luna. For the first time, I feel like I want to explore it all. I never had this desire before. Up until now, all I've ever done was follow my master's objectives. Now, a different focus drives me. Not one that has been given to me but of my own curiosity. Is this your doing, Mr Luna?"

Walking to the manor, he opens its doors and steps inside – gazing around within the dark and lonely mansion. Upon holding his silence, he talks to himself once more – hearing nothing but the ticking of the clock by the wall. "Everything looks so empty here. Every day I've been cleaning this place, for what? I don't want to. I don't need to." Looking at the top of the staircase in front, the robot sees a single portrait of his late creator.

Upon slowly ascending the short flight of stairs, he approaches the picture and stares at it for many moments.

"Dr Stone…"

With both hands, he gently takes hold of the portrait – holding it close to his eyes. "Doctor Stone, I am sorry… I can't stay here." Putting the picture back against the wall, he smiles with ambition and anticipation.

"I want to see it all. I want to explore the world and experience new things. Wait for me, Mr Luna, Ms Ten and Adamas. I'll be joining you all soon."

To his surprise, the front door is knocked twice. The robot pauses for a few seconds – wondering who could be visiting at such a late hour. The only possible explanation would be his recent friends who he just saw off.

"Mr Luna? Mr Luna is that you?"

Wham – at that instant, the entire door is blown to pieces – causing much debris and smoke to cover the front staircase area.

"What in the world…?"

As the dust settles, the defenceless machine sees a single soldier - tall and large, sporting red and black armour, along with golden steel gauntlets and grieves. His head is covered with a large helm that resembles a dragon.

"Sorry to disappoint you, but I am not the man you called for. However, my comrade and I are looking for him just the same."

"Who are you and what do you want?"

At that moment, the large soldier strolls further inside before approaching the nervous robot. With an effortless motion, he takes hold of Malco's head before brutally shoving him against the wall – breaking the portrait of the Doctor in the process. With no sense of remorse, he then slams the robot onto the ground.

"My name is Vast and I am the commander of the Dragoon squad, on behalf of the great Gigas. You are going to tell me where the man called Luna went."

Struggling helplessly, the machine tries to make sense of the situation, as the grinning knight keeps his him pinned to the ground. At that moment, a second knight enters the mansion. Casting his eyes to the front entrance, Malcos sees a shorter soldier of slimmer build, holding what looks to be a hilt with no blade. Addressing the machine, the second soldier speaks with a light yet stern tone.

"Hmmm, a man-made creation, with the ability to communicate with other forms of life. Such an abomination is an insult to our lord Gigas. Your sight sickens me."

The second knight walks slowly towards Malcos, who can do nothing but hope for a saviour.

"I am... I am going to die. Mr Luna... please help me!"

Chapter 12: White

Within the dark tunnel – the three of us try to observe the mysterious path that will hopefully lead to the city of Gin. However, with no light to guide us, all we see is darkness.

"Sigh... how on earth are we supposed to walk through this tunnel? I can't see a thing!" I moan – slapping my forehead with frustration.

"I knew it was a bad idea to depart so soon. We should have stayed with Malcos, until the next morning."

"Quiet Adamas. I only wanna hear solutions. Got that?"

"Bwahaha... oh, relax Lulu. You're not afraid of a little darkness, are ya? Worry not my love. I will keep you company" adds the she-demon, as she proceeds to wrap her slithering tail around my neck. I shiver with disgust before freeing myself from her.

"Stop fooling around, Ten! We don't have time for silly tricks."

"Aww, I am just trying to lighten the mood, honeybee. I realise that you're probably sad about leaving little Tinny behind, but you don't need to take it out on me. Besides, if you need a little light, why don't you just simply use one of your miracles?"

"I can't. I used them all up. I am only allowed to use three, every twenty-four hours."

Covering her own mouth behind a fit of laughter, she replies "Bwehehe... are you serious? So, not only are you useless within pitch black darkness, but your miracles also have a limit? dark messiah my ass!"

"Get bent!"

Chuckling continuously, the she-demon emits a small but radiant flame from her index finger – lighting our surroundings.

"Let's be on our way, shall we?"

We begin our trek through the dim tunnel – staying close together. The air is thick and stuffy, along with a rotten smell of sewage or worse. Of course, I am the only one here that has bothered to notice. The she-demon is breathing in and out like the air were filled with roses, while Adamas, of course, is unable to smell.

"Yuck! What on earth is that smell guys?" Moans the blade, to my surprise and disbelief.

With my nose covered, I stop and ask "You're kidding, right? Do you mean to tell me that you have a sense of smell? You don't even have a nose!"

"I know that Luna, but it's the truth. This tunnel stinks of sewage or something."

Yanking on Ten's single horn – I pull her to me and ask "Demon, I want answers. How in the world can Adamas smell anything, when he doesn't even have a nose?"

"Huh? Oh, don't ask me honeybee. I already told you once before that Adamas is a mystery. He can speak and yet he has no mouth, think yet having no brain, see yet having no eyes and smell yet having no nose. By the way, I take offence at your disgust to the aroma within this place. I for one find it nice."

"Sigh... So you have absolutely no idea as to why Adamas is the way he is? Hmph, I don't believe you."

Shrugging her shoulders, she carries on walking as we follow behind. "I'd never lie to you, Lulu. Then again, perhaps I lied just now? Bwahaha!"

Moving on for some time, the black sword addresses the winged demon.

"Ten, I've been meaning to ask you something, ever since we defeated the Starlight Queen. During our fight with her, she said something about my previous owner, wielding a pair of swords. What did she mean by that?"

Stopping awkwardly, the demon stands still, back turned to us both. I react with a slight flinch – remembering the words of the monster from earlier. That's right, she said that the man known as Septimus wielded two swords.

The atmosphere is tense and uncomfortably quiet, as she remains with her back facing us. At that point, she replies in a smooth and clear tone.

"Well isn't it obvious, Dimmy? You were wielded along with another living sword."

My mouth drops upon hearing her revelation, as my mind races with questions. I step forward – preparing to unleash a bundle of questions. However, before I do, the sword overtakes me and asks Ten "I... I am not the only one like this?"

The she-demon turns around before crossing her arms. Eyes diverted, as though recollecting all that she knows, Ten answers us.

Very well. I might as well tell you, all that I know. Adamas, you once had a counterpart sword named: Platina. Just like you, she possessed a will of her own. She was a pure white sword, who also could kill other immortal beings. Together, you and her were unstoppable in the hands of Septimus: The Miracle Swordsman."

"She? Are you saying that my counterpart was a girl?"

"Not just any girl, Dimmy. Platina was your sister."

This almost sounds too good to be true. Adamas and Platina: sibling blades, wielded by one man, long ago. I wonder if she was as annoying as Adamas is now? More importantly, I wonder where she is now?"

As though anticipating my question, the winged comrade steps forward – places her finger over my lips and says "Don't bother asking me such a predictable question, Lulu. I've been asleep for thousands of years, remember? The last I saw of Adamas and Platina together, was in the land of the gods, along with Septimus. Your guess is as good as mine, honeybee."

Drifting towards me – my companion sword speaks with a desperate and keen manner. Luna, I have a sister... just like you do. Where do you think she is? I really would like to meet her!"

Christ... as if I don't already have enough problems of my own, right now. As much as I find this new revelation interesting and all, it's still not enough to sway me from my destination.

"Adamas - as you know, my journey is to reach the Land of the Gods. I woke you for that purpose alone – nothing else. I am sorry but, I am not interested in finding your sister right now. Perhaps afterwards, when I've forced the Great Observer to revive my sister, you can find yours? Well, let's get going."

Stepping past the pair, I take the lead and begin onwards. From behind, I hear the blade sigh with sadness. Yes, what I said was not the nicest thing in the world. However, it can't be helped. The love for my sister overshadows all overs. If that makes me a terrible person, then so be it.

"Bwhehe... I didn't expect you to be dumb, as well as selfish" Taunts our demon comrade. If you had any sense in that mortal brain of yours, you'd take the opportunity to locate Platina, wherever she is. How else do you expect to survive in the Land of the Gods, without the combined power of both Adamas and Platina?"

Shit, she does have a point. It would be very helpful to have two immortal slayers. However – an attempt at finding the counterpart blade isn't worth taking. Besides, if Septimus perished even while using both swords, I doubt it'd make much difference for me. One is enough.

Ignoring her question, I carry on and she follows behind, along with Adamas. We continue walking for about an hour, in silence amongst the dim and foul-smelling tunnel. This is most likely my doing, mind you. The two can most likely sense my all too often aura of dismissal. They want to persuade me to find the blade known as Platina, yet they are reluctant... – knowing that I will shoot down their attempts to convince me.

Before long, we reach an opening – finding ourselves in a wide area. We seem to now be in a bizarre underground sanctuary. Glancing around: left, right, up and down, we see an abundance of diamonds. With no explanation, they emit and illuminate light which brightens up the entire space.

"What is this place?" I mumble – strolling further inside.

"Beats me, honeybee. Regardless of what it is – it looks kinda pretty. What do you think of this place, Dimmy?"

"Huh? Oh... Yeah... It's nice, I suppose..." The blade replies with a vague tone.

Inspecting the mysterious space further, I scan the area for an exit. However, with so many diamonds and platforms around us, it is quite hard to see. "Hey, Adamas. Do you sense any trouble here?" I ask my blade.

"No... everything seems ok."

"Good. In that case, go and zip around for a possible exit that doesn't involve us turning back. I refuse to believe this place is a dead end."

Upon a brief pause, Adamas responds in a sad and heavy tone. "Ok... As you wish. After all, you're the boss... right?" He glides away, out of sight – leaving Ten and I concerned.

Pulling on my ear, the she-demon scolds me and says "Well done, misery guts! You succeeded in breaking poor Dimmy's heart. What the hell is wrong with you?"

"Me? What have I done wrong?"

"Bah! You know full well, Lulu. Dimmy has just discovered that he has a sister, somewhere in this world. Can you imagine what that must feel like? Yet, all you're concerned about is your own motives. Hell, not even I could be as cruel, and I am the demon overlord!"

Rejecting her attempts to guilt trip me, I stick my chest outward and justify myself.

"I never claimed to be your local helper. My goal has been clear from the very start, and Adamas knew it well. Furthermore, both you and he need to remember that I am his wielder. Therefore, I get to decide where we will go. Got that!"

Shocked by my rebuttal, Ten steps back and glares at me with eyes of anger. Upon biting her lips, she turns her back to me and replies "I hear you, loud and clear. However, with a mentality like that, you'll never be considered a true wielder of Adamas. If you continue to destroy his morale, he won't fight at full strength for you. Hmph, you won't stand a chance in the Land of the Gods!"

Upon a furious sigh, the demon girl storms off – exuding a fiery aura in the process. Left alone, I look up at the ceiling and exhale. "Sigh... why can't I have normal comrades, instead of emotional wrecks?"

With nothing left to do, I decide to look for my blade. Ten's words regarding its morale had struck a nerve. If what she's saying is true, then it's vital that Adamas stays on good terms with me. Opposition from the gods will only get worse, as we draw nearer. The last thing I need is a blade that doesn't respect its wielder. At the same time, can I truly say that I've given Adamas a good reason to respect me?

I eventually find the black sword – in the middle of a large space. I hear crying coming from him and small mumblings that I can't quite make out. Slowly approaching him from behind, I ask "There you are. Are you ok?"

Startled by me, the floating sword turns around and remains silent. Backing away a few paces, he replies "What does it matter to you, how I feel? After all, I am just a sword... Right?"

"Come now Adamas, there's no need to take things so personally."

"That's rich, coming from you. This whole Journey has been personal. The only difference is, it's only about you" shouts the blade – voice echoing from the walls and ceiling. This is the first time I've heard Adamas sound so passionate. I am somewhat lost for words – unable to find an appropriate response. As I stutter to produce a word, the sword continues.

"Luna, do you know how it feels, to not know who you are or where you came from? Why do I not remember anything from long ago? What happened to my memories? All this time, I thought I was the only one like this until Ten told me that I have a sister somewhere. Yet, all you can think about is your sister and your problems. Well, seeing as you're so concerned on nobody else but your situation, why don't you just find the Land of the Gods all by yourself!"

Ouch, I never knew words could hurt this much. I feel as

though I've been verbally struck down. How ironic that the one to do it is an actual sword. He is absolutely correct. This has always been about me and I make no excuses for it. However, If I am gonna expect help, then I should at least be willing to offer the same. Swallowing my pride, I initiate a humble bow and attempt to apologise.

"You're right, everything you said about me was spot on. Listen – if you want us to find your sister, as a team, then…"

Suddenly, a loud crashing sound is heard from above – causing us to look upward at the ceiling. To my shock and dismay, I see a single knight falling towards our position. I've seen that knight before. Sporting black and red fighting gear, it's the slimmer knight who rescued his comrade the other day.

Landing to the ground in between Adamas and I, the foe enters a fighting stance and introduces himself.

"Finally I have found you. Now, prepare yourself against the one and only: Ryu, Prince of Gin!"

Chapter 13: Royalty

Overcome with surprise, I learn that the knight before me is, in fact, the Prince of Gin. If that is so, does that make him Gigas' son?

At that second, I hear sounds of intense fighting and shouting from nearby. It's Ten and that other knight, Vast. Shit, how did they find us?

"Look out!" Screams Adamas - noticing my attention is focused elsewhere. Before I know it, the knight in front is already inches apart from me. Taking hold of my throat he rams me through a series of walls - propelled by his mechanical wings.

"You should never let your guard down!" The enemy states, schooling me as I am continually smashed through harsh surfaces.

We crash through a final wall - entering what looks to be an old and wide, underground graveyard. Upon tumbling to the ground, I struggle as the deadly foe stands many meters apart - holding the bizarre looking hilt with no blade.

"Luna... This place will be your final resting ground."

"Like hell it will. What was your name again? Ryu, was it? I don't know how you found us, but you made a huge mistake."

Standing to my feet, I call for my blade "Adamas!", causing it to zip to my left hand. Producing a fighting stance of my own, I stand elegantly - holding my weapon outward.

"Hmph... It wasn't hard to follow your trail. The broken bridge was a dead giveaway. Also, seeing the remains of a fight by the mansion was a great help in finding you. Unfortunately, the robot wasn't as compliant, so we destroyed it."

My heart stops as the enemy makes mention of Malcos. Did I

hear him correctly? Did he just say that he killed Malcos?

"You did what?"

"You heard me. I killed that annoying machine. Besides, it's not like such a thing was actually alive, to begin with. Its existence was an insult to the gods."

My blood boils and all I see is red. Holding my blade tight I whisper, "I am gonna kill him" before racing forward to Ryu. As I do, he stands with a confident pose which sends me into a rage even more.

"Don't you underestimate me!" I state, attempting to strike at him. To my surprise, I find that I have already been struck, as a small cut appears on my cheek. "What the...?"

"You gotta do better than that... Luna" He says, as my body and clothing are cut without explanation. All I can do is stand defensively, while the knight sways his mysterious hilt from left to right. Is this some form of magic? I can't get close to him.

"Adamas, I need answers. Tell me, what is he doing and how is he doing it?"

"Huh? What are you talking about, Luna? Can't you see the sword he is carrying?"

"No I can't, idiot. All I see is the hilt!"

Blood shoots from out the intensifying scars upon my body, as the opponent runs rings around me. I am helpless against him and his sword which for some reason, I am unable to see. So, I am dealing with an invisible sword.

The attacks quickly take their toll, causing me to stumble and fall to my knees. As I catch my breath, under much pain, the foe halts his attacks and taunts me.

"Haha... how do you like my invisible sword: Leviticus? Its appearance remains hidden from all but its wielder. You do not stand a chance, dark messiah."

"Keep talking, shit head. All I need is one second, to wipe the floor with you" I respond, clapping my hands together to cast a miracle art. However, my sword quickly rants to me.

"No Luna! You already used three miracles, remember?"

"Shit... you're right."

Laughing further - the knight says "Morons. Even if you attempted to use a miracle against me, it still wouldn't work. For you see, I possess something that cancels out your holy powers." To our surprise, he throws off his helmet - revealing his face to us. Bearing short black hair, he looks young - perhaps a few years younger than me. However, the biggest surprise is his right eye, which shines a gold and silver light.

"Behold my dragon eye. This eye of mine was what stopped you from casting your miracles, back in the city of Wellington."

So, he was the one that made it hard for Ten and I to fight within that city. This foe... He is dangerous. However, he is not unbeatable and I refuse to lose against a conceited swordsman like him. Taking hold of my blade, I say to it "Adamas, you said that you could see his sword, right?"

"Right!"

"Ok... well, in that case, I am gonna need you to warn me. Let me know which direction his blade will come so that I can anticipate it. Got that?"

"Got it!"

Standing to my feet once more, I ready my sword as the knight charges towards us.

"Left!" My companion warns. Thanks to his heads up, I defend perfectly - hearing the sound of clashing steel as confirmation.

"Yes!" I let out, as a small smirk upon on my face appears.

Gritting his teeth, the prince says "Hmph... don't get cocky!"

Going all out, he produces a series of strikes and stabs - however, my blade sees it all and reveals to me where each attack is coming from. Sparks fly as our swords consecutively collide within the underground graveyard area.

With each failed attempt at attacking me, Ryu grows more frustrated as I become grow accustomed to his fighting style.

"That's enough Adamas. You don't need to give me any more warnings."

"Huh? Why not, Luna?"

"I have already figured out his fighting style."

With a sure gaze and grin, I breathe a sigh of relief - already knowing how this dual will end. Once I figure out an opponent's fighting style, victory is certain. Although he is quite an accomplished swordsman, he relies far too much on the assumption that his opponents cannot see his blade. As such, his attacks have no weight behind them and are highly predictable. A few seconds to observe his tactics was all I needed.

Going on the offensive, I begin to counter his strikes and initiate attacks of my own.

"What...?" He gasps - stumbling backwards progressively, as I come at him with rapid stabs. The roles are reversed. Now, he is the one who is left confused and baffled.

"How... How can you see through my attacks?"

"Idiot. Your blade may be invisible but your style isn't!"

With a mighty swipe, I knock him back and he hits a far wall. Falling to his knees, he stays exhausted and helpless.

"Sigh... Great Scott. You are a great swordsman indeed" he says, as I slowly stroll towards him - ready to finish him off. "Trista was right about you. Congratulations... you passed the test."

Stopping abruptly, I flinch and lower my sword upon hearing of the witch. "Huh? Do you know Trista? And what test are you talking about?"

Slowly rising to his feet, he bows his head and replies "This was all a test, to see how capable you were. The truth is... Vast and I... We need you to help us take down Gigas and to stop the Seventh Blessing."

Is this some kind of joke? So, all this time they were never our enemies and needed our help? I don't believe it. Besides - I am not interested in forming a merry band of comrades anyway. It's bad enough that I am paired with a demon as it is, let alone a prince and his oaf comrade.

Suddenly, the sound of rushing water can be heard all around us.

"What in the...?"

Within seconds, the walls and ceiling give way and a great flood of water falls upon us. Before I know it, I am gasping for air as we are swept away.

Chapter 14: Emptiness

Ever since that remarkable night, the night where my friend Orion revealed himself to be the messiah of Babylon city, my sister and I have never been the same. It has been six months since that time and since then, my sister and I have not seen him. Our usual gatherings of gazing up at the moons and playing are no more. Now, most nights we spend wondering about him. We miss him.

This wouldn't be too much of a problem for me if it weren't for another grave issue. Lucia has fallen ill and nobody can understand why. For the past five days, Lucia has been in constant agony. However, when I ask her what the problem is, she simply says that her body feels as though it's dying. Her skin has become pale and at times during the night, she sleep-talks in a tongue that makes no sense to me.

Although all the medicine I managed to get my hands on hasn't worked, I still refuse to give up. I have one last option, one that I am certain will save her.

Our friend Orion is the Messiah, which means he most certainly can do something. Just as he healed me, when we were attacked by those monsters, he can do the same for my sister. He will do it for sure because he is our friend.

"Hang on Lucia" I whisper to her – carrying her on my back as we walk through the streets of Babylon City. It is the first time we've both seen the legendary city, from within. It is clean, orderly and a sight to behold – with streets and structures made of shining gold. As we trek onwards wearing our smelly and dirtied clothes, we feel almost insignificant, compared to everything and everyone around us. The people stop and stare at us, with judgmental eyes.

Although they don't say a word, I can almost read their minds. They find us disgusting and unsightly. It doesn't matter though. As uncomfortable as it is right now, I need to keep going. We're running out of time.

Before long, we come to the entrance of the tallest tower in the whole of Babylon city. It is the same tower that we used to always see, from our distant village. It is here where we hope to find Orion. However, as usual, our path is not without obstacles. Standing in front of the large doors, a single priest can be seen, chanting in prayer. As I take minor steps forward, he casts his attention to me.

"May I help you?" The man says, in an unfriendly and hostile manner. Standing my ground, I take him up on his offer.

"Yes, my sister and I need to speak with the Messiah: Orion. She needs his help, quickly!"

Without any sense of urgency or noticeable sympathy, he shakes his head and responds "Sorry, but the church of the holy one cannot help you. For simple injuries or sicknesses, you can go and see a doctor."

"No, this sickness can't be cured. Nothing works for it and if we don't do something fast, she will die! Only Orion can save her. Besides, he is our friend, so please allow us entry."

"Hmph, now little one, don't go telling lies. His Holiness would never be associated with your type. Please leave."

Taken back by his cold and blunt response, my sister and I stay shocked. Why is he being this way? Isn't this place supposed to be a church? No, not just any church but the most famous church in the land. I guess I am left with no other choice then.

Placing my weak and ill sister to the ground, I slowly approach the priest with clenched fists. He looks nervous, as though not expecting my reaction.

"I don't think you understand..." I grumble before pouncing to him. Within seconds I beat him down. "I told you that she will die if we don't something. Do you think I came all this way to turn back...?" I ramble while I continue to knock his head, back and forth. Slanted against the doors of the tower, he sits help-lessly as I relentlessly punch his face. Blood stains my fists from his broken face.

"Brother... Please... That's enough" My sister pleads, causing me to stop instantly. Her voice breaks me out of my fit of rage and I look down at my handy work. The man looks unrecog-nisable, with teeth missing, swollen eyes and drenched with blood. I feel somewhat ashamed, acting out in front of my sister.

"I am sorry Lucia... But..." Gently pushing the doors open, I ready to make my way inside, leaving her outside. "Please wait here, while I find Orion. Once I get him to come out, he'll cure you and everything will be fine. I just need to make sure nobody gets in my way."

Entering the church, the first thing I see are rows of stone pil-lars, all around. "Orion!" I call out – voice echoing through what seems to be a large space. Within seconds of my shout, I hear dozens of footsteps racing towards me. "Here they come..."

Emerging from behind the pillars, I see scores of priests com-ing at me. "What are you doing in this holy sanctum? Leave this place immediately!" They order.

"I just want to find Orion. He's my friend!"

Not backing down, I run past them and delve further into the church. There are too many of them for me to fight, so I'll have to find Orion before anyone of them can catch me. "Orion, where are you? It's me, Cassius. My sister needs your help!" I scream to the top of my voice, hoping he emerges to make everything right. However, with each desperate shout, I begin to grow concerned about his wellbeing. What if Orion is being held here, against his will? That would explain why we haven't seen him for the past six months. "Orion, I am here! Just tell me where you are!"

"Get out of this place!" Screams an oncoming priest – charging at me with a stick. Coming close enough, he waves it around manically. Judging by the sloppiness of his movements, he isn't a fighter. None of them are. None of them has had to struggle and fight to live another day, unlike myself and those like me.

Snatching the stick from his hand, I make quick work of him – thrusting it against his nose. Blood shoots from his face and he falls backwards, allowing me to resume.

Darting by another pillar, the sight of a throne catches my eye. Gazing at it, I gasp in astonishment at the sight of Orion, sitting calmly – eyes locked to mine.

"Orion... Could you not hear me calling you?"

He doesn't respond. Holding his silence, he continues to stare at me, like I was a stranger. What has happened to him?

Upon a deep breath - keeping my wits about me, I slowly begin treading towards him. However, before I can get any closer, he shows a look of disappointment before shaking his head, left to right.

"You... You shouldn't have come here."

"What? Why? Listen, I don't know why you're acting so strange, but Lucia needs your help..."

Whack – suddenly, I am struck from behind by many sticks. Falling forward onto my knees, I see and hear countless priests surrounding me. I try to get up, but before I know it, they pounce on top of me – pinning me to the ground.

"Get off me! Get the hell off me!" I shout – desperate to break free. All the while being watched by Orion who sits still on his throne. "Orion, tell them that I am your friend. We're running out of time!"

He refuses to answer. Instead, he shakes his head once more. Why is this happening? This must be a dream or a nightmare.

"Orion, stop messing around! Lucia is really sick. Please, use your powers and save her before she dies!"

"No... It cannot be stopped. Not even I can stop it" he replies, with a clear tone and face of regret.

Held from head to toe, the priests start to drag me away from Orion. I am helpless against their numbers, no matter how hard I struggle to break free. Watching as he gets further away from me, I call to him once again. "Very well. If you truly don't have the power to save her, then tell me: Where can I find the Land of The Gods!"

He remains silent as I am pulled further away, back to the entrance of the church. "Tell me, tell me... just tell me!"

My words fall on deaf ears, and before I know it I am thrown out. As I tumble back outside, the priests slam and lock the front doors. The echoing thud feels like a final nail in the coffin, to any hope I had of saving my sister.

"Brother, are you ok?" Asks my sister who strolls over to me with a worried look. "Oh no, you look hurt. What happened to you in there?"

Slowly sitting upward, I take a deflated breath – looking away in shame. I am not worthy of looking Lucia in the eyes, right now.

"I... I couldn't get Orion to come out. I am sorry sister... I don't know what to do." Opening her arms, she hugs me close to her. With no hope left, we simply sit together in silence, rejected by the messiah of the gods. Whom are we kidding? It's not just the gods that have rejected us, but the whole world. It's always been this way, ever since I could remember. Born into poverty by parents who would soon die, only then to lose my sister. I wonder why this world hates us so much?

At that moment, my sister stares into the sky - looking as though lost in a trance. With a voice that doesn't sound like her own, she utters mysterious words as though possessed.

"Holy... Holy... Holy. O, Great Observer. I am your friend and loyal servant Selene: Goddess of the moon. Holy... Holy... Holy!"

"Sister? Sister... Snap out of it!" I shout while shaking her out of the mysterious trance. She has been uttering those same unsettling words, each day and night. Why... Why is this happening to her?

Coming to her senses, she realises her bizarre actions just now before bursting into tears.

"Brother... I feel like I am losing myself. What is happening to me?"

"Don't worry, Lucia. I promise, no matter what happens I will never leave you. I will find a cure..."

Two days later, my sister died.

Before a setting sun, I stand opposite her grave, made using my bare and bleeding hands. I lost her, just like mother and father. Now I have nobody. Why... Why did Orion betray us? He was our last hope. If he had healed her or told me where to find that sacred land of the gods, Lucia might have still been alive.

Reaching into my pocket, I take out a small knife and place it against my chest. Seeing as I've lost everything I've ever cared about, there's no point living, right? Worry not sister, I am right behind you.

"It is called the Seventh Blessing" comes an unfamiliar voice from behind. Turning around, I gasp at the sight of a mysterious being - body wrapped in a long cloak that sparkles and shines as if it were made from countless stars. What is even more shocking, however, is the large glowing halo that floats, inches above its head.

"There is a way to see your sister again and rid the world of such a horrid thing. However, in doing so, you will stir the wrath of every god in existence and lose your humanity along the way. So, are you interested?"

Upon a slight pause, I take a single step forward. Nodding my head, I accept the stranger's offer, whatever it may entail. Throwing the knife to the ground, I give my life one last chance and use it to entertain the words of the mysterious god before me.

Chapter 15: Friend

"**H**ey, Mr dark messiah... you planning on sleeping all day?" A voice calls to me – waking me up from my nightmare. As a matter of fact, to call it a nightmare would be an understatement. What I experienced, was simply the accounts of my sister's fate.

Opening my eyes, I find myself laying on soft ground, looking up at the knight I recently fought against.

With his back turned, he sits beside me under a bright and blue morning. It seems to be just us two. Fuck... where is Adamas?

"Uh... Where are we and how did we get here?" I mumble - sitting upward while trying to remember where we were before.

"I am not too sure myself. However, I do know that we're not dead, which is something to be relieved about. When you and I stopped fighting, a great flood carried us out of the tunnel."

"Where are the others?" I ask, scanning my surroundings. To my left and right, all I see are fields of endless flowers but not my friends.

"I do not know. However, I am certain that they survived and are somewhere not too far. Come on, let's look for them."

"And why should I go anywhere with you? If it weren't for you and your friend, we would have been halfway to our destination. Besides, didn't you say that you destroyed my friend Malcos? You're lucky that I am without my blade right now. If I was, I would have already killed you."

Standing to his feet and stretching his arms wide, he yawns before responding "Oh... about that. I simply lied to get you riled up. Rest assured - your robot friend is very much alive."

Closing my eyes, I breathe a sigh of relief. Extending his arm to me, he smiles and says "come on, I'll help you up."

Short moments later, we begin strolling through the field of flowers. Staying a few paces behind, arm's crossed, I keep a firm gaze to the back of Ryu who leads the way.

"Sigh… must you keep glaring at me from behind? I can literally feel the heat coming from your eyes. So, shall we discuss the plan or are you gonna just marvel at me?"

"Plan? Listen - I still don't trust you. We won't discuss anything until you've told me all I need to know about you."

Looking into my unwavering eyes, he asks "were you not listening to me the first time? Vast and I plan to kill Gigas and we need your power to do it. After that, we hope to end the Seventh Blessing. Surely that should be enough information for you?"

"No, not at all. Explain to me why a prince would want to kill his own King? Technically he is your father, right?"

"Not exactly. Although it is true that I am the Prince of Gin, in truth, I am not related to that monster. Originally, Gin was ruled by its true King: My biological father. That was until it was attacked and conquered by Gigas. My father and our empire were quickly destroyed by that horrid dragon, who had its eyes set on taking my father's empire for its own. Clearly, being a god wasn't enough for it. Although at the time I was but a child when the attack happened, I still remember it well. It crushed almost all our soldiers and killed my mother. Gigas was about to do the same to me – however, my father pleaded with it to spare me. Somehow it worked and the creature decided to adopt me as its child. The few soldiers that survived were forced to also join Gigas and supports its new order. So, there you have it… My reason for rebuilding my father's original empire."

"Hmph… Without being too rude, how do you expect to build an empire, when you sacrifice your men so casually? In Wellington, you allowed your henchmen to be killed by me, all in an effort to test my skills. That doesn't sound like someone who cares for his empire at all."

Hands clenched into a fist, ready to strike at me, he holds himself back and replies "They… their lives were already over, six days prior. The ones that attacked you had acquired the Seventh Blessing and were doomed to die anyway. Even still, they chose to trust in me and die for my cause. I swear... I will free the whole world from the hold of all gods and rid Popla of the Seventh Blessing. I will go down in history as the greatest hero of all time."

Holding my silence, I turn my gaze to the distance where the sun can be seen over a faraway mountain. Upon a small sigh, I utter "So... You have lost loved ones too."

"Hmph, haven't we all? This world is littered with things that cannot be undone. The only thing I can do now is honour everyone who passed away by giving my father's country the future it deserves. After all, we can't go back in time and we can't bring our loved ones back to life."

Slightly offended by his last comment, I cast my eyes to him – holding a bothered expression. As though realising my issue with his words, he clicks his fingers and responds.

"Hmm... You don't agree with my statement, right? Trista had already told me about you and your interesting desire, to somehow bring your sister to life."

"That's right. Do you find it laughable, as everybody else does?" I ask – waiting for him to chuckle at me. However, to my surprise, he does the exact opposite. Instead, he calmly strolls to me. Stopping just minor inches from my face, he gently holds my chin and replies.

"No, why would I laugh at that? I have been where you are. I too have once allowed the pain of loss to warp my judgment. It's a long and empty road, which hits you hard when you've realised how futile your actions have been. You're not ready to let go."

Slowly brushing his hand away from my face, I step past him and say "I misjudged you, Ryu. At first, I had you down as your typical conceited royal who looked down on others. I apologise for having the wrong impression of you..." Walking in front, I produce a small grin and finish by saying "...but now I see that you are a hero at heart who thinks his life experiences, gives him validation to educate others. You and I are not on the same road, my friend."

"Hmph, so I am your friend now? Wow... I've never befriended a delusional messiah before. I guess I should be honoured" he says with a taunting smirk.

His mild insult hardly phases me. On the contrary, it humours me, which sends me into a fit of laughter. I am not sure why but something about him feels refreshing. Perhaps it has something to do with his tragedy, which reminds me of my own. He and I are somewhat the same.

Upon walking for many hours, we reach a clifftop. After all that walking, we have basically reached a dead end. Resting by a tall tree, I sit down while the knight stands close by - looking out over the sea of a looming sunset.

"Looks like there's no sign of them anywhere. Let's go back and search somewhere else."

"No, let's catch our breath for a while. Besides, we need to think of a plan as to how to kill the dragon god."

"Very well. Seeing as you know all about Gigas, perhaps you already have a plan?"

With a slight grin, the prince glances at me and replies "As a matter of fact, I do. For our plan to be successful, we're all gonna need to play our part, with no mistakes!"

"Hmph, sounds like an acting role."

"You're not far off. Gigas resides under our castle, behind a heavily guarded fortress. As such, barging in guns blazing will be pointless. My idea is to simply walk through the front doors."

Confused by his plan, I pry and ask "Walk through the front doors? That doesn't sound very smart. Granted, the dragon still believes you and Vast to be loyal soldiers – however, he will instantly attack us once he sees Ten, Adamas and I, right?"

"Not if you're captured. We're going to make Gigas believe that Vast and I captured you and Ten, and bring you directly to the dragon god to be executed."

"Come again? So, you're saying that I need to pretend to be captured and act like a prisoner?"

"Precisely! All I need is one second for him to let his guard down. Although my sword Leviticus can kill immortal beings, it won't be enough to bring the dragon god down. However, together... Our combined power will certainly do the trick. You, me, Vast, Adamas and the demon Ten will be more than enough."

"Sounds like a good plan. However, I am not sure it will work. After all, doesn't Gigas have the power to see the future?"

"Correct. Gigas has the power to see things that are yet to happen, which has made it one of the most feared gods in the world. However, its power does have limitations. For instance, he can only see things about sixty seconds in advance. Plus, his foresight is only active when it's awake. If we arrive when he's sleeping, then he won't be able to foresee our future actions against him."

"Ok... But what about when he wakes up? Wouldn't he then just see the future, once awake?"

Tapping his own head, nearest to his special eye, he replies "No, not if I use this dragon eye of mine, just before he wakes. With this, I can cancel out the dragon's powers and nullify his ability to see the future. By the time he wakes up, he won't realise his powers have been stopped, which will put us at an advantage. Before he knows it, he will be mincemeat."

I gotta hand it to him. The prince thought about it well. So we will be taken to Gigas' castle, under the guise of being captured by Vast and Ryu. Gigas won't know our future actions because we will choose a time to arrive when he's asleep. At that time, Ryu will use his mysterious eye to block his foresight, at which point we will take him down and I will obtain the original map of the world. Sounds simple enough.

"Do you have any questions?" Asks the prince.

"No, not relating to the plan anyway. Let's give it a try... After all, it's the best chance we have. However, I am a little curious about something. If you aren't the biological son of Gigas, then why do you possess a dragon's eye?"

"Oh, this? Haha, believe it or not, this used to be Gigas' right eye until he plucked it out and gave it to me for my loyalty to him. The fool has come to look at me as a real son and has grown to trust me. Little does he know that the truth cannot be any further."

Looks like luck is on my side, for once. With Ryu's powers, I'll be able to find the way to the Land of the Gods in no time – once we kill the dragon god and have explored its hidden vaults. However, something does feel a little odd about the fact Gigas' gave its own eye and essentially half its power to Ryu. In doing so, Gigas' has created a major Achilles heel for itself. Why would an all-powerful god that has lived for thousands of years and able to see the future, do that? Something doesn't seem right.

At that moment, as the sun fully sets – dark clouds begin to loom, followed by heavy rain.

"Shit. We're in for a rough night at this rate. There's nothing worse than sleeping outside, under weather like this" I comment – protecting my head from the rain, using nothing but my robes.

"True. However, with this much rain, we can travel easily without unwanted attention. Besides, if it gets too much, couldn't you just cast one of your miracles to stop the showers?"

"That would be a waste. After all, I only get to use three uses per day. Any more than that and I risk death."

Eyes perked with intrigue, Ryu strolls to my side and sits next to me. "Only three uses? Wow… and there I was, thinking you're on the same level as the Messiah of Babylon City. You heard of the Messiah of Babylon city, right?"

I am slow to answer – wishing he didn't bring up such a topic, as the sounds of pouring rain continue around us. Staring into space, holding a cold stare, I reply in a flat and monotone fashion.

"Yes… of course I have. As a matter of fact, I grew up near Babylon City."

He gasps with shock – eyes shaking with surprise. I can tell by his face that he is assessing me further, perhaps coming to countless conclusions as to what kind of life I used to lead. I wait for him to compose himself before he strings together a question.

"Luna... did you ever meet the Messiah: Orion?"

Upon a deep sigh, I stand to my feet, look outward at the sea and reply "Yes, many times. In fact, I once considered him a close friend, back when I was a struggling child of poverty. Back then, my name was Cassius. However, when I lost my sister, I became like the empty moons above: Luna."

Turning my back to the sea, I prepare to walk through the field before saying "Come on, let's go find the others. I don't want to waste time." As I stroll forward, expecting the prince to follow, he stands and calls to me.

"Wait... so please tell me something. If you were once a struggling child of poverty like you said - how did you become a messiah?"

Before I respond, something catches my eye. By the edge of the cliff, I see a single female, hands held in prayer - peering over as though ready to leap to her death.

"What is she doing?" I ask - alerting Ryu to the direction of the girl. To our shock and dismay, she leaps off the clifftop and plummets towards the ravaging sea below.

"Is she crazy?" Ryu gasps - running after her before taking flight using the mechanical wings of his suit. Catching her just in the nick of time, they ascend back onto the cliff.

He lays her to the ground, as I approach - wondering what would possess someone to take their own life. She looks tired and full of burden - noticed by her bloodshot eyes and messy blonde hair. To our surprise, she looks up at us with wonder and awe, showing an almost deranged smile.

"I knew it. I knew the Great Observer would answer my prayers! You two are angels, right? Please... help me. Please save my brother from the Seventh Blessing!

Chapter 16: The Seventh Blessing

Upon following the lady for many moments, we are taken to a shore where we find a large hut. The lady has been babbling for some time, without even introducing herself. The moment she saw us, she seemed certain that we were helpers sent by the Great Observer. Before we even had the chance to respond, she led us by the hand and practically dragged us here. This already sounds so bothersome. However, at least we'll be safe from the rain.

"Come in, come in!" She says as we enter. Once inside, we see a large and cluttered living space - full of books, clothes and appliances. What a mess.

At the far side, we see a single bed covered by a long and wide, dirtied curtain.

"Wait here. I'll go and wake my brother up!" She orders - rushing around the curtain to see to her sibling who has been afflicted.

"Luna, what on earth are we doing here?" Whispers Ryu - sharing the same concerns as I do.

"I don't know. It's not as though she gave us much choice. It's clear that she's missing a few spanners upstairs and believes that we can help her. Maybe we should leave now before things become difficult? We would only be wasting our time here."

"Leave? Luna, we can't just abandon someone who needs our help."

"There's nothing we can do! There is no cure for the..."

At that second, the lady emerges from behind the curtain and hurries to us, full of good cheer.

"Thank you for waiting patiently... My brother will wake in a few moments. My name is Sonia and I am so grateful for your help. You see, for the past few days, my brother Carlton received the Seventh Blessing. However, I am certain that this was just a test of our faith by the gods. I have tried everything to cure him but nothing seems to work. My last resort was to offer my life instead. On that cliff, I prayed my heart out. I made a bargain and begged the Great Observer to give me a sign, before taking a leap of faith. Before I knew it, you two were there and..."

"Slow down, will you? I can hardly keep track of what you're saying. Listen - what exactly do you expect us to do?" I ask with a stern and impatient tone. Her smile drops and she looks at me with a lost gaze.

"You... You've come to take away the Seventh Blessing... right?"

My initial response is to tell her the truth. We don't have the power to cure her brother of the Seventh Blessing. Nobody in the whole world has a cure. Even with my miracles, they still would have no effect. However, at the mercy of her hopeful eyes, I am powerless to reveal the truth to her. Try as I might, I am are unable to say it.

"We'll do our best" I reply - kicking myself for even offering a slither of hope. She smiles once more and takes us by the hand - slowly leading us towards the bed where her brother lay. As we get closer, we flinch with fright as the boy utters bizarre words.

"Holy... Holy... Holy. O, Great Observer. I am your friend and loyal servant: Seraphim. Holy... Holy... Holy!"

I stop and take a deep breath. I've heard those ramblings from those who have been afflicted, many times before. My sister would often say the same thing, as though possessed by a god or demon. Even now I am unable to explain why such a thing occurs, and it doesn't get any easier witnessing such strange and frightening actions.

Sonia pulls the curtain - revealing a small boy, about nine or ten years of age. With a wet cloth on his forehead, he looks to the pair of us with tired and weary eyes. His clothes are drenched with sweat, as though his body were fighting against a stubborn virus. If only it were but a virus. The all too familiar mark, seen on his left hand is all I need to confirm what has caught him. This is indeed... The Seventh Blessing.

"Are you two supposed to be angels? You don't look like angels" the boy says - unimpressed by our appearance. Of course, anybody with a thinking brain could see that we are far from angels. As sickly as he looks, he seems to still possess a sound mind - unlike his sister.

"Don't say that Carlton!" The young lady scolds - still believing that we are something more than just human beings. "They have come here to heal you and make everything right again..."

"That's...That's enough" I say to her, as she pauses her rant. Gesturing her to leave my sight, I utter "Leave us be, while we see to your brother. Give us five minutes."

As requested, she departs the hut - leaving Ryu and I with the boy. Standing in silence for many moments, looking down at him with a stone and emotionless gaze, I open my mouth slowly and take a deep breath.

"How long have you been overcome with this sickness?"

"Um... For about five or six days, sir."

"Shit..." Tutting under my breath, I look to the prince by my right side. Correction, I look to his sword. Following my line of sight, Ryu gasps before whispering to me.

"Hey, don't you fucking dare!"

"Why not? It's not as though he will live through this anyway. It's the best thing for him."

Just as the annoying prince sussed out, my intention is to kill the boy. I realise that it may seem heartless but... What difference does it make? He only has a day to live. We might as well get this over and done with so that we can all continue with our journey.

Yanking my collar to him, the prince stares into my eyes and says "what about his sister, huh? Are you not the least bit concerned about what happens to her?"

"No bother. I'll just cast a miracle to make her forget everything. She'll be none the wiser and better off for it."

"Bastard! How would you like it if somebody did that to you and made you forget your sister?"

Taken back by his bold words, my initial response is to strike him across his eye-sore of a face. However - realising that we're in the presence of a young child, I hold back and instead roll my eyes.

"Very well, genius. Seeing as you have all the answers, what do you think we should do?"

"Well... I am not quite sure but, as the prince of this country, every innocent life on my father's land is my responsibility."

What a ridiculous answer. There I was thinking the prince possessed some type of maturity. It's clear that he has a lot to learn. Shifting my attention to the young boy on the bed, I proceed to speak in a monotone manner.

"Boy... Do you know the name for what has befallen you? It is called the Seventh Blessing. On the seventh day of acquiring the blessing, you will die. Currently, there is no known cure for it. My comrade and I are not angels. He is the Prince of Gin and all of Biscus, while I am but a wandering messiah. I possess the power to cast miracles - however even they will not work. Observe..."

In order to prove my point, I clap my hands together and utter the word "Cure".

Before our eyes, the mark of the Seventh Blessing disappears from the boy's hand, which gives him brief relief. However, before he can express any joy, the signature mark bearing the word Amicitia appears once more upon him.

"I really am sorry," I say before turning around to walk towards the exit. Just before I open the door to leave, I say to the prince "I am going to look for the others. I assume that you still intend to stay by the boy's side, till the very end. I'll return... When it's all over."

I leave the hut, without so much as bidding a farewell. I can't... I just can't do it. Stepping out under the heavy rain, I look up at the dark clouds and release all of my emotions. My heart grows heavy, my eyes flow with tears and I weep... the same way I wept when I realised how futile my efforts were back then. No matter how hard I try... I just can't seem to save anyone."

Chapter 17: Twin Wings

"**U**m... Good morning Prince Ryu", comes a frail and young voice. Opening my eyes, I find myself on the floor of the hut - looking up at the wooden ceiling. Glancing to my right, I see an opened window that lets in the rays of a bright and serene morning. So, last night's rain finally stopped. Looking to my left, I see the boy Carlton, standing limply - holding a bowl of rice. "Here... my sister made you some breakfast."

Sitting upward, I hold my head and remind myself as to why I am still here. Oh... I remember now. Luna and I were brought here and asked to heal this boy. However, the bastard shortly left, while I stayed the night here. I don't know why I chose not to leave too. After all, I don't have a way of saving him. In spite of this, I just can't leave him to die. What can I do?"

Sitting on the ground, he places the bowl on my knees and stares at me in wonder.

"What? Why are you looking at me like that?"

"You... You really are Ryu the Prince of Gin. I can't believe my eyes."

Rolling my eyes, I reply "I am not that amazing, kiddo. Yes, I am the Prince of Gin - however, I am no different from the next person."

"That's not true. I have read all about your deeds and tales. You were the one who drove back the pirates of Shaheed, the most feared pirates in the world. You also were the one who slew the great demon beast Boros. Of course, who could forget your most notable victory, at the battle of Abbott..."

Wow, he sure does know a lot about me. Not even I remember

half the deeds I did. I think I might have found my biggest fan.

As I finish my food, I say to the boy "With the amount of knowledge you possess about me, you'd make a great comrade someday."

"Really? Do you think so? That makes me feel so happy. Do you wanna know something? My dream was to one day become a dragoon knight, to be one of your most powerful comrades."

His eyes light up with hopes and dreams. I can see in his eyes... He has the look of a great warrior. Unfortunately, none of that will ever be a reality for him, for he has the Seventh Blessing. Why... why does such a thing exist? Because of it, innocent souls like Carlton will never get the chance to live their lives to the fullest. To make matters worse, their friends and family have no choice but to watch as they die.

Noticing the look of concern on my face, the boy holds a brave smile and says "You're not worried about not being able to cure me, are you? If you are, please don't feel bad. I accepted my fate days ago. Besides... To be able the meet the Prince of Gin on my last day of living is more than I could ever ask for."

I am humbled by his bravery. Despite his inescapable fate, he refuses to let that defeat him.

"Carlton, where is Sonia?"

"Oh, she stepped out a while ago to fetch some food for this evening. However, she has been gone for quite some time now. I wonder if she's ok?"

Reminded of her mentally challenged behaviour, I quickly stand to my feet and approach the front door. "Wait here. I'll go and get her."

Leaving the hut, I step outside and scan the sandy shore and the moving tide of the sea. Glancing from left to right, my concerns grow as I am unable to see any trace of her. "Soniaaaaa!" I shout - hoping that she answers. Unfortunately, she doesn't - causing me to bite my lips with frustration. "Shit... That's all we need right now. Where the hell did she go?"

Putting my detective head on, I begin strolling along the beach, following the faint trails of her footprints. Before long, the trail ends by a pair of larger footprints. "This looks bad..." I whisper to myself. These prints are not human. This looks like some kind of abduction.

"Is everything ok?" Comes the voice of the boy. Turning around, I see him - exhausted as ever, as though his body were about to collapse at any moment.

"What are you doing out here? You should be inside resting..."

"Resting? It's not as though I am ever gonna recover. Besides, I am worried about my sister. She's in trouble, isn't she?"

Upon a short and hesitant pause, I reply "I think your sister has been kidnapped." My response was blunt and direct. Under normal circumstances, I wouldn't be so tactless - however, it's clear that this Carlton has an inner strength that would put most grown men to shame.

"Are you... are you sure about that?"

"I am almost certain. Judging by the clues here, I'd hazard a guess that something stole her away. Although, I can't say for certain whether it was a man, monster, god or demon."

"But... But who would do that?"

"Beats me. In any event, I intend to find her... Before you..."

Holding my tongue, I turn around and cross my arms. Focusing on the matter at hand, I ask the boy "are there any suspicious places nearby? A cave, house or castle?"

Clicking his fingers, Carlton replies "Oh... There is an old castle, a few miles away. I think people call it: House of Nin. However, there has never been any bad stories or anything to worry about. There is an old tale about a wizard residing there. However, nobody has ever seen him."

"That's all I need to know. Wait here while I go and investigate."

"Hey wait... I wanna go with you."

"You what? Listen, don't be ridiculous. It may not be safe for you. You might get..."

"I don't care! Don't you see... I don't have much time left anyway. Please... Before I die, I want to experience a real mission. Prince Ryu, please let me achieve my dream... Fighting with you."

Hmph, fighting with me? He will more than likely be a hindrance. Nevertheless, his circumstance and resolve cannot be ignored. As much as I'd like to refuse his plea, I just can't say no. His dream is to fight alongside me. He will never have an opportunity like this one, ever again.

"Very well…" I respond - strolling to him before extending my arm. "… Just make sure you stay close to me!"

Shaking my hands, he smiles and responds "I won't let you down, partner!"

Placing him on my shoulders, we take flight and ascend into the sky. Soaring over the land, we make our way towards the House of Nin, to look for Carlton's sister. Overwhelmed by the experience of flight, the boy laughs with wonder - shouting with pure and utter bliss.

"Hahahaha… We're flying Ryu! We are just like birds!"

The sound of his happiness moves me - filling me with relief. At least I have achieved something to ease his suffering.

Pulling on my ears, he sways left to right - causing us to spiral through the clouds. As I shout frantically, he continues to laugh with excitement.

"Hey, stop tugging on me, buffoon. We're gonna crash land at this rate!"

"Hahaha… This is so fun!"

"This isn't a roller coaster ride! Sigh…"

As I regain my balance, we see a large castle in front. The castle looks dark and forboding - giving off an unsettling vibe, amongst the greenery of the land.

"Is that what we're looking for?"

"Yeah… That's the House of Nin. Say… before we go inside, why don't we think of a team name?"

"Oh give me a break!"

Pulling on my ears tightly, the boy says "Oh come on Ryu! Team names are the best part of fighting for justice. How about… The dragon brothers!"

"No!"

"Super duo?"

"Hell no!"

Ignoring his suggestions, we finally land at the front gates to the dark castle. As he stands behind me, I notice the entrance is already wide open. Looking to the ground, I see the same large and monstrous footprints found on the shore.

"There's no mistaking it. Sonia was taken to this place. Why her?"

Turning around, I look to the boy and ask "Things might get a little rough inside. Do you wanna stay out here or join me inside? It's your call."

"I'll come with you. We wouldn't be a team if I stayed out here, right? Although, thinking of a suitable name is harder than I..."

Shom - at that moment, the boy enters a trance-like state. I've seen this state, far to well amongst the victims of the Seventh Blessing. Eyes rolling to the back of his head, he faces the sky and states "Holy... holy... holy. O, Great Observer. I am your friend and loyal servant: Seraphim! Holy... holy... holy..."

Kneeling low, I take hold of his shoulders and shake him back to reality. "Don't lose yourself kiddo. Your sister needs you!"

Responding to my voice, he regains control of his body and looks to me with embarrassment.

"Sorry, Ryu. I really can't control when that happens."

"Hey, don't apologize. It's not your fault. Come on... let's get moving... Partner."

Together we enter the castle - keeping our wits about us. Once inside, we walk through a series of dark hallways - kept company by dim candles and statues of ghastly creatures. Who would build such a place,?

Amidst an eerie silence, the boy tugs on my attire and speaks.

"Prince Ryu... Can I ask you a question?"

"Not if you're gonna keep calling me Prince Ryu. We're comrades, right? So drop the prince part."

"Oh... Thanks. Well... Do you know why I sometimes lose myself and say those bizarre things? Ever since I caught the Seventh Blessing, I keep spouting stuff about the Great Observer, and being something called a Seraphim."

Stopping in my tracks, I turn to him and take a short pause - figuring out the best way to answer. Like most people in this world, I am without an explanation. Not even that detestable dragon whom I serve, revealed the secret of the Seventh Blessing. Nevertheless, I offer what little information I have observed over the years.

"I don't know why the affliction causes you to go into that weird state. However, I do know that the name you utter, is of a specific holy being, and varies from person to person. Although there is no concrete explanation for it, many have been led to believe that the word of the specific angel or god you utter, is simply a brief period of possession."

"I see. Have you known anybody who also caught this sickness?"

Turning my back before carrying on, I reply "Yeah... I've lost countless comrades to that thing. One day... I will rid the whole world of it. I promise."

Suddenly, the two of us hear the sound of an angered individual, shouting at someone or something.

"You bumbling fool! You took the wrong one!"

The voice doesn't sound too far away. I'd guess it's only a few corridors up ahead. Wasting no time, Carlton and I race onwards before reaching a sealed door. Kicking it open, we rush inside. The room is gigantic and circular - consisting of expansive walls made of steel pipes which rise up for many meters. In the centre, we spot a large throne, where an old man is seated upon. He wears dark robes and sports an oversized pointed hat. Perhaps the only thing that says to us that he is male, is his long and white beard that extends all the way to his feet.

Beside his throne, a large gargoyle kneels before him - holding a single woman upon its back. That is Sonia. She doesn't look conscious. I sure hope she's ok.

With my invisible blade in hand, I take a step forward and shout "What the hell are you doing?!"

The mysterious man and gargoyle flinch, before turning their direction to me. Lifting his large hat to get a clearer sight, the old man asks "Who are you? You shouldn't be here. Furthermore, how did you get inside?" Rolling his eyes to the gargoyle next to him, he scolds it and says "Winston, did you leave the front door open again? You fool!"

As he rants to the beast I take a single step forward and introduce myself.

"I am Ryu, Prince of Gin. I have come here looking for the woman. I demand that you hand her over, immediately!

Stunned by my introduction, the man leans forward and says "Oh? Are you truly the crown Prince of Gin? Please forgive me, your highness. There seems to be a bit of a misunderstanding."

With a worried look, the old man bows his head and continues. "Oh, where are my manners? My name is Nin and I am a wizard and the owner of this castle. The beast is my loyal servant, Winston. Allow me to explain the situation. You see, about three days ago, the woman here delivered a letter to my abode, pleading for my help. The letter explained that her younger brother received the Seventh Blessing and that a cure was desperately needed before it claimed his life. Being the compassionate wizard that I am, I asked Winston to bring the child to me, so that I may save him. Unfortunately, the bulkhead brought the woman, instead of her brother!"

Ah, so that explains it. Desperate to save her brother, Sonia sought this wizard for help. Wait... Although his pet selected the wrong person, does that mean the old wizard knows of a way to cure the Seventh Blessing? Before I question him further, Carlton steps out from behind and addresses the wizard.

"Do... do you really have a cure, to save me?" The boy asks, displaying a hopeful gaze. I too express a look of intrigue - eager to hear the wizard Nin's response.

Now aware that Carlton is the one that his sister asked to help, the old man shows a pleasant grin... Slumping back on his throne.

"Why yes... As a matter of fact, there is a way. However... You're going to have to let it kill you first."

"Kill me? But..."

The boy flinches as I sigh with disappointment. What a let-down. After all of the suspense, I find that we're dealing with an insane magic user. It's no surprise, seeing as he has been locked up in this shoddy place, with nothing but a gargoyle to converse with. I guess there's nothing more to say.

Strolling forward, I say to the wizard "I have heard enough. Hand over the lady, so that we can all leave peacefully. We do not need your help."

"Wait... But... I haven't even..."

"I said hand her over!"

Clenching his fists with frustration, the wizard mumbles to himself as I get closer. Unable to control his emotions, Nin shouts forth "you will all listen to me, whether you like it or not! Winston - destroy the Prince of Gin. Don't let him get in the way of us saving the boy!"

Saving the boy? How does allowing the sickness to kill him, save him? As I try to make sense of his actions, his beast charges at me. Readying my sword, I assume an unwavering fighting stance.

The beast swings both hands to attack. However, with im-maculate precision, I evade and perform a simple swipe - lob-bing its head clean from its shoulders. As the beast falls to the ground, I hear the boy reacting with awe.

"Wow! You are so amazing Ryu!"

With a small grin, I wink to my young comrade before turning my gaze to the wizard. "Do you realise that raising your hand against me is a grave offence? I am afraid that I must judge you accordingly."

"How dare you kill my dear Winston? No... It is you who should be judged. All of you fools who know not of the truth... All of you will be judged!"

Shakoom - with a wave of his hands, the wizard summons a horde of magical spheres, which rain down over me.

"Shit..." I whisper - thinking fast before darting around the large throne room, chased by the projectiles.

"I have spent my entire life, studying the Seventh Blessing! What we think is a death sentence, is, in fact, a benevolent granter... Followed by a dream giver..." the man rants, as his magic projectiles explode around me. Taking flight I soar through the air - still hearing his mindless rambling.

"Your highness - let the boy become what he must. Kill his awakened state and then he shall be free to dwell among the world of Figments!"

"Granter... Dream giver... Figments? What the heck are you talking about?"

Boom - hit by the explosion of a nearby sphere, I fall from the sky and crash to the ground.

"Ryu! Are you ok?" Asks the boy - looking at the damage done to my armour. That last hit destroyed the wings of my suit. Shit... the wizard is stronger than I had anticipated.

Coming off the throne, Nin summons a rod of lightning within both hands. Preparing to finish me off with it, he says "This is the end... Your highness."

With nothing else left to do, I activate the power of my dragon eye - cancelling out his magic.

"Huh? What in the..." The wizard gasps with shock - stripped of his magic. Wasting no time, I lunge forward and stab him through the heart. "Urrrrlll!"

He falls back as I stand over him - breathing with exhaustion from our duel. Looking up into my glowing eye, he smiles and says "A... A dragon eye."

"That's right. Now... Farewell."

"Your highness... if you want to save him... kill that which he utters. Then he will be free."

The man closes his eyes, leaving me to ponder his words. Kill that which he utters? What he utters... Seraphim.

"Ryu! Ryu, you were amazing!" Carlton cheers - running to me with excitement. "I have never seen someone fight so well."

"You did well also... partner."

"Did I? That makes me feel so happy. We really worked as a team, didn't we? Oh, I have finally found a name for us. How about Twin Wings?"

"Twin Wings? I guess it will do. Come on, collect your sister and get out of here."

"Right!"

At that moment, the sounds of steel collapsing is heard all around us. Before we know it, the walls and ceiling begin to give way. The castle is falling apart.

"Shit... This doesn't look good" I whisper - huddling with the boy and his sister. Naturally, my idea is to escape using the same door we entered. However, it is now barricaded. As large chunks of steel fall around us, we remain helpless.

To my horror, I watch as a much larger piece falls directly towards our position. "Fuck... we're done for." Closing my eyes I brace myself... praying for a miracle. "Father... don't let this be the end..."

To our surprise, the sound of the crumbling castle disappears. Instead, we hear nothing but the sound of pleasant waves. Opening my eyes, I find that we are in fact outside of the hut by the shore, under the night sky.

"How did we...?"

Sitting up before glancing around, I see the dark messiah Luna, standing beside us - hands held within a prayer motion.

"There you are. Sigh... I don't even want to know where you went with the girl and the boy."

"Luna... was it you who got us out of the crumbling castle?"

"Yes and because of you, I wasted a miracle. Why am I always surrounded by incompetent people? Speaking of which, I have found the rest of our incompetent comrades" he says - pointing behind us, by the hut. Relieved, I see my comrade Vast, along with the demon girl and living blade. Turning my attention to the boy and girl next to me, I watch as they slowly open their eyes before looking at one another.

"Carlton! Oh, Carlton, what are you doing out here? It isn't safe..."

"Relax sister. You see, Ryu and I saved you from Nin. We formed a team called the Twin Wings and rescued you. I am not sure how we ended up here though."

Pulling him close, she hugs him tightly and says "We can talk about it tomorrow. For now, you need to get inside."

Looking down at his left hand, she realises that the mark of the Seventh Blessing is still upon him. Looking to the Dark Messiah and I with confusion, she asks "Why does he still have the mark? You two were supposed to have healed him? Well... answer me!"

Shaking his head, Luna turns his back and keeps silent, as I look away also. Stepping in, the boy says "Sister, it's not their fault. They never were angels, to begin with. However, because of Ryu, I had the best day ever. It's ok... I am ready to..."

Suddenly, the feared moment arrives. Midway through sentence, the wretched affliction claims him. He lets out a short gasp before slumping into his sister's arms.

"Carlton? Carlton..."

She trembles - clutching onto his lifeless body. I want to comfort her, but I know that whatever sympathy I express will not be enough. Tears streaming down her face, she glares at us and says "Why couldn't you save him? If I had known you never had a cure, then I would have prefered you let me die yesterday. Why save my life in the first place?"

"Sonia that's not the point. Your brother..."

"Shut up! What am I going to do now? How am I supposed to live?"

Hanging my head with shame, I turn my back and walk towards the rest of my comrades. "Come on Luna, let's leave her be," I say - gesturing him to follow suit. However, with an intriguing stare to the sobbing lady, he stays put while replying to me.

"Go on ahead. I'll catch up with you all shortly."

Departing the shore, we leave Luna with the lady and her deceased brother. Short moments pass and Sonia lets her brother's body drift out into the sea. Sitting under a blue moonlight she stares at the ocean waves, as the dark messiah sits next to her.

"Oh, Carlton... what am I to do now? I don't want this feeling. How do I get rid of it?"

"You will never get rid of it. Believe me... I have tried. All we can do is find ways to suppress the pain... and make sense of it. I lost my sister to that very same sickness."

"You too? How do you continue to go on?"

Luna pauses, as though daydreaming of a time from long ago. Upon a deep breath, he replies "I chose to deny my old self and say that I am a new person. Of course, it doesn't really help that much. One cannot fully erase those from their heart. It would take a miracle to do that."

Looking to her knees, she weeps and responds, "I... I wish there was a way for me to forget. I know it sounds cold, but I'd rather forget about my brother completely than live on with the pain of losing him."

Truer words have never been spoken. He knows exactly how she feels. She has lost everything and sees no worth living on. He can see in her eyes that she no longer wishes to live and would most likely take her own life, quite soon. However, he is sure that her brother would not wish that for her.

"Sonia... Although I am no angel, I do have the power to make you forget. Everything about your brother, including all the moments you shared and anything that ever related to him... I can make you forget it all."

"You do? Are you telling the truth? Please... If you do have that kind of power, then I would like you to make me forget" she requests with a tearful smile.

"... Very well..."

Turning to her, the messiah claps his hands together and utters "Forget". She blinks in response and within seconds she notices the tears upon her own face - baffled and lost for words by them. Looking up with surprise, her mood becomes light and cheerful.

"That's weird... Why was I crying? What were we talking about? I don't seem to remember?"

The robed man pauses before displaying a look of sorrow.

Shifting his eyes to the sea, he replies, "It was nothing special."

Standing to his feet, he turns his back and bids her farewell.

With a bright smile, she waves him goodbye as he strolls into the distance, never to be seen again.

Chapter 18: Vengeance of Yesterday

The next morning - walking along a wide-open road, the five of us have been trekking for many hours – making our way to the city of Gin.

"So, remind me: How long will it take to reach Gin?" I ask the party with a blunt tone.

"Were you not listening before? I said it should take us around six hours: Just enough time before Gigas wakes. We are by the east side of Biscus, not too far from Gin."

"Six hours? Sigh... What a drag!" I respond to the prince – rolling my eyes with frustration. Doesn't someone in this sorry excuse for a group have a better way of getting us to Gin?"

Upon a mild chuckle, the overgrown knight Vast replies "Well, our suits got damaged since emerging from that cave back then. If it wasn't for that, we would have flown you straight to Gin."

"Hmph... Useless, the lot of you."

Bursting into laughter, the she-demon slaps my back and cries "Bwahaha! So technically I am the only one here who can fly. I could always carry us all there, you know? However, my services don't come cheap."

"Forget it, demon" responds Prince Ryu. "Even a fool knows better than to trust a demon."

With a cheeky snigger, the she-demon responds "Aww, don't be like that, little prince. Suit yourselves then. Just don't blame me if it rains again and you're left struggling on foot!" With a ghastly laugh, she strolls in front - holding a cocky grin.

"Luna, are you ok?" Asks the ever-friendly sword of mine.

"Huh? Yeah, of course I am. Are you holding up well?"

"Uh huh, yes I am. In fact, I am so excited! Not only have we made friends with Vast and Ryu, but we're also almost at the doorstep of Gin, which should hopefully have answers to the Land of the Gods... and the whereabouts of my sister."

The enthusiasm from Adamas is infectious – which leaves me with a wide smile. "Haha, you really are pumped. It's a good thing. Just don't let your guard down. From here on out, things will get even more tricky."

"I know, you don't need to worry about me, Luna. I won't allow you or any of my friends to get hurt."

"Thanks... I appreciate it."

Suddenly, the five of us stop as we take notice of a large city ahead. I am the first to breathe a sigh of relief, for not only do I wish to take a small break, but I could also do with a bite to eat. "Thank the gods that we found a city. Does anybody here know anything about the place up ahead?"

"Don't get any ideas, delusional one. We are not stopping here" orders the prince.

Shifting my eyes to him in a grumpy manner, I reply "I beg your pardon? I don't remember taking orders from you."

Upon a great and boastful laugh, Vast points to the large town and says "Are you blind, numbskull? The reason we cannot stop here is because that place ahead houses no people. What you see are merely ruins of what once was a city."

Peering closer, I find that it is in fact ruins. Sigh... What a way to get my hopes up.

"It's a shame. I can imagine that the place must have looked pretty, at some point. I wonder how it became a ruin?" Asks Adamas, who looks to us for answers. With a thinking stare, Prince Ryu clicks his fingers as though knowing something about it.

"Aha, I remember now. That place was once called: Ashta. Its full name was Ashta: City of Tomorrow, for its ground-breaking fusion between science and magic."

"Oh and let me guess: they eventually destroyed themselves by creating something that they couldn't control? Such a classic tragedy" I assume, with a cocky smirk. Shaking his head in disagreement, the prince responds.

"Actually, you're wrong. The historical accounts tell of a far more tragic event. I could tell you but perhaps your demon friend would be better?"

Turning to Ten, I await her explanation. However, she seems to hold a bizarre expression. As though frozen, she stands like a statue – eyes pinned towards the ruin ahead. Something about this place seems to have stirred something within her. I wonder what it is?

Suddenly, the she-demon sprints forward and runs towards the ruined city. The rest of us gasp at her action and simply watch as she disappears into the distance.

"What in the world was that about?" I ask, looking to the prince for a decent answer.

As though understanding her peculiar behaviour, he looks onward and replies "long ago, your demon comrade destroyed Ashta." With a quick glance, he asks "Well, are you not going after her?"

"Why would I do that?"

"Because we don't have the luxury of time right now. If we arrive after Gigas wakes up, then our plan will be screwed. Hurry up and talk your demon friend into resuming our journey. We don't have time for sentimental moments."

"Ugh… You're really starting to piss me off with your orders. Very well, I'll go and get her."

Reluctantly, I do as the arrogant prince says and I set out to find Ten. Arms crossed with burden I shift my feet across the ground like a stroppy child, kept company by my loyal blade.

Upon entering the destroyed city, we navigate past half destroyed structures that consist of green marble. An air of emptiness can be felt, as Adamas and I search around for our comrade – hearing nothing but howling of a faint wind.

"This place feels strange, Luna."

"Really? How so?"

"Well, I can't explain it but I feel like I have been here before."

"Oh really? At least your feeling is better than mine. The only thing I feel is hunger, hahaha!" I reply with dark sarcasm, to ease both our nerves. Can't say my little joke worked though. In all honesty, there is a strong presence in this place. For me, it feels nostalgic, as though many things transpired here. The ruins seem to tell a story, by their somewhat alien design. I have never seen anything like it.

Diverting around a small pillar, we come to an open area which seems to contain what looks to be an old fountain. To our relief, we finally find the she-demon, standing beside it, back turned. Careful to approach her, we remain silent and simply watch her still posture. Aware of our presence, she speaks to us in a sad tone.

"After all these years... it still stands. Even after everything I did, along with the passing of five thousand years, these marbles refuse to erode and disappear. Of course, the only things that have disappeared, are the people."

Taking a small step forward, I ask "Ten... What happened here?"

Turning around to face us, she hesitates for a few seconds before answering "I killed them... all of them. You wanna know something? Long ago, I never used to think much about humans. As the demon overlord, I regarded your kind as unworthy of this planet. Us demons came from a place within the inner core of Popla. However, I wanted more... I wanted it all. I wanted to claim every corner of this planet and beyond."

"Ten... you don't have to explain..."

"Yes, I do. You see, in my foolish rampage, I came across Ashta and of course set out to destroy it. The warriors that stood against me were courageous and fearless. It was the first time that I was surprised by the spirit of mankind. They nearly repelled me – however they weren't strong enough and I wiped them all out... all except one."

"One?" I ask – curious to hear more.

Pointing to the black sword, Ten replies "Yes. Amidst all the destruction, one man dared to face me. He wielded Adamas and Platina and fought exceptionally. He won... he beat me. It was at that moment, I fell in love... with the man called Septimus, along with humanity."

Lifting her head with a forced smile, she takes a deep breath and says "From that point on, I officially discarded my title as ruler of the underworld – using it only to assert fear into the gods when necessary. Working together, Septimus and I journeyed across the world, to reach the Land of the Gods."

"For what reason? Why did you both want to reach the Land of the Gods? To bring those you killed back to life?"

"No Lulu. Septimus and I wanted to end the control the gods had over humans. We wanted to create a world where humans were free to live their lives. It was the least I could do, to atone for the life I used to lead. Of course, karma is a bitch and I ended up getting my hide kick in, at the gates of the Land of the Gods. Septimus didn't stand a chance either."

Digesting her revelation, Adamas and I remain quiet. So – Ten really does like us, humans. I can't say I share her sentiments though. As a matter of fact, I've noticed many immortal beings showing a type of envy, towards us humans. What is it about us that they admire and yearn for?

At that moment, we hear a snigger, coming from behind. Upon turning around, we gasp at the sight of a small girl, who holds a sinister smile. Her sudden appearance makes me feel uneasy and nervous. Sporting a fancy black dress, she holds a single parasol within both hands. A long black tail extends from her lower back, along with two petit wings that sit upon her shoulders. Looking to her face, I flinch at the sight of two blue horns by each side of her head, along with a third closed eye that sits at the centre of her forehead… Just like Ten.

"Teehehehe – what are you babbling on about?" The strange girl asks – keeping her gaze centred upon my demon comrade. Ten holds a petrified expression, as though she were looking upon a ghost. Although it's just a hunch, it would seem the two have met before.

"Ten, do you know that little girl?"

Remaining frozen with fright, she replies "Yes, I do. She is… my sister: Nine."

"What? You have a sister too, Ten?" Asks Adamas – swirling around with excitement. I too am shocked by her reply and revelation. However, why does Ten look so defensive?

"Tehehe! I am glad you remembered me. After all, it has been some five thousand years, right sister? However, I am afraid I must correct you on something. I am not just known as Nine anymore. I am Nine: new Demon Lord of the underworld. After all, you discarded your title when you aligned yourself with the humans, remember?"

Becoming increasingly on edge, Ten pauses for minor seconds and replies "Nine, why have you come to the surface? Do you wish to continue my old desire, to destroy the humans and take over the world?"

"Teeheehahaha! Now, why would I wish to do that? In case you have forgotten, I have never been interested in the world of mortals. However..." Shom – at that second, Nine summons a gigantic ball of fire from her hands. The fireball radiates a bright and blue light that is almost blinding.

"...I have come for one reason. To destroy you, sister! Die!"

She tosses the giant fireball towards us, so fast, we have no time to evade. Clapping my hands together, I attempt to cast a miracle. However, I stop myself, seeing as I'll need them for our confrontation with Gigas later. Instead, I shout to my blade and order "Adamas, protect us!"

"Right!"

As my sword soars in front protectively, Ten jumps into harm's way and screams "No you idiots!"

Shakoom! Using herself as a living shield, Ten takes the full blast of the fireball projectile – causing a massive explosion that fills the whole city. Rubble and debris scatter violently through the air before crashing to the ground. As the chaos settles, a bed of smoke covers the fallen city, and as the smoke slowly dissipates, I find that I am unhurt. To our surprise, we find ourselves protected behind Ten's wings. Having taken the full brunt of the attack, she looks injured, with many scares around her body.

"You ok, Dimmy and Lulu?" She asks with a considerate and

weak tone.

"Yeah, thanks to you. Why did you stand in the way?"

"If I allowed Dimmy to get hit, he would have been paralyzed for god knows how long. We need him to be in good shape, for when we confront Gigas."

I guess she's right. We can't fight against Gigas if Adamas is not at full strength. At the same time, I would have preferred if Ten didn't suffer any harm though. Both Adamas and Ten have come to mean a lot to me.

Breaking our brief conversation, we hear clapping coming from above, followed by mocking.

"Aw, how brave of you, sister... - Bravo! You allowed yourself to get hit, all to protect your friends. Unfortunately, being a hero-ine doesn't suit you."

Looking up to the sky, we see the deadly girl, hanging in the air with a look of amusement. Holding a frustrated gaze, Ten asks "Sister... if you don't wish to destroy the humans, then what is your quarrel with me?"

Ten's sister bites her tongue – holding back her reply. After a deep inhale, she cries out "You ruined everything. Everything is all your fault!"

"My fault? How is everything my fault?"

"Silence!"

Swopping down – Nine readies to perform an overhead strike using her Parasol as a weapon. However, Ten blocks using both arms. The force of their collision is so great, Adamas and I are blown backwards by the impact.

"Shit!"

Gaining my footing, I watch as both sisters do battle. Upon each fiery strike, pillars of fire erupt throughout the city, as the ground trembles under the weight of the she-devils.

"Luna, I have a bad feeling about this. If they keep fighting, this place will fall apart!" Warns Adamas, who shivers in my right hand.

"Well, it's not like there's anybody worth saving in this ghost town. In any event, we can't leave without Ten. We're all in this together!"

As the two sisters continue to face off, Ten pleads to her sister "Nine, what have I done wrong? You never showed such anger towards me, ever before."

"Yes – however, you decided to do something so unfathomably stupid. You decided to journey to the Land of the Gods!"

"What? What does that have to do with you?"

"It has everything to do with me. However, you are so stupid and selfish, you'd never understand!"

With her deadly parasol, Nine performs a mighty thrust to Ten's stomach, knocking her backwards across the ground. As she lay grounded, her fierce opponent stands with a bold stance.

"All those years locked away has rusted your battle skills. How disappointing, sister."

Suddenly - choosing the right moment, I leap into the battle from behind and perform an overhead strike with my loyal blade. "To my surprise, the demon foe blocks my attack before gazing at me from the corner of her eye.

"Nice try, human. You wasted no movement with your little sneak attack just now. You must have had a very good teacher. Unfortunately, none of that will be enough to lay a scratch on me."

"Why are you fighting your own sister?" I ask, curious about her intentions.

"That is none of your business. Instead, you should be grateful that I have not come after you. My business is only with her. Had she stayed in her prison, I wouldn't have come to the surface. However, because you let her out, I am now forced to destroy her."

"Forced? I thought you were the new lord of the underworld? Who would be able to force you? Unless in fact, you answer to someone else?" I ask with a cunning and feisty tone. The foe gasps with a suspicious face – the kind a suspect makes when being found out.

"Ugh, you have a smart mouth, mortal!" She shouts before knocking me to the ground and stepping onto my blade. As Adamas and I lay helpless, she shows an even more peculiar stare to the sword. "You... this is all your fault too..."

Suddenly, we hear heavy footsteps storming towards us. Looking to my right side, I sigh with relief at the sight of Vast, charging towards the demon-girl.

"Whahaaa! I was wondering what all the commotion was about. After rushing into this old ruin, the only opponent I see is a little girl!" Shouts the large soldier – swinging his left gauntlet to Nine. However, she blocks his attack with ease, using only her index finger.

"I am far from a little girl, I assure you. Take our differences in strength for example. Do you think a mere child would be able to stop a fist from an adult male?"

"Point taken. However, you've just gotten me even more excited!"

He attempts to strike once again, this time with his right gauntlet – however, she blocks it using her parasol.

"Teehehehe! What makes you think a second attack would harm me? Are you not listening? I am the new demon lord: Nine! You and I are on a completely different..."

Suddenly, the demon opponent pauses with shock, noticing Vast's fists slowly pushing her backwards. Regardless of how hard she tries, she finds herself gradually being overpowered – so much so that she falls to her knees, under the crushing weight of his gauntlets.

"What... What is the meaning of this? How has he become so strong?"

At that second, the second knight Ryu strolls into sight, arms crossed. With a grin, he answers her, while his left dragon eye pulsates with a great light.

"It's not that he has gotten stronger. Rather, you have gotten weaker. This eye of mine allows me to negate the energies of immortal beings like you."

With a cautious gasp, eyes wide with surprise, Nine asks "Wait... is that a dragon eye you possess?"

"Bingo! Even you should know how powerful a dragon's eye is.

You messed with the wrong humans, demon." Unsheathing his invisible blade, he stands behind her, as she remains pinned on the ground by Vast.

Rising to my feet before dusting myself off, I breathe with relief at Vast and Ryu's joint handiwork. I gotta give it to them. They truly are a mighty pair.

"So, Mr messiah – are you gonna finish her off or what?" Asks the prince. Nodding my head, I hold my blade to her neck and prepare to end her life. Suddenly, however, we hear a loud cry from Ten.

"Don't kill her! Luna, don't kill her... please!"

We stand shocked by her request – wondering why she is pleading with us to spare her sister. As I look to Ten who stands many meters away, I see that she is in fact crying. Sigh, I don't get this at all. Why would she want to save the life of someone who tried to kill her?

To our surprise, the foe lets out a great laugh before addressing us.

"Teehehehahahahaaaaa! Ah... do you really think you all have the upper hand against me? Oh, you have much to learn. Behold..."

Right before us, Nine opens her third eye – releasing a terrifying force of energy that blows Ryu, Vast and I apart. A pillar of blue flames surrounds the opponent, which rises to the heavens. The ground shakes violently as the clouds above disperse.

"What is happening?" I mumble to myself and Adamas – to which the blade answers in a scared tone.

"I am not sure Luna. However, I can feel so much power coming from Ten's sister. We need to get out of here!"

The pillar of fire disappears, revealing the demon girl Nine. However, her form is vastly different from before. Gone is her petite and innocent looking appearance. Instead, she resembles a hideous monster. He body is dark and fiery and her height has increased to that of a two-story house. Her horns and wings have enlarged to a gargantuan size, along with her opened third eye that glows a menacing blue light. She roars to the sky – revealing a row of huge fangs within a massive mouth that could devour handfuls of men.

Vast and Ryu show a worried expression – slowly stepping backwards by the second.

"Damnit! My dragon eye doesn't seem to be working against her!" Moans Prince Ryu. "It also would seem this area is becoming increasingly hotter. If we continue to remain here, we will literally burn to death!"

Glaring at us, the monstrous form of Nine grins with an evil gaze. Looking down at us as though we were mere insects, she says "Granted, your dragon eye is very powerful. However, it pales in comparison to that of a demon's third eye!"

She roars once again – releasing a devastating stream of fire from her gaping mouth. Shit, there's no avoiding it. "I must cast a miracle art!"

"There's no need for that… Dark Messiah" comes a voice from around us, followed by a wave of light that envelops us. Within seconds, we disappear into the light and vanish from the ruined city.

Short moments later, we reappear in what seems to be a forest. Huddled together – Vast, Ryu, Ten, Adamas and I glance about our surroundings with confusion. "How in the world did we get here? Wasn't we in the middle of that old city, only moments ago?"

Upon a small chuckle, the same voice replies to me, from a tree trunk above.

"Haha, well duh. You all were about to get roasted by Ten's sister. However, I teleported you all to safety, just in the nick of time."

Together we look up to locate who is talking to us. To my surprise, I see the witch Trista, sitting comfortably upon the tree, holding a pleasant grin. I never thought I'd say this, but I am happy to see her, for once.

As we stay surprised, she twirls her pointed hat around her index finger before addressing us once again.

"Long time no see, my lovelies. It's good to see you're all hanging in there. Now, shall we get straight to business? There is something of grave importance that I must tell you."

Chapter 19: Mentor

"I t's nice to see you again, Trista. Many thanks for getting us to safety. If it wasn't for your magic, we would have likely perished" says Ryu.

"Aww, don't mention it, your highness. At least one of you still remembers their manners. Anyway – I am guessing you're all wondering where you are? We are in a forest, not too far from Gin. In fact, the capital city is roughly an hour's walk away from here."

I breathe a sigh of relief. Not only did she save us from that deadly encounter, but Trista also transported us directly by the doorstep of our destination. Vast, Ryu and Adamas also seem pleased with where we are. However, Ten seems to hold a face of sadness and grief.

"Please forgive this somewhat rushed encounter. We do not have much time."

"I know. The dragon god Gigas will wake in a few hours from now. Hence why we need to make sure we arrive before then" says Ryu – turning his back while crossing his arms.

"Yes, yes... I know all about your well thought out plan. Unfortunately, you may need to quicken the pace. You see... there seems to be a dramatic increase in the number of people who have acquired the Seventh Blessing. In fact, entire countries across the world have fallen victim to it, in one fell swoop."

"Do you have a percentage as to how many people have caught the Blessing?" Asks Vast - bracing himself for her answer.

"I'd say... About ninety-nine per cent of the entire population now have the Seventh Blessing."

Our mouths drop and our bodies freeze with shock. Ninety-nine per cent of everyone in the whole world? That's unbelievable. What could have caused it to increase? No doubt it has something to do with the gods.

"Why is this happening?" Asks the prince. "There are already enough people who are afflicted, as it is!"

"Don't ask me, your highness. Maybe you all have angered the gods by your rebellious actions? However, if you want to save everyone in time, then I would suggest you hurry up."

With a bothered sigh, I step forward and clarify "So, what you're saying is, we have seven days to kill the dragon god and make our way to the Land of the Gods before the blessing kills everyone?"

"That's correct. Nobody is safe."

Not forgetting about our own well-being, Vast, Ryu, Ten and I quickly scan our own hands for the Blessing's signature mark.

"Relax my loves. We are the lucky one per cent that the Blessing cannot approach."

"Hmph... and why is that?" I ask with a cunning gaze to the smiling witch.

Looking up at the sky, shrugging her shoulders she replies "Oh... well I don't really know for certain. Just consider it: women's intuition?"

With a vexed expression, I shake my head with annoyance. As if I'd buy such a ridiculous excuse. That witch knows a lot more than she is letting on. As a matter of fact, I am starting to question whether she is actually a witch. One thing's for certain. She'll never reveal her true motives... whatever they may be.

Placing her hat upon her head, she continues "Things are gonna get even more dangerous from now on, and I won't be around to save you next time. You are the only ones left in the world, capable of making things right. The fate of everybody's soul is in your hands. Well, that was all I wanted to report. Good luck everyone!"

"Wait!" Shouts Ten, who steps forward with a determined gaze. "Trista, please... send me back. I need to see my sister and talk to her."

Taken back by Ten's request, the witch pauses with intrigue. She stares down at the she-demon – looking into her eyes with slight curiosity. After many seconds, she answers with a quick and blunt response.

"No."

Before Ten has any time to react, the witch disappears into thin air – leaving her and the rest of us, alone in the quiet forest. A feeling of disappointment and frustration can be felt from my winged comrade.

"Ten, come on… we need to keep moving forward" I say in a supportive manner. Turning around to face me, she displays an angry face.

"Keep moving forward? Lulu, I am not moving anywhere until I figure out what's gotten into my sister. Something about her has changed and I need to find out what it is."

"What more do you need to find out? She tried to kill you."

"Yes, I know that! However, I have a feeling that my sister's being influenced somehow. You see, as long as I've known her, Nine never wished to do harm to anyone. She was always shy and kind. I realise the importance of our destination, but I must go and see to my her!"

"But what if your sister tries to hurt you again?" Asks the talking blade, with a voice of concern.

Biting her lips, the she-demon looks to the ground with sadness. "I am willing to take whatever pain comes my way. My sister said something about this all being my fault. I need to find out what I have done and hopefully make things right."

Scratching my forehead with grief, I respond "Sigh… so I guess we're one man down, thanks to you. You really are a selfish demon!" I curse with a disgruntled expression. As annoyed as I am right now, I do understand her feelings. If it were my sister, I would have done the same. As much as I wish to stop Ten, it's only right that I let her do as she wishes.

Addressing us with a high and mighty tone, the prince says "Enough of your mindless bickering. If the demon wishes to go and get her tail kicked in by her sister, then so be it."

Vast and Ryu stroll off into the distance, leaving just the three of us. The she-demon looks conflicted. Just by looking at her eyes, I see that she feels disappointed with herself. Not only has she stirred the seemingly unwanted wrath of her sister, but she also is unable to assist us against one of the most powerful gods in the world.

I could use this moment to make her feel worse than she already is – however, I guess I wouldn't be a very good friend if I did. Christ, I am getting soft.

Strolling to Ten, I open my arms and give her an unexpected hug. She gasps with shock, feeling my embrace for the very first time, as I whisper into her ear.

"It's ok, Ten. I understand that you must go. Hurry up and find your sister. Once you're done, please come back to us."

Her eyes blink wide with shock – looking up at the trees as I continue to hug her tightly. Tears begin to emerge from her eyes, as she responds in a heartfelt manner.

"Luna... Thank you."

As I slowly let her go, she steps back and dries her eyes. "Lulu, Dimmy... I promise you that I'll return." Turning her back to us, she expands her wings and takes flight into the morning sky above.

"Goodbye Ten!" Says Adamas, with a cheerful farewell, while I watch as she disappears beyond the clouds. "Do you think she'll be ok, Luna?" Asks the ever-questioning sword.

"Of course she will" I respond casually, with a confident tone.

"Yeah, you're right. Ten is super strong! I can see why she would have such a reputation that has lasted for all these years.

"Yeah... I guess so. However, you wanna know something? Where I am from, the story of the demon lord known as Ten doesn't exist. Nobody knows anything about her. Strange, right?"

"Really? If that's the case, how did you find out about her?"

With a small smile, I turn to my sword and with a wink, I reply "It's a secret."

"Oooooh come on Luna! Why must you always hide things

from me? You're so cruel, you know that?"

"Haha, it's not that important anyway. Come on… we need to catch up with the other two and prepare.

An hour or so later, having caught up with Vast and Ryu, the four of us discuss and confirm our plan, amidst a small space of trees and bushes. Leaning slouched against a tree, arms crossed, I converse with the two knights, as my blade drifts nearby.

"Well, seeing as we can't rely on Ten, should we change our strategy?" I ask, eager to hear Ryu's solution, seeing as he always seems to have an answer for everything.

"No. We carry on and fight the dragon head on."

"Wow… that sounds rather amateurish."

"Well yes, it is - however, we don't have any other choices. Unless you have a better idea, Mr messiah?"

With a bothered sigh, I hold my silence and spare us all any potential suggestions. I am sure the prince had already gone through all other possible alternatives. Even so, I wasn't expecting something so predictable.

"Luna, I won't lie to you - this mission will most likely not go as planned. We may simply end up fighting for our lives and losing them. Hence why, if the going gets tough, you're advised to turn back. He who lives and runs away, lives to fight another day, right?"

Shaking my head with disagreement, I reply "No, there's no turning back."

Vast and Ryu seem surprised by my answer – waiting for me to explain myself further.

"We can't turn back. Were you not listening to Trista? We are the only ones in the whole world, free from the Seventh Blessing. Running away would be futile. Don't get me wrong, I care little for the lives of others in this selfish world. However, I'll be damned if I let things go the way the gods want."

Bursting into laughter, the large knight says "Whahaha! I gotta give it to you, chump. You have a lot of guts that's for sure. I am starting to like you!"

"Be quiet, Vast!" Orders Ryu – showing a stern glare to his comrade before shifting his eyes to me. "Luna, I am pleased to hear your resolve. For me, the upcoming battle is something I could never run away from. My father would curse me from the grave if I ever did. I am prepared to die for my Kingdom."

"Oh... This all feels so scary" Adamas says worryingly.

Paying the blade no mind, I stretch my arms and yawn. "Well, if there's nothing else left to say, shall we get going then?"

"Hmm, we could do. However, thanks to the witch who transported us next to the city, maybe we could use this time to rejuvenate our strength. We are extremely early now. An hour's nap wouldn't hurt, right?"

Sitting down to the ground I reply "Sounds good to me. Just don't forget to wake me. I am a somewhat heavy sleeper."

"Noted."

Closing my eyes, I rest my head against a tree stomp – saving as much energy as possible. Eyes closed, I enter a deep sleep, quicker than ever before. I guess I didn't realize just how exhausted I was.

Within my sleep, I dream, surprisingly not of my sister but of someone else of equal importance. Of course, I'd never say it aloud – however, I'd be lying if I said that this person didn't influence me. After all, it's because of this person that I was able to make it so far. This person was my teacher, and he was the only god I ever respected.

"Awful! Quit leaving yourself so open Luna. And your movements are too slow, especially when transitioning from one form of attack to another. How many times do I have to keep telling you?" Says the majestic being, under a rainy afternoon. Within a small forest, he sits upon a log, judging my fighting stance as I hold a small blade. Ever since I buried my sister, this god has been my mentor – teaching me the way of the sword for the past few weeks. The training has been hard, so hard that at times I feel as though my body were about to break.

"Oh, this is hopeless!" I shout – throwing my blade to the ground and falling to my knees. "Sigh... Armis, I don't think I can keep up. The things you're teaching me are not easy for a human to do."

Standing to his feet before strolling towards me, my godly mentor responds "Well, of course, it isn't easy, especially for a mere mortal. As a matter of fact, it's borderline impossible. However, if you want to stand any chance of survival when up against the other gods, you had better put up with my training. Don't forget why you're doing this."

Extending his arm to my shoulder, he helps me up to my feet before patting me on the head gently. Picking up the blade, he hands it to me and displays a stern gaze. "Now, let's try this again. This time... Concentrate!"

I breathe a deep sigh and look to the ground, not of sadness but of gratitude. "Armis, thank you. Please, tell me: Why are you doing all of this for me?"

Upon a slight look of startle, he pauses before turning his back to me. As his hypnotic robe of cosmic stars covers him, he replies.

"I... I remembered... Who I used to be."

"Huh? Who you used to be? I don't understand" I respond – unable to make sense of his reply.

Turning around, Armis smiles and says "One day... you'll understand. Before that, you need to reach a level of skill that will make me proud to be your teacher. Once you've advanced enough, I'll have one more test for you. If you pass that, then you'll be ready."

The training continued, for weeks, months, and then years. Exactly five years passed, since meeting the mysterious god. Then, one night, my final test arrived.

"Keep up will you?"

"I am doing the best I can, Armis!"

Having snuck into Babylon City, my teacher and I stormed its tallest tower. Inside, we run continuously through its golden interior. We ascend vast steps, dart around corners and sprint through long corridors. Armed with a blade, sporting leather fighting gear, I follow behind Armis. Although the resistance from the guards has been little, my mentor stays strong and focused.

"Armis, you still haven't told me why you've brought us here? What are we looking for?" I ask – eager to know what business we have within the cty's largest tower. "We're not after Orion, are we?"

"Huh? Are you referring to the Messiah? Of course not. If he were here, our mission would be even more dangerous than it is. Thankfully, he is currently away on other matters. The only reason I chose this moment to break in, was to take advantage of his absence. However, we don't know how long he'll be gone for, so we need to be quick!"

"Quick about what?"

"Sigh... You're going to become a messiah and equip yourself with the tools needed to withstand the gods. However, in order to do that, we must locate the correct room which should be around here somewhere."

Reaching the end of the corridor, we come across a single golden door. "Here we are!" the god says with excitement before smashing through it. Upon stepping inside, I look in amazement at a large and wide room within. Inside the expansive space, a circular pool of perhaps the purest looking water I have ever seen resides. Along the walls and high ceiling above, countless statues of angelic beings can be found.

"Wha... What is this place?"

"This is called the Baptism room. Hurry up and get in, will you!" Orders Armis – yanking me by the arm before shoving me into the pool in front.

As my body touches the water, a strange feeling overcomes me. It is not something that I can put into words. I feel as though something bigger than myself is connecting with me, right now. This force or thing is offering me a piece of itself. I can't explain how exactly, but I feel like a part of me is being enhanced. As this sensation heightens, I hear a sweet and loving whisper.

"Please... Don't abandon me."

Its comment baffles me. Although this is the first time hearing the mysterious voice – it feels as though I've heard it a thousand times. Along with its words, a feeling of wanting to belong touches my soul. But who is the owner of this emotion and desire?

Suddenly, as I attempt to reply, I am pulled out from the pool by Armis. Remerging from out the water feels as though I have returned to reality, and as I do, I fall to my knees.

"Luna, do you feel any different? Answer me, boy."

"Uh... I... don't really know. Sorry, my head feels all fuzzy right now. What was in that water?"

"That pool contains the energy of the Great Observer. It's what allows a person to use the power of the gods.

"Really? So, I am just like Orion now? I can perform miracles?" I ask – staring at my hands with wonder.

At that second, the moment is broken, as the ceiling above crumbles – revealing over a dozen gods, along with scores of angels. Descending towards us, bodies glowing with light, they ready to do battle against us.

"Damn, they found us. It's unfortunate we didn't have enough time to locate the weapons you need. Oh well, you'll just have to survive without it. Listen, I'll hold them off and give you a chance to escape."

"Wait... What about you? You don't expect me to leave you alone against them, do you?"

"Haha, you almost sound concerned. Idiot - don't forget that this isn't about me. It's about your goal. Go on, I'll catch up with you later. Now, get moving!" He says before giving me a mighty push that ejects me from the Baptism room. As I tumble back into the corridor, I watch as Armis takes on the opposing gods. Flashes of light and explosions fill my eyes, as I hear my mentor and his foes letting out battle cries.

"Shit, if only I could do something. If I am truly like Orion, how do I use my powers?" Overwhelmed, I turn tail and do just as Armis requested. I run and attempt to escape the tall tower of Babylon city.

"Where's the exit, where's the fucking exit?" I ask repeatedly to myself. Bizarrely, at that moment, I stop by a single door for reasons I myself do not know. The door is wooden and dirty – unlike all the other doors within the tower. Its unattractiveness speaks to me, like a nail being intentionally out of place. I quickly open the door and step inside, only to find a cold and dusty concrete room. On the ground in front, I see a sword within a black scabbard. Something about it seems special, and my curiosity gets the better of me. Reaching down I pick up the weapon and unsheathe the blade. Every inch of the sword is black – emanating a mysterious aura. Perhaps with this, I may be able to fight the gods?

"Hello. Nice to meet you" I hear a voice, coming from the blade. Startled and frightened, I drop the blade to the ground.

"What in the... Am I going crazy?"

Before my very eyes, the black sword begins to move by itself and levitate into the air. "My name is Adamas. What's your name?"

I stare, lost for words at the talking blade that has introduced itself. Could this be the weapon Armis wanted me to find? There's no doubt about it. This must be what we came for.

Skipping the introductions, I snatch the blade by the hilt and make my way, back towards the Baptism room to support Armis.

"I need to help him. Now that I have this weird blade, I can fight!"

"Hmm? Whom are you looking for? Asks the blade sword, as I race around the many passageways.

"I am looking for my teacher. He's around here somewhere and I need to help him!"

"Why?"

"Just be quiet, will you?"

"Ok. Before I do, I think you should know, you're going the wrong direction. The person you're looking for is outside on the roof. I can sense a whole bunch of gods, above us."

Stopping in my tracks, I hold the blade to eye level and gasp at its words. Could it be, the sword can feel the presence of the gods? Incredible! Just what is this weapon and where did it come from? Leaving my questions to the back of mind, for now, I follow its advice.

Outside, on the rooftop of the central tower of Babylon City, Armis is surrounded by a dozen gods. Upon suffering extensive injuries, he kneels, helpless as his opponents stand armed. One of the gods decides to step forward and address him.

"Armis, you truly have brought shame on your name. You were once known as one of the most formidable of gods, especially in the art of the sword. Now, look at you... Reduced to the actions of a criminal, working with a mortal. Before we grant your punishment, tell us: what were you thinking?"

A small smile creeps on Armis' face, despite the might of his foes that have surrounded him. Looking up at the twin moons above, he takes a deep breath and replies "I... I just want us all to be free... Free from this immortality."

"You speak as though you desire to reject your godly existence. You almost sound like a mortal. For your betrayal against us, we shall imprison you, until the Messiah decides what to do with you."

"None of you will lay a finger on my teacher!" I shout forth – having finally reached the roof. As they hear my voice, they look back and stare upon me and the black sword. Within seconds of their eyes noticing the mysterious weapon, they shudder and gasp with terror.

"The... The legendary blade: Adamas. How did he get his hands on it?" One of the god's asks. "No matter, we have nothing to fear. He is just a mortal who most likely knows not how to wield a weapon."

Shocked also by my appearance – Armis stares at the dark blade for many moments, before addressing the opposing gods. "None of you have a clue, of just how amazing that so-called mortal is. I'll have you know, that boy is my one and only pupil who will go to the Land of the Gods!" With a firm glare, my mentor orders, "Luna, this is your final test. Annihilate every last god around and prove to me that you're worthy!"

"Yes, my teacher!"

Within seconds I launch forth and do battle against the army of gods. Using all the skills I have learned over the past five years, I tear through each deity while keeping count of each kill.

"Five... Six... Eight..."

Upon each successful strike, a god explodes into stardust of light. It's working... All the training I endured all this time is working. A smile brews on my face as I continue to dance along the rooftop – allowing not a single opponent to touch me. All the while, the talking sword moans within my hand.

"Woaaah... Why are you swinging me around so hard? I am getting dizzy!"

"Will you stop complaining? I can't concentrate!"

At that moment, the sword breaks free from my hold and clobbers me over the head.

"If you want to get rid of those gods, there's a much easier way!" Adamas shouts to me, before darting through the air – stabbing through the remaining gods like a spear. Watching as it zooms around from left to right – I stand in awe as it makes quick work of them.

"Amazing..."

The godly opponents are no more, and as the final trace of their light disappears, the living sword zips back to my side.

"See... Piece of cake!"

I breathe a sigh of relief, under the now quiet and cool night. Unfortunately, our troubles are not quite over, for at that moment a great golden light fills the night sky - causing me to cover my face with shock and surprise.

"Shit... There's more."

The light folds open like a portal, and from within it another godly being emerges. Seated on a golden chariot - driven by two winged horses, a goddess can be seen charging towards me. Sporting a crescent halo upon her head, she wields a flaming torch. From out the clouds behind her, scores of angels holding harps and trumpets can be seen, which they play as though celebrating the arrival of the benevolent being. A powerful aura is felt from this one, so great that I am having trouble calming my nerves. Amidst the golden sky and music, the foe addresses me.

"Evil one... Prepare yourself. I am the eye of night, all wise and all seeing: Selene!"

Selene? Why does that name sound so familiar? Where have I heard it before?

Wham - as my mind trails off, I am rammed by the two horses and knocked off the tower.

"Fuck..."

As I plummet towards the city below, I panic and shout continuously, as the ever singing angels chant "Queen of Queens... Goddess of the moon. Queen of Queens..."

Shit... is this really going to be the end, already? I only just got the power needed to save my sister. It's too early for things to end now.

As I continue to fall, a sensation brews within me. I don't know why but I have the urge to place my hands together. Going with this feeling, I clap my hands and shout forth "Fly!"

Instantly my fall stops and before I know it I am flying through the sky, like a bird. "Woah! How on earth did I manage to do that?" I smile with wonder - trying to make sense of these new-found powers I possess.

Breaking my thoughts, the blade alerts me and screams "Look out!"

Turning around, I see the goddess and her steads, galloping through the air around me. Holding my blade with both hands, I shout "Come on bitch. I am ready for you!"

"Recieve the judgment of my holy flames!" She rants before unleashing a stream of fire from her flaming torch. Holding my sword in front, I cut into the beam, causing it to pass around me. As I continue to defend against the intense rays of fire, the goddess speaks.

"What is your purpose? Why are you defying the gods?"

"I wish to bring back someone... someone who is more important to me than the whole world. Of course, I wouldn't expect your kind to understand!"

Tossing my blade forward, Adamas strikes the golden chariot -

resulting in a massive explosion of flames.

"Aaaaaaaah!" She cries with agony - now engulfed in flames.

"Gotcha!" I shout victoriously, as the blade zooms back into my hands. As I continue to float in mid-air, I turn my attention to the clouds - looking up at the singing angels. Their sounds are so loud and disorientating, I cannot think straight.

"Shut the hell up!" I shout - throwing my blade to the entire army of angelic beings. Within seconds, the sky is filled with screams as the angels are cut down. Countless instruments, along with their wings fall through the sky, as the magnificent sword darts through the night like a speeding bullet. It truly is a sight to behold. Watching with amazement at the power of the mysterious blade, I feel thankful for having found such a weapon. At the same time, I start to wonder where and how such a blade came to be. Who made the sword and how did my master know about it?

Suddenly I hear laughter from the goddess Selene, nearby.

"Hahaha... How foolish you are. It will take more than that to end the great Selene: Goddess of the moon!"

Turning around, I see the benevolent opponent, riding on the back of one of her winged horses. It would seem that my previous attack was not enough to finish her off.

Within her right hand, she now holds a radiant cloak, while in her left she holds a shining spear. Quickly commanding my sword to return, I face her once again.

"This is the end for you... False one!"

Within seconds she slings her cloak to us - constricting my whole body along with Adamas. The hold is so strong, I can barely breathe. Before I know it, I am dragged through the city and smashed through countless rooftops as the being laughs uncontrollably. As I remain helpless, I look down at the grounds of the city and notice the people of Babylon, watching the spectacle. They are cheering, not for me of course, but for the goddess.

"False Messiah, you should know your place. The will of us gods trumps all. Would you allow the will of an insect to take precedence over your own will? This same principle holds true for your kind and mine!"

Tossing me to the ground, I crash land against a wall and lay slanted against it - injured from head to toe. As she stands inches from me upon her stead, I lay disoriented - wondering why her name sounds so peculiar.

"Where... Where have I heard that name...?"

Making sure I am at a disadvantage, her horse steps onto my blade, making it impossible for me to fight back. As I struggle to recover, I pray to my sister for strength. "Lucia... Help me."

Suddenly, the being freezes with shock - staring with confusion. As though the name has struck a cord, the goddess remains still before opening her mouth.

"Lucia... Who is... Lucia?"

I gasp - wondering why the name of my dear sister has touched her so. How dare she even utter my sister's name? Hold on... does she have something to do with the sickness that claimed Lucia?

As though having jogged my memory, I finally remember where I have heard the name, Selene. It was what my sister used to say, when under those strange trances of the Seventh Blessing. Looking now at the being whom my sister used to call for, I become angry and shout... Holding her responsible.

"So you're the one my sister kept calling for. No, you are the one who most likely gave her the Seventh Blessing and forced her to utter your name! You... This is all your fault. Why did you take my sister away from me? Why did you take away Lucia?!"

"Luna!" shouts my mentor Armis who leaps to my aid from above. Holding a sword of light he strikes the goddess across her chest. Even with the direct hit she still stands. However, her brief stumble backwards was enough to free Adamas from under her.

"Armis, thank you!"

"Shut up, will you? Now's your chance to finish her off!" Wasting no time I leap forth ready to deal the final strike. As I get closer, she holds up her hands and cries with panic.

"No, wait..."

Shom - with no hesitation, I stab her clean through the head - causing her to produce a painful scream to the heavens. "Ahhhh-hhhh!"

She falls off her horse and lands to the ground, as I keep my blade lodged into her. Standing on her chest I glare down at the defeated goddess and say "Tell me, why did your kind create the Seventh Blessing? Why did you do that to my sister? She was all I had left!"

The defeated opponent moans, letting out a small tear before bursting into light. As she disappears, I fall to the ground as my master slouches on his knees. He looks to me proudly, like a pleased father among the now quiet night.

"Well done, Luna. You managed to obtain the legendary weapon Adamas. I am so proud of you." Casting his eyes to the sword, he looks as though he were re-acquainted with an old friend. "You haven't changed at all," He says to the blade.

Slowly standing to my feet, I approach him and ask "Well, have I passed the final test?"

"Hmm... Almost. You see, I asked you to get rid of all the gods. As it currently stands, there's one more left alive."

"What... Where?" I ask with surprise – turning my back to glance about my surroundings. To my eyes, I see not a single enemy around. Then, at that second, I hear a blade piercing into skin – followed by an agonising cry. Looking to my teacher, I gasp in shock and disbelief at the sight of Adamas lodged into his chest.

"Wha... What the hell is going on here? Adamas, what are you doing?"

Looking closely, I see that Armis is, in fact, forcing the sword into his chest even further. Could it be, my mentor struck himself?

"Why?" I ask - eyes bold and wide. Letting out a smile, my godly teacher replies.

"Did you forget that I am a god? Hehe... sorry to break it to you at the last minute, but I never intended to survive this night. I've wanted to die for the longest time, but of course, you never would have granted it to me. Hence why I am using this sword to take my own life. Over these past five years, I've come to know that you are the kindest, loyal and most sensitive person I have ever met."

I am lost for words. As he explains further, my body begins to tremble. I don't believe I've felt this way, since losing my sister.

"Luna, don't give me that puppy look. Besides, you have much to do, right? You need to reach the Land of the Gods and get your sister back. Many hours west of this country, lies a land called Biscus. There you'll find many who possess the knowledge you'll need. There's also an old friend of mine, who for the longest time has been sealed away. Could you do me a favour and release her for me? Whatever you do, just don't tell her I requested it. Well, even if you did, it's not like she'll know who I am, as I exist now."

Leaving me once again with his riddles and cryptic meanings, I watch as his body begins to slowly disappear into traces of light.

"Thank you ever so much, for allowing me... To feel human again."

Chapter 20: Gigas

Upon taking a brief rest, the four of us made our way to the city of Gin, to kill the dragon god Gigas, via our plan. The city is as grand as I imagined – perhaps larger than Babylon City. The design and style of the city itself are rather unique, compared to all the places I visited before. Ghastly monuments of various dragons can be found, practically everywhere I look.

Just as Trista mentioned, the people of Gin all seem to possess the mark of the Seventh Blessing. Watching the prince as he strolls by, they plead with him to help them. They huddle and attempt to block our path - begging for us to save them.

"Please be patient. I will save you all before the seventh day arrives!" Promises the prince - pushing through the vast hordes of people.

It is a sad sight to witness. They are so terrified and lost, with no real assurance that they will live through this. After all, nobody has ever survived the sickness. As much as I'd like to dwell on their thoughts and feelings, my mind cannot help but be focused on something else.

Since waking from my short nap, I haven't been able to take my mind off certain things that transpired within my recent dream. My mentor, Armis took his own life because he grew tired of immortality. His parting words were something along the lines of feeling human, again. How would a god know how it feels to be human? All they've ever known is how to be a god. I also never did question how he knew of Ten. He said something about them being friends and yet that would be impossible. She is a demon and he is a god. As far as I know, Ten never once mentioned Armis at all. The only person she spoke of, was the man named Septimus. Lastly, I never did pay much thought to that powerful goddess I fought: Selene. Her actions when I uttered my sister's name were more than bizarre. Until now, I merely put it down to some kind of bizarre infatuation.

Although I have never vocalized it, my assumption regarding mortals, gods and the Seventh Blessing is one of love and jealousy. Gods love to be served and yet are jealous of our mortality - hence why they created the Seventh Blessing. Offended by the particular mortals who possess a pure desire to succeed, the gods punish them - forcing them to utter their names before taking away their lives. It is the reason why I firmly believe they chose my sister and others like her. Anyone who seems to possess some kind of drive and ambition to push mankind forward is destroyed by the gods. Well, that is my theory.

"You holding up ok, Luna?" Asks Ryu - breaking me out of my daydream.

"Yes, I am fine. How long till we reach Gigas?"

"We will soon be approaching his castle. Once inside, I will active my dragon eye and cancel out his ability to see the future. Once we're inside, give him everything you've got."

"Yeah, you've already explained a hundred times now."

Upon a left turn, we come across a gigantic pyramid structure, made of diamond. The structure is so big, it almost blots out the sun above us. I am guessing that this must be where the dragon god resides. It is at this point, I begin to feel afraid. I have never seen a real dragon before – however, if a dragon needs to be housed in something this big, then it must be humongous.

I am led inside the front doors, before being escorted throughout the castle. The atmosphere inside is dark and gloomy. The walls and ceiling consist of black cement, along with incense sticks that produce a harsh aroma.

"Wow... Some shithole this place is. This place makes Belgrave look like a resort."

"Yes, this is all thanks to that dragon. Ever since he took over, this castle has become a shadow of what it used to be. Ok, let's stop talking now. We can't afford any mistakes" The Prince says, as his dragon eye begins to glow. "I have just activated my eye. This is it... no turning back now."

Carrying onwards, we descend a long spiral staircase, which seems to go down many meters under the ground. Upon reaching the bottom, we come across an enormous door, guarded by a single soldier.

"Oh, master Ryu and commander Vast. You've returned!" Says the surprised soldier.

"Indeed I have. Thank you for playing your part. Please step aside and get as far away as possible. You should already know why we're here" he responds with a wink. The guard nods his head, fully understanding the prince's words. All the soldiers here, are part of Ryu's coup against the dragon. Now the crucial moment has arrived, for all of us.

As we approach the gigantic doors, I wonder just how are we to get inside. The doors are too big and heavy for any man to open.

To my surprise, however, the Prince places his hands upon the doors and begins to utter "To the dragon... for the dragon... grant the dragon... all praise."

Upon his words, the massive doors swing open. Impressive, if I must say so myself. The dragon's quarters are sealed by magic, which can only be opened by a specific set of phrases.

As we walk inside, I am overcome by a strong and powerful aura, which sends my body shaking with fear. It is so sudden that I feel as though my heart were about to explode from my chest.

Once inside, we find ourselves within a large and wide cave, lit with bright candles. Directly in front, we see an enormous dragon, slouched within a deep sleep, on a tall and wide throne. The dragon is pale white, possessing two large wings that cover it like a sheet. A large black horn protrudes from its forehead, along with a dazzlingly bright halo that sits just above its head - displaying mysterious symbols and writings. Behind, a long tail extends to the ground, wrapping around the outside of its throne. So this is the dragon god known as Gigas. As we stand in its presence, it snores loudly – causing the walls to shudder and rock.

"Now's our chance. Luna, Vast…"

Shakoom - suddenly, as we take a single step forward, a spell insignia appears on the ground and surrounds us.

"Shit… a trap!"

Before we know it, our entire body is bound by some form of electricity, which although does not harm us, has sapped our energy nonetheless. Falling to our knees, we watch helplessly as the dragon's snoring stops.

Slowly opening its eye, the dragon yawns so loud, the walls shake violently.

"Eeeekkkk!" Squeals the blade – frightened by the large and reptilian eye of the dragon. As it locks its eye to us, we whisper to one another - trying to figure out how we slipped up.

"Ryu, what the fuck is going on? I thought that your eye was supposed to have cancelled out its magic. Furthermore, weren't we supposed to have the upper hand by arriving during its sleep?

"I know… I know. I don't understand what went wrong. Did we make a mistake somewhere?"

With its eye locked and focused solely on Adamas, Gigas says nothing for many moments, before speaking in a low and heavy tone.

"Ah… finally."

At that moment, the dragon summons a spherical prison of light, which holds and traps Adamas. Reaching forth, the dragon holds the imprisoned blade within his right claw.

"Adamas!" I shout - struggling to break free from the magic hold over us. "You had better give my sword back!" I threaten the gigantic creature, to which it ignores my words. I doubt it could even hear me, judging by how huge it is. I knew it was a bad idea to trust in Ryu's idea. I was better off doing things my way… whatever way that was.

Staring at the three of us on the ground, the dragon god tilts its head and says "Fools… I knew all along of your plan. Did you really think such an idea would work?"

"But... how did you know?" I ask in a calm and collected manner.

With a wide smile, the dragon replies "The eyes of a dragon are far more complex than you mortals could ever imagine. As you know, I gave my right eye to the Prince – equipping him with its power to nullify the energy of others. However, what he didn't realise, was that I am still able to see through it. His eyes were my eyes, all this time."

"So, you were watching us the whole time? Curse you, Gigas!" Cries Ryu. "I should have known there'd be a catch!"

"Indeed, you should have... foolish Prince. Now, I think I will be taking my rightful eye back, seeing as you did such a good job of looking after it for me. Your father will be proud."

By his command, the dragon's right eye, which up until now was possessed by Ryu, flies from out the prince's eye socket. Upon enlarging to an appropriate size the eye returns to its original bearer. As Gigas laughs - now possessing both eyes, the prince screams in pain, holding his now empty eye socket.

"Ahhhh... son of a bitch. Damn you... Gigas!"

With the odds stacked up against us, I accept my defeat. Not only do I not have the power to fight, but I am also without Adamas. Ryu and Vast are also powerless against the dragon, who possesses the ability to see the future and strip the energy of others. Even if Ten were here, I doubt we'd stand a chance.

"You might as well finish me off" I request to the being. "Without my sword to fight, I am at your mercy. Hurry up and make it quick, Gigas."

"Luna no!" Cries Adamas, as he remains trapped in the dragon's prison. I ignore the blade's words and simply close my eyes. To my surprise, however, the dragon laughs.

"Gahgahagaha... oh no. You are far too interesting to kill. After all, you and I have so much in common... Cassius!"

Chapter 21: Birth of Gods

Standing opposite the great dragon god, I freeze with confusion after hearing it address me by my original name.

"How do you know my name?"

"Ghaha. Have you forgotten? You revealed your true name to the prince yesterday, which meant I automatically became aware of it. You also revealed your desire, to reach the Land of the Gods and save your sister. Your intention was to acquire the original map from my keep, correct?"

"Correct. So, cut to the chase, dragon god. What is it you want from me, seeing as you're not going to kill me?"

Peering closer, the dragon holds an amused face and responds.

"Hmmm... I want you to come with me, to the Land of the Gods."

Shocked by its reply I gasp, trying to comprehend its request. The dragon laughs once more before explaining itself further.

"Ghaha... why the surprised face? As I mentioned before, you and I have much in common. You wish to bargain with the Great Observer, while I intend to destroy it and take its power for my own."

"But why would you do that? Wouldn't that be going against your own kind?"

"My own kind? Bhahaha! You, mortals, have so much to learn, about the truth of this world. It is naïve of you to think that all gods are the same and that we have a common goal. After all, look at the actions of the one who trained you: Armis. Why did he go against the other gods? What exactly are gods and how are we born? What is the Seventh Blessing and how does it relate to mortals? Well, you had better listen carefully to what I am about to tell you. You see, all the gods that exist in this world... used to be human beings!"

Eyes gaped wide, I gasp with shock at his revelation. Shaking my head, I respond to the being.

"You... you lie!"

"No, it is the truth. The Seventh Blessing was created by the Great Observer. When a being dies of the sickness, they are reborn as gods, not knowing anything about their past. However, there are some whose will is so strong, they retain a glimmer of their stolen humanity. It was what made your godly mentor go against the other gods. He remembered that he used to be a mortal man."

My mind races with thoughts. Gods used to be humans? So, Armis, used to be a human too and remembered who he was? Now I understand what his last words meant. Hold on... that goddess Selene whom I fought back then. Was there a chance that she was in fact...

"Lucia..." I whimper, covering my face and trembling with disbelief. What if Lucia was, in fact, that goddess and remembered her previous life? That would explain why she held back. Oh god... what have I done? All this time I was wrong about the Seventh Blessing. The name its victims utter is of the god that they will become!

Clutching my chest, I tremble uncontrollably - unable to compose myself. I... I killed my sister. Selene was Lucia. I killed Lucia!

Vast and Ryu also stay shocked - mind racing upon hearing the revelation and secret of the Seventh Blessing.

"Every single god upon this world used to be a human being? So, if the Seventh Blessing isn't stopped, then everybody on this planet will transform into gods. Does that also mean... Carlton is already one of them?"

Observing our reactions, the dragon continues to reveal more.

"Only some of us remember our former lives. Take me for example. I used to be a dragon who was once part of a great family of proud dragons that opposed the Great Observer. We waged war against it, but even with our combined strength, we failed. It killed every single one of my dragon brethren but decided to spare me alone. Before I knew it, I was transformed into a god, whose new purpose was to fulfil the desires of the Great Observer. However, over time, I slowly began to remember who I was and what I originally fought for. Now you know... the true purpose of the Seventh Blessing."

Upon many deep breaths, I lift my head to the dragon and ask "Kill me. I have nothing left to live for, so kill me. If what you're saying is true, then I already lost any chance of saving my sister. I can never forgive myself."

Looking down at me with amusement, the dragon peers its head close to me and replies "Don't be so quick to throw your life away. After all, you have come so far. Do you not want to get even with the Great Observer and save everyone?"

"To hell with all that! I couldn't care less about the world. Everything I did was for my sister and I killed her. I killed the god she became and now she's gone... forever!"

"Oh, you mortals and your simple minds. Do you not know that nothing ever truly disappears? There is one more transition that occurs, after a being that has become a god dies. Although I do not know much about it, I am certain the Great Observer knows. You can still be reunited with your sister. All you need to do is join forces with me. With our combined power, we shall storm the Land of the Gods and finally have justice. What say you?"

Pondering the dragon's request, it only takes a few moments to make up my mind. Of course, whatever chance I have of saving my sister, I will take. I owe it to her, more than ever now. A wave of great anger stirs within me. I will make the Great Observer pay for turning her into a goddess. I will make the Great Observer pay for ever conceiving the Seventh Blessing!

"Let us go... to the Land of the Gods."

"A wise answer."

Placing its head flat on the ground, the dragon gestures for me to climb upon it. I pause and wipe away my tears - filled with new-found hope again. This is my chance to make things right and atone for what I did.

Strolling forward, I proceed to climb onto the dragon's snout before stopping at the centre of its head, underneath its shining halo. As the dragon looks to Vast and Ryu, I say to the being "No... they will not be coming with us. Leave them here. They will only slow us down."

"My thoughts exactly" responds the dragon.

Looking to me with surprise, the prince and his comrade show a hurt expression. "Luna... what in the world are you doing? I... I don't understand?"

"Hey, chump, what do you think you're doing?"

The look in their eyes fills me with mild guilt. After all, I do consider them friends and our intention was to fight together. I could try to explain the reasons for my motives to him, but I am certain it would fall on deaf ears. Instead, I display a cold and stern gaze and reply to him.

"You have your Kingdom back. Farewell, Prince Ryu. Gigas will never again set foot upon this land."

Expanding its great wings, the dragon god releases a mighty roar, which blows the entire roof of the cave open – allowing for us to leave. With myself on board, the dragon ascends upward, leaving the castle and the city of Gin behind. All the while I hear the faint echo cries of Ryu, calling my name. "Luna... Luna... Lunaaaaaaaa!"

Chapter 22: Unstoppable

Having departed the city of Gin, the dragon and I soar through the clouds. Upon its head, I stand with my sword in hand – feeling the wind rushing against my face. The feeling is exhilarating, for, with each passing cloud, I get nearer to my destination. Knowing that there still is a way of saving my sister makes me feel even more hopeful.

"Hey Luna, are we doing the right thing?" Asks the blade – obviously concerned by my actions.

"What do you mean by that?"

"Well… it kinda just feels wrong to have left Vast and Ryu like to work with this dragon."

"Listen Adamas. It's nothing personal, but I can't allow anybody else to suffer harm because of me. I can rescue my sister and stop the Seventh Blessing, without their help. After all, I have the power of a dragon on my side."

"Yeah, I guess you're right. But, what about Ten?"

With a sharp tongue, I reply "What about Ten? Have you forgotten…? She left us to pursue her own things. I only wish I came to the dragon sooner, instead of wasting my time with the she-demon."

Chiming in on the conversation, the dragon laughs and says "Hmph, indeed you should have sought me sooner. Why did you choose to release and use the help of that troublesome demon anyway?"

"I was recommended to Ten by an old friend. On other matters, I've been meaning to ask you something. Why did you choose to attack and take over Prince Ryu's Kingdom? How did that tie in with your revenge against the Great Observer for turning you into a god?"

"Simply put: it didn't. At the time I attacked Gin, I had no idea of who I once was and my original purpose to destroy the Great Observer. I was merely following the same purpose as the other gods: To control and bring order."

"Control and bring order?"

"You heard correctly. Every god in the whole of Popla exists with the desire to control and bring order to the world. This involves a magnitude of things, such as: controlling mortals and keeping the demons in check. My memories of whom I used to be, surfaced when I completed my takeover of the prince's Kingdom. I can't say for certain what caused me to regain my original consciousness, but it happened just after I killed the Prince's father. Seeing as the damage had already been done, I decided to dwell in the city of Gin and become the new King of Biscus – waiting for the right time to go after the Great Observer, once more. At the same time, me being the King of Biscus was probably a good thing. If I hadn't taken over, another god would have done the same and would have treated the inhabitants far worse. After all, I still trained the prince in the art of war and combat."

Giggling to myself, I cover my mouth in a taunting fashion, as the dragon god displays a curious gaze.

"Hahaha... Oh sorry for laughing. It just dawned on me... You're not so horrible at all. In fact, it sounds to me that you trained the prince to redeem yourself. I am willing to bet that you made yourself seem even more terrifying than what you are."

"Hold your tongue, mortal! Although I have not willingly harmed your kind since regaining my memories, that doesn't mean I am not sickened by the sight of humans. I am merely treating you, humans, the way I used to... Before the arrival of the gods. Back then, your kind was still an eyesore – however, we coexisted and even worked together."

With an impressed smile, I look up at the sun as we continue to soar through the skies. "This all sounds too good to be true.

It is almost as if our partnership were destined, as a sort of homage to a time when our kind fought alongside each other. I never would have guessed it."

At that moment, Adamas shivers in my hand and says "Something... Something big is coming!"

"Huh? What is it?"

At that moment, Gigas becomes alerted also – sensing something close by. Stopping in the air he says "Hmmm... I guess it was only a matter of time before we were apprehended. Cassius, get ready!"

At that moment, an entire army of gods and angels appear from behind the clouds. Varying in size, each brandishing a weapon, the deities sit upon a Cherubim. As they encircle us, I try to count their number. It is well in the thousands.

"Wow, I've never seen such an army before. They must really not want us to reach the Land of the Gods."

"Indeed, boy. After all, you and I pose the biggest threat to the Great Observer. Regardless of their numbers, we can't allow them to waste our time. We'll have to push our way through."

Upon a sudden pause, the dragon's revelation about the truth of the gods' echos within my mind. I feel overwhelmed and conflicted. All of those gods... they used to be human beings. Every last one used once was a person who fell to the Seventh Blessing. If I kill them, wouldn't that make me worse than the one who turned them into such things, in the first place?

Sensing my apprehension, the dragon says to me "This isn't the time to second guess yourself, boy. Indeed they all used to be mortal men, women and children. However, by destroying their godly forms, we would be freeing them from such a tragic existence. We will think of a way to save them all, once we confront the Great Observer. For now... the best thing you can do is throw your humanity to the wind!"

With no hesitation, Gigas soars directly ahead towards the army of gods. Upon a mighty roar, the dragon god releases a wave of light from its mouth, which obliterates thousands of opponents before us. The army begins their attack – unleashing rays of light to our direction. The incoming projectiles are vast in number, making any form of evasion near impossible. Astonishingly, however, not a single ray of light touches us. As though having eyes at the back of his head, the dragon weaves around effortlessly – as the sky erupts into chaos.

"Incredible... How are you able to dodge so well?" I ask as rays of light are continuously shot to our direction.

"You haven't forgotten, have you? I can see the future!"

With a strong glare, Gigas tears through the army like a rampaging juggernaut – sustaining not a single scratch. His claws and tail are like thunder, which upon each swipe destroys hundreds of deities.

Being careful not to lose my footing, I hold onto the dragon's head tightly – as cries of gods, angels and cosmic explosions fill my ears.

"Uh... Christ... at this rate, I'll fall off. Gigas – although you are the strongest comrade I've ever had the privilege of working with, you make a lousy steed!"

"Fool... That's because men were never meant to ride us dragons. How typical of mortal men, to assume that which is not like yourselves, must be tamed. Consider yourself grateful for me allowing you to touch my sacred scales at all!"

"Believe me, I am grateful. However, throwing-up due to all this movement is not what I have in mind." Clapping my hands together, I shout the phrase "Fly!"

With my miracle cast, I obtain the power of flight. Taking hold of my companion blade I order "Come on, Adamas. We can't let this dragon have all the fun!" Soaring through the air to battle the gods also. Like an arrow, I pierce through their ranks – slicing through them, as the dragon charges onwards. As much as it hurts to know that I am killing what used to be innocent people, the dragon's words are helpful. In order to see this through to the end, I must abandon my humanity.

Soaring side by side, we take on the forces of the godly army, like the unlikely duo we are. Watching each of their comrades fall by the second, the army grows ever scared by our very presence.

"Just how many gods are there? Adamas, how many have we killed so far?"

"So far, we've taken down around three hundred."

With a taunting chuckle, the dragon god mocks "Is that all? I am able to destroy five hundred, with but one swat of my tail!"

"Well, nobody asked you. Besides, even with the amount you're managing, it still hasn't stopped them completely."

"Indeed. However, what did you expect? By now, every god in the world is probably on their way to us. Don't hold back... Even for a second Cassius!"

The battle carries on for many long moments until the army is finally no more. Descending back onto the head of Gigas, we all breathe a sigh of relief.

"Finally. I thought that would never end" I say to the dragon and Adamas.

"Indeed – however, this is no time to stop moving. That was only a small fraction. It won't be long until another wave comes against us again. And if you thought this was bad enough, we haven't even set foot upon the sacred land yet. There, their numbers are practically limitless."

An overwhelming feeling of impossibility overcomes me, as I digest the dragon god's words. As powerful as we are together, our success is far from certain.

Sensing my worries once again, Gigas says "Overthinking is useless at this point. You'd do well to remember this... Cassius."

"Stop calling me by that name, will you? I have long since thrown that name away."

With a slow and wise tone, the dragon god says "Boy... You really should not be so quick to abandon that which you were born with. After all, some of us have long forgotten our original names. I myself had a name before I was forced to become a god. However, it has been so long since I was but a simple dragon, I am unable to remember it. I would give anything... to remember it again."

Looking away, I feel a slight ounce of shame. As much as I wish to disregard my birth name, at least I have the luxury of knowing it.

At that moment, a single voice calls to me from amongst the clouds.

"Cassius... Luna... Cassius... Luna. You could give yourself over a hundred names, and it still wouldn't make a difference. The outcome will always be the same."

I flinch as the voice reverberates through the wind. I've heard this voice before, from a long time ago. Although my mind tries to deny it, my soul knows who the voice belongs to, all too well. Then, at that moment, a golden door appears directly in front of us. As it shines bright, the dragon shakes with terror and says "Boy... We have trouble. We are in grave danger."

Adamas trembles too, as we continue to stare upon the dazzlingly bright door. "Luna... What is this weird feeling?"

The door of light opens – revealing a single male, looking roughly the same age as me. He sports a gold and white robe, decorated with many unreadable symbols made of silver.

He smiles with a familiar smile, which sends my mind recalling all the times that he, my sister and I used to spend together. Holding my chest, I lose my breath at the sight of my childhood friend Orion: Messiah of Babylon City. His smile drops and becomes expressionless, as he proceeds to address me once more.

"It has been awhile... - Wouldn't you agree, old friend? I really didn't want to come here, but you've left me no choice. As the one and only true Messiah, I have no choice but to bring righteous judgement... Cassius."

Chapter 23: False

As Orion hovers opposite from the three of us, I stand on guard – trying to predict what he might do. Although in the past, he and I were once friends, at this present moment we are enemies. He never helped Lucia and I when we needed him, and even now he wishes to obstruct my path. Why?

"Luna, who is that person? I sense such powerful energy from him. It feels like yours but even greater..."

"Adamas now's not the time for explanations. All you need to know is that he is an obstacle, got that? Besides, you don't need to worry. After all, he's up against you, I, and Gigas."

Interrupting my response, the dragon god says "Boy – our numbers mean nothing when up against The Messiah of Babylon City. He is on a level that not even I can compete with. Even my power of foresight is useless against him. You had better prepare the best Miracles you have!"

Clearing his throat, Orion says "You did many bad things, Cassius. Not only did you steal Adamas and unlawfully take a fragment of the Great Observer's power, but you also used it to kill countless gods, awaken the former demon overlord and spread rebellion throughout the land."

"What of it? I have no shame in any of my actions. It's not as though I could count on you to help me save Lucia!"

"Lucia... now there's a name I haven't heard in a while."

Suddenly - by a simple click of his fingers, everything around us freezes. The clouds, distant birds, sea, land and all who dwell within it, stop. Even Gigas, as powerful as he is frozen like a statue. The only ones who can move are myself and Adamas.

Glancing around, I try to calm my nerves, knowing exactly the type of miracle he cast.

"He... He stopped time..."

At that second, Orion disappears before reappearing behind my back. I gasp with shock at but a taste of his powers, which he seems to display effortlessly. Unlike myself, who has always needed to clap my hands and utter a phrase, he simply can cast a miracle, as though reality were his playground. Standing back to back, he speaks calmly.

"A true Messiah can perform miracles by simple faith alone, and the amount I am able to use is limitless. Do you see the difference between us? You must understand... you are nothing but a false messiah!"

"I'd rather be a false messiah than a false friend!" I shout – turning around to perform a horizontal strike. As my attack goes into motion, he remains defenceless and open – as though uninterested in fighting back. I halt the blade, inches from his neck for reasons I am too embarrassed to admit.

With sympathetic eyes, he says "You can't do it, can you? Even after all this time, you're still the same. You are sensitive and loyal – especially to those dear to you. I am honoured that I still inhabit a special place in your heart."

"Shut up! Why... Why didn't you free Lucia from the Seventh Blessing when you had the chance? She didn't deserve to die!"

"Die? Come now Cassius, I am sure you know by now that Lucia didn't die. She transitioned to the goddess Selene and you killed her, remember?"

His words cut deep into my heart, confirming the reality that I killed the goddess my sister became. Sharing the blame, I shout to him "I... I wasn't to know! However, I am willing to bet that you knew the truth all along... about the Seventh Blessing and what it did to Lucia. Well answer me, damn you!"

To my surprise, a look of sadness appears on Orion's face. It is only for but a second, but I see it. The brief second revealed a vulnerability that I had only seen upon him once before. It was when I first begged him to save Lucia, all those years ago.

Locking his eyes to mine, the old friend asks "Cassius, what will you do to the Observer, if or when you make it all the way to its abode?"

"What kind of silly question is that? A perfect outcome would be to kill it after forcing it to bring Lucia back and rid the world of the Seventh Blessing."

"I see… That's a shame. You know, I really expected better from you."

At that point I become enraged. His answer sends my blood boiling and I shake frantically.

"You, expect better from me? Do you know what I've been going through these last five years? You know nothing… Nothing all!"

Throwing away all hesitation, I attempt to attack him a second time. This time I know I won't hold back. For a moment I was distracted, by sentiments and feelings from a time long gone. The mere fact that I am wasting time on someone that wishes to see me fail, is proof enough where we stand.

Anticipating my attack, Orion steps forward and simply taps my chest. As light as it looks, it feels as though a mighty giant has just sucker punched me. Like a doll, I am blasted backwards, off the head of Gigas before spiralling through the air.

Clapping my hands, I attempt to cast another miracle of flight - however, I remember that I cannot use the same miracle in one day. Shit - I am helpless.

As I continue to plummet towards the sea below, I try to think of another miracle instead.

"I am not gonna lose!" I declare, clapping my hands together a second time before uttering "Float!" just as I hit the seabed. Thanks to my quick thinking, I do not sink but instead, stand upon the water. Catching my breath from the fall, I assume a kneeled position while my sword stays close.

"Luna, are you ok? Be careful… That was your second miracle!"

"I know… I know!"

On alert, I blink from left to right, trying to catch sight of my foe. From the distance, I see him skating upon the water as though it were a sport. With his hands behind his back, he holds a jolly smile as though this were all but a game.

"Here he comes..." I say – clapping my hands together before shouting "...Maelstrom!" Summoning a gigantic whirlpool to swallow Orion whole.

Before our eyes, Orion disappears into the Maelstrom. With him gone I stand with relief, holding an excited gaze. "I got him, I finally got him!"

Suddenly, a huge amount of pain overcomes my chest and I fall to my knees. It is hard to breathe and my vision begins to fail me. Damn, I reached my limit.

"Luna, oh no!" My sword worries – spinning back and forth through my blurry line of sight. "Are you ok?"

"I'll be ok. I just only hope that last miracle got rid of him."

Astonishingly, before our very eyes, Orion floats to the surface, being only a meter apart from me. He stands upon the water, bearing not a single look of injury. His robes drenched and full of seaweed, he laughs while draining his sleeve.

"That was a nice trick, Cassius. A miracle like that would have killed any normal man. Fortunately for me, I am favoured by the very elements of nature."

"Damn you, god damn you!" I curse - clapping my hands a fourth time. Anticipating my actions, the sword rants to me.

"Luna, what do you think you're doing? You're not supposed to use anymore!"

"Shut up! Don't you see... I don't have a choice" I reply before shouting to the heavens "Meteor!"

Upon uttering the name of my fourth miracle, the sky dims as though the sun were blotted out by something great. A loud sound of something falling can be heard, as the world begins to tremble. Within moments the clouds above disperse, revealing a gigantic meteorite the size of a whole city.

"What in the..." Adamas gasps, as I stand with a grin on my face to Orion. Orion, however, seems to hold a look of wonder - impressed by my miracle.

As it descends more and more to the ocean, he smiles and says

"Wow, you're really not holding back, are you? However, how do you hope to survive your own miracle? Once that thing hits this whole area, you will perish also. Furthermore, the effects of it disrupting the waters will most likely cause a tsunami that will submerge countries."

"I couldn't care less about all that. As long as it takes you out in the process, I'll be more than happy!"

Shaking his head with disappointment, Orion says "You don't mean that. You're just speaking out of anger that's all."

Looking up at the ever falling meteor, the opponent folds his arms and utters to the object "Return to the stars", commanding it to stop in mid-air before shooting upward, back into the universe above.

Falling to my knees I stay lost for words, having witnessed my fourth miracle to have no impact whatsoever. Shit, will nothing work against him? No... I need to keep trying!
Refusing to let up, I clap my hands again, only for the irritating blade to complain once more. "Luna, what are you doing? You just went over your limit!"

Eyes focused solely on victory I reply "Silence! If it means getting rid of him, then I am willing to cast over one hundred miracles!" I can't give up. Even if it means losing my life, I'll fight till the very end.

"I'll handle this Lunaaaaa!"

Before my eyes, Adamas leaves my side and darts straight to the Messiah. What is the idiot doing? I've told him countless times, not to act without my orders.

As the sword gets closer, Orion smiles and says "That's right... Come at me and embrace my lullaby" before pulling out an empty scabbard. I gasp, for the sheath looks worryingly familiar. Wait... That was the very scabbard Adamas was found inside. Why is Orion using it?

Adamas spears forth to stab the Messiah – however, with a well-timed action, Orion catches the blade within the sheath. To my surprise, Adamas doesn't break free.

"Sleep well, little one," Orion says – holding my sheathed

companion under his arm. Somehow, the scabbard has trapped Adamas. How... How is it possible for a simple sword holder to imprison such a powerful blade?

Seeing the confusion on my face, Orion turns to me and says "Remember this sheath? In your effort to steal Adamas from Babylon City, you neglected to take his cradle. It is the only thing capable of keeping him under control. Within it, he sleeps – unable to hear anything from outside of it."

I freeze, hearing Orion's words regarding the power of the scabbard. I am such a fool. Why didn't I take the sheath with me? Armis never warned me about it either.

Smile dropping, my adversary takes a step forward and continues. "Old friend, you have lost. You lost, the very moment you decided to go against the wave of change. Contrary to what you may think, I don't wish to see you suffer. I love you and Lucia. However, the world will change and it is my duty to ensure that it changes. The Seventh Blessing has touched everyone on this planet. The world will eventually become gods... including you. We will know no death and will be free from earthly desires and wishes. There will be no poor, rich, suffering or injustice. Only peace and love... Under the watchful eyes of the Great Observer."

Unbelievable. They want to turn this world into nothing but one big planet of gods where nobody is mistreated. With such a world, there will be no more tragedies like mine. Everybody will be happy - not having to struggle. I must admit, this sounds like a dream come true... - And yet there is something about it that causes me to reject such an outcome. Living without a will of your own is not the way the world should be.

Standing to my feet, I take a deep breath and shout "Adamaaa-aaasss! Wake up!"

Upon a slight flinch, Orion says "What do you think you're doing? Have you not been listening to me this whole time? Adamas cannot hear you. You have no choice but to give up and submit to the world that will eventually take place."

"Like hell I will! I don't know where you got it in your brain that the gods wish for nothing, but the gods I have met on my travels all wish for something! Whether it's feeling alive, tasting death or being like a mortal, the gods I have met yearn for such things! Adamaaaas... wake the hell up!"

Suddenly, the blade begins to rattle and shake within the scabbard, causing Orion to gasp with shock. "What... How is it moving?"

"Come on Adamaaaaass! You can sleep after this is over. You and I need to find our sisters, remember?"

To my astonishment, Adamas frees himself from out the scabbard. Shocked with dismay, Orion stands lost for words. "How... That's impossible!"

Caught off guard, I use this opportunity to attack. Pouncing forward, I take hold of my released companion and perform a vertical strike, shouting aloud "How's this for miracles!"

He leaps backwards, just as my blade makes contact against his face. It wasn't a clean strike, but it was a strike nonetheless. As quick as he tried to dodge, he still couldn't evade the tip of my blade. A clear straight scar appears upon his forehead, releasing an outpour of blood.

"Yes!" Adamas and I both say at once, as the once smiling opponent glares with disbelief at perhaps the first injury he has ever received. "How does that feel, old friend? It's not nice to feel pain for once" I say with a sinister smile.

Touching his own bloodied face before viewing the blood within his hands, Orion stays speechless. He begins to shiver and tremble. Under his breath, I can hear him say "You hurt me... you hurt me... how dare you?"

His eyes turn to anger. This is the first time I have seen eyes so full of feeling. As I stand in a fighting stance, he continues ranting "Do you realise who I am? I am the messiah of the Great Observer!"

Reaching into his robe, the furious opponent pulls out a second, white scabbard, containing a sword inside.

"What... Another sword? Could it be...?"

With no hesitation, Orion unsheathes the blade and holds it

up high. It is dazzlingly white – exuding an aura that is almost identical to Adamas. Smiling at the blade with almost deranged eyes, Orion says "Behold, the sister blade: Platina!"

Together, Adamas and I freeze with disbelief upon seeing and hearing the name of the sword in front of us. That sword is Adamas' counterpart!

"Luna, that's my sister Platina right? She looks just as Ten described: Pure white and shiny!"

"Yes, indeed that is your sister. However, she is currently being wielded by our enemy. Before you think of any kind of reunion, we need to first deal with him!"

Shifting his gaze to me, Orion shouts "Get ready to die, Cassius!" Launching forth to attack with the white blade. Leaping forth also, I ready to strike.

The two weapons collide and as they do, something miraculous happens. A ringing sound is emitted from between both weapons, followed by a sound wave that blasts the two of us apart. I fall into the water, as so does Orion. For some reason, we are no longer able to stand upon the sea. Looking up, I notice that the flow of time has also resumed as I begin to hear the waves and wind. Something cancelled out the effects of our miracles.

"Boy! There you are!" Shouts the familiar and great voice of the dragon, Gigas. From the clouds, he soars down to my aid. "Get on!"

With his gigantic fingers, Gigas scoops me and Adamas into his claws, while Orion struggles to stay afloat in the water. Splashing about, he panics, seeing as this is the first time he has had to do without his powers.

"Help, I can't swim... I can't swim!"

Safely on board the dragon god, we ascend into the clouds as Orion stays helpless in the ocean. Looking to Gigas, I say to the dragon "Finish him off, will you? This our best chance!"

Upon an agreed head nod, Gigas releases a gigantic ball of light from his halo, which falls all the way down to the ocean. Hitting Orion head-on, the entire sea explodes. It feels as though the whole world is shaking from the powerful explosion that rises into the heavens.

Wasting no further time, we leave the chaotic scene and resume our flight. Taking a small glance behind at the devastation, I whisper "Farewell... Old friend."

Chapter 24: Black and White

Since the battle with the messiah of Babylon City, I have been recovering - sleeping in fact for over twenty-four hours. I fought with everything I had - even going as far to go over my miracle limit. Now awake under a looming sunset, I sit in the hands of the dragon who greets me pleasantly.

"Good afternoon boy. I hope you slept well?"

"Huh? Are you always this polite?"

"No. However, you have earned all of my respect. I don't know what you did but it looked like you got the best of the messiah of Babylon City."

"Somehow, Adamas and I caught him off guard. Something happened when our weapons clashed though. A loud ringing occurred, and then our miracles vanished. What do you think, Adamas?"

"Well... I don't know. However, when my sister and I made contact, I could feel how she felt. She was confused... Not knowing why she was fighting. Luna, do you think she'll be ok? After all, she was caught in the blast. We should have taken her with us."

With a look of slight guilt, I reply "Yeah, sorry about that Adamas. The only thing on my mind at the time was getting away and making sure Orion didn't follow us. However, if she's anything like you, then she would have withstood the blast.

In a wise and deep tone, the dragon says "Adamas and Platina... The greatest weapons ever to be crafted. Born from beyond the stars, the two have been allies of mortals since the days of old. They remain a mystery, even to my knowledge. However, I remember in times past I used to pursue the demon lord Ten, along with her partner: a man named Septimus. He wielded both swords and used them to withstand even me. Against Adamas and Platina, my powers had no effect."

"In that case, I really should have taken the opportunity to acquire the counterpart blade. We'll need all the strength we can get if we're to survive the Land of the Gods."

"Rubbish. We have more than enough strength to succeed. With your miracles and my power, we will crush all deities that come against us and will be the only ones standing!"

As confident as he sounds, I get the feeling that the dragon is speaking out of pure pride. A personal vendetta drives Gigas. Revenge for the Observer killing his entire dragon brethren perhaps? Although the dragon realises it needs my power to assist it, it wants to be the one to take the throne of the Great Observer, with his own hand.

Breaking me out of my thoughts, the dragon says, "Here we are... We have reached the entrance."

I show a confused face – wondering if I heard the dragon correctly. Did he just say that we have reached the entrance... Of the Land of the Gods? All we see before us is a large cloud.

"Are... Are you sure about that?" I ask, stand up before squinting my eyes. "It's not exactly what I had imagined."

"Fool, what were you imagining? Golden gates and trumpets? The cloud before us is the door that will take us to our destination. Before we go any further, you had better prepare for the worst. Once we go through, there's no coming back."

I stand quietly, holding my sword within both hands. I am shaking. So many emotions are running through me right now. Excitement, fear, hope... it all feels a bit too much. I have finally reached a place thought impossible. I don't want to come this far, only to fail. The key to saving my sister and everybody else... lies inside.

At that moment, I feel an arm resting upon my right shoulder as a familiar voice speaks forth "Wow... so this is the place, huh? I was expecting much more."

Turning to my right side, I gasp with fright at the sight of the ever-annoying witch Trista. "Christ! Must you always jump up on me like that?"

"Hahaha, sorry my lovelies. You know I just can't help myself sometimes, especially with you two!"

In a curious manner, Adamas asks "Trista, how did you know where to find us?"

"Oh, my dear... I always know where to find you. All I need to do is follow your trails of destruction, then bingo!"

As convincing as she sounds, I don't quite buy her explanation. Regardless, this isn't the time to be pondering on such things.

Addressing the witch, Gigas shows a hostile stare and asks, "Who are you and what do you want?"

As always, the woman takes off her pointed hat and spins it around her index finger. With a jolly smile, she replies "I am Trista the witch, at your service. It's a pleasure to meet you, dragon god Gigas. Forgive my sudden arrival. I have come to give my lovely friends here my final piece of information." Glancing around, she shows a bothered face and says, "Hmmm, but someone else is missing. Where is Ten?"

"She went off on her own to handle some personal affairs."

Placing the hat upon her head, she folds her arms and responds "Sigh... such a troublesome girl. Her leaving wasn't part of the plan. Didn't you try to stop her?"

"No, I didn't. It's not like I would have the power to do so anyway."

"Sigh... you could've at least cut her wings off. That would have stopped her from flying away. I guess there's also no point asking about Ryu and Vast aswell then? Sigh... I guess they will have to do without knowing... the purpose and origin of Adamas and Platina!"

Adamas, Gigas and I gasp, upon hearing her words. With a cautious look, I wait to hear her burst into laughter. After all, she does like to play tricks on us. However, she continues to hold a genuine expression.

"Trista... Do you know about Adamas? You're lying!"

"Nope, although it is up to you if you wish to believe me or not. You see, in days of old, this world was kept company by four moons... not two. Perhaps Ten had already mentioned it to you, once before?"

Turning her back to us, she looks up at the twin moons that can be faintly seen, past the orange sky. "Blue... Red... White, and Black. Believe it or not, each moon used to be inhabited by a race of highly advanced beings. The beings were called: The Locistals. Although they had their differences, they lived in harmony with one another and stayed out of the affairs of the inhabitants of Popla."

"Locistals? I have never heard of such a tale!" Interrupts Gigas – holding a face of disbelief in Trista's words.

Looking up at him with a strong glare, she responds "Were you not listening? I just said that they stayed out of the affairs of this world. Naturally, you and your dragonkin would not know of their existence. However, there was one group of humans, who were visited regularly by the beings from the moons. Do you remember the ruined city, where you were attacked by Ten's sister?"

"Yes. It was called Ashta, correct?"

"Yes, Ashta: City of Tomorrow. Somehow, a bond was formed between the people of Ashta and the beings from the moons. Over time, the Locistals understood much of mankind's struggle. They came to understand their biggest threat, being that of the immortal beings: gods. To support the humans, the Locistals of the Black and White moons decided to intervene. They created two weapons, made for the purpose of destroying immortal beings. Their names were: Adamas and Platina."

I stand lost for words at Trista's revelation. Holding the blade close, all I can do is stare. Looking up at the twin moons also, I respond "Adamas and Platina... they come from beyond the stars."

"So, I was created by people from the moon. I wish I had a memory of them, at least?"

Winking at the black sword, the witch replies "You did, in the very beginning. However, your memory was erased. You have your sheath to thank for that. You see, in the unfortunate event you went out of control, the Locistals created a sheath that would tame you. Once inside, you would fall asleep and dream, just like the rest of us. The catch is, the longer you're inside, the more you forget about everyone you had met before. Don't ask why, but the Locistals of the black and white Moons thought it necessary."

"You speak a lot of the black and white Moon's involvement. I assume the beings from the red and blue moons chose not to create swords to help mankind?"

"Precisely... and for good reason too. Although they interacted with the people of Ashta, they didn't want to get caught up between the affairs of gods and mankind. It's the reason their moons still exist now."

"What happened to the other two?" Adamas asks.

Gently placing her hands together, Trista replies in a nonchalant manner. "They were destroyed by the Great Observer. Your previous wielder, Septimus tried to confront the most powerful god in existence, using yourself and Platina. You all failed, however, and not only were you and Platina cast out, Ten imprisoned and Septimus killed, but the black and white moons were also destroyed as punishment for creating you both. The Great Observer is not one to be taken lightly, right?"

Chiming in, the dragon makes a frustrated sigh and adds "Indeed, it goes without saying. One need only look at what the Great Observer did to my whole kin and myself for daring to challenge it, millions of decades earlier. It left not a single dragon alive. Only I, who was forced to become one of its godly minions."

An overwhelming feeling comes over me. We are all up against a being that can destroy moons and races of beings. If we fail this time, who knows what punishment lies in store. It just might decide to wipe out half of the planet if it suits it, or I may end up becoming one of its minions. Do I really have the power to do this?

Approaching me before yanking my left ear, the woman

chuckles and says "Now, I know what you're thinking. You probably have lost confidence, right? Well, I am here to tell you that there is a way... as slim as it may be. When you fought Orion earlier, both Adamas and Platina clashed. Remember the effect it caused? It cancelled out your powers."

"Ah, yes! I had a feeling something bizarre happened after we struck our weapons against each other. Something released which wiped out the miracles we used."

"That force you experienced, was the true power of Adamas and Platina. Once struck together, both swords emit a sound that completely nullifies the gods and their powers."

Shocked with disbelief, I hold Trista's shoulders, unable to control my joy at her last revelation. "Trista, so... if I used it against the Great Observer, I could nullify its powers?"

"Yes. But you need to obtain Platina, which so far is still in the hands of Orion the Messiah."

"Shit, does that mean we need to go back to where we left Orion?"

"No, not necessarily. Your old friend is already inside, waiting for you. All you need to do is find a way to take Platina from him. Your next tussle will probably be even harder than before. Don't go over your limit again, like last time."

Clenching my fists, I hold my head high and respond, "I can't make you any promises... haha."

With a surprising look of sorrow, the witch produces a forced smile before taking a single step back. "Yeah... I am sure you can't. Well, I shouldn't keep you waiting. Do your best in there. I'll be rooting for you."

"Wait... before you go, I want to ask you something. Did you know the truth about the Seventh Blessing all along? Did you know what became of my sister?"

Looking overwhelmed and embarrassed, she does not answer. Her silence is all I need to know. All this time, she knew about the truth and yet played ignorant. With a disappointing sigh, I turn away and respond.

"You too huh? Don't worry, I won't take it personally. I've gotten used to two-faced people anyway."

"Sorry... Luna. Well, I really shouldn't be keeping you. After all, the world only has six days left", she says before turning her back to us and disappearing into thin air. Standing still for many short moments, I whisper "Six days... plenty of time."

Looking up at the dragon, I say to him "Apologies for the unexpected visit from my witch friend. Shall we get going then?"

"Hmph... if that woman is a witch, then I am a caterpillar. I have seen many magic users, witches and wizards alike in my time, and I can assure you... that friend of yours in no witch."

"Well, what is she then?" Asks Adamas.

"That question, I am afraid I can't answer. However, it might be a good thing. Some truths are better left in the dark. I digress... let us claim victory this day!"

Upon the dragon god Gigas, we head straight into the cloud – ready to storm the Land of the Gods.

Chapter 25: Warm Welcomes

Travelling through the cloud, all I see around me is fog. Preparing myself for anything, I hold Adamas close to my chest. This is it, this is the moment I have waited so long for.

"Luna… Guess what?" My chirpy sword asks, causing me to sigh with irritation.

"What now? Can't you see that I am trying to focus?"

"Oh… Sorry. You see, I wanted to tell you that while I was briefly inside that scabbard, I had a dream!"

Flinching with shock, I gasp with surprise. Adamas has been unable to sleep, ever since we met. I must admit, I am intrigued as to what kind of dream he had.

"Well… What was it about?"

"Oh, it was incredible! I was a human being, just like you Luna! However, I was a little human. You, Ten and I were running throughout a town, causing all sorts of trouble!"

"Hehe… Sounds like a good dream."

"It was. Even now, I can remember the feeling of breathing air and the sun rays. Later, we went home where our sisters were. We spent the whole evening laughing together. It felt so real."

Taken back by his accounts, I let out a small smile – imagining what such a scene would look like. His dream sounds beautiful.

"Luna, I know that I haven't been the best comrade on this journey. I am always saying stupid things and I have sometimes made things worse. But… I just want to say that I have had the best time with you. Going around with you and Ten has been a blast. I hope that after this, we can all live together and be happy."

My heart becomes heavy and my eyes grow moist. Wow, I never imagined Adamas could bring me close to tears. I too would love for all of us to go somewhere far... and live happily.

Keeping my gaze away from him, not to display my emotions, I close my eyes and reply "Adamas... you have been the most loyal friend I ever had. Let's try to make that dream you had come true... somehow."

Shom – the fog disappears, just as I reopen my eyes. With a deep breath, I lay my eyes upon the sacred land. A golden sky hangs above, filled with countless shooting stars. Below us, a rich and deep forest can be seen, decorated with sparkling fruits that hang on each tree. Mountains and waterfalls of many colours sit in the background. At the far distance ahead, I see a grey spire which extends all the way up to a shining sphere, resembling a sun.

Pointing to the glowing wonder, the dragon says, "The Great Observer will be found in that cocoon of light. There's no doubt about it."

"Good. Now let's go for it!" I state – standing upon the head of the dragon comrade.

Going full speed ahead, Gigas soars up, towards the abode of the Observer.

As expected, however, our visit is not without a warm welcome. The stars suddenly begin to fall to our direction. Upon close inspection, we find that the stars are not stars at all, but in fact each a celestial being.

"Fucking hell!" I shout – holding Adamas readily. "It looks like we're up against the very sky itself!"

"You're right Luna... But it doesn't matter. We can win, no matter what!"

The legion of celestial beings descends closer – each bearing two pure white wings and heads of falcons, wielding a glowing sword and shield.

As though sensing my wonder at the incoming enemies, Gigas says to me "They are angels. They too were once human beings who have been transformed to protect this land from intruders.

Although their strength is nothing to worry about, they serve as an irritant due to their unyielding numbers."

With his lightning claws ready, Gigas tears through the legion of angels. Upon each furious swipe, hordes of winged opponents are tossed through the air. Focused on the gigantic sun structure afar, the dragon charges through the army at blistering speeds – leaving behind a trail of dead corpses and thunderous explosions.

"Keep it up Gigas! At this rate, nobody will be able to stop us. Our moment of victory is near!"

"Indeed, I have waited so long to return to this place and seek my revenge. I will make my fallen brethren proud, by laying waste to everything within this realm!"

"Wait… Something is coming!" Warns Adamas. Within seconds, a large being descends from the golden sky. Bearing the form of a gigantic right hand, along with a glaring eye within its palm - the being glows fluorescent lights that are almost blinding. The dragon stops its flight – displaying a worried expression.

"Curses. As always, the royal guard of the Observer never takes its eye off an intruder", mumbles Gigas.

Curious, I ask the dragon, "What is that being before us? I have never seen such a thing."

"That is the great hand and protection of the Observer: Hamsa. Its body is unfathomably powerful, which can halt almost anything from getting through!"

With a mighty and earth-shattering tone, the being says "The net of heaven is large and wide but allows nothing through. I am Hamsa!"

"Stand aside!" Shouts the dragon – releasing a mighty ray of light from its mouth. The light hits Hamsa directly – resulting in a mighty explosion that rocks the very realm we're in.

As the light clears, however, the enemy before us still stands – with not a single scathe or scratch. Upon a short pause, the glowing being says "Nothing formed against the Great Observer shall prosper."

Wham – at that moment, the being slams into Gigas like a battering ram – sending him spiralling back through the air. Holding onto his scales as we are pushed back, I shout "Shit... such force..."

Regaining his balance mid-flight, Gigas shakes his head out of disorientation. Looking upon the divine obstacle before us, we show a frustrated stare.

"Hamsa's strength has not waned at all, since last we met. It took thousands of my brethren to get it to move just an inch, and it cost a thousand more of their lives to allow a small fraction to pass through."

Up against such a foe, my usual reaction is to cast a miracle. After all, it has been twenty-four hours. However, I can't afford to waste a single miracle - especially knowing that Orion is somewhere within this place.

Gigas, give me and Adamas a chance to strike at it!"
Nodding his head, the dragon charges forward and tackles the divine hand - holding onto it tightly.

Wasting no time, I sprint up the dragon's arm and leap to the opponent - sword ready to strike. With all my might I perform a clean cut – slicing into the divine being like a hot knife through butter.

"Aaaaahhhhhhhhh!" The being screams, while I bear a sinister grin as though enjoying its death cry.

As I continue to cut further into it, I shout to the foe "Get out of our fucking way!"

Boom – the once impenetrable being explodes into light, which showers the sky. Breaking my fall, I am caught by the dragon before resuming our flight.

"Bravo! That was an excellent display of victory!"

"Much appreciated – however it is too early for praises right now."

Not letting up, the legion of angels descends upon us once more.

"They just keep coming!" Adamas says – being held tightly within my hands. Holding a strong fighting stance, I hold my head proudly and show an excited and adrenaline filled glare.

"They can keep coming against us, all they want. It won't change a goddam thing. We have come too far!"

Suddenly, I hear a familiar voice, coming from nearby.

"Indeed you have come too far. However - what exactly are you fighting for, Cassius?"

My heart stops for but a second, upon hearing the familiar voice. There's no doubt about it... That was Orion's voice calling me. Bizarrely enough, it feels as though he is speaking into my very mind. He must be around here somewhere.

Glancing around, I try desperately to find my rival. However, it's hard to see anything, past all the angels in my way. "Where are you hiding, Orion!"

"Look down..." He says once again - voice speaking directly into my mind. As requested I look directly down, where the deep forest can be seen below. I see him sitting atop a tree, waving at me. As friendly as it looks, it is clear that he is challenging me to a second bout. Very well.

Without warning, I leap off the dragon and plummet through the air – leaving Gigas speechless.

"What are you doing, boy? Have you gone insane?"

"Leave me be, dragon. I have an important matter to attend to. Once I have settled my personal matters, I will rejoin you."

"Buffoon! We stand a much greater chance of success by sticking together!"

His words fall on deaf ears – for I have already fallen many miles through the sky to challenge the messiah of Babylon city, once more.

As pesky as ever, the angels attempt to rush at me as I fall. However, I cut them down, one after the other. As I slaughter the winged foes, my sword babbles further.

"Luna, are you sure it was a good idea to separate from Gigas?"

"Of course it was. We need to get your sister, don't we? The dragon would not have been interested."

"Oh yes, you're right. Luna, thank you for helping to get my sister - even if it means fighting your own friend."

"Don't mention it. Besides... you and I are a team, remember? Before Gigas, Ryu, Vast, Ten and Trista... it was just you and I. This friendship that we have, is a miracle in itself!"

Yanking one of the angels from the air, I force it under my feet – using it as a cushion to break my fall as I crash into the forest. Taking the full force of the fall, the angel explodes into light – leaving me mostly unharmed, save for a few bruises.

In a crouched fighting stance, I glance around the forest. The ground beneath me seems to be made of blue and red marble. The trees, which house an abundance of fruits, seem to be humming... singing to be exact. However, their words I cannot make sense of.

"Luna, watch out!" Adamas warns – signalling for me to look up above. Yet again, I watch as the legion of angels descends upon me. They land to the grounds of the forest – circling around us. Standing to my feet, I hold an elegant fighting stance – feet held together and sword outward by my left side.

"Well, what are you waiting for? Come on!" I shout – urging the winged opponents to come at me. Wasting no time they charge towards me... to their demise.

Every attack they throw is met with an evasive manoeuvre from myself. And upon every evasive manoeuvre I perform, I strike back with a fierce stab. Try as they might, the foes are unable to keep up with my vast skills and techniques. Each attack is vastly different from the other – testament to my ability as an accomplished swordsman. Of course, I am not just any swordsman. My swordsmanship is that of a god, thanks to my teacher: Armis.

As I cut through more and more angelic beings, using all the battle skills available to me – my mind is taken to the five long years I spent with my former teacher. Each day would begin hard and yet would end with me learning something valuable. All those days and nights were not in vain. For it is because of those days, I can stand in the face of such adversity.

"Here I come, Cassius!" Shouts Orion in a playful manner. Quickly turning around, I spot him falling towards me - white sword in motion to strike.

"Orion!"

Our weapons clash - resulting in a release of energy which blasts the surrounding angels into the distance. As we keep our swords pressed against one another, I display a focused glare while Orion holds a smile of excitement.

"Our weapons are quite extraordinary, don't you think? The combined energy they give off negates even my holy powers."

"Stop treating this like its all one big game. We have come here to end your god's ambition and bring our sisters back!"

Somersaulting over his head, I attempt to strike him from above and lob his head off. However, he blocks against my attack masterfully.

The powerful force from the clash of blades releases another great energy, which knocks both of us backwards before tumbling along the ground. As though having the same thought process, Orion and I recover into a fighting stance at the exact same second.

"Hmph, Armis taught you well, Cassius. Clearly, his efforts were not wasted on you."

"Since when were you skilled at using swords, Orion?"

"Haha... did you really think that miracles were all I had? I also have been blessed in the art of swordsmanship. Let's find out who's better, shall we?"

Revelling in our confrontation, he runs straight to me, wielding his white sword while holding a challenging and exciting grin. Upon each footstep he takes, schools of white roses bloom from under his feet.

Upon a great exhale, I engage him once more - racing forward with my black comrade held in front. With each footstep I take, a group of red roses sprout and follow behind me.

We duel - clashing sword against sword, throughout the living forest. Upon each collision, rows of singing trees are tossed to and fro, as though caught amidst a violent whirlwind. As our battle intensifies, the two of us converse.

"Cassius, your sister was chosen by the seventh blessing. Who are you to get in the way of something so great?"

"I am her god-dam brother, and I want her back!"

"Haha, you want your sister back... to what? A world of poverty and suffering? No, such a fate belongs to you, Cassius. Lucia, on the other hand, was destined to die and awaken... as a new being. Billions of people all around the world accept this fact. Everything that lives will eventually pass away to something else. It is the natural order of things!"

Shakoom - upon another great collision, the two of us stab each other straight through the chest. Gallons of blood shoot from out our mouths as we let out a collective cry. Even under such agony, we rant to the other.

"I... I don't care about the natural order of things!"

"Then you are a fool, Cassius. Not just a fool... but a dreamer. You are dreaming to return to a time that is no more. Even if you were to somehow bring everybody you wanted back to life, it would never be the same. You have become a cold and merciless slayer of gods. For the past five years, all you have known is how to kill the opponent. What would you now have in common with Lucia? What moments would you both be able to share today? Open your eyes and face the truth of what you both have become. You have both been led through divergent rivers of change. Accept it!"

Pulling each sword from out the other's chest, we stumble backwards and fall to our knees. Breathing heavily, I cover my deep chest wound to stop the blood. As I do so, my sword panics.

"Luna, be careful!"

"I know. Damn, his skills are as good as mine."

"Don't give up. Come on... Hurry and use a miracle to heal your wounds!"

Following his advice, I clap my hands together and cast a healing miracle. Within seconds my near to fatal wound is no more and I breathe a sigh of relief. However, before I have time to even stand up, my opponent points the tip of his blade to me, having already recovered.

"Shit!"

"Indeed. Now, let me ask you once more. If you were to make it to the Great Observer, knowing that it was the one responsible for the Seventh Blessing in our world, what would you do?"

"Why do you keep asking such dumb questions? I couldn't give two shits about anything else other than killing it!"

A look of deflation overcomes my opponent who shakes his head before sighing. For some reason, he hopes to receive a different answer from me. Not sure why though. Revealing further the motive to his question, he asks "Would you not even try to understand it? After all, you were capable of understanding me once: a child from a completely different walk of life. You have understood a living blade and have made it a loyal comrade, among many other individuals you have met on your journey. If the opportunity were to present itself, why wouldn't you try to reach out to it?"

I don't know what he is babbling on about, but all I am hearing are suggestions of sympathy and empathy. Not in a million years.

"Enough with the bullshit already. I already told you what I would do. If there's nothing left to say, then hurry up and make your move!"

"Uh... fine then, Cassius. If you won't even try to help, I might as well just finish you now!" Orion responds furiously - swinging his blade to my neck. Suddenly, however, the white sword stops mere inches from me, acting on its own accord.

"Huh? What in the..." I mutter as Adamas watches the sister blade also. Before we can react, the sword speaks for the first time, in a gentle and light tone.

"Stop it... I don't want to fight Adamas. I am not supposed to be fighting Adamas!"

Lost for words I pause with shock as Orion stands surprised also. If I remember correctly, both Adamas and Platina had their memories erased after being within their sheaths for thousands of years. How is it possible for Platina to remember?

"Platina, what are you doing? Furthermore, how have you recovered your memories? Nevermind. It is clear that you will only be a hinderance right now." Pulling out the white scabbard, he sheathes the white sword and tucks it into his robes.

"Platina! Let my sister go!" Shout Adamas - zipping from out my hand to stab our foe. Just before the sword can make contact, Orion simply breathes a mild sigh - summoning a fierce gale that blows us and the entire forest backwards. Crashing many meters away, I lay half buried, under piles of broken logs and barks. The entire forest is no more but a wide golden expanse of open ground.

"Shit... he's back to using his miracles again I see."

"Look out!" Screams Adamas, signalling for me to look upward. To my shock, I find that Orion has already cast another miracle - summoning a pillar of fire from the heavens to fall down directly towards us.

"Teleport!" I utter while clapping my hands - causing me to disappear in the nick of time. The pillar of fire falls to the ground, resulting in a mighty and wide explosion that covers the area. As the debris of flames falls all around, I reappear nearby - just outside of the blast radius.

"That was close" I utter, looking up at the scene of destruction. Just above the flames of the burning devastation, we see Orion - drifting in the air, hands held behind his back in a calm manner. His smile no longer present, he looks down at us as though we were but insects in his presence. Opening his mouth, he calls to me.

"I am afraid this is where the fun stops. Cassius, you had better think of your best miracles, because I will not be holding back."

"Give it everything you've got, Orion!"

Chapter 26: A Thousand Miracles

Our battle resumes, and just as expected, Orion wastes no time throwing everything at me. By his command, the very ground erupts like a volcano - releasing streams of light that fire all around us.

"Fly!" I utter - casting a miracle of flight to escape the hazardous grounds. Of course, my efforts are almost futile, as the constant beams of light follow me through the sky. "Shit... too many things are happening all at once!"

"Luna, you just used your third miracle!" Rants the talking blade, as I continue to desperately evade each projectile.

"Huh? Already? Looks like I have no choice but to go over my limit."

"No, you can't do that. You may die if you overuse your miracles!"

"I am gonna die regardless if I don't use them!"

With a great clap, I shout forth "Time stop!" freezing everything around me. With the numerous projectiles and Orion frozen still, I use my chance to soar to him - sword ready to strike.

"Checkmate!" I shout while performing a vertical swipe. However, before the sword makes contact, Orion breaks free from the time freeze and evades in the nick of time. "What in the..."

Wham - with a simple strike from his palm I am sent spiralling backwards. The blasts of light resume their deadly pursuit, and as I struggle to outrun them, the sword and I converse.

"Damn, he was able to break through my time stop miracle!"

"Now what do we do?"

"We keep fighting, that's what!"

Upon another great clap, I utter "Tsunami!" summoning an ocean of water to fall over him.

Looking up at the flood of water, Orion simply says to it "Get thee behind me", commanding my miracle to pass over him and wash into the distance. I don't let up and proceed to command a gigantic mountain, perhaps the biggest mountain I could imagine to appear and fall on top of him. However - much like before, he lifts his head and says "Move", launching the mountain behind him. Crashing into the far distance, the mountain crumbles into pieces - filling the ground with rubble, smoke and debris.

"Nice effort. However, your miracles are too simple. You should try something a tad more wondrous. Behold..."

By his command, Orion summons a legion of comets to rain down from the sky, along with thousands of miniature suns, moons and stars. The sight of the collective projectiles is terrifying and yet magnificent at the same time. I have never seen anything so powerful and godly. It looks as though the very universe were falling towards me. Lost in awe, I simply stay frozen - knowing that there is no way of getting out of this one. Orion... He really is one of a kind.

"Amazing..." I whisper - no longer fighting back, ready to accept my defeat. Against him, I simply have no chance. I guess this means I have thrown in the towel?

Shom - inches before the collection of stars, comets, suns and moons make contact - Orion stops the miracle before proceeding to speak in a jolly manner. "Hehe... looks like I won this round, old friend."

With a click of his finger, the magnificent legion of projectiles disappears from the sacred realm. Looking to him with a suspicious and confused face, I ask "You're not going to kill me?"

"I have already defeated you. Ending your life now would be meaningless. However, seeing as I was the clear victor, I have only one request. Meet me within the highest floor of the spire and listen to what I have to say."

Reluctantly I hold my tongue and slowly nod my head in a

compliant fashion. Of course, the idea of my life being spared by Orion of all people doesn't sit well with me. I would prefer to die than to now be in his debt.

"See you later," he says - disappearing from the area - leaving only Adamas and I, stunned by the whole confrontation.

"Wow. We are so lucky, right Luna? I thought we were finished!"

"You're telling me. It would seem he wants to explain something, possibly about the Great Observer. None of his actions makes sense at all."

Looking straight ahead, I see the dragon in the distant clouds, still battling the infinite army of deities and angels. Nearby I see the spire, which seems to have only one entrance, found at the bottom.

"Let's keep going."

Chapter 27: Holy Guardians

Due to going all out against Orion, much of my energy has been exhausted. However, I am not nearly as concerned as one would expect. For some reason, although I went over my limit, I have not suffered the usual repercussions. Somehow, being in this realm allows me to cast more miracles than usual. However, I'd be a fool to assume that the uses are limitless.

We finally reach the base of the spire and see an open entrance which leads directly inside. However, guarding the entrance, I notice two large cherubs. As well as bearing the typical: lion body, gryphon wings and human face – each creature seems to wear a single crown, unlike the other cherubs I have encountered before.

"Looks like its show time again."

Gaining their attention, the two large cherubs peer down at me. The left creature spots me first and tilts its head before addressing the blade and I.

"As feared, the cursed sword has managed to find its way here, once again. This time, it has brought a different mortal."

The right-hand guardian tilts its head to me also and speaks forth. "Yes... This one is called Cassius. He is the one that is fighting for nothing."

"Indeed, his existence is a sad one. Only the weak wish to partake of fruits from yesterday."

The crowned cherubs seem to speak as if they know all about me. Perhaps they do? An air of all-knowing wisdom exudes from the pair, making me feel as though I were in the presence of knowledge itself. Nevertheless, I brandish my sword and threaten the duo.

"Spare me your conceited words. Who wants to die first?"

The left guardian takes a step forward before formally addressing itself.

"I am Lamassu: King of all cherubs."

Strolling beside him, the second being says "I am Apsasu: Queen of all cherubs. O cursed sword Adamas and foolish Cassius – allow us to show you, what real purpose looks like."

Within seconds the pair sprints towards us at blinding speed. They are so fast, I barely have time to react and instead am knocked backwards. "Shit!"

As I tumble across the marbled ground, the guardians gallop around me – challenging my purpose with words of doubt.

"Cassius, what are you fighting for? Your sister no longer exists. She had already become the great goddess Selene who you eventually killed."

Struggling to my feet I respond, "There has to be a way. There has to be a way to bring her back, as well as save everyone from the Seventh Blessing!"

Wham – once again I am knocked off my feet and kicked along the ground. They are just too fast and strong. The moment I focus on one of them, the other comes at me from a blind spot.

As I lay on the ground, they attempt to trample over me with their mighty hooves. Fortunately, Adamas thinks fast and blocks each crushing stomp. The cherubs laugh and mock, as their attacks continue.

"You are a pitiful liar. Do not pretend to care about your fellow man, Cassius. Your heart longs for your sister alone... nobody else. However, as we stated before: she no longer exists!"

"Bullshit! You are the liars. My sister exists as a Figment... whatever that's supposed to mean."

Wham – with a great kick, I am sent spiralling through the air before crashing to the ground, near the entrance of the spire. Full of pain and injury, all I can do is remain within a crouched position as my sword floats defensively in front. As I cough forth a ton of blood from my injuries, the mighty opponents speak further.

"Who told you about such a thing? That word is taboo amongst us. To be a Figment is a fate worse than death itself."

A fate worse than death itself huh? Now, what exactly is that supposed to mean? Either way, their acknowledgement of it offers some hope of reaching Lucia. Now I am more determined than ever to make it to the Great Observer. I just need to get through this gruesome twosome here. Shit, I really don't want to have to waste any more miracles, but I don't have a choice.

Suddenly we hear a short chuckle, coming from above. The sound is familiar, causing Adamas and I to gasp with surprise. Looking up we watch as a suited individual descends from the sky. Landing by my side, I stare in disbelief at the sight of Ryu.

"Hehe... why do you always get yourself in this mess, only for me to get you out?"

"Ryu! Am I seeing things?"

Almost lost for words, I stand shocked. What is he doing here? How did he even get here in the first place?

As though anticipating my questions, he reaches to the waist of my robe and picks out a small metallic device. Holding it to eye-level, he says "I had a feeling that you'd do something crazy and ditch us, so I bugged you with this little tracking device here. I have come to know you very well. You're the type of person to go it alone, only to end up relying on help from others."

"Idiot... You should have stayed where you were. This place is too dangerous for you!"

"Hmph... says the guy who is getting his ass pummelled right now. I didn't come here for you. I came to save my people from the Seventh Blessing."

Wasting my breath no longer, I step past him and face the direction of the twin cherubs. "Fine... suit yourself. Let's just hurry up and get rid of these eyesores, shall we?"

"That will not be necessary" He replies - looking upward with a small grin. At that moment, a second larger knight falls from the sky, wielding a pair of gigantic golden gauntlets. With a mighty downward swing, he crushes the two guardians into the stone ground – causing a great shower of debris and smoke to fill the area. As the dust settles, I am astounded even further at the sight of Vast, standing over the fallen beings.

"Whahaha! Do you mean to tell me that these two overgrown pigeons, almost got the best of you Luna? Hah… what a chump!" He says – looking to me with a friendly grin. An overwhelming sense of gratitude overcomes me. As much as I wish they were not here, their presence alone encourages me.

Holding onto my arm, the prince leads me into the spire and says, "Come on, let's keep going while Vast holds those guardians back."

"Wait, isn't he coming with us?"

"No, he will stay out here and defend the entrance. Worry not, he and I have come here, anticipating our death. This is our choice to make."

As we race inside, I take a small glance back at Vast. He holds an ever-present smile before producing a thumbs up to me. As much I hate to say it, he really wasn't that bad of a guy, after all. Granted, our first encounter wasn't the best, but if I was ever a King or leader, Vast would be one of my closest comrades.

Watching us disappear into the tower, the overgrown knight stands firm – whispering to himself. "Goodluck, lord Ryu and Luna."

Shom – at that moment, the two cherubs rise from the ground and release a burst of light from their wings. The man is blasted along the ground before hitting against a stone pillar. Body shining with light, Apsasu and Lamassu stand tall – expanding their radiant wings, ready to challenge Vast. Supporting them, a legion of angels also descends from the golden sky – surrounding the single knight.

"I swear, by the name of my Kingdom… None of you will get through me!"

Chapter 28: Holy Justice

Having entered the spire – Adamas, Ryu and I look around the innards. The structure is made up of purple marble, from the ground to the walls. To our right, we see the start of a spiral staircase that goes far up to a bright ceiling above.

Floating to the stairs, Adamas moans, "Whoa, do we really have to climb all these steps? It will take forever to reach the top."

"What does it matter to you? It's not like you have legs dimwit" I respond – taking hold of the blade before wasting no time ascending the flight of stairs. Following closely – Ryu stays by my side. My bones and muscles are screaming - yet I refuse to back down. Because I had already cast a healing miracle once already, I won't be able to cast the same for another twenty-four hours. Even so... As long as I have even an ounce of strength in my body, I will keep moving.

"Oh no... Something's coming!" Adamas alerts us. Looking upward, we watch as numerous wheels made of flames descend upon us. Each wheel possesses eyes, which stare piercingly at the three of us. As though having a collective mindset, the bizarre looking beings speak in unison.

"We are Ohanim... We never sleep. We are Ohanim... We never sleep!"

Ready to take on the wheeled beings, Ryu and I assume a perfectly combined fighting stance – standing back to back. With my feet elegantly placed together, I raise my sword to the side as Ryu stands in a partially crouched stance – holding the hilt of his invisible blade within both hands.

"Here they come Luna, don't let your guard down."

"Speak for yourself, Ryu!"

Upon a joint smirk, we take on the fiery wheels – cutting them down while racing up the stairs. Fighting together, Ryu and I cover each other's back – protecting each other's blind spots.

Despite their efforts, the Ohanim are powerless against the combined skill of Prince Ryu and I, and like a pair of juggernauts, we charge through the masses of enemies. To my surprise, however, I hear the foes collectively chant another saying... - one that instantly makes my blood boil.

"You killed her... You killed your sister. You killed Selene... You killed Lucia... You..."

I pause for but a moment – losing focus as their statements continue to ring throughout the walls of the spire. How dare they? How dare they speak of my sister!

"Shut up, the lot of you!"

As though toying with me, the eyes of the fiery wheels display a mocking and sinister gaze, as they continue to rain down over us.

"Don't listen to them, Luna..." Ryu says in a supportive manner.

We continue ascending up the stairs, laying waste to the opponents before us. By now, I have lost count of how many foes I have defeated. The only thought on my mind is reaching the top where Orion and the Great Observer awaits.

Before long, the enemies are no more, and upon slaying the final wheel, we stop to take a breather. Unbeknownst to us due to all the fighting, I realise we have advanced more steps than expected. It would seem we're halfway towards the top. The glowing ceiling above is closer than ever. Just a few more flights of stairs to go.

Slanted against the wall, the prince exhales constantly as he attempts to catch his breath.

"I thought they would never stop coming. Thank goodness we defeated them all" He says with relief.

"Yes, you're right. However, we still have bigger challenges ahead. We're running out of time" I respond sternly - ready to continue onwards. "Although we have seven days to halt the Seventh blessing, we shouldn't waste a single second."

"I know that..." Ryu affirms - preparing to resume the long and winding steps.

With a gasp of worry - Adamas states "Something is coming!"

From above, a single angel descends into our line of sight. However, this one looks far different from the rest. Upon its back, six magnificent wings shine brightly. Its face is covered by a golden helmet, and within its right hand, a flaming sword is held.

"Holy... Holy... Holy" The angelic being says as it drifts slowly towards us. Assuming our fighting stances, Ryu and I stand ready to face the new foe. Swaying within my hand, the black sword grows nervous.

"This angel... Something feels off about this one."

"Off? Adamas, you'll have to be a little more specific about that."

"I don't quite know how to say it. I... I feel as though this isn't the first time we have met this one."

Gliding through the air, the angelic being calls to us and says "I am the newest friend of the Great Observer. Behold... I am Seraphim!

Much to my surprise, Ryu gasps - mouth open wide as though having seen a ghost. "Seraphim...?" He whispers to himself, as though mind racing with certain thoughts.

Nudging him with my elbow, I whisper "Hey... What's gotten into you? Why have you let your guard down?"

"Luna... I think that angel is..."

Shakoom - attacking us while we converse, the angel flaps its wings - releasing a powerful blast of light. Together, Ryu and I tumble back down many flights of stairs before finally gaining our footing.

"Great Scott. Such power..." I express - as we both fall to our knees from the attack. Landing a few paces in front of us, the angel exudes a strong and cemented aura, while we struggle to stand.

Glancing to the knight, I say "Ryu, we won't be able to survive another hit like that. Come on... get up."

"Yeah... but..."

"Why are you being so hesitant? Stop pissing around, will you? Sigh... This is the reason why I didn't want you to come along in the first place!"

Upon another sway of its wings, the being releases a second wave. Fortunately, Adamas gets into harm's way - taking the full brunt of the blast. Still, the very force itself propels all three of us back even further.

Laying flat on the marble stairs, Ryu and I can only look up at the foe. Standing on the spot, the being raises its sword of flames and proclaims "Holy... Holy... Holy..."

Looking up at the opponent, the prince interrupts the opponent and says "So, this is your godly form... Right Carlton?"

Chapter 29: Divine Judgments

Outside the Spire, high above the clouds of the golden sky - the dragon advances closer to the beaming sun that is the resting place of the Great Observer. Despite the millions of angelic foes that continuously come against him, the dragon lays waste to scores of opponents, like an unstoppable comet.

"I am almost there... I've almost made it. After all these years of being manipulated and stripped of everything that I once was, I will finally get my revenge!" Gigas shouts aloud - as numerous angels and gods fall like flies upon every thunderous strike he makes.

The sun grows brighter and brighter, as he flies closer - withstanding the increasing onslaught.

"Five million... Eight million... Ten million, down!" He states - counting the number of foes slain by each attack he inflicts. Upon a mighty roar, he shouts to the heavens "Enough of your lackeys, Observer. Stop hiding and face me!"

Finally reaching the shining sphere, Gigas lands against its solid surface. With his mighty claws, he attempts to rip it apart.

"You... You took everything from me!" He rants - striking continuously at the shell of the hard sphere. However, each thrash proves futile - for not a single scratch appears upon it. Still, the vengeful dragon refuses to let up. "Like a candle being snuffed out, you took the lives of my brethren, without a second's hesitation. You stole my will and forced me to become one of your godly henchmen. You even snatched my original name from me - making it impossible for me to ever remember. I hate you!"

Suddenly, the cocoon rumbles and shakes - causing the dragon to pause with shock. Within seconds, the golden shell unfolds and opens up - becoming a large and magnificent flower. Looking into its centre, Gigas freezes - marvelling at the greatest of gods. Sitting within the flower, he sees the embodiment of the entire universe. Its appearance is beyond comprehension to the dragon, who can do nothing but stop and stare.

"So... So... beautiful" Gigas whispers - frozen still by its mere countenance.

Extending its hand forth, the being places its fingertips against the snout of the dragon, and with a loving and soothing tone, it produces a single word.

"Zilant."

The dragon flinches - slightly baffled by the word spoken by the Great Observer. However, something deep inside feels familiar about it. With another serene tone, the being says "Zilant was your original name before I stripped it from you. Now, it is yours to claim once again. Hold it close to your heart, as you sail through the stars where all your brethren await you."

By a mere brush of its hand, the being causes the dragon to let out its final breath. The flower refolds into its cocoon form, and the dragon known as Zilant falls from the sky - passing away with a smile upon his face.

He crashes to the ground below, not far from the entrance of the spire, where Vast can be found, battling the two Cherubs and the army of angels.

"Shit... Even good ol Gigas has fallen" Vast utters, as he glances at the defeated dragon's carcass.

Overwhelmed by their strength and numbers, the large knight stays in a kneeled stance - glancing around at the foes around him. "They just keep coming, no matter what I do" He mutters to himself, as the Cherubs Apsasu and Lamassu circle around him.

"Mortal, your bravery and strength are commendable. The mere fact that you're still breathing, after being struck numerous times by us is noteworthy. You will make a fine warrior, to the Great Observer."

Standing tall, the man replies "No thanks. The last thing I'd ever wish for is to be like the rest of you sad fuckers. I also don't intend to die here. Me and my buddies will live through this, and each of us will have our names carved in the pages of history!"

Within the spire, Ryu and I continue to lay helpless at the foot of the powerful angel. To my surprise, however, the being stands as though petrified - transfixed solely on the prince. Its movement halted, the moment he uttered the name, Carlton. Carlton... that was the child we met some days ago, who died of the Seventh Blessing. Wait... Is this what he has become?

"Ryu - is that thing really Carlton? How do you know for sure?"

"Trust me... It's him all right. I remember the name he used to say, when under those weird trances."

I don't believe it. Rather, I don't want to believe it. Not only has Carlton been made to become a god, but he is also now our enemy. Shit - what are we supposed to do? None of us wishes to fight him. However, if we don't do something fast, he'll wipe the floor with us.

Shaking its head with confusion, the Seraphim takes a step back and says "I... My name is not Carlton. My name is Seraphim. But... Why does that name feel so..."

Standing to his feet, Ryu calls to the opponent and says "No, you are Carlton. You have a sister who loves you and would do anything in the world for you. Luna and I are your friends. Try to remember who you really are!"

Crouching while holding his head in both hands, the angel moans as though under much agony. "My sister... My friends. Ryu... I know you all" he says, causing us to stand with surprise and hope. He's starting to remember. Carlton is starting to remember who he is!

Suddenly - a great and mighty voice enters the spire. It addresses the Seraphim with an all-powerful tone which causes us to tremble.

"Heed my order. You are my loyal friend: Seraphim. You are not and never was Carlton. Fight for me... My magnificent angel."

"Yes my lord. Holy... holy... holy" the winged foe responds as the mysterious voice commands him to take up arms against us.

As the echos of the voice fade, I ask my blade "What was that? Where is that voice coming from, Adamas?"

"That was the Great Observer. It's trying to stop us from getting through the Carlton!"

"Damnit! The Observer must be threatened by..."

Wham - before I can finish my sentence, the angel goes on the offensive - performing a great tackle which sends us crashing against the wall. Because of the Observer, Carlton is back to being a will-less angel. His free will is being held hostage.

Blocking our advancement, he stands unmoveable - flaming sword ready to attack us with no hesitation.

"Curse that Observer. It really wants to make sure that Carlton forgets everything about himself. Such a cruel being. I will not let that happen!" Declares the prince.

"Any bright ideas?" I ask - hoping he comes up with one of his usual genius plans.

Standing in front, Ryu says "Yeah... As a matter of fact I do. It's quite simple really. I will act as a decoy and buy you time to reach the top."

Gasping with surprise, I say to the knight "What kind of plan is that? If I leave you behind, alone you won't stand a chance!"

"That may be true. That is why you need to hurry up and reach the Great Observer. The sooner you put a stop to it, the sooner we can save Carlton and everybody else for that matter. You're the only one who stands a slither of a chance right now!"

"But..."

"Get moving!"

My mind races with thoughts - trying to think of a better solution presented to me. I don't want to lose this friend of mine. I am tired of losing those whom I cherish!

Soaring upward before swooping down towards us - the Seraphim swings its blade of fire and proclaims "Holy... Holy... Holy!"

Pushing me out of harm's way, Ryu faces the adversary and

shouts "Come on Carlton. Let's have some fun!"

Their weapons clash - resulting in a mighty sound of steel which echoes through the tower.

"Go on... Now's your chance, idiot!" the prince orders - struggling against the deadly angel.

Realising the opportunity given, I race up the stairs and leave a supportive farewell. "You had better not die before I finish up!"

As I continue - a heavy feeling weighs down on my chest. I have felt this, once before. It is the feeling that comes with saying goodbye to a loved one. To my surprise, I notice my cheeks are wet. Wait... Are these tears? I am... I am crying. I never imagined I had any tears left within me. I guess I surprise myself sometimes.

Reaching the top of the spiral stairs, Adamas and I see a single door of light. Wasting no time, we charge through it and finally exit the spire.

Stumbling through to the other side, we emerge within the middle of a wide and expansive field. The sky above is blue and white, looking like a scene from a painting. Such a stark contrast to where I was before, makes me doubt if I am still in the Land of the Gods. What is this place?

"Adamas, are we still in the Land of the Gods?"

"Yes, there's no doubt about it. However, I don't exactly know why everything looks so natural. Wait... Someone's here! Behind you!"

Without thinking, I spin around and perform a horizontal swipe to whoever has approached me. Feeling the blade cutting into flesh, I hear a loud scream coming from the unknown individual.

"Aaaaaaahhhh! Brother..."

I gasp, realising the person struck was none other than my sister. Oh god... - I just killed...

"Luciaaaaaa!" I scream - looking into her tear-filled eyes as I quickly pull the black sword from out her side. She spews blood before falling back to the ground. I stand, shaking with disbelief. This can't be happening. How could I have killed her...

Again?

Falling to my knees, I lean over and say "Lucia, I didn't mean to. Please, just hang in there."

Her pupils begin to dilate, as she produces a warm smile. No, I won't allow this to happen. I won't lose her, not again!

Clapping my hands together, I shout "Recover!" casting a miracle of healing. However, I am unable to, seeing as I already used it before. Even so... I have to try!

"Recover... Recover... Recover..."

"Luna, stop it!" Yells Adamas - clobbering me over the head with such force I almost black out. Falling backwards, I look up at the sky - hearing my companion sword rant to me. "That isn't your sister. That was just an illusion, cast by a deceptive magic trick. Someone is trying to fool you. Luna, I am gonna need you to use that logic you always tease others of not having!"

"Adamas... Are you sure that it isn't her?"

At that second, the dead body of my supposed sister begins to erode and fade into a dark mist. As we watch the mist evaporate, we hear a troubled sigh, coming from nearby.

"Sigh... After all the effort I made trying to get you to take your own life out of guilt. You really have no shame, do you?"

Turning to my right, I look with surprise at the sight of a familiar foe. Dressed in black, equipped with two blue horns - wielding a single parasol, I shudder at the sight of Nine: Ten's sister. The last time we encountered her, we almost lost our lives. What is she doing here and why is she aiding the Great Observer? She isn't a god. On the contrary, she's the new demon overlord. None of this makes any sense!

Slowly rising to my feet, holding the blade tight, we stand in silence - hearing only the gentle breeze. Twirling her parasol playfully, the girl asks "Why are you so stubborn? Do you not know that your efforts are in vain? All you'll do is make your loved ones suffer even more. Even as we speak, your friends are on the verge of losing their lives. The dragon has already perished, and it will only be a matter of time before the other two follow suit."

Listening to her words, I keep silent - still troubled by her appearance before us. Wait... Wasn't Ten supposed to be after her?

"Nine... what have you done with..."

Shawoom - before I have the chance to finish my question, a pillar of fire bursts up from the ground, meters behind me. Those flames... I know those flames. Sweat begins to fall from my forehead. Not from the heat but of nerves. An aura of hostility is coming from the pillar of fire.

"Luna... that is..."

"I know Adamas... I know."

The flames disappear, revealing none other than my comrade: Ten. However, her eyes are aggressive and challenging - the way they used to look when we first met. Sniggering with amusement, Nine seems to be enjoying the confusion upon my face. Paying no attention to her, I address the fiery she-demon.

"Ten... You're here too. Are you ok?"

Raising her arms forth - she emits a ball of fire between her hands, and with a vengeful glare, she replies.

"Luna... This is all your fault. I... I have to kill you!"

Chapter 30: Nothing Personal

"**W**hat... What did you say?" I ask - questioning my ears. If I heard correctly, she said something about killing me. However, that wouldn't make any sense.

"This is all your fault. This is all your fault!" She screams - tossing the fireball at me. Thinking fast, I leap out of harm's way, causing it to explode against the ground. The force of the explosion sends me tumbling through the field.

"Ten, what are you doing!" Asks Adamas - equally surprised and lost for words.

"Shut up Dimmy. This is your fault too!" She replies, racing towards us as I recover into a fighting stance.

With a strong and stern glare, I shout "Talk to me... Help me understand. Ten, we have been through so much together. I don't want to fight you!"

"In that case, stop resisting and let me end your life. It will be easier that way!"

Ka-pow! With a powerful thrust of her knee, she strikes my stomach with such force, the entire ground vibrates. As I let out a painful scream, the she-demon grabs hold of my throat and slams me to the ground. Kneeling on my chest, Ten tightens the hold as I struggle to break free.

"Ten... Please... Stop it."

"Shut up Lulu! The more you talk, the harder it is for me to make things right. You never should have released me. Had you kept me locked away, my sister would not be suffering like this!"

Coming to my aid, Adamas darts towards her while warning

"Get away from him, Ten!"

Evading the blade, she leaps off my chest as the sword comes within mere inches of her. Pouncing a few meters back, she pauses as I regain my breath. As I stand to my feet, she speaks once more.

"Lulu... My sister told me the truth. Have you ever wondered, why the Great Observer decided to imprison and not destroy me? Well, I have Nine to thank for that. You see, the Great Observer was indeed about to destroy me. However, without my knowledge, Nine pleaded with it to spare my life. Her words somehow convinced it to keep me alive. However, there was a catch. The Observer instead demanded her life, as a forfeit. Although she was allowed to retain her existence as a demon, it told her that she had to obey its wishes, whenever it desired. To top it off, it warned her that if someone were to ever release me than it would revoke the deal and punish her."

Entering our duel, Nine strolls to her sister's side and says to me "Lo and behold, you were that someone, and as a result, I was punished..." Opening the palm of her right hand, she reveals the sign of the Seventh Blessing. As we stay surprised, she continues. "The Observer cursed me with this awful thing, six days ago. If we kill you, there's a great chance I would be free from this, before it turns me into a god. I only have an hour left, before the blessing activates."

So that's it. Now I understand why Ten is fighting against me. She wants to save her sister from the Seventh Blessing. Can't say I blame her. If it were my sister, I would be doing the same thing. Shit, if I knew this was gonna happen, I would never have released her, to begin with. Wait... Didn't my old master advise me to do it as a favour? Damn... Why did you tell me to search for her in the first place, Armis? All I can do now is keep going forward. If that means I have to cut down a former friend, then so be it. It's a tragic turn of events to be in, however, it's not like I have many choices.

Readying my sword, I hold a focused glare and say to my former companion "I truly am sorry, for everything that you're going through. However, I too have someone that I must save and I can't allow you to stop me."

With a compassionate frown, she looks to the ground in silence before lifting her head to respond "I know... Honeybee. And I am sorry too."

At that moment, Ten's third eye, which had remained closed all this time finally begins to open. Adamas and I are shocked, as we witness Ten's true power for the first time. Flames dancing around her, she transforms into a gigantic red beast. Her mouth has now become large fangs and her nose is now a long snout. Her hair, which was once short and boyish has grown long and fiery. Arms and legs oversized - she stands tall with two humongous wings and a thick tail which cover half the sky. Following suit, her sister opens her third eye also - transforming to a similarly large and terrifying creature.

The aura emanating from them are terrifying - which causes Adamas and I both to shiver and shake. Despite this, I do not back away... Not even an inch. With a deep breath, I hold my fighting stance and whisper to my blade.

"As impossible as it looks, I promise you that we will not lose!"

Meanwhile - within the spire, Prince Ryu and the Seraphim continue their duel. Soaring up and down the tower, they constantly collide against one another. However, with each collision, the prince sustains a multitude of injuries.

"Shit... You've gotten really strong - haven't you Carlton?"

"Holy... Holy... Holy!" The angel chants - speed and strength increased by the minute. As he overpowers the prince more and more, the faint voice of the Great Observer can still be heard, constantly commanding the invincible angel.

Trying his best to hold back while at the same time stay alive, Ryu whispers to himself "What's taking Luna so long? I can't keep defending like this. It's only a matter of time before I am forced to fight seriously."

Upon another blast of light - Ryu is sent crashing down the stairs as the very top half of his suit shatters into pieces. Hitting the ground, he pleads with his opponent and says "Fight it, Carlton. I know you're in there... Somewhere!"

Outside the entrance of the spire, Vast is pummelled by the twin Cherubs before being kicked across the ground. Exhausted and badly injured, he struggles as the multitude of angels continues to encircle him.

"Looks like I am done for..."

To his surprise, Vast finds he has landed next to the corpse of the fallen dragon, formally known as Gigas. Initially paying no mind to the dragon's body, Vast gives it only a short glance. However - just before turning away, a glistening object catches his eyes. Inspecting further, the man finds the object to be one of the dragon's eyes. Aware of its capabilities, he realises that this could be his only chance of survival. He also knows that in order to use it, he must sacrifice one of his own eyes.

"To hell with it!"

Wasting no time, he takes a deep breath before plucking his own eye out.

"Eyaaaaahhhhh!"

The knight screams as he reaches forth to claim the feared power of Zilant. As if by magic, the eye miraculously shrinks - just enough to fit into Vast's empty eye socket. Upon inserting it into his face, he lets out a sudden sigh as a mysterious feeling overcomes him. Standing to his feet, he looks up at the golden sky - whispering to himself.

"I can see it."

Sensing a change within him, Apsasu and Lamassu pause before galloping towards him. However, as they get closer, they find he isn't the least bit phased by their presence. He simply stands openly - repeating himself once more.

"I can see it. I can see... the future!"

Shapoom - evading their tackle with ease, the man spins around and performs a mighty clothesline strike, which sends them crashing backwards. The surrounding angels shake with fear at the knight who can now see the future.

"Remember my name well. I am Vast, the invincible warrior who has already defeated you all!"

Back amongst the mysterious field, the demon pair combine their fiery powers - summoning a giant ball of blue and red fire. The flame is bigger than anything I have ever seen before. Looking akin to a miniature sun, Adamas I brace ourselves. Interestingly enough, I am not worried. Instead, I see this moment as our only opportunity for victory.

"Adamas, I have a plan. However, you're not gonna like it."

"Does it involve me getting hurt?"

"Something like that."

With a collective shout, Ten and Nine throw the gargantuan projectile towards us. To their surprise, I do not attempt to retreat but instead, I run to it, head on.

"What are you doing, Luna?" Screams my sword, to which I reply with a stern and focused tone.

"Trust me!"

Summersalting forward, I perform a continuous vertical cut - spinning through the air like a yoyo. Making contact with the fireball, I cut it into two halves - sending it to ricochet into the distance. Lowering their guard, the sisters stand astonished as I spin towards them, almost completely unscathed, save for my burning attire.

"Yaaaaaa!" I shout - striking the she-demons with a quick and fatal stab. They let out a gasp - unable to comprehend how I managed to pull off something so impossible.

"Magnificent..." Utters my former comrade - held in disbelief.

With our backs turned, we remain silent for many painful seconds. Closing my eyes, I address her.

"You fought well... Ten."

Resuming their normal form, the sisters fall to the ground as blood begins to emerge from their fatal wound. As much as I would like to help them, I know that it would be pointless. We were involved in a battle to the death. We both knew the stakes. Even if I could, healing them now would simply add embarrassment to their defeat.

"Come on, Adamas. Let's keep going."

Strolling onwards, head held high, Adamas and I approach a

second door of light, not too far ahead. Entering the door, we leave Ten and her sister within the quiet field. Lifeforce fading by the minute, they can only hold onto each other's fingertips - laying helplessly on the ground.

"Sister... I am finding it hard to see. Are you still here?"

"Of course I am, Nine. I am so sorry. If I had never come here in the first place, you wouldn't have gotten caught up in all of this."

"I know... - but there's nothing we can do about it, now. At least I won't lose my identity and become a god. Sister, do you remember when we were young and all the games we used to play? There was one game in particular, where we had to pretend to be humans. Do you remember it?"

Letting out a weak laugh, Ten replies "Bwehe... how could I forget. It was your favourite game. You and I would pretend to be mortal women and run around with overgrown dresses. As usual, father would scold us for imitating the humans. Those were the days, right Nine?"

A small smile opens on the younger sister's face, as she asks "Say, I had always wanted to ask you something but never had the chance to. I always wanted to know: why did you come here, to the Land of the Gods in the first place? What did you want to wish for?"

"Hmm... You wanna know the truth? I came here... Because I was in love... With him. I would have followed him to the stars if he wanted. I was never interested in anybody else or for world peace. I just wanted to be close to him. I wanted to be a normal human... So that he could someday love me back."

"You would abandon your demon hood, all for one man? Sister... I never did understand your fascination with Septimus. Speaking of which... isn't it funny how similar the boy fights to him?"

"Oh, you mean Lulu? Yeah... I often found it interesting. Say... If you had the chance to have a wish granted, what would yours be, Nine? Nine...?

Chapter 31: Testimony

Emerging to the other side, Adamas and I find ourselves within an empty white space, save for a single house in front of us. The house is not particularly of any interest to me. However - what I do find important, is the person upon its roof. Although his back is turned, I am able to discern the individual before us. With a deep sigh, I take a strong step forward and grunt his name.

"Orion."

He continues to sit relaxed - knowing full well of my presence, but unthreatened nonetheless. His calm and collected body language angers me, as though I were not worthy of his sight. Quivering in my hands, the blade points out, "Luna, there she is... My sister!"

Next to Orion, the white blade can be seen, within its sheath. He makes a polite hand gesture while addressing only myself. "Cassius - come and join me on the roof. The view is exceptionally beautiful tonight.

View? What on earth is he talking about? The only thing surrounding us is pure white space. At that second, however, Orion clicks his fingers - transforming the white void. Before our very eyes, it becomes a familiar village under a night sky, kept company by the twin moons above.

"This is... my old village."

"Not exactly, old friend. As a matter of fact, we are in the cocoon of the Great Observer. However, within this room, we're able to create whatever surroundings we wish. Well, don't be a party pooper. Hurry up and join me!"

He turns his head to my direction, with a wide and genuine

smile. Looking at his cheerful face, I drop my guard. Orion always did have such a beaming smile, so bright it could pierce the heavens. Of course, it goes without saying that I shouldn't entertain him any longer than I already have. Despite this fact, there is a part of me that is telling me to accept his request. After all, he did win our last fight. Seeing as he spared my life, I will hear him out. Letting go of my blade, I say to it "Wait here, Adamas."

"Say what? Luna, have you lost your mind? Are you really gonna face him, without my help? You saw just how powerful he was when we fought him earlier!"

"Relax. I know what I am doing."

Of course, that was a lie. I haven't a clue what I am doing. Here's to hoping this gut feeling of mine is onto something... for once.

Strolling to the house, I slowly climb up before reaching the top. Sitting next to my old friend, we look up at the star-filled sky and soak in the nostalgia. It feels just like old times.

"Cassius... I always knew the truth about the moons and their involvement with our world. Naturally, as a born Messiah, there wasn't much I didn't know... About the universe. Be that as it may, I enjoyed pretending that it was all a mystery. Guessing and debating with you and Lucia every night, made me feel like a normal boy and offered a temporary escape... From my purpose."

"Orion... So you always knew about the Seventh Blessing and what would happen to those who caught it?"

Looking down at the ground, he nods his head slowly and holds his silence. His troubled look is all I need to know, of his knowledge pertaining to such an infliction. At the same time, I sense another reason for his expression. It is one of conflict - as though he were torn between two things.

"Orion - I want to know why you're facilitating this? If you enjoyed being a normal person with us, then why are you helping to stamp out humanity from the world and make everyone as gods?"

"Because if I don't, the Observer will be all alone. Cassius...

Have you felt true loneliness? Not the kind that occurs when nobody is around, but the kind where your very existence is rejected by everything and everyone?"

I am not quite sure where Orion is going with this, however, his question is an easy one to answer. Instead of simply opening my mouth, I click my fingers and command our surroundings to change - seeing as this place obeys our visual wishes.

We're now under a dim sunset, looking over a nameless tombstone, where a small boy can be seen standing opposite - placing the tip of a knife against his chest.

"Do you see the younger me, down there having lost all desire to live? My parents were killed, leaving me and my sister to fend for ourselves in a shabby old village. My sister was then taken from me, while my only friend stood by and allowed it to happen. I know all about loneliness, Orion. Does that answer your question?"

With a look of sympathy, he tilts his head and replies "Not quite, I am afraid. Watch... Observe... And feel." Clicking his fingers, Orion counters my chosen image by revealing a scene of space. Amongst the stars, I see four moons: Red, blue, white and black. This must be a vision from a time long ago when all four moons existed. Circling around our planet, they look majestic and beautiful, like cosmic guardians of Popla.

From the distance, a shining star catches my eyes. The star is large and moves through the solar system at blistering speeds.

"What in the..."

At that moment, an overwhelming feeling of loneliness overcomes me. This specific type and intensity is one that I've never felt before. This feeling... it does not belong to me.

As though reading my mind, Orion glances to me with a smile and says "What you are feeling now, is the despair of that star, wandering through the coldness of space. It has been travelling for an untold amount of light years - cast away by its own kind. It didn't know what it did wrong to be rejected so harshly. All it knows is that it was not wanted. It is so very tired and just wants to find a place it can feel accepted and call home."

Orion and I watch as the mysterious star falls to Popla.

"Upon entering our world, the being was met with hostility from the inhabitants of Popla. As much as it tried to be accepted, the star was quickly hated and rejected, for being different. Can you fathom it, Cassius? Imagine travelling from place to place, only to be shunned by everything in existence, not making a single friend... For billions of years?"

"Orion - is that star the Great Observer?"

Clicking his fingers, we find ourselves once again in the white space. Upon a mild pause, he replies "Yes... What you witnessed and felt, was the day the Great Observer entered Popla. Although it tried to integrate into this world, it was never accepted. Its appearance and powers were too frightening for the original inhabitants. Tired of its fate, the Observer figured that if it couldn't live like mortals than it would force the mortals to live like it. Hence why it created what we know as The Seventh Blessing. If it couldn't obtain friendship by modest means, then it would simply take it by force. The Observer refused to allow fate to have its way. Does this sound like someone familiar?"

I stare with shock by his question. I know exactly what he is trying to say, and I can't argue against it. The Great Observer sounds just like me. Like me, it refused to accept loneliness and tried to find a way out at all cost. Like me, it didn't care about the people it hurt along the way. I get it now. The Observer created the Seventh Blessing and forced godhood on them so that it could feel belonging. However, something seems wrong about this. Clearly, it wasn't happy with just doing it to one or two people. It wanted to force everyone to be as gods. Whereas, all I want is my sister. Well... At least that's how I feel now. But who's to say that I might not desire something else in the future? What if I want more? If I had the power, what would stop me from getting my whole family back? There would be no limit.

"Bingo," my old friend says - clearly seeing the trail of thought upon my face. "Cassius... It would be nice to end this cycle of loneliness, don't you think?"

"Well, what exactly do you expect me to do, Orion? I am not a saviour, and I don't have the power to fix everybody's problems. Especially long time insecurities of a god."

"Oh, Cassius... But you do have the power. Right here..."

To my astonishment, he hands me the white sword. Placing it on my lap, he continues "I firmly believe that the people of the moons created Adamas and Platina, not to destroy the Great Observer, but to make it happy... Truly happy. For years, I struggled to think of a way that would help. As you and I fought and our weapons collided, my powers... The powers given to me by the Observer were gone, briefly. If you were to make the swords knock heads again, in the presence of the Observer, perhaps you could take away its godhood and give it what it always wanted?"

"Which is...?"

"Which is... To be accepted, as a mortal."

To be mortal, huh? Why does almost every immortal being, god or demon wish to be like us? It's not like we're particularly powerful or smart. We are foolish, ignorant, naive and imperfect. Taking his words into consideration, I gaze at the counterpart blade to Adamas. Finally, I have the power to get what I want. Speaking of which, not to be distracted, I open my mouth once more.

"Where is she? How can I get to see Lucia again?"

He doesn't respond. As if a stone were in his throat, Orion fails to produce a single sound. A painful look of sorrow overcomes him, as though saddened by a hidden truth.

"Cassius... There is a way to see her again. But it means that you..." Stopping himself, he stands to his feet and takes a deep breath - turning my attention to another golden door in front.

"The final door lies just before you. The Great Observer will be on the other side. However, you won't be able to open it, like the others. That door needs a key, and there's only one... - Me. The truth is, I was never a human, to begin with. I am merely an extension of the Observer, given just enough will to feel somewhat human. Although my form and appearance has changed over the decades, my job has always been to act as the key."

Opening his arms wide, Orion faces me and nods his head with a determined smile. "Well... - What are you waiting for? This should be easy for you, seeing as I made you suffer so much. Come on... Take my life."

Lost for words, I stare with shock at his request. The only way through the final door is by killing my childhood friend, who was never a human, to begin with. He was just a tool - tasked with making sure that nobody entered the final door.

"Cassius... - Meeting you and Lucia, was the best thing that ever happened to me. I don't regret those moments for a single second. Of all the ages I have existed, if I could stay in one moment, it would be the times we shared together."

"Me too" I respond with a low voice - gesturing for my companion sword to zip into my right hand. "Thank you... For everything."

I thrust the sword into his chest, causing him to let out a mild whimper. Stumbling forward, he falls to his knees - inches from my face.

Too much to bear, I avert my gaze and look to a blank space as he places his hand against my cheek.

"Cassius... You are and always will be... My best friend, right?"

"You don't even have to ask. You and I will always be friends, and no one can ever take that away from us."

With a relieved sigh, he tilts his head backwards, as his whole body becomes particles of light. He disappears before our eyes and as he does, the golden door in front swings open.

"Thank you, my friend" I whisper - wiping away my tears with my robes.

"Luna, are you ok?" Asks the sword, as simple as ever.

"Yeah, I'll be fine..." I reply, before reaching to the sheathed white blade. "This isn't the time for tears. After all, this is a reunion, right? Let's wake up your sister, shall we?"

Whoosh - unsheathing the white blade, it produces a loud and great yawn. Holding her skyward, I chuckle and say "Wake up sleepy head. Your brother has been waiting a long time to see you."

She jolts within my hand, as the black sword slowly drifts closer. Upon a mild mode of silence, the white blade says "You are my brother, Adamas. I never forgot about you, even after this time."

"Really? I am sorry I kept you waiting" Adamas responds softly.

Holding my silence, I remember the words spoken by that annoying witch, explaining the cause of their amnesia. Each time the blades are sheathed for long periods of time, they lose their memory - save for their names. However, although Adamas lost his memory, Platina didn't. For whatever reason, she refused to let go. Not even the passing of five thousand years was enough to break their bond.

Placing the sheaths by my waist, I turn towards the opened door and address the reunited blades.

"I am gonna need both your help, to get my sister back."

"Luna... Are we gonna kill the Observer, or are we gonna help it, as your friend asked?" As good-natured as ever, Adamas just had to prick my conscience. I can already sense that the blade wishes to help it. I, on the other hand, am not as merciful and why should I be? It's not as if it was merciful to me when it took my sister.

Leaping off the roof, twin blades in hand, I slowly enter the final golden door - where the truth awaits.

Meanwhile - back within the spire, the battle between the prince and six-winged Seraphim reaches a head. Unable to defend any more, Ryu has no choice but to fight with everything he has.

"Looks like Luna still hasn't finished yet. Damnit, I can't afford to wait any longer!"

They charge into one another to perform one final strike. The sound of steel cutting into flesh resonates throughout the walls of the tower. Breathing heavily, the two opponents stand back to back, not saying a single word. Before long, the prince falls to his knees.

"Looks like I failed... Yet again."

Still standing, the angelic being looks down upon its chest - spotting a deep and fatal wound. To the prince's surprise, the Seraphim glances around with shock, as though released from the Great Observer's control.

"Where... where am I? What's going on?"

Lost for breath, Ryu's mouth drops with joy as he sees Carlton regaining his memories. However, his brief happiness falls, remembering the fatal strike he gave him. Holding his head low, Ryu utters "I am sorry... I couldn't save you."

"What do you mean? I don't understand. Why do I look like this? Where is my sister?" As he begs for answers, his body slowly fades into traces of light... Till he is nothing more.

Left alone within the empty spire, the prince weeps - whispering to himself, full of guilt.

"I am sorry Carlton. I am so very sorry... Uh..."

Injuries proving too much from perhaps the strongest opponent he has ever faced, Ryu falls flat to the ground. Almost every single bone in his body is broken, which has taken its toll on him.

"Looks like I won't be far behind you, Carlton. Father, mother... I'll be joining you all soon..." His vision becomes blurred as his breathing grows weaker.

To his slight surprise, however, he hears footsteps approaching him. It most likely is an enemy, he thinks to himself - knowing that within his state, he would be powerless to defend himself. The approaching sound stops before a familiar and monotone voice addresses him.

"Never fear... Malcos is here."

"What in the..."

Opening his eyes, Ryu looks up and sees an angel. However, this angel is not like the rest. This one is man-made - fitted with bulb-like eyes and hide made of steel. The prince recognises the machine - wondering the reason for its appearance.

"Get out of here... - This place isn't safe."

"Negative. I made a promise to see Mr Luna again. Have you seen him? Oh... Where are my manners? It is clear that you have suffered many injuries. Don't worry. I will fix you up in no time!"

Throwing down a medical kit, the robot picks out its contents and sings to itself cheerfully, as Ryu stays flabbergasted. From the corner of his eye, the prince sees his comrade Vast, slanted against the wall - having also claimed victory. Relieved to see each other alive, the two wink at one another.

"Now... All that's left to do, is to hope Luna succeeds."

Chapter 32: Gospel

Having entered the heart of the cocoon, we find ourselves within a black space - illuminated with colourful stars. It feels like we are standing in the middle of space and all its wonders.

"Adamas, Platina... Get ready for anything."

"Got it, Luna!"

"Ok."

At that second, we feel a great and overwhelming presence, all around us. I want to pin the source of it to one place, but I can't. It would almost seem as though we are within it.

"I can't make sense of this place!"

Shom - at that second, a pillar of light falls from the sky and strikes us head-on. The three of us scream before falling flat to the ground. It feels as though my whole body is paralysed, save for my neck upwards. At that moment, a grand voice fills the space we're in.

"Unclean mortal. You are the first to have entered my home, without having already transitioned."

Its voice travels through the air - coming from every direction as I lay helpless. Addressing us once again, the voice fills my ears.

"You... You committed acts of unspeakable violence against my friends, just to get your once mortal sister back. Why should your desires have more importance over the will of a god?"

I open my mouth to respond - seeing as it is the only part of my body that can still function.

"I couldn't care less who you are. Why did you take my sister away?"

"Why, you ask? I made her transition because I observed her to be a person of great character. She was wasted as a mere human - so I turned her into the Goddess Selene. She became one of my most beautiful friends. No, she became like a sister to me. Unfortunately, you and the cursed blade ended her life and sent her to the world of Figments."

"Figments? Enough with the riddles. I just want to know where the hell she is! I won't repeat myself again!"

A sense of frustration exudes from the being, as though struggling to deal with my lack of understanding.

"Sigh... It is such a burden - communicating with mortals. Your lack of knowledge is painful to observe. Look around you, at the countless stars, mortal. What you see is where I used to abide: My home. It exists over a billion light years away. My kind was blessed with the power to manipulate and facilitate the transition of energy, although we were forbidden from doing so. I committed an unforgivable crime and as such, I was cast out, with nowhere to go. Upon entering your galaxy, I observed the principles that this world was bound by. Everything in existence is made from energy, and when one form ends, another is reborn in its place. The energy of mortals within Popla is one of eternal birth and rebirth: Reincarnation. When a human dies, his or her soul is recycled into another body and born again - usually having no memory of his former life."

I gasp - blown away by the revelation of our world. So, if all humans are continuously Reincarnated, does that mean I too had a former life? How many lives have I lived in that case? The being carries on.

"Humans are reborn as humans and beasts are reborn as beasts. However, I altered this principle, when I introduced the Seventh Blessing to this world. When a life ends by my blessing, the mortal is reborn as an immortal being, rather than starting its life as a human once again. However, in the unfortunate case of a god dying... It becomes nothing more than a Figment - living on in a plane of dreams and memories. All the gods you slew, on your journey of darkness became nothing more than Figments... Just like the being who once was Lucia."

So, my sister is lost somewhere, on a plane of dreams and memories? In many ways, I should be relieved by this. For at least there, nobody will be able to hurt her again. No... Lucia deserves more than that.

Putting thoughts aside, using every ounce of strength in my body, I slowly grab hold of both blades before rising to my feet. "I understand more or less, what the Figment world is now. Nevertheless, I am still gonna need you to take my sister out of it. While you're at it, I want you to free everybody within Popla from the Seventh Blessing, before they turn to gods!"

"That is not possible. The mortal once known as Lucia dwells within a plane of existence that even I cannot reach. Regarding the Seventh Blessing: You're already too late. My blessing has already transformed the whole of humanity into gods and I have no intention of reversing their state."

"You lie!"

At that second, a large glass screen appears before us, allowing us to see the state of our world. My eyes shoot wide with disbelief, upon seeing the land, sea and air, overrun with gods with not a trace of a single human. "What in the..." I shake with shock as the screen reveals to me all of the places I visited. Belgrave, Brightin, Wellington and Gin have all succumbed to the Seventh Blessing. Now, nothing but countless gods remain.

"I... Don't understand. The Seventh Blessing usually requires seven days to take effect. We've only been in this land for a few hours at least!"

"Were you not informed earlier? The time within this sacred land is unique from the world outside. A day within my realm is over two weeks outside. You are already too late."

What kind of sick joke is this? So, two weeks has already transpired since being in here? Plus... not only is there no way to get my sister back, everybody outside this realm has become gods? If that's the case, what use is there in fighting anymore?

"Young mortal, of course, there is one way for you to see your sister again. All you need to do... Is become a god, then perish as one. Before you know it, you will be residing within the land of

Figments, where your sister will be."

Its suggestion fills me with curiosity, as I now ponder the only option given to me. After all, if the world is already lost, then there's not much point dwelling in it, right? Furthermore, I never cared too much for others anyway. Sensing my thoughts - Adamas says "Luna, don't you dare think about it. I won't allow you to give up like this!"

His words are surprisingly sharp and stern - gaining my attention as he continues.

"Trista, Ten, Vast, Ryu and a whole lot of other friends, helped you get this far, not to wimp out by becoming a god. You showed us all, just how amazing being a human is. If you become a god, I will never forgive you!"

"That's easy for you to say, now that you have found your sister. What am I expected to do, now that she is gone?"

"She is not gone! She's just someplace else, for now. We can find her... I know we will! Even if it takes five years, ten years... Even a hundred years, I promise to help you find her!"

My heart is overcome with a certain warmth. His loyalty humbles me, with an assurance that I feel unworthy of. Nevertheless, I am grateful. The blade is right. There must be a way... Somewhere in this big old world of magic, miracles and wonder. Seeing as the Great Observer doesn't have a suitable answer, then we'll just have to look somewhere else. However, before any of that, we need to get everyone back to the way they were.

As much as I detest the world, there are some good things about it. More importantly, if there is another way to get my sister back... If there is someone in the world who knows of a way, then I am first gonna need to force the Observer to reverse the Seventh Blessing over Popla.

Filled with a newfound goal, I take a single step forward and say "To hell with your offer. My friends and I will find another way of saving my sister after we have made you turn everybody back to their original state. I swear, by the end of this confrontation, the Seventh Blessing will be no more!"

"You fool! It is you who will be no more!" The being shouts -

summoning another pillar of light to fall towards us.

Already anticipating its response, I swing both Platina and Adamas into one another - activating the hidden power Trista told me about. As both weapons collide, the soothing chime reverberates outward... - Disintegrating the descending pillar of light. The alluring sound and shockwave do not end there, as it expands far and wide - shaking the very realm itself.

"Eeeeeeyaaaaaaahh!" The being screams, as though dealt a major blow. We can feel it... Its power fading.

"Stop that!"

"Not a chance!" I respond with a smile - hitting my companion blades against one another, with even more force than before. A louder and even more mesmerising sound flows forth - shattering the walls and roof of the cocoon. Losing its omnipresent form, the once all-powerful god appears before us, in a kneeled and weak stance. Its body resembles a young child, whose body consists of miniature stars and planets. Its eyes are like the sun and hair like that of the milky way. It is beautiful from head to toe.

To my surprise the Observer trembles, as though it were the most sensitive thing in existence. "My... my powers are leaving me!" it gasps to itself, crying tears of stardust. Pointing towards me, it tries to release another pillar of light to attack. However, no projectile of any sort is fired.

"Give it up Observer. As long as I have Platina and Adamas, you have no chance against me. How does it feel to have lost against a mere human?"

"No, I haven't lost! You can't do this to me!"

Overcome with fear, it can only flail its hands outward - like a defenceless toddler, in the presence of a stern parent.

"Ok... I'll make you a deal. I'll reverse the Seventh Blessing if you'd allow me to keep just a handful of my friends!" Its tearful tone and desperate face are enough to move any man to tears. Its plea is genuine and true - however, I remain steadfast and unyielding.

"No deal. All the friends you obtained, were forced into becoming your godly minions."

"Please!"

Ignoring its words, I strike the blades a third time - causing the sound to escape even the sacred realm and reach the lands of Poplar. The whole world shakes violently, and we can sense each person, reverting back to their original state. The being feels it too and cries continuously while I whisper to my blades.

"Well done you two."

Responding gently - the white blade says "That being... It is in pain. We're not going to kill it, are we?"

Replying to her, Adamas whispers "No, we won't kill it. We're just gonna grant it something it wished for... For a very long time."

With blades held tight, I slowly approach the being before us: the source of all my struggles. The Land of the Gods, which was once populated by countless angelic beings, is now quiet. There are no more angels left and as such, a distinct emptiness can be felt all around.

"Luna... - The Observer's powers have almost completely disappeared. One more sound from my sister and I should be enough to take away its powers completely... As well as your own" Says the blade.

"Noted" I utter, before raising the swords above my head - ready to deal the final melody.

"Don't... Don't take away everything I worked for. I... I don't want to be alone again."

"You won't be alone."

"Yes, I will! Your feeble mind cannot possibly comprehend my loneliness. If you were to taste an inch of it, you would surely die. I tried my best to get along with your kind. However, no matter what I did, I was pushed away and hated. Why can't anybody just love me for being me?"

Lowering the blades, I halt my action as the being continues its tearful rant.

"I did nothing wrong. I just wanted to survive and live in a place that I could call home. After all, I was banished from my original home and then spent billions of years, roaming endlessly through space. You would have done the same, had you been in my position. In fact, you have been doing the same, all this time. You had your way countless times, not for the purpose of a greater good, but for selfish and personal reasons. Just who do you think you are!"

I stand quietly, fascinated by the god who once had a monopoly on the whole world, begging for mercy. I owe it no further explanation. However - be that as it may, I feel that I owe it to an old friend to remind the Observer that it too was genuinely loved.

"Orion knew... He knew how much you were suffering. As a creation of yours, he only wanted to make you happy. He knew how much you wanted to be accepted by the world. It pained him to see you go down this road. However, he still stood by you."

"You... You don't know what you're talking about. If you take everything away from me, you may as well just go ahead and kill me because there's no way I could live amongst you mortals. I'll only get rejected again, like before."

Surprising both blades and the being in front - I kneel down and wrap my arms around the Observer. Holding it close to my chest, I whisper into its ear "Back in Babylon City, when I first acquired these powers by falling into that holy water of yours, I heard a voice. it said 'please... don't abandon me'. That was your voice... Wasn't it?"

Stunned by my embrace and words, the being reciprocates my hold before crying aloud.

"I don't want to be alone... In this cold and selfish world."

"You won't be. I am sure there is someone in this world, who is looking to meet another, just like you."

"Do you really believe that?"

"I know it. With this final melody, all your powers will be gone and you will be like me: a human being."

Lifting my head high, I strike the blades against each other with all my might. The sound is almost deafening - releasing a shock wave that is so great, the sacred realm shatters like glass. The golden sky falls away, as the spire and ground below give way. As the Land of the Gods begins to crumble around us... We panic.

"Shit... why is everything falling apart? Adamas, start talking!"

"Why are you surprised, Luna? Our melody was intended to take away the Great Observer's powers. With no more powers to sustain the sacred land, this realm has no choice but to disappear."

"Fuck! Once we leave this realm, we'll basically wind up falling through the sky, to our deaths!" Clapping my hands together, I attempt to cast a miracle of flight. However, nothing happens. Kicking myself, I remember that the melody from the blades stripped all miracles from the world... including mine. I no longer have the powers of a messiah.

"Ahhhh!" The now mortal Observer screams as the ground beneath it collapses. Instinctively, I leap forward before catching the being's arm.

"I got you... Hold on!"

Looking up at me, the Observer stares with wonder at my actions - surprised that I didn't let it fall. Already anticipating its question, I utter "Don't give me that look. Orion considered you a friend. Any friend of his is a friend of mine!"

Eyes wide with disbelief, it freezes as though I were a god. As more tears fall from its eyes, the Observer responds "You are... My friend?"

As if our situation couldn't get any worse, the entire structure breaks away, causing us to plummet. The Land of the Gods fades away, like an apparition as we emerge back to the world of Popla. The sky is now dark, and the twin moons hang boldly in the air.

Holding onto the Observer, we continue to descend through the sky, as my blades can do nothing but watch by my side. From the corner of my eyes, I see Ryu, Vast and Malcos falling also. I hate to say it - but I don't think we're gonna survive this one, save for Platina and Adamas here. Once we hit the water, we'll die from the impact. Jeez, what a way to go.

Suddenly, at that second, time is frozen in place and our descent is halted, although it would seem that myself and the blades are the only ones conscious of this. I know this miracle and I've used it, many times before. However, who used it? It definitely wasn't me, and it couldn't have been the Observer either. Furthermore - miracles should no longer exist, right?

"Adamas, Platina... - Why has time stopped?"

"I am afraid we don't know. Wait... Something's coming!"

To our surprise, a certain red witch appears from out of thin air, just in front of us. With a small smile, she stands on the wind - eyes fixated on me. Something about her aura feels different somehow. It is not hostile - however, the energy from her feels cosmic and otherworldly.

"Congratulations. You did it. You ended the Seventh Blessing and granted our child's wish. We are truly grateful."

Chapter 33: A world without You

I stay confused, not only by her sudden appearance but by her vocabulary. Why is she referring to the Observer as her 'child'? Who is 'we?'.

"Trista... - Who are you?" You are not a witch and you've never been a witch, right? come on... out with it."

With a nod of surrender, as though being found out, she claps her hands - releasing a great light which surrounds her. As the light disappears, her appearance changes. Her eyes look like suns and her hair like that of the milky way. She is... Another Observer.

"Please forgive me, for not telling you the truth earlier. I too am an Observer, whose task was to stop the young child in your hands from dominating your world. However, we Observers are not allowed to tamper with worlds directly, hence why I assumed the form of a human woman. I also was the one who first gave the Locistals of the Black and White moons, the idea to create Adamas and Platina, before gifting the weapons to your kind."

"Trista, why did you cast out one of your own in the first place?" I ask with a slightly strong tone. After all, if it was never cast out, it wouldn't have reached our world, to begin with.

"That is a valid question. Unlike the rest of our kind, the child possessed a strong desire... To touch, feel and communicate with other life forms. This went against our nature, as Observers of the world. As such, it had to leave and find a new home."

Looking down at the little Observer in my arms, a feeling of pity and empathy overcomes me. The more I hear of its story, the more I understand its reasons for doing what it did. We both really are the same after all.

"Trista... You do realise that this is all your fault, right? You sent away one of your own, because of its wish to connect with others."

"Yes, we realise that now. Since then, we have changed much of our ways and have tried our best to make up for our own ignorance. As a way of making amends, please allow me to take the child off your hands, along with the swords. Your world will never again be troubled by them "

I show a defensive stare, by her request. So, after all the work I put in, she's just gonna swoop along and collect the spoils of my victory? Not a chance. Surprisingly, the black sword shouts to her in response.

"Now way, Trista. My sister and I will not be going anywhere with you. Besides, we already made a promise to help Luna find his sister."

"But that wasn't your purpose, Adamas. You were created to strip the child of its benevolence and rid the world of its influence. Your power is too much for this world. Who's to say that your next wielder won't aspire to harm others?"

"That won't happen!"

Addressing the loyal sword, I say "Quiet Adamas, I can handle it. Listen - could you and your sister do me a favour and go back into your sheaths? I want to have a private conversation with Trista."

Reluctant to follow my command, the black sword pauses before replying "But... I don't want to. Besides, wasn't we told that staying in our sheaths for too long will erase our memories?"

"Yeah, but of course I'll let you out before that happens. It will only be for a moment, while I iron a few things with little miss false witch here. Go on... Get some rest. You both earned it."

As commanded, the twin blades enter their respective sheathes - leaving Trista and I. As though able to read my intentions, she produces a small frown and says "Luna, you really are a terrible liar. You have no intention of releasing them, do you? You know, you could have simply told them the truth. Regardless, I thank you for your cooperation."

She reaches her arms forth, expecting me to hand them to her. However, I shake my head with refusal and utter "Don't thank me just yet. Granted, I have no intention of unsheathing them again. However, I also have no intention of handing them to you either. Well... Not as they currently are."

She looks confused by my response, which amuses me. Looking up at the twin moons above, I continue further.

"I don't know why the Locistals decided to create Adamas and Platina with a conscience, but it is clear that what they wish for the most, is not to live as swords. The first thing I want you to do is to separate their consciousness and place it into a mortal body. I don't care how you do it but just do it. The second thing is: I will not be handing over the Observer to you. It's gonna stay here, within Popla. Give it a chance to start over, as a human being. Give it a nice name too. Something that represents a beginning."

With a slight huff, she asks "And why should I grant any of your requests?"

"Because you owe me that much, that's why. Now... Listen carefully to my final request..."

"If it's about your sister, then I am afraid I won't be able to help you. As the child already explained, Lucia is now a Figment. She exists in a plane of existence, consisting of memories and dreams. She has always been within you, within your dreams - looking up at the moons under the night sky. She will always be safe, in your heart."

"I am well aware of that. All this time, she has been within my dreams... Sharing our treasured moments, over and over. However, when I wake up, she is not with me. That's why I want you... to turn me into a Figment."

She freezes with shock - not responding to my request. Looking me up and down, she flinches and asks "Are you sure about this? If you become a Figment, then there will be no way for you to return to this existence. You will be a wandering memory. Death will be a kinder fate."

"Hmph... No thanks. If I remembered the Observer's words correctly, it said that humans who die are reincarnated into a new mortal body and mind. I don't want to forget, ever knowing my sister."

"But, what about those who still remember you and wish to have you in their lives, Luna? Ryu, Vast and Malcos consider you a great friend."

Closing my eyes, I respond "That's why I want you to make them forget. Make every living soul forget that they had ever met me. It will be easier that way."

Unable to control herself, she opens her arms and wraps them around me. Her hug is loving and strong, a little too strong I might add.

"Trista... You don't need to hold me so tight."

"Luna... Cassius - don't do it. Don't turn your back on this reality. There are so many people who love you now."

Resting our heads against one another, I smile and say "It's ok, Trista. I really don't want to carry on in this world. I just want to go back, to the times I shared with my sister. Please... Will you grant me my wish?"

"Ok... As you wish. As a reward for all your efforts, I will: Reincarnate Adamas, Platina and the child into human bodies. I also will turn you into a Figment and make everyone who ever met you, forget. Well... I guess this is goodbye then?"

"Yeah... I guess so."

From her hands, she releases a surge of energy that flows into my body. The feeling is beyond comprehension. My body, it feels s though it is losing itself and becoming something cosmic. Oh, that's right, this must be how it feels to become a god. Another surge of energy enters my body, but this feeling is not pleasant. It feels as though my very being is dying - leaving this whole existence. As my body, soul and mind disappear, I hear the faint echos of Trista's trembling voice speaking to me.

"You will always be loved. You will always be loved..."

Shawoosh - before I know it, my body explodes into rays of light, which disappear into the clouds. She looks up at the sky and whispers "Have a safe journey… Cassius."

Holding the sheathed blades and Observer in her arms, she holds a brave face and utters "Adam… Paulina, and Genesis. That will be your names."

Clicking her fingers, she unfreezes time before soaring into the stars.

As the world begins to resume once more - the inhabitants of Popla are finally free from the Seventh Blessing.

Still falling through the clouds, Vast, Ryu and Malcos hold onto one another - preparing to hit the seabed below.

"Shit… This is bad. Vast, do you have any more juice left in your suit to fly?"

"I am afraid not, your highness. I am all out of steam! How about you, little robot?"

"Affirmative. I am able to fly - however, I do not possess the strength to carry you both. A possible chance of survival is to dive head or feet first. Incoming… I detect possible enemy hostile!s"

"What? But I thought we defeated all of those bastards!"

To their surprise, two winged individuals enter their line of sight. The first has dark wings, a long tail and a single red horn upon her head. The second has much smaller wings and two blue horns. Within seconds they catch the three and laugh with delight.

"Bwahahaha! Never fear, Ten and Nine the overlord sisters are here!"

"That's right! Ahahaha!"

Soaring through the sky, they swoop down to a nearby island, where they drop the trio onto its shore.

"Bwahaha! That was some rescue, right guys? I bet you didn't expect me to come saving your hides!"

Surprised to see them, Vast, Ryu and Malcos stay wide-eyed - dusting the sand from their bodies.

"Well, I'll be damned. I didn't expect to see you two here. Were you also in the Land of the Gods?" Asks the prince.

Stretching her arms wide before pulling out a small can of

beer, Ten yawns and replies "You bet we were. Although my sister and I wasn't much help. We were more of a burden than anything."

"Well... Whatever the case, it looks like the blade was success-ful in ridding the world of the Seventh Blessing. I think we all should be very proud."

With a chirpy nod, the red horned demon glances around and asks "Say... Where is the little brat anyway? I hope he is ok? Have you seen him, Tinny?"

With a confused head tilt, the robot strolls to her and replies "Negative, Ms Ten. If I may... Wouldn't it make sense to first lo-cate Mr Luna first? After all, they're always together."

Responding with a baffled face, Ten, Ryu and Vast scratch their heads.

"Luna? Who the hell is Luna? Have your circuits fried, Tinny?"

"Hmph, perhaps the time spent in the sacred realm somehow confused the machine?"

Stepping backwards - unable to process or explain their col-lective lack of memory, the robot says "No, my processors and circuit units are fine. Mr Luna was... Our friend."

Shrugging her shoulders, she turns her back, looks up at the sky and responds "I don't know much about a lot of things, but I know I have never met anyone with that name."

"Me neither" adds the prince - also looking up at clouds above. With no explanation however, he finds a single tear, falling from his eye by the mere thought of the name. "Luna. Why does that name give me such a bizarre feeling...?"

Epilogue

Within a place beyond reach, I find myself travelling through a current of light. Where it leads, I do not know. However, one thing I do know is that there is someone special, waiting for me. Wait... Who am I again? Oh, that's right... - I am Cassius or Luna. Cassius was my birth name, given to me by my parents. Luna was the name I had given myself, upon deciding to challenge the gods. With a bit of help from some friends, I managed to finally discover where my sister went to while saving the world in the process. How long ago did that happen? I can't seem to feel the passing of time at all. Is this what being a Figment is like?

At that instant, I feel a familiar presence next to me. The feeling is warm and protective - like a parent to a child. Looking to my left side to spot the individual, I am surprised to see a man whom I have never met before. However, his aura feels so familiar. Wearing fur fighting gear, he stands with a nervous grin.

"Hehe... Looks like we both were destined to end up in the same place. The apple doesn't fall too far from the tree, right?"

"Why are you talking as if you know me? You don't look familiar. As a matter of fact, you don't look like somebody that I'd ever associate with either."

"Ouch... Must you always be so cutting with your tongue, boy? However, it makes sense that you don't recognise me. After all, I am without my godly form. As a Figment, I am able to once again resume my original look. As a mortal man, I was once known as Septimus the Miracle Swordsman. As a god, however, I was known as Armis... Your teacher."

I gasp with shock, as the man reveals to me his identity. I get it now. The god who trained me and turned his back on the other gods was Septimus all along. That explains a lot.

As we both drift through the light, my former teacher nods his head, as if reading my thoughts. "Sorry about getting you involved, boy. You see, once my original memories returned to me, I desperately tried to think of a way to stop the Great Observer. I figured that you would be the best choice, seeing as you possessed so much resentment to the gods."

"But... When your mortal memories returned, why didn't you tell me of whom you used to be? Of course, it's not as though it would have mattered. However, you knew that I would have encountered Ten, right? She should have known the truth about what happened to you."

Shaking his head, the man replies "No... She didn't need to know that part of my fate. Having her believe that I perished in the Land of the Gods is fine with me. Besides, at least as a Figment, I can be close to her... within her dreams. I hope she didn't cause you too much trouble?"

"Haha, I'd prefer not to answer that. However, I don't regret releasing her."

"Thank you. As my one and only pupil, you made this teacher proud."

Floating opposite each other, my master and I stay silent - both holding a pleased grin on our faces. With an appreciative head nod, I say "Thank you too... For everything you did for me."

Turning his back, the man begins to drift away like a feather, as I am carried to a completely opposite direction, by the stream of light.

A deep sleep overcomes me, as my eyes grow heavy. Upon a wide yawn, I close my eyes - embracing this feeling.

"Hey, Cassius! I asked you a question!" Comes a sudden voice - snapping me out of my slumber. To my surprise, I am no longer in the stream of light. Instead, I find myself within a familiar town, upon a rooftop, looking up at the endless sea of stars and twin moons. This feels so real, like everything up until this point was but a dream. Was I really within a tunnel of light just a moment ago? What about the journey I experienced beforehand? Did I really meet such bizarre people, on a journey to a sacred land? No... I must have been daydreaming.

Looking at the one who addressed me, I see my sister Lucia, sitting beside me."

"Lucia..."

"Haha, you just spaced out for a moment. Are you ok? I wanted to know what you thought about the moons up there?"

Shrugging my shoulders, I close my eyes and sigh "Who cares, sister. They're just a pair of boring old rocks, floating in the sky." Laying on my back, I absorb the gentle breeze of the night - hearing my sister whisper assumptions about the Blue and Red Moons.

"Well... I think they're made of blueberries and strawberries" comes a second voice - causing me to flinch with shock. Opening my eyes before sitting upward, I see my friend, Orion, by my right side. I don't know why, but a slight urge of surprise overcomes me. Although I have no explanation for it, I didn't expect him to be here. Haha, I must be getting tired. I should already know that Orion comes here every night, offering his ridiculous guesses.

Closing my eyes and falling back once again, I smile to myself - soaking in this treasured moment.

"Let's go to the moons... Someday."

Meanwhile, in another place and time, within a reality that no longer knows of the one known as the Dark Messiah, a small cottage resides, surrounded by a lush forest. Upon the rooftop of the cottage, two girls and a boy look up at the faintly seen moons of a gorgeous sunset.

"Hmm... I think the moons are made of candy. That would explain the beautiful colours" Says one of the girls, at which point, the second girl responds.

"No way, Paulina. If the moons were made of candy, then you'd need to explain who managed to put so much candy up there. I think the moons are just like Popla, where many people live..."

Yawning impolitely, the boy interrupts the two and says "For crying out loud, you two. What's so special about a pair of boring rocks? It's not like they can do anything, at all!"

"Stop being so mean, Adam! Otherwise, I'll tell Trista!

"Oh come on Paulina. I was only saying..."

At that moment, the door to the cottage opens and a red witch steps out to address the three children.

"Adam, Paulina and Genesis. You three have been up there for hours. Hurry down now and get inside before it gets cold!"

"Ohhhh... Ok" The three express with reluctance - shimmying down before running into their home. Before the woman closes the door behind, she looks up at the sky - thinking of an old friend who no longer exists.

"Rest well..."

The End

Printed in Poland
by Amazon Fulfillment
Poland Sp. z o.o., Wrocław

55086612R00176